D0054306

THE SURROGATE

THE SURROGATE

a novel

TONI HALLEEN

HARPER

An Imprint of HarperCollinsPublishers

THE SURROGATE. Copyright © 2021 by Toni Halleen. All rights reserved. Printed in Italy. No part of this book may be used or reproduced in any manner whatsoever without written permission except in the case of brief quotations embodied in critical articles and reviews. For information, address HarperCollins Publishers, 195 Broadway, New York, NY 10007.

HarperCollins books may be purchased for educational, business, or sales promotional use. For information, please email the Special Markets Department at SPsales@harpercollins.com.

FIRST EDITION

Library of Congress Cataloging-in-Publication Data has been applied for.

ISBN 978-0-06-307007-3

21 22 23 24 25   GV   10 9 8 7 6 5 4 3 2 1

For Larry, Branch and Linnea,

with love

[W]e are the breakers of our own hearts.

—*Eudora Welty*

PART ONE

CALLY

Night

I wrapped the baby in pink flannel blankets, tightly like they taught me. To cushion her, I stuffed my extra clothes in the duffel, plus the white hand towels I stole from the bathroom. As I zipped the duffel shut over her face, she was quiet as a corpse. Digger was supposed to flash his lights when he got to the parking lot outside my window. I set the bag on the floor next to the bed and leaned back, watching the wall clock. The second hand jerked forward in sync with the thumping beats of my heart. I was terrified the night nurse would return or someone else would waltz into the room like they'd done all day long and all day yesterday after they'd moved me from the birthing wing to my recovery room.

"Hold on, just hold on," I said to the duffel bag, willing it not to jiggle, not to whimper. In my head I called her Nell, even though the contract said the intended parents would have sole naming rights. Only two days old, she must have been exhausted. When Digger's headlights finally flashed, I crumpled the blankets on the bed to confuse the nurses or the food service guy or the priest or anyone else who might happen to stroll in on their rounds. Tomorrow was the day of transfer, and I needed time.

Pains jabbed at the base of my belly as I shuffled to the window, tugged on the latch, and slid it open. Snow and cold air blew in and stung my face. I lifted the duffel, wobbly with Nell inside it, and placed her on the stone ledge, about two feet deep and ten feet off the ground. I crawled out next to her as quickly as I could. My eyelashes caught giant snowflakes that melted as I blinked.

Below us were deep drifts, but where was Digger? I needed him to get over here and catch this baby. My nostrils were sticking shut with each inhale, and I was shaking. I'd climbed out of windows before, but never in weather as cold as this. Once I'd escaped an overnight camp my aunt sent me to when she got tired of me being out of school for the summer. And a few times in high school I climbed out of Digger's bedroom when we were about to get caught making out. But now I was seriously scared.

Soreness throbbed in my groin. Nell was big, over eight pounds. The doctor said my hips had probably cracked open when the baby's head passed through, and I was feeling it. Out in the parking lot, thick flakes fell down like rain under the light of the lamppost. My heart was racing. Come on! Finally I saw someone trudging along, and I recognized Digger's hooded outline. He was walking in the wrong direction, toward the side doors.

"Hey!" I yelled, and he turned around, confused.

"Cal?" he said.

"Get over here and catch my bag," I said.

"What in the hell?" He moved closer, throwing up his hands as he marched through the snow.

"Get below me," I said, looking back at the hospital room. "Take this first."

He reached out his arms, ready. "Give it to me," he said.

I leaned forward and lowered the bag toward his open arms. Even though the baby and I were about ten feet off the ground, the distance to Digger's hands was less. She'd fall only two or three feet, we'd make it.

"Be careful," I said as the freezing ledge seeped through my pants and numbed my thighs.

"Drop it," he said, gesturing for me to let him have the bag. The wind blew the hood off his head, and he squinted into the falling snow. "Do it!" he said, and I did.

He caught it like a football, with give, and then chucked the duffel to the side, into a snowbank. Then he turned back and looked up at me, as if waiting for instructions.

"You can't catch me," I said.

"No shit."

"Well, get out of the way, then."

Digger stepped back, looking behind him as car lights swept the parking lot. "Hurry." He shuddered and blew into his hands.

I inched myself farther along the frigid ledge till I found a landing spot that had a big enough pile of snow. My wet pants were half frozen, and my hands burned. Taking a deep breath, I pushed myself forward, fell about four feet, and landed.

"Ow!" I said, and Digger reached over to pull me out of the snow.

"You okay?" he said in the way people ask but don't really want to know.

"No," I said, but he was already walking in front of me, taking the duffel to the parking lot.

He opened the passenger door and shoved me up into the warm truck, which he'd left running for us, at least. The inside of the truck was exactly the same as I remembered it, and I had that sad flashback feeling of when I was his girlfriend. He put the bag in the backseat, slammed shut the driver door, and shifted into drive.

"Thank you for doing this," I said, touching his arm.

"Yeah." He adjusted the rearview mirror and my hand fell away. "It's good to see you," he said, not looking at me.

"Been a while." I cleared my throat and reached for the seat belt.

"So where are we going?" he asked, pulling out of the parking lot and onto the road.

"North," I said. "Maybe to that place we went for New Year's that one time."

"Duluth?" he said. "That's three hours away!"

"Yeah, I know," I said, kicking off my shoes and wiping snow from my ankles. "I need to get away. Where no one can find me."

"Why?"

"I'll tell you," I said, reaching back for the duffel. "Do you have utility scissors in here?"

He nodded toward the glove compartment. I dug around in there until I found the Leatherman, Digger's handy all-in-one pocket tool we'd used to open bottles of beer and other emergencies.

"Just drive and we'll find somewhere," I said.

"I know a place," he said.

And we were off into the night.

Two

RUTH

2001

Here's how it is with me and other people, meeting new people: when I don't care, I usually love them. But when I especially hope to like someone and want it to go well, that's when problems inevitably emerge. I'll find something to nitpick, even a small concern like a grammatical mistake, a poor handshake, or dirty hair. A faux pas, like failing to push in one's chair after leaving the table, and any number of other small or large flaws will grate on me, build up and fester, and prevent me from instantly connecting. That's how it was with Cally.

She looked great on paper, when she sent us an email in response to our ad on Craigslist. We said we were looking for an ambitious, brave young woman who was willing to donate her egg as well as carry the child for us: in other words, a traditional surrogate. We said we preferred not to work with an agency because it allowed us to have a closer relationship with the surrogate, and because Hal would provide the legal services, the fee to the surrogate could be higher. We emphasized that we wanted someone who was between nineteen and twenty-four, an unmarried woman with young, healthy eggs.

My eggs were, apparently, of "poor quality" due to my age. Of course, I hadn't calculated this when I was younger; I'd been single and immersed in my career, so the timing would have been wrong. What a lousy curse, then, after I met Hal and we (or mostly I) wanted to get pregnant: my body wouldn't cooperate.

Then came Cally. She had just turned twenty, the perfect age. She worked at a popular doggy daycare, which was a steady job, and it sounded like she was good at it. But she wanted to go back and finish college, to get a better job; she wanted a career, and I admired that. Before she'd run out of tuition money, she'd completed one semester of college, which is where, on the back of a toilet stall door, she'd heard about egg donation. In pursuing egg donation, she explained to us over coffee, she'd found our ad. She considered herself an ideal candidate and seemed very motivated to jump right in.

So I looked for defects. I looked for ways to reject her, which wasn't easy.

She was pretty and slender, although her nutrition habits left something to be desired. She had adequate posture, smooth skin, and balanced, even features. At five feet seven, she was only a half inch taller than me, and just like me, she had thick, wavy dark brown hair. This was ideal, because I preferred for our offspring to have some chance of resembling us. Resembling me. To cut down on the questions and the assumptions. To help me bond with the child.

As a girl, I'd always had a vague idea that someday I would have kids. I babysat here and there during high school. I held babies at church and weddings. After college, then grad school, I was busy building my career. And I hadn't found the right man. If I waited too long, I'd have to do it alone. Fortunately, I met Hal.

When I met Hal, he was married. And slightly drunk. I was covering the 1997 Legal Aid awards dinner where my college professor was being recognized for her work analyzing wage disparities based on gender, focusing on the working poor. I'd asked my editor for the assignment even though it wasn't my normal beat. I'd write the story about Judith, and wouldn't my alma mater be proud. As it turned out, Hal was there receiving a "lifetime achievement" award for his volunteer work with Legal Aid. When he accepted the award in front of five hundred guests, he said, "Thank you, but I hope this doesn't mean my lifetime is over." The crowd groaned. Of course we'd all heard that joke a hundred times, but something about the way he said it made me laugh.

Later at the photo shoot, when all the award recipients lined up, I swear he winked at me. I snapped a few extra shots of him for myself, which, according to journalistic standards, may have been slightly unprofessional. I was looking down at my viewfinder, making sure I had the shots, when I sensed his presence.

"Did you get what you needed?" he said.

I looked up and fumbled to switch off the camera, afraid he'd see what I was looking at. "Yes, I think so," I said, and smiled, sweeping my hair out of my face because, as usual, I hadn't bothered to get it done, and I was overdue for a cut.

"Hal Olson," he said, offering his hand, and I took it. A perfect handshake.

"Ruth," I said, momentarily forgetting my last name. "Ruth . . . Martin."

"And you're a . . . photographer?" He pointed to the camera hanging around my neck.

"Sort of." I laughed. "I'm a journalist. Judith was my politics professor in college."

"Lucky you," he said in a smooth baritone. "She's impressive. And has done so much for women's rights."

"Yeah, she's a . . . hero," I stuttered, thinking that he should be on the radio with a voice like that. Then there was this awkward pause while I looked around the room hoping someone would read my mind and hand me a glass of cabernet, but no one did. "I liked your speech," I said, finally thinking of something to say.

"Oh, that old thing." Hal waved his hand. "My wife told me it was—what was her word—'tired.'"

His wife? Of course. Where was she? I scanned the room again, as if she might be glowing orange or wearing a crown or something else that would make her easy to locate. With a man this good-looking, she should be attached to him at all times.

"Okay, well . . . I'd better get back to work," I said, because, tick-tock, I couldn't waste my time on unavailable men.

"May I have your card?" he asked.

"Uh . . ." I tried to think about all the reasons why it would be wrong to give him my card versus all the perfectly okay reasons to professionally network with a local lawyer who volunteers with dis-advantaged members of the community who need legal advocacy from a really handsome tall married man.

"You could interview me," he said, as though he'd heard my thoughts. "For your story. I assume you're writing a story?"

"Uh . . . yeah," I said, digging in my camera bag and finding a crumpled old card. "Here ya go. The address isn't right, but the main number is."

Hal flipped his business card out of his hand like a magic trick. "Call me," he said.

I took the card and shook my head, exhaling. This guy had a lot of nerve. Vibrant and confident, he had an energy about him, and his blue eyes were intense. He looked like a model in an Eddie Bauer cat-alog: red-blooded but kind. He looked great in a suit, but I bet he'd also be great on a hike. And funny. Like George Clooney, he had a troublemaking grin. A killer combination.

"I'll think about it," I said.

He walked away, lifting his arm up, his glass still in hand, as if to say "cheers," as he waltzed out the door alone.

I thought about him the rest of the night, as I said good night to Professor Judith and packed up my gear. I thought about him as I walked to my car in the parking garage, and as I drove back to my house, and I thought about him as I brushed my teeth and combed my hair, and as I slipped under my down comforter, and as I switched off the light. I'm sure, if you had analyzed my brain waves, I was thinking about him while I slept.

All of that with Hal was unexpected. I must have had my guard down to let him in like that. And four years later, married and infertile, I must have had my guard down with Cally, too, when we finally met in person, at that coffee shop. Within ten minutes of sitting down together at a rickety little table in Caribou Coffee, and just as I was allowing myself to think I liked her, she did it: She sneezed without covering her mouth. Without excuse. Just sprayed germs all over us, our hot drinks, and our papers.

"Bless you," I'd said, finding a Kleenex in my purse and handing it to her. Such a simple thing, hygiene. Maybe I could help her, I thought. I wanted her young eggs, her hospitable uterus. I wanted her to carry our child, but I also wondered about her. Who had raised this girl? What else didn't she know to do?

Three

CALLY

FRIDAY, DECEMBER 6, 2002

Night

I pulled the duffel onto my lap. The weight of the bag strained my groin, but I needed to make sure the baby was okay. Most of all, I needed to cut that ID bracelet off of her in case the hospital could still trace it. Digger took a harsh turn around a corner, and the truck bumped over icy ruts, and all of it was painful for my sore butt and thighs. The entire lower half of my body was a mess.

I gently pulled open the zipper of my duffel. There she was, still bundled, but she had shifted sideways, and her face was in a towel. I fished her out and lifted her to my chest.

"Holy SHIT," said Digger, swerving as he gawked at the baby.

I grabbed the dashboard to stabilize myself, pinning the baby close with my other hand. "Jesus, careful," I said.

"What the hell is that?" said Digger.

"It's a fucking baby," I said, holding on.

"I can see that," he said, swerving again, catching glimpses.

"Keep your eyes on the road," I said.

"Goddammit," Digger mumbled as he slowed down and pulled over.

"Why're you stopping?" I said. "Hey, keep going."

"No." Digger slammed the shift into park and turned to face me. "What the fuck are you doing, Cally?"

I didn't know what to say. The baby whimpered and made a coughing sound. I adjusted her hat and loosened the blanket around her neck. Her face was so tiny and squished. Her eyes were closed, but she frowned and fussed, as if angry at what we were doing, as if she knew I was out of my league.

"So this is that guy's baby?" said Digger with a hint of hurt in his voice. "You went ahead with it?"

"Yeah," I said. "Obviously." I felt myself getting defensive, because this was basically the reason we broke up. I turned to look out the rear window of the truck, partially defrosted. We were alone on the shoulder, snow falling all around us. Even in Minnesota, drivers knew to stay off the roads unless they really had to be somewhere.

Bouncing the baby lightly in my arms, I turned up the heater.

Digger turned it down.

"Hey," I said, "I need to keep it warm in here." I slid the baby's little hand and wrist out and snipped off the bracelet. I rolled down the window to chuck the bracelet away, then quickly rolled it back up. The truck smelled like cigarettes, oil rags, and McDonald's, but the heater worked. Digger sat with his head hanging down, hands on the steering wheel, like he was trying to concentrate.

"I thought the whole point was to give the baby to that couple—"

"—Hal and Ruth, yeah," I said.

"I thought they'd take the baby home, and you'd get the money," said Digger.

"Yeah," I said, stroking her cheeks.

"Then why the fuck are we going up north with it? To, what, hide it in the woods?" he said, mocking me.

"She's not an 'it.' Her name is Nell," I said, gaining strength as he started criticizing me. Gaining strength as I remembered what it was like to be with him, as if the past ten months apart hadn't happened. He was the same old Digger.

"Don't you want the money?" he said, as if I were stupid. "I thought you wanted to go back to college?"

"I do," I said, and that was true. "But when I saw her, and the way she looked at me, I just . . . couldn't."

Digger shook his head like I'd made the hugest mistake he'd ever seen. "Didn't they already pay you some of the money?"

"Yeah."

"How much?"

"Like half," I said, but I didn't want to tell him the exact amount, especially if he was gonna pick it apart.

"Half? So this is, what, some kind of ass-backward attempt at a ransom? You trying to get them to pay you even more?" said Digger, as if that would be a possibility.

"No!" I said. "I just need more time with her, and they weren't gonna let me."

"Did you even ask?"

"Yes, I asked Hal," I said.

"Who the fuck is that, the sperm donor?" Digger sounded jealous.

"Yeah," I said. "I called him, I asked if I could spend, like, another week with the baby, and he said no. He said the two days was generous enough as it was."

Digger scoffed. "What a dick."

I paused, and it felt good that Digger had my back. "And then, when I held her—" I tried to explain something that was unexplainable. "It was like it all happened so fast. I just felt like I didn't have enough time, and Hal and Ruth were, like, breathing down my neck. And they were always hanging around in the hallway and coming in my room to hold her. So . . ."

"Motherfuck." Digger squeezed the steering wheel as if that would calm him down. "I can't believe this," he said finally. When he rubbed his chin, I knew he was coming around. He was almost gonna say yes. "You really drive me crazy, you know that?"

"I know. But you were the only one I could ask," I said, cradling Nell. "I just need some time to figure this out. Please?"

Digger sighed and looked away. When he faced forward again, he yanked the shift into gear. "Fuck it," he said, and pulled onto the on-ramp, speeding up.

"Thank you, Digger," I said, exhaling. "Really."

We merged onto the highway. In the quiet air of the truck, I could almost feel Digger's brain working. After a while he asked, "Do you think they'll pay you the rest?" He glanced at me and I shrugged. "Or would they offer you more?"

"I don't know, Digger. We'll find out, okay?" I hated how he focused on the money part. I leaned down to Nell and swayed my legs to rock her slightly. Her cheeks were pimpled. I pulled back her hat and touched her black hair. Her entire face was smaller than my palm. When she yawned, her tiny lips formed a perfect O.

Digger took a swig from his travel mug. The smell of coffee was strong, and I felt a flash of nausea. I kept my hands on the bundled baby and looked out the windshield, wondering what was ahead. Digger hadn't told me exactly where we were going, but it would be at least three hours to Duluth.

We drove like that for miles, not talking. Black sky, big white snowflakes flying at us, hitting the windshield and melting, then the squawk of the windshield blades wiping away the wet. The rhythm of the wipers at odds with the tires bumping over pavement cracks, and the in and out of breath in my chest.

I leaned my head against the cold window and closed my eyes, listening to the soothing sound of the road. This was the hum I'd often fall asleep to when my father would bring me with him on his late shift in the tow truck. I'd try to stay awake, strapped in on the big bench seat beside him, promising to be good. But being up past my bedtime, I could never stay awake for long. I remembered the rattle of that old engine, the buzzing of the wheels, and the vibration from the center differential underneath the seat. Sometimes he'd turn on the ball game, if the Twins were playing late enough in a time zone two hours behind us, like in Oakland or L.A. Sometimes he'd put on the oldies and sing along to a sappy song. "I'm just an old cornball," he'd say. Then we'd arrive at the broken-down car, and he'd pull over, hop out, and talk with the driver. I always stayed in the truck, as instructed, and watched as Dad jumped the battery or changed the tire or attached the tow, and whatever else needed to be done, before we'd go back to headquarters, sometimes with me squished in the middle between my dad and the grateful, stranded driver. Then Dad would clock out and take me home for bed.

A bump in the road jolted me awake, and I blinked and wiped my face. Had I been snoring? Had I dropped the baby? I checked my lap. She was still there. Was she still breathing? Yes.

I looked at Digger, staring ahead, lit by the glow of the dashboard, and I admired his profile. Rugged. He wore his ratty old DEKALB Corn cap backward, with a few curly locks poking out. He'd been wearing that cap the first time he kissed me, up against a tree behind school. I thought about that kiss as I watched him drive. I always liked his face best when he hadn't shaved for a couple of days, and that's how it was that night in the truck. Maybe he sensed me looking at him as he drove, or maybe he read my mind, because at that moment, he rubbed his chin and scratched his cheek like he was anxious to shave. He adjusted the rearview mirror. He glanced at me, and I blushed. He smiled and shook his head, and I looked down at the baby. Something about this felt nice.

Four

RUTH

Morning

The day we signed the contract, I was mildly queasy, which I liked to think of as my own version of morning sickness. The pile of papers was half an inch thick. There was no way Cally could digest all of that in one sitting. Hal had sent the contract to her in advance, but do you think she'd read it? How could we make sure she understood her obligations? I could barely understand it, and Hal had been pedantically explaining it to me for weeks.

We met at Hal's office, in the green-carpeted conference room. All glass. Heater vents clunking.

"I like your sweater," I said to Cally as she took off her puffy jacket. I was trying to find some common ground, to establish rapport.

"Thanks," she said. "It's cold today."

I faked a smile; I hated talking about the weather. I believed her conversation skills could be improved. Maybe this was something I could help her with.

"Did you make it?" I asked, bringing the conversation back to her sweater. I was looking for ways to connect and get to know her. Did she knit? Perhaps part of me saw knitting as something a fertile, soon-to-be-pregnant woman could do.

"No," she said, looking at her cardigan. "I got this at Kohl's."

I paused and smiled. What could I say about Kohl's? I hadn't expected that. "Well," I said finally. "It looks handmade." Although this was meant as a compliment, I cringed at how it came out sounding like an insult. This was me trying to bond with our young surrogate, make her like me, but somehow it kept backfiring.

Hal joined us and took a seat at the head of the table. His secretary—sorry, administrative assistant—followed Hal into the room and set down an extra stack of papers.

"Anything else you need?" she said.

"Not yet," said Hal. "Thanks, Pat."

After Pat left the room, Hal cleared his throat and straightened some of the papers, as if to say, Things are going to really get serious now. His body language was giving me the sense that Cally and I were meant to sit quietly and listen. To him. Like what, a couple of schoolgirls in trouble with the headmaster? This adventure was supposed to be me and Hal, as a couple, hiring this young woman. But instead, it felt like I was a hapless client, Cally was an enchanted fertility goddess, and Hal was the hero who could make it all happen.

It's possible I was reading more into it than was there.

"Okay, team," he said, and we smiled. That sounded better.

But were we a team? The fertility doctor called us a team, "Team Let's Make a Baby," and he had included Cally in that, in some of our meetings. But making a baby, in my world, in the world where I thought I would live, was never supposed to be a team sport.

It certainly wasn't the way I'd imagined starting a family, having a baby. As part of a "team." I don't think any woman dreams of growing up and hiring a surrogate. You might joke about it as a way to avoid childbirth, but it's different when you come to the conclusion that it's your last chance, the only remaining possibility. Surrogacy, with another woman's egg, was not what I really wanted, down in the molecules of my deepest womanly hopes. I wanted to feel the baby kick inside me; I wanted the birth experience.

Of course, I assumed I'd be able to get pregnant the minute I wanted. Why else had I worried so much about birth control all those years? I didn't want to adopt, because you're never sure what you're getting, genetically. I'd had friends tell disaster stories of medical issues, mental illness and behavior problems, fetal alcohol syndrome, and the list goes on. We considered IVF, but my doctor had made it clear my chances were slim. So I went down the path of alternative medicine for a year. Tried acupuncture and yoga, meditation. I eliminated processed sugars, ate lamb, and visualized a fertilized egg in my uterus. But nothing worked, and I finally had to face the fact that I'd waited too long: I was of "geriatric maternal age."

Hal already had his two boys, who were twelve and fourteen when I met him, and he might have assumed that we'd become an instant family, and wouldn't that be a sufficient motherhood experience for me? Because, after all, we'd have his sons every other week. Hal might have been hesitant to start over again with the nighttime feedings and diaper changes, and that would have been reasonable. But regardless of how he personally felt about becoming a father for the third time, it was clear to me that he loved me and wanted to make me happy. And that, he said, was enough of a reason for him.

For me, however, I'd been surprised by my desire to reproduce. It was different, falling in love with this man. Sex was fun and we were making love, yes, but for the first time, I also wanted to make a baby. With him. Combining his sperm with my egg, blending us together. I believed it would be the ultimate bond, and I yearned to see him father my child. My biological clock was ticking: I wanted to be a mom. But, of course, we don't always get what we want, or in the way we think we should, or at the time we're ready for it.

Hal was ready for us to read and sign this surrogacy agreement, an agreement which, as an additional bonus, he, a real estate lawyer, was quite proud of having written himself. The conference room heater whizzed and rattled into action and caught our attention. I laughed nervously as all three of us turned and stared at the heater vents at the base of the floor.

"Geez, Hal, the heater," I said, teasing about the rackety old utilities in Hal's office building. "Should we take cover?"

Cally didn't laugh at my joke. She didn't seem to mind the noisy heater. But I wanted everything to be smooth and easy. Why couldn't we have a warm and quiet heater, a heater that worked?

"It's fine," said Hal. "They tell me they'll be fixing it soon."

"It's already winter. It's November," I said, stating the obvious.

Ignoring me, Hal continued, "Shall we review the TSA?"

"Yes," Cally and I said in unison. Here was something we could agree on: the preliminary small talk had been torture.

Hal pushed a copy of the contract toward each of us and pointed to the title. "This is the traditional surrogacy agreement," he said. "Actually, hold on." He leaned back in his chair and reached his long frame toward the door, opened it, and called out, "Pat, will you come in here and bring your notary stamp?"

Cally and I exchanged glances, and I wondered if she'd ever been an administrative assistant. I'd been a temp for two summers during college. Not terribly qualified as a steno, I'd patched together a few skills to make it through. Fast handwriting (but not shorthand, like Pat), fast typing (thanks to a typing class in junior high), and excellent proofreading (thanks to reading lots of books).

Pat returned with her stamp, pen, and steno pad. Hal asked her to sit in on our meeting to take notes but also to be a witness. In case, I guessed, there were ever a legal dispute over this.

Our team had just gained another member.

Five

DIGGER

Night

Driving to the hospital at eleven at night, in the snow, was not exactly my idea of a good time, but when Cally called and asked, I said I would. Even though she had dumped me. And we hadn't talked in almost a year.

Cally and I had been making each other crazy on and off for five years. But that's what we did. We fought, made up, fought, made up. It was like coats of paint, and it had been that way forever. Since we met, really. In high school.

Both of our middle schools sent kids to Willaton High, one of the biggest in Minneapolis. I hated the principal and most of the teachers. They would catch me smoking. Or they'd tell me to take down my hood so they could see my face. They said they had a policy. Well, I had a policy of putting my hood up specifically so no one could see my face. Sometimes I took naps in class. Mostly I wanted to be left alone.

I got held back a year because they wanted me to improve at reading. So that meant I was older and taller than almost every other guy. I hated sticking out like that. I was the first to get facial hair. I was one of the first to get a job, get a beat-up truck, get a fake ID.

I told kids to fuck off when they bugged me about stuff. They bugged me about my clothes, but I didn't care. So what if I wore the same pair of jeans every day? So what if my shoes were old? So what if I smelled like cigarette smoke? I didn't give a rat's ass. I lost a fingernail using a power drill. My hands were always dirty. Big fucking deal. It was no one's business whether I combed my hair, and I wasn't about to quit chewing toothpicks.

But I never had a problem finding girls. They hung around me, like mosquitoes. Always asking questions like I was a mystery they were trying to solve. Who were they trying to impress? I didn't listen to half the shit they said. But Cally was cool, and I knew she liked me, too.

I knew because Noreen told me. First week of eleventh grade. I caught Cally staring at me. She was standing at her locker before lunch. I walked by and leaned a little in her direction. Just so my arm brushed hers. A few steps down the hall, I looked back. She was smiling, so I gave her the peace sign. She laughed and flipped me off. I liked her hair, the way it hung in her face, and how it was long and thick.

We had finger sex at Noreen's Halloween party. We'd been taking vodka shots while standing around the Ping-Pong table. I took her hand. Found a dark corner of Noreen's basement. I had a good buzz on. She was tipsy. There was always a party somewhere on the weekends, and there was always plenty to drink. It was easy to find a place to make out.

Cally was good at kissing. We had a good time, but I respected her wishes. It was easy to talk to Cally. She must have trusted me, because one day she showed me her Goal Cards. Inside her locker, at the back, she taped up index cards with messages to herself that she'd written with colorful pens and glitter and crap like that. I said I thought it was cool that she gave herself goals. But one of them made me laugh. It said, "GARB."

"What's GARB?" I'd asked, but she was embarrassed. "Come on, what is it?"

She was blushing and getting her books out. "It stands for . . ." She shook her head.

"Just say it." I poked her underarms.

"This was before . . . you and I . . . it was what I wanted, you know . . ."

"Okay." I leaned in so our bodies were touching and my face was close to hers.

"Get A Real Boyfriend," she said in a quiet voice, looking up at me with those big brown eyes.

I leaned closer. "So am I your boyfriend now?"

"I don't know," she said, like a dare. "Are you?"

The bell rang. I winked. Then turned and walked away.

She chased me, grabbed my arm. I turned around and she kissed me in the middle of the hallway.

"Oooooh," said someone, and I flipped them off.

That was it. Next time I saw her locker, she'd taken down the GARB card. Never saw it again.

We held hands in the hall. We hung out between classes. After school, we'd sit in the bleachers in the empty gym. She helped me with homework. We made out. We talked. She asked me questions. We had sex in my truck, in her bedroom, in my bedroom, anywhere we got a chance.

During the rest of high school, we broke up a couple of times. She accused me of cheating. I hadn't. Then later, I didn't want to go to prom. So she went with someone else. That chapped my ass. Then she graduated in June, and I finished up over the summer. We got together again. That fall she went to Inver Grove Community College. She wasn't around much. I thought she was cheating, found a college guy. She swore she hadn't.

She thought I was jealous of her. Seriously? I didn't give a crap about education. Waste of cash. She wanted to finish. Wanted a "career." I felt bad when her dad died, and she needed funds. But being a surrogate? Having a baby for money? That was creepy as hell. I didn't trust the lawyer and his wife who wanted her to do this. His sperm? No, thanks.

But they offered her fifty grand. Jesus Christ. That was more than I made in a year. Cally thought I was "threatened" by that. Bullshit. She claimed it wasn't just about the huge fee. I didn't believe her. We argued about that. Cally said this was something she could do that I couldn't. Like she was better than me. That really pissed me off, and I lost it. I'd been hanging out at her place. I might have thrown some shit. She told me to go and never come back. So I grabbed my stuff and left.

We didn't talk again. I honestly didn't think she'd go through with it. I thought it was worse than a bad idea. She didn't care what I thought, though. She was gonna do what she was gonna do. And I had to take care of myself. My uncle offered me construction work out of state. Good pay. So I went to Missouri for the summer. She stayed in Minnesota.

Months went by and we lost touch.

And then, out of the blue, she asked for the ride. I'd been back a couple of months when she called. She left a message with my room-mate, who gave me a look when he passed it on. He thought I should stay away. Ignore it. I might have said some things to him about her in the past. He thought she was jerking me around. Using me. My roommate was a good guy; he was trying to look out for me.

I called her back. She said she liked hearing my voice. I said what's up. She said she was in the hospital. "Why? Are you sick?" I said. I was surprised to hear that. I worried about her even though we weren't together. I didn't want her to be sick.

"No, I'm fine," she said, but she didn't tell me she'd had a goddamn kid. She just said she wanted to go but the doctors wouldn't let her.

"Why won't they let you?" I asked. It didn't make sense. "Maybe you're sicker than you think. Are you sure?"

She said she was definitely okay, and the doctors were just being pussies. She said she really needed to get the hell out of there.

Fine, I said. I'd pick her up.

She said to park behind the main building and flash my lights before I got out of the truck. Then come get her. She asked if I could take her out of town and stay with her for a few nights. I thought, Here we go again. She's gonna try to get back together. My roommate had called it. But I wasn't sure. Something in her voice. She said she had a lot going on. Needed time to "process." She sounded nervous. She sounded desperate. So I went and got her. Hell, I had the time. My uncle didn't need me again until February for a job down in Florida. So what the hell.

And I gotta say. That night with her in my truck, on the highway. It was like old times. Except that she had that sperm lawyer's kid, and she was breastfeeding it the whole way. Every time I glanced over, they'd either be sleeping or she'd be sticking her boob in the baby's face.

"Don't watch me," she'd say.

"I'm not," I'd say. "I'm fucking driving." But I caught a peek at her tits, and they were huge.

Cally must have been thirsty, because she emptied my water bottle. Plus another one she found on the floor. I told her I didn't know how old it was. She said she didn't care.

After we passed Rush City, she wanted to make a pit stop. In the middle of nowhere.

"Do you see anyplace to stop?" I said, pointing outside to the dark.

"No, but when you see a gas station, please?"

I said nothing.

Eventually, there was an exit and a mini-mart. I drove up to the front door and dropped her off. After she hopped out, I lit up a cigarette.

"Want one?" I said to the kid.

Six

RUTH

1997

I'd kept Hal's business card on my bedroom dresser, caressing it from time to time, as if the embossed letters were his lips or a Ouija board, telling me it was okay. Finally, I summoned the right rationale: my story was done and needed a companion piece.

"Hal Olson, please," I said to the male voice who answered on the second ring.

"Speaking," he said, and I felt a twinge in my breasts.

"Oh hi, this is Ruth Martin, we met at the—"

"Hello, Ruth," he said, cutting me off with his sexy confidence.

"Oh. You remember me?" I tucked my chin to my chest, and the back of my neck tingled.

"I sure do."

"Um, okay. Good . . ." I got up from my desk and closed the door to my office. Didn't want Kristin hearing this, or any of the other newspaper employees nosing around in my personal life. I wanted this man all to myself.

"I'm glad you called," he said, and I believed him.

"You are?" I hated how flirty I sounded. "Okay, um, good, um . . ." I heard myself breathing into the receiver.

"Hmm-mmm. I was hoping you'd call," Hal said in a smooth voice as warm as roasted chestnuts.

"Oh, okay, um," I said, regaining my composure. "Have I caught you at a good time?"

"Yes, this is a very good time," he said. "How've you been, Ruth?"

"I'm great, I'm great." I sat in my chair and swiveled side to side. I was enjoying this.

"Have you finished your article about your professor?" he said. It was kind of him to remember Professor Judith.

"Oh, um, yes, and that's why I'm calling." I grabbed a pen and a tablet of paper and pressed my shoulder to my ear, squeezing the phone in place.

"It is?" he said, sounding surprised. Was he challenging me?

"Yes, I thought I could explore a piece about, you know, successful attorneys doing pro bono work in these challenging economic times," I said, drawing doodles on the paper.

"I'm glad you think of me as successful."

This flirting was thrilling and disarming all at once. I wanted to keep him on the phone just to listen to that deep voice. His voice in my ear, so close to my brain, so close to the thoughts I'd kept of him, his eyes, his smile and his broad shoulders, the images I'd kept replaying, my own private movie, wondering what it would be like to have his arms around me, his peppermint breath near my cheek, his lips close enough to kiss.

"I'd say so, I mean, you're a partner at a big law firm and—"

"Would you meet me for dinner tonight?" He cut me off again, taking charge. Every instinct I had wanted to say yes to him.

"Uh . . . I don't know," I said.

"Or tomorrow night, if that's better."

"I don't know if that's a good idea, I mean . . ." I looked at my closed office door, wondering what everyone would say about me dating a married man. We were a tight team, mostly women, and we were small enough to know what everyone else was up to. To do our job well, we had to be in touch frequently and help each other; our work was entirely collaborative. There wouldn't be a way for me to keep this from them for long.

"Why not?" he said.

I wanted Hal to tell me he wasn't really married. Maybe he'd gotten divorced since the awards dinner. "Because dinner with you sounds like, you know, it sounds like—"

"—sounds like what? A date?" he said.

"Yeah, sort of," I said, but I wasn't ready to admit that. Or to admit that's what I wanted.

"You're aware that, technically, I'm married." His words landed with a thud.

"Yes, I am aware of that," I said, trying not to let my disappointment show. "That's why I wanted to clarify—"

"It's fine," he said. "I'm sure, as a journalist, you'll understand that things aren't always as they seem."

"Well, yes, but," I said. I didn't really want to hear his shtick.

"Have dinner with me, please. I'd like to explain," he said. "Or, we can focus on the inherent injustice in our system of unequal access to legal advocacy."

I could feel him smiling on the other end of the line. "Well, that last part sounds like an intriguing hook. I'm always in for a good story," I said, wanting to see that smile in person.

We made plans to meet the following night. I didn't want to sound too anxious, and I wanted to think about it. Maybe I'd change my mind? Also, I needed time to research issues related to access to justice. Think about what to wear. Wash my hair.

I could hardly wait.

When I arrived at the Winston steak house, I felt like splurging, so I drove up to the valet. I thought about all the other times I'd eaten at this particular restaurant. When you live in a place long enough, you attach experiences to landmarks and then string other memories on top of those, forming an unexpected necklace. And it's hard not to revisit those past selves when you swing by again. At the Winston, I'd had a job interview lunch, a girls' night out during grad school, and a miserable blind date. Tonight would be either a good interview or a good date. But hopefully a good date.

I opened the door and Hal was already sitting at the bar on a red leather stool, as cool as Pierce Brosnan, watching for me. His smile pushed dimples into his cheeks, and I'm sure I blushed. He looked so sexy in a crisp suit and tie, and I could smell his cologne as he took the coat off my shoulders. His skin glowed in the dim lights reflected in the giant mirror behind the bar, and I wanted to touch his hair.

"You look nice," he said.

"So do you." I glanced past the bar toward the dining tables, with formal white linens and real candles.

"Would you like a cabernet? Or something else?"

"That sounds perfect," I said, and it was as if he already knew me, knew what I wanted.

Hal nodded to the bartender. I knew I was in good hands. And this was definitely a Good Date.

Seven

CALLY

THURSDAY, DECEMBER 5, 2002

Evening

Being a surrogate had been a good job for me; it paid a lot and didn't require a college degree. To be honest, it made me feel important, that I could do this big thing: grow a baby for a couple who couldn't have their own. Being pregnant was easy for me. My body was healthy and all my parts were working, and that was something special I had. At the doctor appointments, all the attention was on me. People helped me up onto the table, always asked how I was, and praised me for doing a good job. The nurse weighed me, and I was proud of how the baby was growing. The doctor listened to the strong heartbeat, and I smiled because I could take credit for that.

As my belly got bigger, though, I started to worry about how much it would hurt to give birth. But there was no turning back; this thing had to come out. I didn't have a mom or grandma or sisters to ask for advice, but millions of other women had done it, so why couldn't I? Plus Ruth had taken me to all the Lamaze classes, and everyone said it would be fine.

When I went into labor, I didn't have time to worry. Ruth got me to the hospital and they hooked me up. Things moved fast and it was kind of a blur. I do remember the pain, though. It hurt a LOT.

No other way to describe it. Just insane amounts of pain and confusion. Tired, with nowhere to go except forward. There was a crowd around my legs, cheering me on. So many people in the room, the doctor and three or four nurses, all wearing blue paper hats, plus Hal and Ruth, and all of them were focused on my privates, holding my feet and legs, telling me to push. Finally, the doctor said I was almost done, one more push. When the baby came out, all the attention shifted from me to her. I heard her cry and she was gone. The doctors and nurses huddled over the baby, passing her around to wipe her off and check her. No one really cared about me after that point. They were all focused on the baby. I sank into my pillow to rest.

Hal and Ruth were always there, somewhere in the background. I could feel their nervousness, the intrusion of them lurking, huddled against the wall. They'd seen my nakedness, they'd seen the thing come out of me, and who knows what else? The sounds I'd made, what I might have said or the look on my face. I didn't know how to feel about any of it, honestly, but I ended up thinking both Who cares? and Why should they be here?

Nothing about this was normal. Nothing about this was routine.

The blue hats and rubber gloves finally wrapped up the pink-hat baby and handed her to Ruth, who held the tiny bundle like it was light as a feather and breakable as glass. I'd never seen Ruth cry before, never thought I would. She was crying and smiling and holding the baby that I'd grown for her.

Exhausted, I turned my head and slept. When I opened my eyes, I saw Hal studying me. Like he was worried. Was he happy, too? Tomorrow would be a full day at the hospital with the baby, and then the next day was the transfer ceremony. He'd reminded me of his rigorously planned drill so many times: after one full day of recovery, his pastor, Jim, and their social worker, Carol, would arrive at ten o'clock the next morning to say a blessing and honor me, the birth mother. Then we'd sign the final papers on parental rights. I'd have a chance for a final goodbye, and at one o'clock, the new parents would leave the hospital with the baby. I'd stay one more day for observation and recovery. This was generous, Hal liked to mention, because it was more than what ordinary birth moms got under their standard health insurance.

I watched Hal and Ruth in their new family circle. He had his arm around her as he leaned down and looked at the baby. Ruth loosened the blankets and touched her legs, pulled one out and touched the toes. She wrapped her back up and bounced her. She put the baby on her shoulder, then quickly took her down again as if she couldn't decide or didn't know which way was better. She and Hal both stared at her. They smiled and kissed each other, and I wondered if that was what it had been like for my parents when I was born. I wondered if it could've been like that for me and Digger if we'd stayed together. Or how he might react if he could see this baby. I wished he could see her. He'd gone to Missouri, but he must have returned by now. His construction work was supposed to end in October.

After a few minutes, Hal gestured to Ruth and said it was time to go, and she frowned. He took the baby from her and set the pink bundle down next to my face, between me and the metal bars on the bed. He touched my shoulder and said, "She's beautiful."

I nodded. The baby opened her eyes and seemed to be looking right at me. She looked so pathetic and weak, like a tiny puppy.

Ruth cleared her throat, and Hal looked up. "Gotta go," he said to me. "Get some rest, and we'll be back tomorrow."

I looked at him and squinted. I couldn't see his face well because the ceiling light was above him, making a halo. "Okay," I said, and I put my hand on the baby. I didn't know if she would fall off the edge or what.

Hal walked over to Ruth. She had been standing near the door, watching us. Her arms were crossed. She looked away, and they both slipped out the door.

Then it was just me and the baby, dark and quiet and alone. A while later, a nurse came in and closed the curtain around my bed. She picked up Nell and put her in the bassinet. "Try to sleep," she said. "Press your call button if you need us."

"Where will the baby be while I'm sleeping?"

"She'll be right here in the bassinet or in the nursery," said the nurse.

I'd already asked the nurses lots of questions, like how they kept track of the babies, because didn't they all look alike? She explained our matching bracelets and the alarm system, and the DNA tests, but they rarely needed to use those.

"Don't worry," she said; maybe she saw something in my face. "We'll take good care of her. And you."

"Thanks," I said, and closed my eyes.

Eight

HAL

NOVEMBER 2001

Morning

When drafting a contract of any nature, I always begin with a template. A template contains the standard boilerplate language, the generic yet necessary clauses that I don't need to spend time drafting. No need to re-create the wheel, so to speak. The traditional surrogacy agreement (hereinafter, the TSA) was no exception.

Since I didn't practice in the area of family law, which is where surrogacy law would reside, I consulted a family law treatise and form book. Once I had the form, I tailored the clauses to be specific to us, such as names and addresses, and also the topics that were important to Ruth. She had some particular proscriptions about Cally's behavior during pregnancy (e.g., nutrition, safety), as well as concerns about the delivery itself and the naming of the child. That sort of thing.

My practice with getting documents signed is to bring the parties together in a room and walk through the details. In this sense, I'd usually be talking about real estate deals, but the document review and signing process is effective regardless of the topic. The result is that any sticky issues can be identified and any unclear provisions can be clarified immediately.

In our case, I called a meeting for Ruth and Cally and me to meet at my office, and we gathered in the large conference room with copies of the documents ready to go. I asked my assistant, Pat, to join us and take notes. I'd been working with Pat for over fifteen years, and she knew how I liked to document my files. So . . . we were all present. We had the paperwork in front of us. And, after the standard small talk, I began the review process.

Pointing to the first few paragraphs, I wanted the team to know how the contract was structured: the main agreement plus three attachments, which are incorporated by reference into the whole. I began with a statement confirming that Cally had been advised to seek her own lawyer on this matter, which had been her prerogative. Since she declined, I had her initial that part, for our own protection.

"Are you sure you don't want a lawyer?" Ruth leaned closer to Cally and scrutinized her face for any clues of discomfort. Cally seemed fine to me.

"I'm fine," said Cally. "My manager at the dog daycare helped me. Her sister was a paralegal, and she walked me through it."

I furrowed my brow. A paralegal giving legal advice would contravene the rules of professional responsibility. And constitute the unlawful practice of law. "What's her name?" I was ready to jot it down, in case there was a dispute.

"Gwen," said Cally.

"Last name?" asked Pat. Good ol' Pat. She knew I'd want the full name for the file.

"I don't know," said Cally, and we watched Pat frown.

"Does she have the same last name as your manager, maybe?" asked Ruth. Ruth was clever and a good investigative journalist. She was trying to be helpful.

"I don't know if she's married or what," said Cally. "But she's a paralegal, so . . ."

"I see," I said, disappointed. I'd already offered to pay for Cally to consult a licensed attorney. In fact, I'd repeatedly offered that, but you can lead a horse to water . . .

I looked over the table at Ruth. She seemed agitated. I half expected her to ask Cally to disclose the "advice" she had received. Had the unnamed paralegal urged Cally to seek more money? Or to change the deal? We didn't want to change the deal at this juncture, so it was best to move on. I could tell from Ruth's expression that she was having similar thoughts.

"All right," I said, "but a paralegal cannot give legal advice, just so you're aware of that."

"Yeah, I know," said Cally.

I glanced at Pat, nodding so she'd take note of my comments and Cally's response, to include them in the record of our meeting. It was important to avoid liability. Ordinarily, I didn't like to venture outside the bounds of my real estate expertise. In an ideal world, I might have consulted a surrogacy attorney, but it was what it was. I hadn't strayed far from the template. And a contract was a contract.

I turned to page two and indicated for the team to follow along. "Everyone," I said, "please fill in your current age there where the blank line is, and initial that. Cally, you are twenty, if I'm not mistaken, and I am forty-eight, and Ruth, you are forty-two, right?"

The women nodded and initialed.

"Good," I said, and the mood was lightened with my teasing, as though any of us wouldn't know our own ages. I continued to the introductory declarations. "Okay. Reading here: 'This is a legally binding contract which the parties have entered into of our own volition and free from duress.' That means no one is forcing you to do this." I turned to Cally and explained, "Cally, in this section it says that you, the surrogate and donor, agree to carry and deliver a live child, okay, either by artificial insemination or via in vitro fertilization of eggs, and that I am the genetic father, okay? This will be accomplished as soon as possible, at an approved fertility clinic, within a fifty-mile radius of your listed residence. Okay?"

"Yep," said Cally. She seemed comfortable with it all, happy to help, and certainly ready to begin the procedure.

I explained the attached schedules (A, B, and C). All of the schedules were equally enforceable, but if for some reason, one part was

invalidated, the others would still apply. "Make sense?" I asked, seeing them nodding. "You with me?" I always preferred a verbal response if I could get one.

"Yep," said Cally.

"For example," I said, flipping to the tabbed sections, "here is
Schedule A, which lists all the things you cannot do, okay? You
agree to abstain from aerosols, artificial sweeteners, obviously drugs
and alcohol, hair dye, coffee or any caffeine, cat litter, okay, medici-
nal herbs, antibiotics, pesticides, okay, it's all listed here."

"Yep," said Cally.

Ruth cleared her throat as if annoyed. She may have been react-
ing to Cally's use of the word "yep." This had become a pet peeve
of Ruth's as they'd been spending time together. I smiled to assure
Ruth that it was going well and to hang in there. She took a sip of coffee and flipped ahead to scan the pages. Ruth's way of calming herself was to get information and take action, traits I greatly admire.

I continued with the behavior section. "No lifting weights, no
X-rays, no hot tubs, no sports, okay, you can't leave Minnesota,
etc. . . ." I didn't read the next part aloud, but they could see the
rest of the sentence for themselves. It said "no sexual intercourse."
I didn't need to embarrass Cally by getting into detail on that. And
since Ruth had informed me that Cally had broken up with her high
school boyfriend, the sexual prohibitions were most likely moot.

Cally blushed and said, "I'm not planning on doing any of those
things."

"Okay, good." I moved on. "This is traditional surrogacy, meaning you are also donating your egg. That's why you're getting the
higher fee, okay, which we'll cover at the end."

Cally nodded. Ruth shifted in her chair, and it groaned. We'd
been having problems with our conference room chairs: the hydrau-
lics were unpredictable; the chairs were either too high or too low,
and the squeaking sounds could be embarrassing. Ruth ignored the
chair's noise as she reached for her pen and made some notes.

I skipped a few sections and turned to the ones I'd marked for special emphasis. "Okay, next page," I said. "You, the surrogate, affirm that you are not aware of any reason you would not be capable of conceiving and bearing a healthy child in the future. You also attest that your sole intention is to assist me, the intended father, and Ruth, the intended mother, in adding to my family."

"To our family, right, Hal? Shouldn't that say 'our' family?" said Ruth.

"Yes, Poppy, sorry about that," I said, using her nickname, which made her blush. "Okay, then, the rest of this is legalese and disclaimers," I explained. "'Surrogacy is an unsettled area of law in the state of Minnesota,' et cetera, and 'no warranties can be made as to the outcome of judicial proceedings which may result,' et cetera, and let us know if you have questions about this last part, Cally."

"I will," she said, but I wasn't entirely confident of that, and I didn't think Ruth was, either.

"Maybe run it by your manager's sister, or whatever we should call her," said Ruth.

"Her name is . . . Gwen," said Pat, checking her notes.

"I already did," said Cally.

"Okay, good." I waited a beat for any questions, but hearing none, I continued. "Shall we turn to the money part? Schedule C."

As the women turned to the fee section, Cally leaned her elbow on the table. At one point, she covered her mouth with her hand, presumably in awe of the dollar amounts. The numbers were there in black and white, but I thought it was important to read them aloud, and I did.

"That's more than I'd make working full-time for, like, two years," Cally said in a low voice.

In fact, at the end of ten months, assuming the baby was healthy, she would be paid, in addition to all medical costs, enough money to cover four years of tuition at a decent community college, plus housing, food, and expenses. Cally could finish her degree and start her life with no debt. This was an advantage that any young person would surely appreciate.

"Everybody okay?" I said, peering over my reading glasses to catch a glimpse of their reactions.

Ruth reached over to hold Cally's elbow.

"Yep," said Cally, pulling her arm away and folding her hands in her lap.

Nine

CALLY

FRIDAY, DECEMBER 6, 2002

Night

"Are you gonna go pee or what?" Digger yelled through the passenger window as I stood next to the truck in front of the mini-mart.

"Yeah." Standing still, I looked into the gas station store, brightly lit and well stocked for all the night drivers. I looked back into the truck. The baby lay on the seat, making a face like she was getting ready to cry.

"Go, then." Digger motioned for me to get a move on, like I was a bad smell he wanted to push away.

I opened the passenger door and picked up Nell. Something told me I shouldn't leave her in the truck with Digger. "I'm taking her with me." I unzipped my parka and stuck the baby inside, then zipped it up again, like how Digger and I sometimes smuggled beer and Cheetos into the movie theater. I put on my fleece Minnesota hat and slammed the door behind me. It hurt to stand up tall, so I slouched over slightly.

The baby bulged out in front of me as I waddled into the mini-mart. Two large women stood next to the banana case and stopped their conversation to watch me enter. They smiled at my chest, and I realized Nell's pink hat was sticking out of my parka. I covered her head and walked as quickly as I could to the back of the mini-mart to find the ladies' room.

Once inside, I didn't know what to do with the baby; she was fussing, but there was no place to put her. Maybe the sink? On top of the trash bin? I spun around trying to decide, then pulled out a bunch of paper towels and made a spot on the floor for her in the corner. I lifted my parka to undo my pants, but I was too late, and I peed myself. I pulled out my sopping wet pad and tossed it in the trash, happy I hadn't put Nell on top of the bin. I needed clean pants and a new pad, but my supply was in the duffel bag, back in the truck. I stood there straddling the toilet with not a lot of options. Maybe the mini-mart sold adult diapers?

"Hey," I said, then louder, "HEY, CAN I GET SOME HELP IN HERE, PLEASE?" I pulled up my pants, crept over to the door, opened it a few inches, and peeked out. The baby was still on the paper towels. She twisted her tiny head back and forth like she was furious about being left on the floor. She made cranking noises, getting ready to cry, and then let it rip, releasing angry wails, red-faced and toothless.

One of the women, the one who was wearing a purple Minnesota Vikings sweatshirt, was standing right outside the bathroom. She must have been waiting for me.

"Um, can you get me, um, like an adult diaper or a maxi-pad or something?" I asked.

"Oh, sure thing," she said, sounding surprised. "Everything all right in there?" She heard the crying. It sounded bad.

"Yep," I said, wishing she'd mind her own business, and I caught her trying to peek into the bathroom.

"Hey, Roz, where the adult diapers at?" she asked.

Roz, the cashier, was in a conversation with the other woman, who wore a gray and white snowflake sweater. "Whaddya need, hon?" said Roz.

"Adult diapers or maxi-pads," said the Vikings woman, who had started to browse the aisles.

"Next one over," said Roz.

Digger honked the horn outside and that annoyed me. The baby sobbed, and I picked her up and bounced her, keeping the bathroom door open with my knee and foot.

The snowflake sweater came jogging over, out of breath and holding a box of pads. "Here you go," she said.

"Where'd you get these?" I was panicking, paranoid she might have somehow gone out to the truck and rummaged through my duffel bag.

"Over there," she said, pointing to the hygiene aisle.

"Oh, thanks." I took the pads and closed the door. I set the baby down again and let her cry. I wished I hadn't brought her in with me. It made everything difficult. After I cleaned myself up, I looked in the mirror. I took off my hat and puffed up my flat hair. My face was pale, so I pinched my cheeks. I looked like a cancer patient. I looked like a drug addict. What was I doing?

Digger honked again, and I picked up the baby. This time my groin ached when I lifted her. I paused and waited for the sting to fade. I wiped the baby's wet face and bounced to get her to settle. I opened the bathroom door and slowly walked out. The two women were keeping the cashier company, like they were sisters and this was a fun night out on the town. I'd wanted a sister, but I was an only child. Digger was the youngest of four kids, and he always said be careful what you wish for.

"How old's your baby?" asked one of them when she saw me.

"Two weeks," I lied. I didn't have time to think about what I should say. I just guessed at a good lie. All I knew was that I didn't want them to know anything about me that was true.

"She's beautiful," said the other one.

"What's her name?"

"We haven't named her yet," I said.

The women seemed surprised, but I think they believed me. It was partly true. A nurse had given me a form to fill out for the birth certificate, but then another nurse told me to wait because of the intended parents' instructions, so I never got a chance to write anything on it.

There'd been something about the birth certificate in the surrogacy agreement, but I didn't remember what it was.

"Do I need to call the cops, or are you gonna pay for those pads?" said Roz, making me panic for a second, as if she knew I'd taken the baby. How could she tell?

"She's joking," said the Vikings sweatshirt.

I exhaled and probably blushed. "Ha! Yeah," I said. "I'll get my wallet and be right back."

When I got out to the truck, Digger was smoking and messing with the radio. "They don't have shit for stations up here," he said. We must not have been close enough to Duluth to pick up a signal. I set the baby down on the seat and rummaged around in my backpack for my wallet.

"You shouldn't smoke in here. It's not good for the baby."

"Where am I supposed to smoke?"

"Outside," I snapped, because wasn't it obvious? I sighed and grabbed a pair of clean maternity jeans from the duffel.

"She's fine," said Digger, snuffing out his cigarette and flicking it out the window.

"Did you get gas?" I asked.

"No, we still got a quarter tank."

"Will you get some anyway? I don't want to take any chances with this weather."

He grumbled, which meant he would do it.

"And will you watch her? I'm gonna go back in and get supplies and stuff for us to eat."

"Get me some beef jerky and a Coke," he said.

"Okay." I checked the baby, still resting on the front seat. It would be too difficult to bring her in with me and do shopping and change clothes, so I left her in the truck. I closed the door, and Digger drove slowly over to the gas pumps. I marched back into the mini-mart, and the doorbell rang as I walked in. I headed straight for the bathroom. "Hi again," I said. I knew they were staring, but I didn't care.

Ten

RUTH

1997

I didn't normally go to bed with a man on the first date. Or even during the first month. And I didn't with Hal, either, but I wanted to. I wanted to very much. And so did he. I know he did. We practically ate each other's faces off when we kissed, and we kissed most of the time we were together. In his car, in mine, in elevators, stairwells, at his place, anywhere we could be alone. Our attraction was intense, but I waited as long as I could. I let the tension build while I sussed out his character and gauged whether we'd be a good match. This had been my strategy every time there was a new man in my life.

In college, I found the men to be immature. In grad school, I was busy working. The real saga of my grown-up love stories began after I started working for the *Duke Herald* in St. Paul. I'd rented a carriage house in the historical district with two friends from grad school, and I rode the bus downtown every day. My job was hectic and entry-level—I was a proofreader, basically—but I loved it. Occasionally, I'd get an assignment to research, and sometimes to write.

I wanted a career, and I didn't want to worry about finding a man, so I kissed a lot of frogs in my thirties. Roger was an ear, nose, and throat doctor, and on weekends he played bass in a jazz combo. I hated jazz, and it didn't last long. I ended things with Gary when I learned he was a vegan and a sex addict. Nils was a symphony violinist I met on assignment in Sweden. We danced all night, and in the morning, he explained he was in an "open relationship." We had a magical weekend in Stockholm, and that's all I'll say about that.

There were a few others, dates that never went anywhere, guys who weren't my type. And then there was Hal.

Hal and I both felt a simmering something's-different-about-this, and we purposefully took it slow. The night of our first date, at the Winston, I drank too much, which was slightly embarrassing, but Hal was a complete gentleman about it. He took me home and tucked me in, and I remember the walls were spinning when he kissed me goodbye. I closed my eyes and fell asleep dreaming of that kiss. The next morning, I found a handwritten note on my bedside table. "Ruth," it said. "Thank you for a refreshing evening. You are smeautiful—a rare combination—and I can't wait to see you again." After coffee, I'd read the note over and over again. I knew that "smeautiful" was "smart" and "beautiful," because, frankly, I'd heard it before. But something about Hal's earnest desire to explain his situation had me disarmed and wanting more.

That night at the Winston, we'd been sitting at the bar, chatting about the awards banquet where we'd met, and waiting for our table to be ready. After our first round of drinks, Hal cleared his throat. He turned to me with folded hands, his signal, I learned over time, that he was preparing to explain something or make an announcement. "I have two kids," he said, as if beginning a fascinating story. "Two boys. Caleb and Jake."

"Nice names," I said.

"Thanks," he said, but the cleverness of their names was not the point. He ordered another cocktail for himself. "Another cabernet?"

"Sure," I said, and the bartender got busy. I saw him glance at us, and I wondered how many conversations like this he'd heard over the years.

"Jake is fourteen and Caleb's twelve," Hal said. "Both have birthdays coming up."

"Hmm," I said, thinking, Shoot, adolescents. "Tough ages?" Just in time, the bartender placed our new drinks in front of us.

"We have our moments," he said. Clearly, this story was not going to be about raising teenagers.

"I have no kids," I said, wanting in on the let's-tell-our-life-story game and not quite ready for the next chapter of his. "I've never been married."

Hal nodded as if none of that information was good or bad and he was just taking it in. Or he could have merely been waiting for me to stop talking so he could continue describing his demographics. "As you know, I am . . . married."

"Yes."

"Excuse me, your table is ready," said the hostess, who had approached our bar stools. "If you'll follow me?"

We picked up our drinks to bring them with us. It felt good to stand up and stretch my legs, as if my weakened blood circulation might have been impairing my judgment. Hal motioned for me to go ahead, and we fell in line, snaking through the candlelit tables to a two-top against the wall, toward the back of the room. I'd never been seated at this particular table, which was a relief. No unnecessary baggage to carry. "This is perfect, thanks," Hal said to the hostess as he helped me settle in. He had given me the seat with the best view, and I wondered if he was aware of that.

I opened the menu. "I'm hungry, are you?" Perhaps talking about food would give us a respite.

"If you'd allow me, I could order for us," said Hal.

I'd never been with a date who'd tried that. It was so Neanderthal and yet fascinating. "Oh, gosh. Thank you, but I'd rather order for myself," I said, already eyeing the filet mignon.

"As you wish," he said.

After I ordered, Hal simply said, "I'll have the same as the lady." He seemed anxious to get back to his story.

We both took sips while maintaining eye contact, as if in a trance or on a dare. Hal said, "May I continue? May I actually tell you about my wife?"

"Of course," I said, but the *W* word seared me, so I went into journalist mode, walls up, ears primed. Big sip.

Hal said his marriage had ended years ago. His wife struggled with manic-depressive illness. She had a top-notch psychiatrist. She was on medication. Sometimes it worked, sometimes it didn't.

I listened. Hal kept talking. I held onto my glass of wine. More sips.

He explained how they'd been through counseling and marriage encounter weekends at church, and how both Hal and his wife had been unkind. Had grown apart. Both of them were unhappy. Audrey (what a name, I'd always liked that name) had agreed to separate, live separate lives, but stay married. Until the youngest reached eighteen.

"Eighteen? That's six years from now," I said, because it didn't make any sense.

"I know." He took a long sip of water and gulped. "And we'd divorce sooner if either of us wanted to remarry," he added, "but that hasn't happened yet." He winked, and we sat with that hanging in the air for a second or two.

I smiled. "Do the kids know about your arrangement?"

"Oh, yes. It's impossible to hide. Kids pick up on everything, anyway," he said, grabbing a piece of bread and reaching for the butter.

I watched him trying to spread it, his long knife pushing the too-hard patty into doughy craters on his slice of French bread, and eating the thing even though the butter hadn't melted. He looked at me as he took a bite and smiled. He had a beauty mark near his temple on the left side, and crow's-feet from years of sincerity.

"So tell me about you," he said, still chewing and gently wiping his mouth with the black cloth napkin the waiter had earlier swapped out for the white when he saw Hal and I were both wearing dark colors.

"Tell you about me?" I said, considering where to start. Audrey was still on my mind, and I wondered what it would be like to live with a bipolar family member. I knew about having a mother with health issues and possible Alzheimer's, but I'd already moved out when the worst of those symptoms began.

Our filet mignon arrived, and we both took a deep breath as the servers set down our plates. "Careful, they're hot," they said, and it was a nice diversion from the Audrey chronicles. Hungry, we dug in with pleasure. We sat there, savoring the meal together and sipping our drinks, just letting it all sink in. I had so many questions. I thought about taking out my notepad.

Hal read my mind and answered one without me asking. "I have my own apartment," he said, looking up from his fork and knife. "The kids live in the house, and Audrey and I alternate weeks living with them there. Although somehow Audrey seems to have more time with them than I do."

The more he said her name, the less I liked it. One more glass of wine wouldn't hurt. "You don't see them as much as you'd like?"

"Oh, yes, we have a great time when they're at the house. But I'm at work. The kids come and go. They have their activities, that sort of thing." Hal must have seen my confused face. He added, "They're busy. Homework. Friends. Concerts. They're in sports."

We chewed on that. Hal shrugged. I smiled and watched him skewer a couple of potatoes and swirl them in the bloody juice from his piece of beef. "So it sounds like you're basically living and acting as if you were divorced."

"Yes, I guess you could say so."

"Then why not go ahead and do it?" The words came out before I had a chance to stop them.

Hal choked and took up his water glass.

"Sorry," I said.

"No, it's fine." He composed himself. "I like your directness."

"I shouldn't have . . ."

"No, I'd like to answer you. I would. I just don't know how to explain it."

"Let's talk about something else," I said, but I made a mental note.

The marriage and divorce situation would be important to resolve before getting serious with this man, no matter how charming and handsome he was.

"There are a number of financial issues that would need to be addressed, so that's one thing," he said, keeping the topic going.

"But people do that every day. That's what lawyers are for, right?" I was curious (and right), though I also hated how it sounded like I was pressing for marriage. I wasn't.

Hal paused and gazed at me. "Yes," he said, furrowing his eyebrows. "That's right."

I'd finished eating the insides of my baked potato, so I cut into the skin, which was hard and crusty, just the way I liked it. As I lifted the fork to my mouth, I realized Hal had been watching me. As I chewed, I covered my mouth, afraid that pieces of food might escape. "Sorry," I said. "You've gotta eat the whole potato to get all the nutrients. And I love the skin."

"That's fine. Go ahead."

"It's none of my business," I said, giving up on the potato. "Sometimes I cross the line. Hazard of the job." I lifted my empty wineglass. If only there had been a few more drops in there.

"Do you want another? Or any dessert?" he asked.

I shook my head. "This was perfect," I said.

When the check arrived, I watched him sign his name. I had a theory about the correlation between signature style and personality or character. Hal's signature was large and clear and slanted to the right. He pressed down hard on the pen as he wrote. I liked it. "So is your real name Hal, or is that a nickname?" I asked.

"The real name is Harold," he said, putting away his credit card and returning his wallet to his pocket. "Harold August. But I've gone by Hal since college."

"Interesting. There's a story there."

"Is everything a story to you?"

"Pretty much."

"Well, mine is rather dull," he said. "I didn't like the name Harold.

And at college, no one knew me. It was a fresh start. So I gave myself a new identity. And 'Hal' was younger, more . . . fun."

I smiled. I liked Hal, and I liked fun.

The waiters had cleared our plates and gently scraped the crumbs from the tablecloth with a small aluminum blade. The table was a white landscape of possibility, and we let our hands and forearms rest dangerously close together on the soft surface.

"You know," Hal said, walking his fingers over to mine and brushing the tips, "I've done most of the talking tonight. You haven't answered my question."

"Which one?"

"About you," he said, his face glowing warm over the candlelight. "I'd like to get to know you."

"Oh, really?" I grinned, and I opened my hands, palms up.

"Really," he said. "You have beautiful teeth, you know that?"

"Thank you."

"And beautiful hands."

"Thank you." I looked down.

Hal placed his large hands over mine. His skin felt warm and silky and tingly. "I'd like to see you again," he said, stroking my wrist and hand. "Would you give me another date?"

I lifted my hand, and our fingers interlocked. The hair on the back of my neck perked up as my fingers slid against his and he caressed the skin between my fingers. I drank in his touch and felt a hum under his skin, or was it mine? I pressed my hand up against his as if to mirror it, but his was much bigger and I blushed. "Yes, I would give you that," I said, looking up. I didn't want to be unreasonable.

He stood and reached out; he helped me out of my chair. We walked to the parking lot without talking, and when we got into his car, the buzzing between us was palpable. We didn't need words. The car doors closed, and in the quiet black leather, we turned to face each other and kissed.

Eleven

CALLY

FRIDAY, DECEMBER 6, 2002

Night

I grabbed the beef jerky and Coke for Digger right away, so I wouldn't forget, then made my way through the aisles of the mini-mart, trying to think of the basics we might need. Toilet paper, instant coffee, water, chips, cereal, and milk.

"Forget something?" said the snowflake sweater.

"Yeah," I said.

"Where's your baby?" said Vikings.

"In the truck," I said. I was searching for something that looked good to eat. Suddenly, I was starving. I grabbed some cans of soup and put them on the counter, then went to the hot-dog warmer.

The women were looking at the truck parked next to a gas pump, and Digger standing beside it, smoking.

"Is that your husband out there?" asked the snowflake lady.

"Huh? Yeah, no," I said. I paid for my items and got the hell out of there, making the bell on the door chime extra-loud. I shuffled toward the truck as fast as I could, only twenty feet away, but my legs and crotch were weak.

"Can you help me with these?" I asked Digger as I got close to the truck. He took his time putting out his cigarette on the snowy ground, stomping it with his work boot, and finally taking one of the bulging plastic shopping bags out of my hand. I grabbed the door handle, but it was locked. I tried the backseat door, but it wouldn't open. "Digger!"

"What?" He was on the other side of the truck, and I saw him frown at me through the windows.

"It's locked!" I said, panic rising.

Digger tried the doors on his side. "Shit," he said.

"The baby's in there!" I pressed my forehead up against the glass.

"Don't you think I know that?"

"Do you have the key?"

Digger patted his coat and jeans, feeling for the keys, but then looked at the steering wheel. "They're in the ignition."

"Oh my God, Digger!" My heart tightened. I felt like I couldn't breathe. I looked back into the brightly lit mini-mart and saw all three women inside watching us. "Digger! Do something!"

"Calm down, calm down," he said, moving to the back of the truck and reaching over the snowy cover.

"How can I be calm when you locked the baby in the damn truck?" I said, not calm, tears in my eyes. I dropped my shopping bags in the snow and walked all around the truck as if there might be another way in. "Look, your window's open a crack."

"Yeah, I know," he said.

I stared at the baby, wide awake and alone on the passenger seat. "Can you open it? She's crying!"

"Working on it," Digger said, pulling a smaller toolbox out of the large built-in box and pushing me out of the way.

A voice squawked from the gas pump speaker. "Need any help?" said the cashier from inside.

"No, we got it," I said loudly, and waving, unsure if anyone could hear us. What if they'd been listening all along?

Like a thief, Digger stuck some wire into the window and tried a screwdriver on the lock mechanism, and I bounced in place, trying to keep warm. Finally, he opened the door, and I hoisted myself in and picked up the baby. I unzipped my coat and held her up to my warm clothes, pulled out a boob, and put her on it. Right away, she settled down.

Digger finished paying at the gas pump, then loaded the bags of supplies and food into the backseat. Someone knocked on my window, and I jumped. There was the Vikings sweatshirt, wearing no coat and marching in place. She motioned for me to unwind my window, which I did.

"Is this yours?" She stuck a red fuzzy mitten in my face.

"No."

"Okay, well, it was near when you—"

"Yeah, it's not mine," I said.

Digger was arranging stuff in the backseat, and I wished he'd hurry up.

"Hey, where's your car seat?" said Vikings, peering inside.

"Oh, um," I said, twisting to look in the back as if it might be there.

"You're gonna need one," she said. "It's the law."

"Okay, thanks," I said, nodding and waving her away. I wound up my window and she stepped back, closer to the rear of the truck. Was she looking at our license plate?

Digger hopped into the driver's seat. He was adjusting the rearview mirror and grumbling under his breath. He started the ignition, but the woman didn't move. Just stood there with that stupid mitten, staring at our license plate as we pulled away. The cold made her breath visible like smoke from a purple chimney. The truck bounced as Digger took us up and down a curb, then swerved to get into the turn lane and finally back on the highway.

"That nosy bitch with the mitten," I said. "She took down your license number."

"For what?"

"Did you hear what she said? We're supposed to have a car seat for the baby."

"Okay, Officer."

"Seriously, we need to get one," I said.

"Look around you. I don't see any car seat stores."

"Well, no, I realize that. But tomorrow," I said, almost excited about the idea.

"And how much is that gonna cost?" He sounded anxious.

"I don't know," I said, but I wasn't worried about money. Hal had preloaded a credit card for me with a huge balance, close to eleven thousand dollars.

"Well, I'm not paying for that. I just spent thirty bucks on gas."

"I can use the baby money," I said. "Hal gave me a special credit card."

"Is that what you used in there?"

"Yeah, why?"

"Just asking." Digger put his cap back on with the bill facing forward, which meant he was focused on driving and didn't want to be disturbed. He'd taken the cap off to run his fingers through his hair, as if it helped him settle down. But now the cap was back on, so he was back to being the driver, and I was the passenger holding the baby.

After a few miles, the truck was warm again, my heart rate had returned to normal, and the air had cleared. We got into the rhythm of the road, with occasional little gasps from Nell. I smiled over at Digger, hoping he'd heard them, too, but there was something else going on in his head.

"How much money is on that card?" he asked after a bit.

"I dunno," I lied. My eyes were closed. I was half sleeping. "But I can check it at an ATM."

"Okay," he said, and I let myself fall asleep again.

It was two-thirty in the morning when we reached Duluth, and the road curved down a long hill toward the city and the big black Lake Superior. The sky was clear and midnight blue. Below us were shadows of ships, containers, and cranes, all resting for the night, and the familiar slope of land on the left. The hills were dotted with hundreds of tiny lights on small but rugged homes, where, inside, the local people were sleeping, and tomorrow they would wake up and start a new day, go to work and take care of their children. Why couldn't we be one of those families? Weren't we just like anybody else?

We crossed the bridge from Duluth to Superior, and on the other side, I rested my forehead against the glass. The seat belt cut gently into my neck, and I saw the sign that said "Welcome to Wisconsin."

"I'm not supposed to leave Minnesota," I whispered to the window.

Twelve

RUTH

1997

The first time I met Hal's sons, we'd just come back from a movie date. We tumbled into the mudroom from the attached garage, laughing and kissing, and then spilled into the kitchen. Caleb was sitting on a stool at the far counter, and Jake was on the sofa beyond.

"Boys?" said Hal, clearly surprised to see them. "I thought you were going to Chicago with your mom."

"Got canceled," said Jake.

"Oh . . . great," said Hal, faking it. "Well, this is Ruth," and it was a terrible way to meet them.

"Hi, guys," I said, trying to telepathically express that I came in peace, I'd answer any questions they had, and I was no threat to them or anyone they loved.

"Hi," they grunted, barely audible, barely decipherable. Typical for thirteen- and fifteen-year-old boys. Caleb barely raised his eyes to briefly meet mine. Jake was watching a television show, looked like an episode of *Baywatch*, but was that show even still on?

"I've heard a lot about you guys," I said.

No response. Caleb wiped his nose on his arm.

"Caleb's fighting a cold," Hal explained.

"Oh, that's too bad," I said, but also I didn't want to catch it. "We just saw *Titanic*, have you seen it?"

Caleb smirked. No response from the TV watcher; finally, Jake tossed me a bone. He said, "We liked *Scream 2*."

"Oh," I said. A horror movie.

Caleb got up and went to sit by his brother.

"Hey," said Hal, clearly trying to break the tension, "do you guys wanna order pizza?"

"Sure," they both said as they switched screens to begin playing a video game.

"Great," said Hal. "Excuse me, I'll be right back." He went down the hall to the bathroom, leaving me alone with the moody monkeys.

"So . . ." I took a few steps closer to them. "Do either of you play school sports?"

They were facing the TV, controllers in their hands. "I play soccer," said Caleb. "And Jake doesn't."

"I don't want to, you little wuss," said Jake, side-checking Caleb. "I snowboard. In competitions."

"Oh," I said, not knowing how to respond to that.

"Broke his collarbone last year," said Caleb, laughing.

"You busted your leg," said Jake. "Doing nothing."

Caleb punched Jake's arm, and Jake stood up as if ready to fight. Hal returned and calmed them down and apologized to me. Jake sat down again, and the boys glowered at each other until one of them started the video game again, then all was well. Hal invited me to stay for pizza, but I declined, so he plopped some cash on the counter for the boys and took me home. And that was the first of my many attempts to gradually crack the code to understanding Hal's boys. The first glimpse I got of what kind of father Hal was.

While we were dating, Hal often wanted me to come for dinner at "the House" during his week with the boys. This place was huge. The kind of house with lofty ceilings to impress its visitors, or intimidate them. There was an echoey emptiness inside that seemed to hold the pain of Audrey's emotional struggles, which I'd been hearing more and more about. Even when she wasn't physically there, I could sense Audrey's presence in each room, the way it was decorated with yellows, pinks and florals, frilly pillows, scented candles, the Talbots in the closets, Clinique and Calvin Klein in the bathroom: she was everywhere.

From time to time out in the community, I'd run into Audrey. Hal had introduced us early on. She didn't make me feel terribly comfortable, and I understood that. Once I saw her in the grocery store parking lot. She was leaving just as I was getting out of my car, so I walked toward the other entrance to avoid her and make things easier for us both. Food shopping was already miserable enough without adding the unwanted ex-wife encounter. But there she was.

"Hello, Ruth," she called from the parking lot.

I turned around and feigned surprise. "Oh, Audrey, hi," I said, stepping down the curb and back into the parking area. "I didn't see you."

"Yes, you did." She simpered and opened her purse, pulling out her keys and a pack of gum. She was digging for something.

"Okay." I stepped out of the way of cars and up onto a median that separated the parking lot. A safe zone.

"And how are the boys?" She put her keys away, plucked out a cigarette, and lit it. "Is Caleb over his cold?" she asked, exhaling smoke to the side, but the wind blew it back in our faces.

"I think it was just allergies," I said.

"No." Audrey shook her head. "Caleb doesn't have allergies." She was the only one allowed to diagnose her sons' ailments, and I had crossed a line.

"Anyway, he seems fine," I said.

"And Hal?" She looked me up and down as she took another drag. "I know he has a big closing coming up, or has it happened already?"

"It was last week. Went fine." I hated how Audrey snooped for intel about Hal's work. When they divorced, she negotiated some deal where she got more alimony if Hal closed a big transaction. Fortunately, the alimony obligation would end when Audrey remarried. Unfortunately, she had no marriage plans on the horizon.

"Well, I'd better not dawdle." She winked and sashayed away, holding the lit cigarette in her right hand. "Good seeing you, Ruth." She flicked the ashes and didn't look back.

I always told Hal about my encounters with Audrey, because I wanted him to know, but also because she would inevitably tell him her version of things in one of their periodic phone conversations about bills to pay or decisions to make. Sometimes she would show up unannounced at the House during Hal's week with the kids, because she was in the neighborhood or because one of the boys forgot something, or simply because she was having a fit and needed to see Hal.

Once he'd invited me over for Hungarian goulash, his famous dish. I rang the bell and was waiting on the front stoop. The door opened, and there was Hal, tall and handsome, smiling and warm and wearing a chef's apron. "Come in," he'd said, pulling me toward him and kissing me in the threshold. The warmth of his mouth and the heat from his body against mine contrasted against the cold of the outdoors and created a thrill that seeped in from three sides.

"Dad, something's buzzing," called a voice from the kitchen.

Hal let go, and I almost fell back onto the front stoop. "Sorry. That's Caleb," he said. "Okay!" he yelled to the kitchen.

"Go ahead," I said, tossing my coat over the banister and fixing my hair and lips in the hallway mirror.

In the kitchen, Hal had turned off the oven timer and was washing his hands. Caleb was leaning against the kitchen counter with a sandwich in his hands.

"Hi, Caleb," I said.

Caleb took a bite and waved hello with a limp hand, his mouth full.

"Is Jake here?" I asked, because it was an easy topic for me and Caleb to connect on.

"Yeah, he's downstairs," said Caleb, chewing.

"Oh, that's right," I said, remembering: Jake had fallen in a snowboarding competition, injuring his shoulder and suffering a mild concussion.

"He's banished to the basement," said Hal in a fake-evil voice as he pulled open a drawer for a spoon.

"How much longer does he have to be in darkness like that?"

"The doctor said a few more days," said Hal, tasting some of his goulash and then rinsing the spoon. Caleb ambled to the fridge and filled a glass with milk.

"I hope you're more careful, Caleb," I said to his back, an attempt at teasing.

"That's why I play Final Fantasy VII on PlayStation," Caleb deadpanned. He chugged the milk, set the glass on the counter, and scuttled to the sofa in the great room, plopping into place in front of a giant-screen television. His video game was waiting, characters hovering in animated suspense, and he donned his headphones and picked up the controller.

"Sorry about that," said Hal, opening a bottle of cabernet.

"No, I get it," I said. "Scary about Jake, though."

"Thank God he was wearing his helmet." Hal poured me a glass.

"Must be hard for him to stay in the basement." I took a long sip. I felt a twinge of guilt for being happy he was out of our hair. But the poor kid had taken a pretty bad fall. "He's down there full-time, huh?"

"Yeah, but Audrey set up a nice bedroom for him, with dim lights, and he listens to music." Hal smiled, and we both sipped.

I nodded at Hal. Since Jake was in the basement and Caleb was immersed in his game, we had a few minutes alone. I flashed my eyebrows up and down with a smile. Hal set down his wineglass and sauntered toward me, never letting his eyes leave mine. I set down my glass, too, and in one motion we swooped into an embrace. His arms around my waist, we wrapped ourselves together, and our mouths met. We kissed this way and that way, over here and over there. He kissed my neck and earlobe, my lips. I drank in his scent and we swayed gently, dancing without music. I smiled, and I was blushing.

I was tingling. He stroked my hair. "I love you," he said. We kissed again, swaying and dancing. Hal lifted his arm and I twirled under. He pulled me close and held me.

"Hello, it's me," a woman's voice trilled, the door slammed, and we heard footsteps. High heels. Audrey.

Hal separated from our embrace, quickly let go as he had done at the front door, and gave me an apologetic face. I shrugged and picked up my wineglass.

"Just checking on Jake," she said as she entered the kitchen. "Hello, Ruth. Hi, Caleb! So how is he?" Audrey directed her question at Hal.

"Jake? I'm sure he's fine. I haven't been down in the last hour or so," said Hal, wiping a bit of lipstick from his cheek.

Audrey glanced at me as if I were the reason for Hal's distraction.

"Mom," said Caleb as he hopped up from the sofa and removed his headphones. "Can we go to Burger Town?" He shuffled toward his mother.

"Sure, but it looks like your dad just made goulash," said Audrey.

"Yeah, but I don't wanna be on their *date*," said Caleb lowly, his head pressed into Audrey's hug. I worried that he'd been watching us. Audrey kept her arm around him as if he were a poor creature who needed extra love and attention. In her clasp, his posture changed, his face relaxed, and he became strangely younger, sweeter, before our eyes. There was an ease between them, and he didn't mind when Audrey tousled his hair; he shrugged gently and fixed a few strands.

Hal stood watching Audrey and Caleb, proudly grinning at his younger son and at Audrey's ability to soften him. Even though divorced, these three were a family, and anyone would know that just by looking.

I knew I wanted that. I wanted to be someone's mom. I wanted to be inside a microsphere like that with Hal. Where we could have our own clever teenager to tousle and hug and spoil. I didn't want to stay out here on my own. I wanted in.

"It's fine with me," said Audrey, a question in her voice for Hal. "Do you mind if he eats at Burger Town?"

"Fine with me," said Hal. And although I thought he let Caleb off the hook too easily, it did give us more time to be alone.

"Okay," said Audrey, "just let me go see your brother and then we'll go." She smiled at me, and Caleb followed her down the stairs.

Hal followed Caleb and Audrey, but I stayed put. Somehow I knew this group visit to the basement wasn't for me. Alone in the kitchen, with Caleb's game still paused on the big-screen TV, I surveyed the overflowing quantity of goulash. "Looks like we'll have plenty of leftovers," I said to the Final Fantasy warrior.

Thirteen

CALLY

FRIDAY, DECEMBER 6, 2002

Night

When we got to the cabin, it was pitch-black outside. Digger parked the truck at the bottom of the driveway, shining the headlights onto the locked gate. He got out but left his door open, and cold air blew into the truck. It was too far for me to reach and pull shut, so I snuggled the baby close and waited.

In the headlights, Digger unlatched the long metal gate and pushed it open, skimming across the tops of drifted snow. He tossed his winter gloves at my feet and shifted into four-wheel drive, which was one of his favorite things to do. The long uphill driveway was covered with about a foot of fresh powder, only a few deer tracks, no signs of humans.

"You never told me you had a cabin," I said, wondering if we were trespassing.

Digger focused on the snowy climb, leaned forward toward the windshield, and switched on the brights. "Yeah," he mumbled, "it's my uncle's place."

"The same uncle you worked for in Missouri?" I leaned forward with him, trying to see it.

"No, my uncle Charlie, on my mom's side."

"Oh," I said, trying not to sound disappointed. I didn't like Digger's mother, and she didn't like me. Didn't like when I came to their house after school. That was one of the reasons we found other places to be alone together. That was also the reason I'd escape out his window and climb onto the roof of the garage whenever she came up the stairs calling his name. I'd get plenty of warning: her footsteps were loud under her large body. Her voice was like a man's. She and I did not get along. But this cabin would be a perfect place for us to camp out.

The truck moved easily over the snow, and soon we were at the top of the hill. The trees were like dark statues, thick and tall. In the headlights, I strained to see: a simple rustic cabin and a shed, and more trees beyond.

"This is it," he said.

"Does it have heat?" I said, peering as if I could tell by looking at it.

"Hold on, hold on," said Digger. "Wait here while I get the key." He left the truck running but got out, and I turned up the heat. He opened the back door and rummaged around in the backseat.

"What are you doing?"

"Getting a flashlight," he said. He marched back to look in the truck bed. Digger was in love with his F-150 and had been really pumped when he found a four-door with a hard-shell "truck cap," to protect his stuff. He kept tons of junk back there, gas cans, tools, jugs of wiper fluid, an air compressor, boxes of nails and screws, firewood, a dirt shovel, bags of car towels, Turtle Wax, a wool blanket covered in wood chips and dust, Spackle, motor oil, gloves, cheesecloth, cans of Mountain Dew, shims, a piece of plywood, a couple of five-gallon buckets, and his ongoing pile of cardboard boxes.

On the drive, he'd told me about the Missouri job and the next one coming up in February, in Florida. He liked having time between jobs like this. He was okay with traveling for work, getting temporary housing. It didn't sound fun to me.

"Got it." Digger switched on the flashlight and closed the back hatch. He shined his flashlight at my feet. "Got my gloves?" he asked. I reached down and passed them to him. Digger hiked around the side of the cabin until he was out of range of the headlights. Soon he trudged back to his side of the truck. He hopped in and shut the door. "Dammit," he said.

"What?"

"Can't find the fucking key."

"What?" I said, confused, upset.

"Yeah, I know." Digger held his forehead, lifted off his DEKALB cap, and put it back on.

"Where is it supposed to be?"

Digger slammed the steering wheel. "There's a goddamn peg it hangs on."

"It wasn't there?"

"No, it's not there, Cally. That's what I just said."

"Where could it be?"

"It must have fell in the snow, and I couldn't fuckin' find it."

"Oh my God!" I said, panic rising in my chest.

"Goddammit!" Digger slammed the steering wheel again, and the baby woke.

At this point, things could have gone two ways: I could have yelled at Digger, gotten angry because he was losing his temper, which probably would have gotten him angrier and made him do something stupid. Like the time he punched the wall and broke his hand. Or when he kicked his bike and broke the spokes.

Instead I decided to stay calm and ignore his bullshit tantrum. Something about having Nell there told me this was the better choice. "It's okay," I said. "It'll be fine. We can sleep in the truck."

"For fuck's sake," said Digger.

"When it gets light, we can look for the key." I bounced the baby. "Shhh. Shhh. It's almost morning, anyway." Sure enough, Digger started to relax. So did the baby. "Do you have a blanket back there?" I said.

Digger got the blanket and laid it over us. We reclined our seats and I brushed the wood chips off the blanket. Digger switched off the headlights and turned down the heat to medium. We closed our eyes and listened to the sound of the heat blower and the engine humming. It wasn't our first time sleeping in a car. In high school, we'd spent several nights together like that.

But with the baby in my lap, I didn't sleep very well. I closed my eyes but was always half aware of Nell's little gasps and coos. I must have finally fallen asleep, which I needed, until she wailed and woke me up. I tried, but this time I couldn't make her quiet just by bouncing her.

"Okay," I said, "okay, now." I raised up my seat in the dark truck and lifted the many layers of clothes to find my breast. Groping for my own nipple, I made a path for the baby and positioned her crying face into my chest. Even though the heater was still running, the air felt cold on my exposed skin. Nell's warm mouth would make it better.

Digger rolled over and grumbled, pulled the blanket all the way up to his ear. I leaned forward slightly to meet the baby halfway, to help her find the nipple. "Come on," I said, "come on, please." When the tiny wet mouth finally grabbed on, it was thrilling. Nell's mouth was strong, and she pulled hard on my breast. Tingles ran from my shoulders down my chest and into my nipples. The sensation was like nothing else I'd ever felt: amazing. It blew my mind, and the sound of her suckling was like a miracle. Something was very different this time. She sounded like she was really drinking, slurping something. Milk! I tried not to move. I didn't want to mess it up.

As I nursed the baby, I looked out the windshield into the snow and trees, pinkish blue from the light of dawn. I thought I saw things in the shadows, shapes of things, and pictures. I looked to the sky and then to Digger, sleeping. He still snored loudly, that hadn't changed. When the baby pulled off the nipple, she was completely relaxed. I tried the other breast, but she wasn't interested. I held her to my shoulder, and she burped. I was so happy because I felt like I knew what I was doing: I could feed her. I kissed her little head and closed my eyes and hoped she would sleep again. Maybe I could get a few minutes more. Awake or asleep, we rested together, and I didn't need to know the difference.

Fourteen

RUTH

2002

My plan had been to take six weeks off from work after the baby was born. I'd already used up several hours of PTO going to Cally's doctor appointments and ultrasounds, but I was entitled to maternity leave, and I planned to use it. The legislature would be going back into session in January, so the timing would be perfect.

Hal and I had moved into our new condo, and I had the nursery ready. The theme was an underwater wonderland. Taupe walls accented with bright colors of the sea, orange and ocean blue, sunset yellow. I had a selection of onesies and diapers stacked in drawers under the changing pad. A solid wood crib, a brand-new mattress, a green flannel blanket, and pink and yellow fish-themed sheets.

I'd wanted to put starfish-shaped knobs on the small dresser, but Hal told me to stop with the crazy overboard. I tended to overdo things, especially things that I cared about, and especially when I was feeling out of control. There's only so much preparation one can do for a baby arriving in one's home before it starts to feel like it will never happen. Empty crib. Empty rocker. Everything clean and tidy. Then the dust starts to settle. The stuffed animals take on a horror-movie vibe. Enough, I told myself.

When Cally got pregnant, I didn't want to tell people at work. Not right away. But when? And how? All together at a meeting? One on one? There were milestones I'd wanted her to pass for "safety." Pass the eight-week mark, then fourteen weeks, then twenty-two, then twenty-six. So much could have gone wrong. So much we didn't know.

And the whole question of how we got our child, and the underlying topic of infertility. Was I afraid of their reactions? Their opinions about surrogacy? Not afraid, but I dreaded what they might do, like blurt out questions or give me well-meaning advice. And were they secretly judging me, talking behind my back? Did they think I was too old to become a mother? It was none of their business, and perhaps my fears were exaggerated, but those were the things I thought about. Eventually, of course, I had to tell the team. We had to work out coverage and communication. We had to address the calendar and deadlines, reassign responsibilities while I'd be out. I was a workaholic. I loved my work.

In fact, I had an idea for a story I wanted to do. I'd been gathering sources and jotting down thoughts as our journey progressed. The concept was a woman's need to be productive, her need to be valued as a contributor to society, compared against the options available to her, especially without an education. I'd noticed that many of the surrogates I'd researched were relatively uneducated or unskilled, which limited their options in our society, for many reasons. But with surrogacy, young, healthy women could earn good pay and step into a powerful, impactful role: carrying a child for another family. There were great physical (and emotional) risks involved, and the area was poorly regulated. Surrogates were rather poorly protected, I thought. I wondered what led women to take such risks. Someday, when this was over, I thought I'd interview Cally about it. I wanted to check out my instincts on the topic.

I often sat in the empty nursery with my journal and made notes about my stories, lists of questions to ask. The baby was almost here, and I'd have to find another place of inspiration. Hal was supposed to hang the mini-blinds, but he kept putting it off. He acted like we had all the time in the world, but I knew how to work a deadline. He played the experience card a bit more than I appreciated. He'd been through this all before, he kept reminding me, and the nursery would be fine. None of this was new to him.

But it was new for me. And when I finally told my team about it, they were ecstatic. They didn't say anything critical or rude. I wondered how I could have imagined that they would. In fact, they didn't seem to care one way or the other how we got our child. Most of them didn't seem to know much about surrogacy; to them, it was just something celebrities or wealthy people did when they wanted to have biological children, like William Stern and Baby M. If my coworkers had questions or opinions, they didn't say anything to my face. They only cared about the extra work they'd have to do to cover my absence. They only asked when I was coming back. I'd been slightly surprised by this. I imagined that if the roles had been reversed, I would have had more questions.

Kristin asked if it was a boy or a girl. Thank goodness for Kristin. She made me feel like a normal mom-to-be. I explained that we'd wanted to know the sex, and how happy Hal had been when he'd heard it was a girl. I told her about the ultrasound (where we stood next to Cally) as the technician danced the wand around (on Cally's belly) and we saw the fetus in the womb, a gray-and-white Rorschach image, and how we listened to the heartbeat.

I didn't tell Kristin that my eggs were no good, or how I felt about an embryo being formed with an egg that wasn't mine, or that I'd have no genetic connection to the child. I didn't mention that we'd used artificial insemination or any of the other gruesome details. Just the fact that we were having a baby girl.

I found out later that Kristin was the one who tied a pink balloon to the little tree in our front yard and placed a sign there that said "It's a Girl." Very sweet.

"When is she due?" she'd asked.

"December."

"So the legislature will be in recess."

"Exactly. We got lucky there."

"That makes our lives a lot easier for sure."

I'd been covering the legislature for about six years, and before that I'd done health (which I was tired of), energy policy (which I hated), and education (which I loved). The legislature was only in session for half the year. Which meant that during the other half, I covered other stories, and usually, I was able to pick my own features to pitch. Of course, I had to stay in touch with my sources, the lobbyists, the agency heads, and most of all, the governor's office.

In the back of my mind, I did worry that I'd want something else. Would I want to stay home for the entire maternity leave? Maybe I'd hate it and want to come back to work sooner? Maybe I'd miss the energy and the intellectual stimulation? Or I'd want to telecommute, and how would that fly? If I wasn't in the newsroom, I wondered if people might forget me, if I'd be passed over or be selected for the next rounds of reduction when they inevitably came.

None of this stressed out Hal. He stayed calm as a sea cucumber. He knew what to expect, and I didn't. But I was doing my best to see his experience as another resource for me. And for us.

Fifteen

DIGGER

Morning

Cally was shaking me. We'd reclined our seats, but I hadn't slept well in the truck. "Wake up," she said. "I need to pee."

"Go and pee, then." I squinted and sat up. It was so early. I could barely see the cabin, the shed. All covered in snow.

"Where?" Cally was wide awake.

"There's an outhouse." I pointed to the right. "Over there, down the path. Take the flashlight."

She wiggled herself out of the blankets and clothes we'd slept under. She tried to pass me the baby.

"No, just put her on the seat."

"No," she said. "Hold her till I get back."

"Hang on," I said, sitting up and adjusting my hat. I wasn't getting out of this. So I put my hands out, palms up, like a beggar. Cally placed the baby's head in one hand and the butt in the other. Felt like a Slinky.

Cally took high steps through the snow. She found the trail and disappeared in the woods, the light from the flashlight jumping around.

I looked at the baby. She yawned and opened her eyes. They were wide and dark. Like walnuts but black. "You look like an alien," I said to the kid. "Anybody ever tell you that?"

Cally was quick. She came walking back with a big grin on her face.

"What's wrong with you?" I said when she opened the door and climbed in.

"I found the key!" She dangled it in my face.

"Where?" I traded the baby for the key.

"In the outhouse," she said. "On a hook!"

"Oh yeah." I rubbed my eyes. "I should have looked there."

"It's all right," she said, smiling at the baby. "We survived."

"I need to go back to sleep."

"No, let's go inside," she said.

"God, you're a pain in the ass." I shut off the ignition and checked my hair in the mirror. "Fine."

I went first, and Cally followed with the alien. This was your basic one-room hunting cabin. The walls were stacks of rounded logs. On each side, there was a small window. The place hadn't been touched in a while.

"It feels colder in here than it was outside," said Cally.

"Yeah." I was already at the woodstove, pulling newspaper and kindling from the pile.

"Is there any heat?" she asked.

"You're looking at it," I said, loading the stove with firewood. I'd need to get more. "Matches?" I asked, as if Cally knew where things were. I found them in the kitchen and got the thing going. The cabin was about twenty by thirty. Double bed in one corner, small kitchen in another. Open shelves for pans and shit. Foldout sofa, small table, rocker. Simple, but it got the job done.

"Are there any lights?" Cally asked.

"Hold on," I said, looking around. I'd been here many times with my uncles or brothers when we'd come to hunt or just come drink on a weekend. I lit a candle and the oil lamp. There was a battery-powered lantern, but the batteries were old.

Cally sat on the rocker and bobbed the baby. The fire caught and roared up nice.

"Will you bring the stuff in?" Cally asked.

I groaned but went along. It wasn't much. Her duffel bag and backpack and five or six bags from the mini-mart. My backpack. After fifteen minutes, the place was warm enough. Cally got up and changed the baby's diaper, then wrapped her in blankets and put her on the bed. Both of my older brothers had kids, but they didn't visit much. Their kids were elementary-age. And bratty.

"Come here," Cally said.

I walked over and stood by the bed. "What?" I looked at the kid.

"See how helpless and cute she is."

Her walnut eyes were open again, and she was staring at the ceiling. "Sort of like a baby raccoon."

"Digger!" Cally punched me, laughing. But it was true.

I went outside to the shed for more firewood. While I was out there, I shoveled the path to the outhouse. When I got back inside, Cally had swept the floor and was wiping down the kitchen and pans. She'd emptied a wooden crate and made it into a baby bed. I put another log in the stove. Cally emptied out her backpack and all the mini-mart bags. She put some stuff on the table and some on the floor. Then she explained it to me. Didn't ask if I wanted to know. Which I didn't.

"Okay, we have ten diapers, only nine now, so we'll need more. One package of wet wipes. This is a bulb syringe." She squeezed the blue ball. It made a puff of air on my face. "Kinda fun," she said.

"Okay, okay," I said, waving it away.

"Bottles, nipples, pacifiers, and formula. These are only free samples from the hospital. We have to get real ones and extras. Ointment, baby powder. This is travel-size. We'll need more."

"What for?" I said. "We're only here a couple days, you said."

"Well, I don't know how long this stuff will last."

I frowned at her. She'd better not be up to something.

"Thermometer strips, that's fine," she said, holding up each item as she named it. "Look at this tiny hairbrush and these little nail clippers."

Cally was acting like she was playing with a doll. When I was a kid, I had to share a room with my sister, Deena. She'd had baby dolls and plastic accessories and stuffed animals all over the place. I'd wanted my own room so bad, but our mother took the extra one for her office. This was when Mom was trying to be a Realtor. What a joke. When she finally gave up, I convinced her to let me have the room. But for all of first grade and part of second, I'd had to put up with Deena's play sets and make-believe shit.

"I don't really care about all that," I said as Cally showed me her supplies.

"We have water, coffee, cereal, beef jerky, Coke, and these sandwich cremes," said Cally.

I took the package of cookies and ate a handful. When the baby cried, Cally picked her up and nursed her. That made her stop crying. Rocking on the rocker. I poked at the fire. After ten minutes, I said, "Did you still want to go to the store?"

"Yeah, as soon as she's done." She looked down at the baby pressed against her chest. The only sounds were the rocker creaking and the baby's sucking noise. "The main thing is a car seat," said Cally.

"Fine," I said, looking at the door. There was a small pool of melted snow on the floor. "I found you a pair of boots you can use if you want." I pointed to the extra pair I'd brought in from the truck. Cally and I had almost the same size foot. Hers were a bit large and mine were a bit small. We used to sit on the floor facing each other with our legs sticking out and match up our feet.

"Thank you," she said, as if this was the nicest thing anyone had ever done.

"They're just boots," I said.

"That's sweet."

"Yeah," I said. "So are you ready to go?"

"Can't you see I have a baby hanging on my boob? I can go as soon as she's done."

"Then I'm going out for a smoke."

"Okay."

I walked out and tried to light up. The fucking wind kept blowing it out. I hunched over and cupped my hand on it. Finally, I took a drag and got it going. I saw something from the corner of my eye. I looked into the kitchen window. Cally was just standing there, watching me.

Sixteen

RUTH

Instead of a honeymoon, Hal suggested a ski trip with his sons. They were getting older, and he wanted us to become a family. Plus, it was prime ski season, and his boys were snowboarders. We could honeymoon later; Hal loved to downhill. Their favorite place was Vail, so we splurged and spent a week there in a four-bedroom chalet.

Apparently, with Audrey, they'd vacationed in a single hotel room, with the couple in one bed and the two boys in the other. Now that the boys were larger, and with me being a new and nonbiological member of the family, we had a healthy debate about whether to book two hotel rooms or to rent a house. In the hotel scenario, I would have a room to myself, and Hal and the boys would share a room because the boys weren't yet eighteen. Hal promised we would ask for adjoining rooms and that he'd sneak into my room at night. When the hotel couldn't guarantee rooms together, I booked us a house.

From the beginning of the trip, there was tension. At check-in, through security, in the airport food court, the newspaper shop, then walking to the gate, the boys bickered and punched each other, grumbled under their breath, slouched, moaned, and burped. It was as if they were trying to punish me and embarrass Hal, or both, and it was working.

"Stop it," Hal said.

"You stop it," said one of the boys.

"No, you stop it," said the other.

"Boys." Hal furrowed his brow and lowered his voice.

They copied him: "Dad."

"That's enough," said Hal.

"Is it really?" said one.

"No, I think we need more," said the other.

"Stop it, now." Hal made a karate-chop motion on the word "now." We'd been walking through the terminal, heading to our gate. As if to purposefully annoy, the boys had been walking closely behind us, and we'd felt their sophomoric remarks land on the backs of our necks. But then they were silent. Gone. I turned my head to find them. They had stopped several feet behind us, standing still in the middle of the walkway, with streams of travelers parting around them to avoid a collision.

"Hal," I said, turning my head back while walking briskly to keep up. "They literally stopped moving when you told them to stop."

"Good." Hal charged forward, weaving through strangers.

"No, I mean they stopped walking. They're standing still back there. Look," I said, touching his elbow, "they're blocking traffic." Hal stopped, sighed, turned around, saw the boys frozen like they'd seen Medusa, and then Hal resumed walking toward our gate. I followed Hal's lead and kept trudging. After a few steps, I asked, "Do they have their boarding passes?"

"That's their problem." Hal adjusted the shoulder strap of his laptop bag and kept walking.

I was pretty sure we'd been assigned seats all together across one row, so this was going to be an awkward two-and-a-half-hour flight to Colorado. As we approached our gate, I heard the stomping thuds of running feet and recognized their out-of-breath voices, racing and laughing and calling each other names. Their hair flying, they landed in front of us in line to board the plane and plopped their backpacks on the floor, bent over red-faced, and caught their breath.

"You're such a woman," Caleb said to Jake.

"Idiot." Jake recovered enough to shove Caleb, almost toppling him over.

The two attendants at the gate watched us, probably calculating whether to address the situation or let it settle. One of them lifted the phone receiver and talked to who knows who on the other line. Perhaps she was warning the flight attendants about the rowdy family about to board. Maybe she was faking a call so she wouldn't have to deal with us. I wondered if it was too late for me to turn back and stay home. The other attendant took our boarding passes and tore off one end, smiled, and pointed to the backpacks still on the floor.

"Jake. Caleb, get your backpacks," said Hal.

"Sorry," I said to the gate attendant.

"No problem," she said. "Have a nice flight." She moved on to the next traveler in line. I wondered if the gate attendant could tell that we were a "blended" family and that I was completely ill-equipped as a stepmom. Were we that obviously different from the other families on this flight? Was I the only one who didn't know how to handle these dynamics, this behavior? I wondered if I was being naive to marry a man with children. And whether I'd made a mistake in marrying him so quickly. Or at all?

It got worse.

Because we were in a chalet with its own kitchen, Hal thought it would be fun to cook our own meals. But the boys didn't like any of my ideas. They picked at the meals I cooked, claiming they weren't hungry or saying they were allergic. They said they wanted to eat out, like they had done when they came with their mom. So for the rest of the week, we agreed on dinners out, lunch at the ski resort, and breakfasts at the chalet. The boys scarfed down bagels and cereal each morning before we headed to the slopes but left their crumbs and dirty bowls on the counter for me or Hal to clean up.

Hal waved it off as a minor blip in the big scheme of things. At least they were willing to get up early and get dressed for skiing, which was impressive enough, in his book. At sixteen, Jake wanted to drink wine with dinner because all of his friends apparently did, and besides, we were on vacation, so we should make it special. Both sons brought their portable Game Boys to the restaurants so they could rescue Mario and Pikachu under the table, while grunting at the waiters and eating with their hands. I believe I was the only one at the table who used a napkin. The boys made very little eye contact with me, speaking only to their father, even in response to questions posed by me.

"How were the slopes today?"

"Did you find your other glove?"

"What's the best kind of snow for snowboarding?"

I tried. They answered approximately every other question. They looked up once or twice. It was lonely. Several times they wove in references to their mom and memories of times they'd had on previous family vacations with her, and what a great skier she was, and other stories of Audrey, which was fine.

But it wasn't enough.

I knew I wanted my own child with Hal. I wanted my own child, period. My body knew I didn't have much time. My libido had been going bonkers, telling me to get pregnant and to hurry up. But whenever we kissed in front of the boys, they'd groan and say "Get a room" or "Gross." I learned to keep private our displays of affection.

I was determined to make this trip at least a bit of a honeymoon. So I organized a schedule and created my opportunities. Our agreement was to meet up with the boys for lunch at eleven-thirty and then again at the end of the day for dinner. Afterward and in between, Hal and I could be alone.

The chalet had a beautiful large stone fireplace wall, plate-glass windows, and a six-person hot tub on the back deck. The boys wanted nothing to do with the hot tub, so that became our oasis. We donned thick white terry-cloth robes and tiptoed to the hot tub each night, with sleeping mountains in the background and twinkling lights surrounding the deck. Those were the best moments of the week.

And that was where and when we agreed we'd make our own baby together.

Seventeen

CALLY

MARCH 14, 2002

I learned that there were a lot of ways to do an insemination. I never thought the turkey baster thing was real, but apparently, lots of women did it that way, and apparently, it worked. And there were fancy, more technical versions of the baster. Or some surrogates, like in the Bible, actually had sex with the intended father. But that wasn't how we did it, thank God. I liked Hal, but he was too old for me. And Ruth never would have allowed that. Nope! Ruth chose the clean and sterile way. At a clinic. With a syringe.

When Ruth and I arrived at Dr. Salovich's office for the procedure, I had to wait in line before I could check in. To give me privacy, Ruth sat in the waiting area. This was a nice one. Bright and modern. It had a happy feel; after all, this was a place where babies were made. The receptionist seemed glad to see me. "Have a seat, Miss Scott. We'll be right with you," she said. Clearly, she recognized me from previous visits, when I'd gotten my shots and prenatal checkups.

I sat next to Ruth and flipped through the parenting magazines. I'd been in a waiting room like this before, when I went in for a Pap smear and exam at my ob-gyn's office, and they also had a bunch of parenting magazines. But these magazines were different, with titles like *American Journal of Fertility* and *Surrogacy Today*. Sitting next to Ruth, I could have been mistaken for her daughter, and I wondered how I could let the other people in the waiting room know I was a surrogate. I wanted them to know I was here for insemination, not infertility.

I picked up *Surrogacy Today* and held it open in front of me, like a sign. I skimmed the pages until I found an article I liked. "Stories of Success: Bringing the Gift of Life to an Infertile Couple." This was a profile of two different surrogates who both loved being able to make another couple's dream come true. The first surrogate did it once and then moved on to have her own family. The second lady did surrogacy as a career. She'd already done it three times, and she hoped to squeeze in one more if her body would let her. She must have made enough for a house and a car. All I wanted was to finish college debt-free, and as much as I loved everybody at the dog daycare, I wanted a better-paying job.

I looked around the waiting room to see if anyone noticed what I was reading. I held the magazine a bit higher. There was an article about the medical costs, a list of legal dos and don'ts, and lots of ads from surrogacy agencies. Hal and Ruth hadn't used an agency, they'd told me, because it would have limited their options for finding the right surrogate. And Hal had told me later that it would have resulted in less money in my pocket, since the agency would take a cut of the fee.

Hal had asked me what kind of career I was thinking about. I told him accounting because I was good at math. He seemed pleasantly surprised by that answer, and he offered to help me find an internship after I got back in school. I got a sense that he wanted me to put his money to good use. He seemed to actually care. Once we met at a coffee shop near his office, and he gave me a list of accounting firms he'd researched that had summer internships for college students.

"When is Hal getting here?" I asked Ruth. We couldn't do this without him.

She looked at her watch and shrugged. "Should be any minute."

Finally, a nurse walked out and said, "Cally Scott."

"That's me." I dropped the magazine and smiled at Ruth. She would wait for Hal and see me afterward.

"Come this way, honey." The nurse walked in front of me and I noticed her wide hips.

I stepped on the scale for my weight. In the exam room, I stuck out my arm for the blood pressure wrap, and I undressed and hopped up on the table as instructed. Someone knocked on the door, and I adjusted the blue paper to cover as much of me as possible.

"Come in," I said.

Dr. Salovich burst into the room holding a folder. "How are we today?" he asked. Dr. Salovich had a bushy full head of gray hair, a large mole on his cheek, and a take-charge attitude.

"Excited," I said. "Today's the day."

"Yes, it is," he said as he washed his hands at the tiny sink and ripped out too many paper towels. He lowered his glasses halfway down his nose. "You are here for artificial insemination, eh?"

I didn't know what kind of accent he had, but it was thick. "Yes," I said. I pressed my knees together, and we both pretended I was fully dressed.

"Do you have any questions for me?" He peered over the top of his black-framed glasses.

"Not really," I said. "I'm here to get pregnant."

He chuckled and must have decided that I should have asked a few questions, because he answered them. He described the procedure for using either a cap or a syringe to place the sperm on and near the cervix. He talked about the alternative, which was to use a catheter going into the uterus. Before we decided, he said he'd take a peek and see which method he would recommend for my body. Either way, I was not to move much afterward and should limit my activity. Did I understand? I did. "May I examine you now?" he asked.

"Yes."

The doctor scooted his rolling stool toward my legs and positioned a bright light to shine between them. He lifted the blue paper and folded it back a bit so he could see. I felt the heat of the light on my vagina and heard Dr. Salovich snapping the rubber gloves on his hands. His eyes appeared over the top of the paper sheet.

"All right," he said as he reached over to his side table, "this may be somewhat cold," and he inserted the speculum. It was. "Some pressure now," he said as he cranked it open. It hurt. "I'm looking," he mumbled.

I held my breath during this part. After about thirty long seconds, he released the speculum and slid it out. I exhaled and relaxed. Covering me with the paper sheet, he moved the lamp away and said, "We're gonna try the syringe."

"Okay," I said from the pillow. One of the ceiling tiles had a water stain.

"You're not currently pregnant?" he asked, yanking off one rubber glove with a snap, then the other.

"No," I said. "But they took a blood test to be sure."

"Good."

For a second, I thought I heard Hal's voice in the hallway. Could he just now be arriving? Walking by my exam room? I wanted to shout hello to him, and I hoped he might stop in, since this was the big day. Here we were, doing it.

"Everything's ready," said the doctor, "except the sperm, of course." He chuckled as he took off his glasses and wiped the lenses clean with a tissue.

"Yeah." I laughed at the joke, but he could probably tell I was faking.

"I'll be back in a bit," he said.

A knock at the door and a nurse entered, bumping into the doctor as he left. "There are a few questions here you didn't answer," she said to me.

I hadn't seen this nurse before. She had a nasal tone in her voice, and she acted like paperwork was her favorite thing in the world. "Sorry," I said.

She handed the questionnaire to me on yet another clipboard. "The most important one is here." She pointed to the middle of the page. "Next of kin."

"Oh," I said, bummed that she'd caught it.

"We need full names of two relatives, along with their phone numbers, plus one emergency contact who is not a relative, also with a phone number."

"Okay," I said, but it wasn't okay. I didn't have any relatives that I wanted to be involved in this or much of anything else, not since my father died. That was why I'd left it blank. I wanted to ask this nurse: so what do you want me to say? That my mom left me and my dad when I was six? And that for a while my aunt tried to help us, but she gave up on me when I was ten, because she got busy with her own kids and she figured I was old enough to take care of myself? And should I explain that it was just me and my dad until I was eighteen, when, in the summer after my first semester of college, my dad had a heart attack and I found him at home in the hallway? Or that I had to drop out to take care of everything that needed to be done, and that there was no more money for school? Is that what this nurse wanted me to write?

Or should I have lied? Lied and given her a nice name or two? With a happy story. I could have said, Oh, yes, my parents are Ron and Donna Nobody and they live in Wonderful, Massachusetts. My dad is a genius dentist and my mother stays at home. They raise horses and donate to the Red Cross. But right now they're on vacation in Hawaii, so no, there's no need to worry.

In the end, I wrote down Hal and Ruth's information. This was their child, anyway. They should be the ones to deal with any problems. Then I added Digger, because there was one more blank to fill in, and I'd always used him as my emergency contact on job applications. I didn't mention that two weeks earlier, we'd finally broken up once and for all. And just like with every other breakup between us, we'd had amazing goodbye sex. It was a bittersweet end, but I believed he'd always be there for me. So I wrote down his name and number, and I wanted this nurse to get off my back.

"All set?" asked Dr. Salovich when he returned with the sperm.

"Yep," I said, noticing he had mustard on the corner of his lip. He must have just eaten lunch.

"Pregnancy test was negative," he said, not looking at me.

My stomach growled, and I punched it.

The nurse with the hips walked in with a cart. She stood at attention, waiting. The doctor placed the tools on the tray, ripping open sterile packages and getting everything ready.

The nurse held my wrist to read the ID bracelet they'd given me. "I have to do this, okay, honey?" she asked.

I nodded. I was getting nervous.

"You are Caroline Ruby Scott?"

"Yes," I replied to this and the other questions. Birth date, address.

"You are here today for an artificial insemination, correct?"

"Correct."

"The donor is Harold August Olson?"

"He goes by Hal," I said, "but I never heard his middle name before."

The room went quiet for a second, as if the hips nurse was deciding whether I should have known that Hal's middle name was August. Apparently, there were no more questions. The nurse glanced at the doctor, who was busy setting up between my legs. He wasn't fazed at all by my lack of knowing Hal's middle name.

"August, hmm? That'd be a good one for the baby, a good boy name, wouldn't it, darlin'?" said the hips nurse. She winked at me and moved back to her post beside the cart, ready to assist.

I ignored her.

The doctor began, announcing his every move one second before he did it. I felt the heat of the light again, and him, focusing between my legs, his gloved hand on the inside of my thigh. "No second thoughts, right?" he said. Was this another one of his jokes?

I held my breath. His question made me wonder. Maybe this wasn't as simple as I'd thought. Was this a good idea?

"No second thoughts," I said, and he plunged in.

Eighteen

HAL

Morning

Ruth is a remarkable person: talented, tenacious, and bright as can be. But she also tends to get anxious. She certainly got worked up over the birth of this child. I thought if anyone should be worried, it would be Cally. She was the one who would be in labor, after all. And I'd been there before, in the delivery room. I'd seen it. Twice. It is indeed thrilling, but let's be honest: there's a lot of waiting involved. So I'd planned to carry on with a normal work schedule until the part when they called the doctor and the baby popped out.

I had a deposition scheduled. It wasn't a big deal. Wouldn't take more than a few hours. But Ruth nearly lost it when she called me at work. The deposition was on a break and I'd been standing near Pat's desk when the call came in. Pat handed me the phone.

"Cally's water has broken," said Ruth, breathing heavily. I could feel her smiling, the joy in her voice. I asked Pat to transfer the call so I could talk in private.

"Where are you?" I asked, closing the door to my office.

"At home," said Ruth, sounding panicked. "But I'm leaving . . . I'm going to pick up Cally . . . at her apartment and I—"

"Okay, slow down. Just breathe," I said, as if Ruth were the one going into labor.

"I gotta go," she said. "Can you meet me there?"

"When?" I asked, checking the small marble clock on my desk.

"Now!" she said, as if that were obvious.

"Well, not now, obviously," I said.

"Why not?" Ruth had that demanding tone in her voice that I dislike, but I understood this was a big day.

"I'm in the middle of a depo, for one thing."

There was a pause on the other end of the line, the longest bit of silence in this conversation by far. She exhaled, breathing hard into the phone and not in a sexy way. Finally, she said, "I wish you wouldn't have done that."

"What, Poppy?"

"Scheduled a stupid deposition this close to the due date!"

I swiveled my chair to look out the window. The sky was blue, and the ground was covered in thick snow, narrow lanes plowed for cars on the streets, heaps piled high on the edges of sidewalks and corners of parking lots. The sun was out, but it was twenty degrees. "I understand," I said. "It will only take another hour or so, and then I can be there. At the hospital. With you. Okay?"

"I just want you to be as excited about this as I am."

I pressed the receiver tightly to my ear, bringing Ruth as close as I could. "I am excited. Of course I'm excited. I just, you know, I've been through it before."

Ruth scoffed and I knew to be careful with this. She hated that I'd had experience with childbirth and she hadn't. "I know," she said.

"And it can take a while, even after her water's broken, okay?" I had so many memories flashing up from when the boys were born. But I knew better than to go into detail about it with Ruth. I'd learned that the hard way. A few times when Ruth had come home all aglow after attending Cally's doctor's appointments, she'd report on Cally's progress, and I'd tried to explain false contractions, medication for inducing labor, and the whole centimeters thing. Well, let's just say Ruth hadn't been receptive to my knowledge. I only wanted to caution her. Soften the blow just in case things didn't go perfectly. I knew lots could happen outside Ruth's carefully prepared birth plan. "Try not to get your hopes up," I said. Outside my window, an airplane left a contrail behind, high in the sky. "We could be there for hours, into the night, who knows?"

"Please don't lecture me," said Ruth. "Just get there as soon as you can."

"I will." And suddenly, I remembered another thing I'd learned from taking Audrey to the hospital. "Watch out for potholes!" I said, but the line was dead. Ruth was long gone.

RUTH

For months I'd been keeping a journal. I wrote on and off during the time we signed up with Cally, before and after the insemination, and regularly during the pregnancy. I'd made notes of Cally's progress and concerns during doctor visits, lists of things to do, and summaries of our conversations. My journal was stuffed with various drafts of our birth plan and included ideas for the transfer (adoption) ceremony that was to occur at the hospital two to three days after the birth, if the baby was healthy and all was well.

But my journaling ceased when Cally went into labor. After she'd called me, I couldn't think. I didn't know who to call. Nothing was ready. I wasn't ready.

I marched into the cold garage and slammed the door behind me. Examining the stacked boxes of baby equipment and supplies, I moved and repositioned boxes until I had access to the important one. Using only my frozen hands and hardened determination, I ripped open the box with the car seat inside. Lifting the thing out with a whoosh, I got a whiff of chemical packaging and felt a sense of superpower. I pulled off the plastic wrapping, yanked at the tags and gathered the warnings and government safety certification cards. I feverishly flipped through the owner's manual, looking for English.

I saw my breath as I exhaled. Why hadn't we assembled this behemoth before today?

I didn't have time to deal with the installation, so I loaded all the pieces (and the instructions) into the backseat and slammed the door. "What am I doing?" I said to myself, angry that I'd wasted ten minutes. "I won't need the car seat for two more days!"

I ran back into the house and searched for the birth plan, but it wasn't on the dining room table where it had been, not in the living room, not on my bedside table or in the nursery or in any of the other obvious places. I ran to my desk and searched for my journal, pulled out some of the folded papers stuffed inside. Which one was the most recent version? I wanted to have it with me in case the nurses hadn't gotten a copy like they were supposed to. I couldn't tell which was which, so I picked the one that looked complete, jammed it in my purse, and grabbed my coat. My hands were shaking as I struggled to fit the key into the ignition. I adjusted the rearview mirror but then adjusted it back. I hit the garage door opener too soon, and it nearly came down onto the hood.

A block down the street, I remembered I had forgotten the video camera. Turned around and raced back, parked in the driveway, and left the car door open with the warning bell ringing as I ran into the condo and grabbed the camera case and tripod from the closet near my desk. Ran back to the driveway and into the car and felt for my purse, making sure my wallet was there, and my glasses.

At the stoplight, someone honked at me. I drove forward, turned left and a different car honked. For the first time in a long time, it seemed like everything I did was wrong.

Later that morning, when Cally and I arrived on the maternity floor, the nurses checked her in and checked her over. They got her hooked up and comfortable in a birthing room. I draped my coat on one of the guest chairs and piled my camera equipment and purse on top. The nurses had pointed out the free coffee and water station for me, and fortunately, the vending machines accepted credit cards. I showed the nurses the crumpled-up copy of the birth plan and reminded them that they should also have a copy in their file.

I went out to the nurses' station and told everyone who'd listen, "I'm the intended mother. Cally Scott is the patient. She's our surrogate. We have a birth plan." I went down the hall to get a cup of water. I walked as gently as I could, as if my footsteps might disturb all the unborn babies and cause added pain to all the birthing women nearby. When I returned to Cally's room, the door was open, and I peeked in. She was nowhere in sight. I felt my throat tighten as I tried to contemplate what this meant. Then I heard voices. In the bathroom. A flush and the door opened. Cally shuffled out, the nurse beside her. "There you are," I said, relieved.

"Yeah. Can't really go too far," said Cally, waddling toward the bed, a strained look on her face. The nurse had two hands on Cally, guiding her. Cally was wearing a hospital gown and white tube socks.

"How's it going?" I sat in the guest chair that wasn't overloaded with my stuff.

The nurse smiled at me briefly, then helped Cally sit and swing her legs onto the bed. The nurse fussed with the sheets, pulling them up and covering Cally's midsection. "It's okay," said Cally. "Kind of scary."

"Are you having contractions?" I asked, wanting so much more information than I was getting.

"Yep," she said.

"I'm just about to check her cervix," said the nurse, picking up a pair of latex gloves and putting them on. "Can you come back in a few minutes?"

"Oh, yes, of course," I said, getting the hint. "Cally, I'll be right down the hall."

"Okay," said Cally. "Is Hal here?" She always seemed to be looking for him, asking about him, and I wondered if her reason was because, like her, he had the biological connection. He was the father of the child inside her.

"He's coming from work," I said. "He'll be here soon." Maybe saying it would make it true.

HAL

When I got to the hospital, it was late afternoon and, as I had predicted, Cally was still in labor. I stopped at the visitors' desk and sensed, as I was filling out my name tag, that the receptionist was flirting with me.

"My wife's already upstairs," I said, putting an end to the receptionist's little game.

"Good luck," she said with a smile.

"I'll take it," I said, rapping on the desk as I left. This was a habit I'd picked up from my first supervising attorney, a man who would become a mentor of mine. Funny how we pick things up without always being aware.

I found Cally's room. Ruth was sitting in the side chair, holding a crumpled copy of the birth plan. She was clutching that paper so hard, I thought it might disintegrate. The birth plan indicated that, to the extent possible, the parties preferred a natural delivery, with as little medication as possible. This was Ruth's idea. If it'd been up to me, I would've deferred to Cally and the doctors, but this was Ruth's baby, possibly her only child, and I wanted her to have everything she wanted. The prevalent factors guiding medication decisions were to be (in this order): health and safety of the baby, health and safety of the birth mother, comfort of the birth mother, and desires of the intended parents. Ruth wanted me to cut the umbilical cord, which I'd done with both of my boys. That was fine. A tradition of sorts. And it gives the father something to do. The plan then instructed that Ruth would be the first to hold the infant, to facilitate bonding.

However, that didn't happen. That got lost in the heat of the moment. In the shocking way that a baby's birth seems to make time stand still, we forgot. Suddenly, there was a new person in the room and nothing else mattered. So what happened was the doctor placed the baby on Cally's chest, and Cally put her hand on the wiggling little creature. The nurses wiped her off a bit and then prepared for me to cut the cord, which I did. It was a minute or two before Ruth got to hold her. And those two minutes probably felt like hours to Ruth.

But later, after Ruth had recovered from her disappointment, she was floating on air, completely taken with the new child, and she described that moment in her signature poetic manner. She said it was as if a galaxy had landed in the room. And it was true.

The birth was a marvel, and I wished my boys could have been there. Cally had asked that we keep the group of witnesses small and discreet, and who could blame her. And I don't actually think Jake and Caleb would have wanted to see a live birth even if they'd had the chance. They're great guys, and of course I love them to death, but they aren't always as mature as I might like. Even so, this was a family event and I wanted them there. To meet their sister. Well, their half sister.

After the nurses washed and wrapped the newborn, we took turns holding our little bundle, passing her back and forth like a good-luck charm. We were, all three of us, in awe of her.

She was beautiful, and we must have taken a hundred pictures of her. When Ruth snapped a shot of the proud father, she compared me to a photo she'd seen of a gorilla cradling a fallen bird. I took it as a compliment, although I already knew I was a natural. Even Cally said so.

Ruth and I sat there grinning at the sleeping baby and lost all track of time. We were in love, in love with time itself, in our own new world. It could have been storming outside or flooding inside, and we wouldn't have noticed. We had our little girl.

And then they kicked us out. Politely, of course. The nurses said the birth mom needed her rest, and they'd soon be moving her to a recovery room. They suggested we get a bite to eat and come back in a couple of hours. But since we both had a car at the hospital, I suggested we drive home for supper and then return in one vehicle. Which was what we did.

RUTH

Later that evening, back at the hospital, we found Cally in her new room, the recovery room. She was groggy, but she smiled at us when we tiptoed in. We lifted our daughter out of the bassinet and sat in the visitor chairs. I placed her on my lap for a good look.

I had expected the baby to be more awake and less wrinkly. Her eyes were squinted shut, as if the world was too much, too soon. For some reason, I'd imagined her nose to be more like a tiny rosebud, like in commercials. But hers seemed a bit big for her face, like a mushroom, and she had no chin. Her forehead was low, and she had so much black hair. Overall she looked like a shrunken-up miniature weight lifter. Her skin was purplish red and uneven, blotchy. She had pimples on her face, a bruise-like stain on her neck, and a smaller one on the back of her left hand.

"Strawberries," the nurse had explained. "Very common. They'll fade away, and her complexion will clear up."

"How soon?" I asked.

"Usually within the first few weeks," said the nurse.

Otherwise, she was perfect. Ten toes. Ten fingers. She was sweet. I don't know how long I'd been studying her when Hal came and took her away. He said it was probably time for us to leave and that Cally needed to rest. I didn't hear the nurse say that. I couldn't think of any good reason we should leave. But Hal was convinced we should get out of their way. "Fine," I whined, picking up my coat and purse.

"We'll see you tomorrow," said Hal, taking the baby over to Cally's bed and setting her down gently, like an extra pillow next to Cally's head. Cally reached over and put her hand on the baby, keeping her from falling.

"I thought you said Cally was gonna rest?" I said to Hal. "Why'd you give her the baby? You should have put her in the bassinet."

Hal frowned at me and shook his head as if I were talking non-sense. I'd been overruled. He smiled at Cally, and she weakly waved goodbye.

As we rode home together that first night after meeting our baby, we were alone in the car and silent. This was supposed to be the best night of our lives, the night our child was born, but Hal had ruined it. He didn't even know what he'd done wrong. He had no clue how he was acting. Or how I was feeling. I leaned toward the passenger window and turned away from him. I wanted to get as far away from him as I could, and I didn't want him to see my face.

"What a night," he said finally, at a red light.

"Yeah," I said without enthusiasm.

"She's perfect, isn't she? Just perfect."

"Yeah." My breath fogged up the cold window. I didn't mention the pimples or the splotches or any of the things I'd noticed about her that weren't perfect. Her nose. Her massive head of hair.

"What is it, Poppy?"

I could sense him looking at me. I didn't know where to start. While I was holding her, he'd decided my turn was up, and he'd taken the baby out of my arms and given her to Cally. He'd touched Cally's shoulder. And I didn't like the way he'd looked at her: it was like she was the mother, not me. Like he was saying, Good job. The simple fact was that he'd made a baby with this woman, not with me, and I was supposed to be happy about it.

"Nothing," I said. "Just tired."

"Well, you'd better get your rest," he said. "Soon you won't be getting much."

"Mm-hmm," I said. Hal loved to complain about the sleep disruption.

"Just think," he continued. "In thirty-six short hours, our little angel will come home with us. We'll become our own family."

"I thought we already were," I said as quietly as I could.

"What'd you say?"

"Nothing." I closed my eyes and leaned back. My cheek touched the cold leather headrest. One of these days, I thought, I should quit my lonely habit of going silent when I'm hurt. Hal wasn't curious enough to ask me how I felt. He wasn't perceptive. Or aware that I was sad. Had he really not known that I wanted to hold the baby longer? And that he shouldn't have handed her over to Cally like that? He would have made a terrible journalist, I thought. And I wondered whether he was any good at parenting. If I'd misjudged him. Maybe this had been a mistake. I turned my head to peek at Hal. He was tapping on the steering wheel like a drummer, playing some song in his head. This was one of his habits of which he was not aware.

"Can you please stop that tapping?"

"Sure," he said, and started whistling.

We seemed to catch every red light on the way home. I peeked at each intersection, vaguely recognizing the places we'd driven past so many times. They looked different now. Empty parking lots ready for tomorrow's shoppers. I couldn't think of a single thing I needed to buy. Nothing that I wanted in any of these stores.

"I can't wait to call the boys," Hal said. "And bring them over to meet their new sister."

"Yeah," I murmured, trying to sound like I was excited for them. "But Jake's up north snowboarding, remember?"

"Oh yeah," said Hal. "But when he gets back, he'll be so excited."

I wasn't sure about that. Neither of Hal's sons seemed particularly jazzed to be getting a half sibling. They weren't thrilled with having a stepmother. To be fair, this whole thing had been foisted upon them, and it'd been rather a whirlwind. Hal and I had met, dated, married, and had a baby all in the span of five years, which is fine if you're in your thirties and your stepkids are toddlers. But when you're fortysomething and your husband has teenagers and an ex-wife, things are more complicated. Things take more time.

Hal's boys had been fighting tooth and nail to get out of being there for the transfer ceremony. So when Hal informed me that Jake had a big snowboarding competition on the same weekend, I wasn't surprised that Hal had given Jake permission to miss the ceremony.

And I wasn't upset.

Nineteen

CALLY

THURSDAY, DECEMBER 5, 2002

Morning

I remembered my dad telling me the story of how I was born. He liked to tell it every year on my birthday. Apparently, my mother was very strong. In high school, she ran track (because she loved to run), and at the meets, when the team had to do the field events, the coach convinced my mom to throw the shot put because no one else was any good at it. According to my dad, my mother had great running speed as well as upper-body strength. This was always the way my dad would start the story.

Then he'd say, "But she didn't have a lot of common sense," and that was the line I was supposed to laugh at, because we both knew what was coming. The story of her going into labor and not even realizing it, then nearly giving birth in the front seat of a Pacer (which was a small car my dad thought was funny) while being driven to the hospital by a stranger who had been a customer at the Perkins where she was working when she went into labor.

Where was my dad at the time? On his way to the Perkins to pick her up after her shift. What did he do when he got there and found out she was on her way to the hospital? He drove so fast he got pulled over for speeding, then talked his way out of a ticket because his wife was in labor, even though she wasn't in the car. This was another cue for me to laugh, because, as my dad explained, driving a pregnant woman to the hospital was one of the very few ways to get out of a ticket. And even then it wasn't a guarantee.

"There are no guarantees in life, Little Pea," he liked to say. "So pay attention."

And when my dad got to the hospital, it was too late. He'd missed my birth, but he was amazed by me and my speed at being born. He said he admired my fire to arrive in the world at exactly the moment when I wanted to arrive.

After hearing that story so many times, I knew I would have more sense, pay attention, and do it better than my mom had. Plus, I had Hal and Ruth breathing down my neck, especially during those last four weeks.

"You look ready to pop," Ruth would say. "How are you feeling?"

"Fine. The same," I'd say, and it was true.

She'd been coming with me every week for my check-ins with the doctor. He'd listen to the heartbeat and squeeze my hard belly, locate the baby, and give an estimate for the baby's size. He'd feel inside to guess how ready I was for delivering.

"Any issues this week?" he'd ask.

"It's hard to sleep." It was also hard to get in and out of cars, put on shoes. I went to the bathroom a lot. I waddled. People stared at me.

"Any pain in your groin?" said Ruth.

"Not usually," I said, but Ruth frowned. She couldn't help herself. I was carrying her precious child.

The doctor smiled at Ruth and raised his hand to stop us from talking, then took off his glasses and explained how everything was normal, he wasn't concerned and we shouldn't be, either. The baby was in a good position and I was on track. He'd see us next week, and we should call if anything changed. Day or night.

I thought about my mother, what she'd have said if she could have been in the room with us, hearing that fierce heartbeat, watching my giant belly. Would she have approved of what I was doing? Or would she have said I was selling a baby, which was what Digger told me his mother had said behind my back. Maybe my mother would have been proud of me for making so much money. I didn't know her well enough to guess what she'd have thought. I was too young when she left.

Ruth had taken me for a tour of the maternity ward, to see the rooms where women gave birth and those where new mothers recovered afterward. The facilities were homey but still hospital-like. Ruth thought it would be good for me to be prepared and to "visualize" myself in these rooms, so it would be less stressful when I got there for the big event. We saw the bathtubs where some women chose to give birth, but we both knew this was not for us, and we had a laugh about that. At one point on the tour, Ruth asked about getting a room for herself on the maternity ward, could she check in and stay there?

"This isn't a hotel," said one of the nurses. "The rooms are for patients."

Ruth blushed. "Oh, I realize," she said. "I'm just asking about the facilities for the parents. The family."

"The family is free to stay in the room with the mother and baby." The nurses showed us how the bedside chair reclined into a cot, how the padded window seat held pillows, sheets, and blankets, and how a small person could also sleep there. But I could tell that Ruth wanted her own bed where she could wear a hospital gown and check her blood pressure and order room service.

When I did go into labor, I knew it was happening.

That morning, I'd gone to the community college to pick up registration forms and check the class schedules for after the baby was born. I was standing outside the registrar's office, looking at the bulletin board, when I felt a pop inside. I stepped back and saw a puddle of water on the floor. Immediately, I called Ruth, and she wanted to come get me.

"But first I need to get my stuff from home," I said.

"Okay, if you think you can, I mean, can you drive yourself to your apartment? I'll meet you there and take you to the hospital, if you're sure," said Ruth, breathless.

"Yes, I can do that," I said, but I wasn't sure. I didn't really know what I was capable of.

"Okay, I'll see you there. Thirty minutes." Ruth's voice had an intensity that made me nervous, less sure. But what choice did I have?

Half an hour later, Ruth rang my buzzer, and I let her up. I'd been waiting at the kitchen table, my coat on, my bag by the door. When I opened it, she had the biggest grin on her face. I just wanted to get going. "How far apart are the contractions?" she asked, picking up my duffel bag.

"Like ten minutes, maybe less."

"Oh my goodness, oh my goodness," said Ruth, jumping in place, jumping without leaving the ground.

We went down the stairs together, side by side and almost too wide for the space. Ruth held out her arm for me to hang on to, dragging the duffel behind us, and we waddled down, two feet on each step.

Outside, the sidewalk was still snowy. My landlord hadn't shoveled after the last storm, so we slowed down over the slippery spots. Ruth helped me into her car, and she drove more carefully than anyone I'd ever been with. Digger always drove so fast, I hadn't thought I'd hate going slow even worse.

"Can you go faster?" I said. "It hurts."

"Oh, sorry," she said, leaning toward the windshield, as if that would get us there sooner.

I thought about my mom in the Pacer and clenched my groin area, holding the baby in. I didn't want to give birth in a car, but I had no idea how long my labor would take. When we got to the hospital, I realized I had nothing to worry about. I changed into a gown and the nurses hooked me up to monitors, and after checking my cervix, they said it would be a while before I was ready to deliver.

I wondered why my mother didn't have so much time. Why had I come so quickly? The nurse gave me something for the pain, and I dropped in and out of awareness. At some point Hal must have shown up. He and Ruth were bustling in and out of my room, and I decided I would ask the nurse my questions when Hal and Ruth weren't there. If I could find a moment alone with the nurse or the doctor, I'd tell them the story about my mother in the Pacer. Maybe they'd want to know about her labor. Maybe I'd inherited something important.

Twenty

RUTH

Morning

Traditional Surrogacy Agreement, Sect. 9(b)(ii)

After delivery, the birth mother shall be allowed a Transition Day with the newborn child prior to the Transfer Ceremony. This twenty-four-hour period with the birth mother is intended for the well-being of the child. Prior to the Transfer Ceremony (or concurrent with it), the birth mother shall execute the affidavit relinquishing her parental rights, and the intended parents shall thereafter promptly execute the adoption and parental rights declarations attached hereto. None of these documents may be signed prior to the birth or they shall be deemed null and void.

Since the birth was on a Thursday, we designated that entire Friday as "transition day" with Cally. Even so, I was under the impression that Hal and I would have access to our daughter that day. After the baby was born, I called Kristin and my editor, Jerry, from the hospital to let them know. He agreed to start my six weeks of maternity leave on Friday, the transition day. Hal planned to take a full week off starting on Monday. He still had some things to finish up at work on Friday, so that made sense.

Friday morning was cold and snowy. The world was white outside my car window, weighing down trees and blowing across streets, then veiling in silver all the buildings I passed on the way to the hospital. I stopped at Caribou to pick up a couple of slices of coffee cake and two decafs, to share with Cally. I brought my journal, as well as copies of the *New York Times* and the *Pioneer Press*, so we'd have something to read. And I brought the pink-and-white-striped newborn jammies I'd picked out at Baby Gap. I couldn't wait to see how they fit.

We'd have to decide on her name soon. I thought I wanted Elizabeth, my mother's middle name. And it was a classic, after all. I'd imagined calling our baby Libby, Liza, or Tess. But now that she was here, I wasn't sure the name suited her. I studied her tiny, creased face, but I couldn't quite recognize her.

The baby lay in the plexiglass bassinet, swaddled in elephant-patterned flannel blankets and a pink hat. Cally was asleep with her back to me. When the nurse came in and saw my "spread," she told me Cally shouldn't have coffee, even decaf, so I drank both cups. I saved a piece of coffee cake for Cally, though. Pretty sure she could eat that. I pulled out my journal and wrote:

"Baby Girl Olson" was born on Thursday, December 5, 2002, at approximately 4:51 p.m. She weighed in at 8.2 pounds and measured 20 inches.

Cally didn't have an epidural. She requested pain relievers, which were administered (although they did not appear to make any difference). Flowers and balloons were not allowed in the recovery room. Room H-258, extra-large en suite, big window overlooking the back parking lot and a snowy marsh. Weather is hideous but— Minnesota. It's quiet here. I keep my eye on the nurses' stations, where they sit, heads down, busy on computers, or stand huddled together, chatting in low voices. Wish I knew what they were saying.

There are three family lounge areas, carpeted, comfy sofas, plus kiddie tables with books and puzzles, and a television tuned to the

Golf Channel. I asked the staff to switch the channel to the news. United Airlines might go bankrupt, so how would that affect our local Northwest Airlines? Minnesota was considering a concealed carry law, and Governor Ventura was expected to comment. Not much else going on. I left to use the restroom, and when I came back, someone had switched the channel back to golf. Ugh!

I don't think the staff took our birth plan seriously. Not sure if there is a bias against surrogacy or if they just hate all birth plans. I may interview some other new mothers to get a sense of whether there's a story here. I may want to follow up on the usefulness of birth plans being followed in general, and possibly do a hospital-to-hospital comparison.

Today (Friday) is the transition day, but we are allowed to visit. Tomorrow Cally will sign the papers and we'll have our pastor here for a ceremony. Then we'll bring home baby girl. It's been stressful. Hal and I have been having sex three or four times a week for the last couple of months, because, I'm sure, we both need to release all this tension. Early this morning, I had this dream:

Someone told me to climb stairs. They're sparkling white and clean. They go up steeply and I can't see the top. Someone says there will be a reward beyond description. I climb the stairs into the sky, but it's dark and there are no handrails. I want to turn back, but there's no exit.

When I get to the top, there's a ledge with a long slide. I realize I must take it, but I'm afraid I'll move too fast. At the bottom, I see children in a playground. If I slide down, I might hurt them. Then I look again, and some of the children are dead.

When I woke up, I looked around the dark bedroom, half expecting to see dead children on the floor. God, I wondered what it meant. Where am I headed? The only sound in the condo was the ticking of Hal's clock, each tick reminding me that I was home, and I was safe. I hadn't crushed anyone. But I was antsy to get to the hospital. And here I am.

10:47 a.m. Cally is still asleep. I just ate both the coffee cakes I was saving for her. In addition to sex, I'm using food for stress

*relief. Been eating a lot. Better watch that. Oh! Baby is waking. So
precious!*

I closed my journal and reached into the bassinet. I had just picked
up the baby when I noticed Cally starting to stir, opening her eyes.
"Good morning, momma," I said sweetly.

Twenty-One

DIGGER

SATURDAY, DECEMBER 7, 2002

Afternoon

Like a psycho, Cally watched me light my cigarette, so I turned my back to the window. My truck was about fifteen feet away. Everything was white and cold. I was wearing my work boots. They were lined with flannel but still not great for this depth of snow. I shifted back and forth to keep warm while I finished my smoke, then dropped the butt in the snow and headed for the door.

When I got inside and stomped off the snow, Cally was standing in the kitchen with the baby on her shoulder. She patted the baby, still looking at me.

"What the hell are you staring at?" I said.

"I dunno . . . you."

"You like playing house like this, don't you?" I shook my head.

She flipped me off, just like she did in high school.

"Don't get any ideas," I said.

"I won't," she said but in a teasing way. Cally knew how I felt about having kids and settling down. I wasn't interested in any of that until I was set. Probably not till I turned thirty. My mother had drilled it into me: kids take money. Kids can drown you. And I was just getting my head above water. That was one of the things Cally and I agreed on: we both wanted to wait, whether we were together or not.

"You ready to go yet?" I said.

"Yeah." She was wrapping another layer around Nell. I waited for her to walk outside.

"Holding the door for me?" she said in that voice I hated. A flirty-ass, know-it-all voice. And I hated when Cally tried to make me into something I wasn't. Romantic. Smart. Polite. She saw things no one else saw. Because they weren't there.

"Stop it," I said, getting pissed. I locked the cabin, and we got in the truck, still messy from us sleeping in it. When I turned the ignition, the clock lit up: 2:41 p.m.

"So late already," said Cally.

"That's another reason I don't want kids," I said. "Everything takes longer."

"Did your mother tell you that?" Cally balanced the baby as she fastened her seat belt.

I ignored that question. Cally and my mom didn't get along, but I never liked Cally criticizing her. "So where am I going?"

"We just need a Target or a Sam's Club or something like that."

"So, Duluth," I said. Duluth was about twenty minutes away.

"Sure," she said.

Cally held the baby in her lap as the truck bumped over the snowy roads; the trees were covered in white, the gas station, pie shop, all covered in white. I took the same route from last night, but this time we could see where we were. The main street, center of Superior, the farms, then the landmarks of Duluth: the harbor, the container ships, and the High Bridge.

We crossed into Minnesota, and Cally smiled at me. I knew what she was thinking. We'd been to Duluth a few times before, on a field trip from school, a skiing weekend with a bunch of my friends, once for Thanksgiving at my cousin's, and once just the two of us for a New Year's Eve at the Radisson.

The night we spent at the Radisson was a lot of fun. All we did was fuck and order takeout. We'd turned on the TV only to watch the ball drop in Times Square. We slept in late, and when we woke up, we got busy again. We were in the middle of fucking when a cleaning lady walked in on us. We laughed after she left, but it was a turn-on, to be honest.

Now we were surprised—and not surprised—to see people on the streets. It had to be about eight degrees outside. People were bundled up and waiting at the corner for the stoplight to turn. Where was everyone going on a frigid Saturday? "I think the mall's up this hill," I said.

"I can ask this guy," said Cally, rolling down her window.

"No," I said, speeding ahead as soon as the light turned. "I know where I'm going." The truck handled the snowy hill easily, and sure enough, there was the mall. The parking lot was a fucking mess. Giant mounds of snow and crooked rows of cars. I found a spot and shut off the engine.

"This is pretty far away," said Cally. "You could have dropped us off."

"Oh, for Christ's sake," I said, turning the engine back on. Cally grabbed the safety strap and braced. I yanked into reverse, drove up close to the mall doors, and pulled over to let her out.

"Meet me inside, right there," she said, pointing.

I peeled off and found a place to park. Got out of the truck and slammed the door. I just wanted to get this over with. And I didn't want to stay mad. As I stomped through the snow and around the parked cars, I thought about my dad. When he lost his temper, he couldn't get it under control. I didn't want to be like him.

Once he threw me down the basement stairs. He found out I'd skipped school that day. They were making the whole seventh grade take a career interest survey. I didn't want to take the stupid test. I didn't know what it would ask. Or how to answer. But I'd already skipped so many times, I was on the truancy list. The school called home, and my dad, who'd been drinking because that's what he did during factory layoffs, answered the phone. He didn't say anything.

He hung up, walked over to me, picked me up, and threw me down the steps like I was a pile of dirty clothes. I shouted at him. Called him a drunk. And he locked the goddamn door at the top of the steps. Just left me down there. Until my sister, Deena, came home and unlocked me. No one said anything about it. Not my dad. Not my mother, because she always acted like she didn't have a clue. My older brothers had moved out. It was just me and Deena. And Deena never said a word.

It was a good ways across the parking lot. By the time I got to the mall entrance, my head was clear and I was sweating under my coat. Cally was standing inside the doors, waiting. She led me through the maze, past Victoria's Secret, the crappy Gap, idiotic American Eagle. The place was covered in red banners and silver glitter. Christmas trees everywhere. Christmas songs blasting. Lights. Wreaths and shit. And an old guy dressed as Santa so kids could sit on his lap and say what they wanted. Not that I ever did. Creepy as hell.

I stopped in front of Penney's. "How about this?" This was where my sister shopped. She lived in northern Wisconsin, not far away.

"I'd rather find the Target," said Cally, and we kept going. Strangers pointed at us. Said things to Cally about the baby. How small, how cute. Cally nodded at them. I tried to ignore them. "There." Cally pointed and we sped up, like Target would protect us from the mall people.

"Let's get the shit and get outta here," I said, pulling out a red cart and pushing it into the aisles.

"First the car seat," she said, searching.

I heaved the giant-ass box into our cart. She cruised through the aisles and picked up diapers, formula, bottles, anything that looked important. Burp rags, washcloths, and clothes. Everything was expensive.

My brothers and sister and I had gotten most of our clothes secondhand. Garage sales, thrift stores. And as the youngest, I got the hand-me-downs from my older siblings, so my clothes were third-, fourth-, and fifth-hand rags.

"Oh, and a winter coat," said Cally, pulling a miniature sleeping-bag thing into the cart.

Finally, we got in line for checkout, and Cally gave me a look as if she liked having me there. I frowned and looked away. I didn't want to encourage her. She was playing house again. I didn't want to be a part of that. I hoped she wasn't thinking she could keep this kid. She'd be on her own.

I unloaded the shit onto the conveyer belt, and the cashier started scanning. "Looks like baby came early?" said the nosy-ass cashier as she bagged our items.

I gave her a smirk to let her know I wasn't into this. Cally took out the special Visa card her sperm lawyer guy had set up. For Cally to use for personal expenses and medical visits and whatever miscellaneous crap she needed. This was the card we'd used for everything so far on this trip. Except for the thirty bucks of gas I bought before I knew.

And this was the card Cally had said she would use to get a cash advance and pay me five grand.

Twenty-Two

RUTH

FRIDAY, DECEMBER 6, 2002

Morning

"How long have you been here?" Cally rubbed her face and tried to sit up.

"Not long," I said, still in my quiet baby-talk voice. Whenever I held the baby, I automatically bounced, and my voice changed involuntarily to baby talk, which I objectively despised in others. Maybe it was maternal instinct? My words were meant for Cally, but I said them in that voice, as if talking to the baby. I nestled the baby on my lap and tickled her cheek, saying, "I brought you a cup of decaf, but they wouldn't let you have it, would they? No! And I brought you some coffee cake, but I ate it, that's right, I sure did."

"She can't understand you," said Cally.

"I know," I said, "and I'm sorry about the coffee cake."

"That's okay," said Cally. "They bring me three meals a day plus snacks. I'm fine."

"Look, I got her this Baby Gap sleeper. She'll look so good in pink, with her dark hair and her . . . What color are her eyes?"

"I don't think we know yet."

Cally watched me rocking the baby. We sat for ten or fifteen minutes, the only sounds being the squeak of the rocker and the beeps of the monitor. The curtain opened, and a nurse came in. "How's it going in here?" she asked, and her voice sounded extra loud because the room had been so peaceful.

"Good," we said in unison. I wasn't sure who the nurse had been asking.

"I'm Mindy," she said, as she stood in front of the whiteboard on the wall that read, "Today is Friday, December 6, Walk 2X, All foods, Snow." Mindy erased the other nurse's name from the board and wrote hers in all caps, and she dotted the I with a smiley face.

"Hi, Mindy, I'm the intended mother, Ruth."

Mindy nodded as she put the pulse machine on Cally's finger. She squeezed the IV bag and looked at the monitor, then marked something on her clipboard. "How are you feeling?" she asked in her loud voice.

"Tired," said Cally.

I rubbed the baby's tiny little back and wondered if she'd burp.

"How about the stitches?" said the nurse. "Any pain in that area? We'll check for bleeding in a sec."

"I think it's fine," said Cally. She'd had a few tears during birth.

"That's what we like to hear," Mindy said as she wrapped Cally's arm with the Velcro cuff and pumped the bulb till the cuff squeezed tightly. "One twenty-five over eighty-six," she said, releasing the remaining air.

"Is that good?" Cally asked.

"Mm-hmm," said the nurse, coiling up the tubes and placing them back in a cubby. "We're checking for signs of postpartum preeclampsia, okay? Shall we go to the toilet?"

Cally nodded, and Mindy helped her rise from the bed and waddle into the adjoining bathroom. The baby started fussing and grunting, as if she, too, were annoyed with the nurse. "Uh-oh," I said, repositioning the baby. She fussed more, so I stood up with her and bounced. "There, there . . ." When Cally emerged from the bathroom, the fussing turned to crying. "What should I do?" I said, still bouncing.

Cally walked over to us and stroked the baby's head. "I don't know," she said. "Change her diaper?" The baby complained, as if frustrated with our incompetence.

"Want to try latching on?" the nurse asked Cally as she helped her back into the bed and straightened her sheets.

"Umm," said Cally, "if you think I should?"

"Yeah, if you're up to it, it's a good idea to try," said the nurse, not fazed by the crying. "If we can get some sucking motion, that tells the body it's time to start the next phase, start moving on."

"But she wasn't planning to breastfeed," I said, holding the baby out in front of me as if she, too, might weigh in on this question.

"At this point, it's not about feeding her," the nurse said. She took the baby from me and placed her in Cally's lap, stacking pillows under the baby and helping Cally sit up. It was like I wasn't in the room; the nurse spoke only to Cally. "You won't produce milk tonight anyway. Only colostrum, which is, like, the thick cream at the top of the milk bottle, it kind of 'uncorks' the flow, that'll come in a day or two. Maybe tonight." The nurse helped Cally find the opening in the hospital gown, revealing the breast.

"We were going to use a bottle," I said.

"Will you close the curtain?" the nurse asked me, ignoring my comment.

"Oh, sure." I yanked on the curtain, pulling it shut.

The nurse positioned the baby's face directly onto Cally's nipple, and it looked like the poor child would suffocate. But she didn't. She grabbed on to the breast, began to suckle, then fell off. The nurse helped reattach her.

"Should I go?" I asked. No one answered for a few seconds, and I thought about just leaving.

"You can stay," said Cally.

"Okay." I stood in front of the curtain and watched.

"Will you look at that?" Cally said, eyes wide like a child herself.

The baby latched on and repeatedly fell off the breast. "When she falls off, just put her back on," said the nurse.

"It doesn't feel like anything's happening."

"That's okay," said the nurse. "We're learning."

I wanted so badly to ask, What does it feel like? I held back because I'd been pestering Cally with that question all along. During the pregnancy, I'd constantly be asking questions. "How does your belly feel?" (Same, just bigger.) "What do kicks feel like?" (Kinda like stomach gurgles.) "What do labor pains feel like?" (Menstrual cramps but worse.) I was dying to know how breastfeeding felt, but I liked watching it, too. Besides, there was no good way to describe another woman's feelings. I would have to fill in the blanks with my imagination. Fortunately, I had a very good imagination. It certainly had helped me to think of interview questions, develop story ideas, and pitch narratives to my editor. In my career, I had created a lot of what-ifs to pursue.

Finally, the nurse said, "That was a good start. We can try again later."

"Later?" I said. "Tomorrow is our transfer ceremony. Cally won't be nursing; we'll be using a bottle."

The nurse looked at me with politeness and a tinge of pity. "Breastfeeding helps the mother's body," she said softly. "The sucking triggers the uterus to shrink back."

Cally smiled and closed her gown. The baby was asleep, nestled in next to her on the bed. I wanted to pick her up again and hold her some more, but it didn't seem right. I wished Hal were here. After all, this was his daughter, too.

"I'll let you rest," I said as I backed out of the room. I went to the family lounge, where there was a story about a press conference given by Ari Fleischer. Something about Kissinger. I felt a twinge of sadness about being behind on the news. Hal was at work, but this was my first day of leave.

Alone in a generic waiting room, in the recovery wing with nothing to recover from.

Hal had said he'd try to swing by over the lunch hour but not to stress if he didn't make it. All the clocks on the maternity floor showed slightly different times, but the one in the family lounge said 12:07. I thought about going to the cafeteria for a bite to eat, but I didn't want to miss Hal in case he arrived. I stepped into the hallway, and there he was! My heart raced when I recognized the outline of his frame, as well as his casual gait. I'd recognize him anywhere, the way he strode along without a care in the world. "Hal!" I called, walking as quickly as I could toward him.

"No running," said one of the nurses, maybe as a joke.

I fell into Hal's arms, not realizing how much I needed him. Not knowing how important it had been to me that he would appear. This was our child. This was our miracle. We needed to be together. I caught one of the nurses watching us, watching Hal. I was used to Hal catching the attention of women. He was immune to it.

"Let's go see our daughter," I said.

"Lead the way," he said, and I pulled him by the hand back to Cally's room.

"Shh," I said, "she's asleep."

"Cally or the baby?" Hal whispered.

"Cally," I whispered back, smiling.

I led him to the bassinet, and he reached down to pick up our girl. "Come on," he said, like a pro.

"You're good with her," I said.

"Had some experience," he said as he positioned the bundle of joy into the crook of his arm and wiped something off her face. "Aren't you a beauty?" The monitor beeped, and there were no nurses in sight. It was absolute bliss.

"Look," I said, quietly pointing to the end of the bassinet.

"'Baby Girl Olson,'" Hal read the sign taped there. "It's got a ring to it."

"Ha-ha, but honey, seriously, we need to decide on a name."

"Not really. We have thirty days by state law."

"Always the lawyer's point of view."

"Let's take her for a walk," said Hal, motioning toward the door

We'd been talking in hushed voices so as not to disturb Cally. It hadn't occurred to me to take the baby out of the room. "Can we?" I whispered back.

"Why not?" He shrugged and walked out of the room into the hall, holding the baby.

I walked next to him and tucked my hand under his arm. We strolled into the lounge, but there was another family there with toddlers, and I didn't want any of their germs. "Let's go down there," I said, pointing to our second-favorite lounge on the other end of the hall.

A nurse approached us. "Excuse me, may I please see your wristband?" she asked me. "Just a formality."

"Uh, I don't have one," I said. The nurses had put matching ID bracelets on Cally, Hal, and the baby.

"I'm the father," said Hal, showing his bracelet.

"And I'm Ruth Olson, and this is Baby Girl Olson," I explained. I tried to pull out the baby's wristband, but it was tucked deeply inside a well-folded wrap. "Can you help?"

I held the baby while the nurse unwrapped the tight blankets to free the baby's wrist. She found the bracelet and matched it with Hal's.

"So you're the Olsons," said the nurse, apparently recognizing that we were the intended parents. "Can I ask you to bring her back into the bassinet? It's okay if you move around, but we like you to have the bassinet with you."

"Sure," said Hal.

"No problem," I said, although it was a big problem, and I didn't like it at all.

The nurse helped me wrap up the baby again. Tucking her wrist back in, she said, "And be sure to remove the baby's bracelet before you take her home. It has a chip in there that'll set off the door alarms if it's not deactivated."

"Who deactivates it?" I asked.

"The staff," said the nurse nonchalantly. "When they give the discharge papers. But every once in a while, someone will forget and—" The nurse made a gesture indicating alarms going off.

"Sheesh," I said, imagining that.

"Come on, honey," Hal said, shepherding me away.

"I hate this place," I said under my breath.

When we got back to the room, Hal put the baby down on the visitor bed on the other side of the curtain. This was a double, but Cally was the only occupant, so the extra bed had been made but stayed dark and empty. I pulled the curtain around to give us our own space with the baby. Hal unfurled the blankets and peeled off the newborn T-shirt, which was only a wraparound, with no snaps, no ties. We gazed at the beautiful body of our tiny wriggling wonder. Hal touched the bottoms of her wrinkled little feet and examined her toes. He traced her chunky arms and studied her long delicate fingers, like matchsticks, and her miniature fingernails.

Hal slid the pink hat off her head and stroked her matted black hair. Something about her hair struck me as odd, like a kitten that had fallen in the toilet.

"Look at her ears," I said, and I untucked the tiny flaps of skin that had been pressed down against her head. "Like little buds of tulip petals."

"Have you changed her diaper yet?"

"No! Should I?"

"Sure, why not?" said Hal.

I searched around for the stash of newborn diapers. "Look at this little thing!" Hal lifted the baby's legs and I slid the clean diaper under, just like I'd learned at the Lamaze classes. We wrapped the flaps around and stuck the tape on the sides. "Lemme try the blanket thing," I said, laying out the square flannel blanket and giving myself audible instructions, from our training. "Fold this part over here, then this over here, and tuck this under, and . . ."

"Voilà!" said Hal, helping me with the final tuck-in.

"Good job," I said, and we high-fived.

"Uh-oh," said Hal, noticing my tears.

"Yeah," I said, wiping my cheeks.

"Come here," said Hal, and he pulled me toward him.

I kept one hand on the baby, who was bundled up on the empty bed. "Hang on, I want to get her," I said, and I picked her up.

"You make a beautiful mother," he said.

"Oh, Hal," I said, and the tears came again.

"It's all right," he said, putting his arms around me and our daughter.

"Hello?" said a voice from the other side of the room. "Hello? Who's there?"

Hal opened the curtain, and we saw Cally sitting up in her bed. "How long have you been awake?" I asked.

She pulled on her sheet and straightened the blanket. "Where's the baby?"

"With us," I said, holding her out for Cally to see.

"Why is she over there? What are you guys doing?" said Cally, making both Hal and me bristle.

"We just wanted to see her," said Hal, as if it were obvious.

"Yeah, and we changed her diaper," I said, cradling the baby.

"Oh, okay. Thanks."

"No problem," I said, a bit irked, because we weren't doing Cally any favors. This was our child. "We have to get used to doing that."

"Yeah, I guess you do."

I put her back down on the empty bed and unwrapped her. I slipped her into the pink sleeper I'd brought from Baby Gap. "Look!" I said when I'd finished. "So cute!"

"Yeah," said Cally. "It's a little big for her, but . . ."

"Yeah, but it's better to be too big than too small, right?"

"I guess," said Cally.

"Well, ladies," said Hal. "Lordy, I'm outnumbered here, aren't I?" We smiled.

"I should go," said Hal.

"Oh, but you just got here," I said.

"Yes, and it's a workday. And I have to get back to work," he said. "I will see you at home."

I put the baby in the bassinet and followed Hal out to the hall, kissed him goodbye, and watched him stroll away, waving his hand up in the air the same way he'd done on the night we met. I stopped at the drinking fountain and filled a paper cup with water. I stood and sipped it as I examined one of the bulletin boards hanging on the wall. It had been decorated with the nurses' photos and "fun facts" about their personal lives. Jenna had a dog named Barky. Bill had a degree in computer science. Kate liked fencing and also studied tae kwon do. The photos were glued onto squares of faded construction paper cut with zigzag scissors. This was a low-budget display.

The clock in the hallway said 1:55 p.m., but I wondered what time it was in Cally's room. I headed back over and saw new people there. Someone was clearing her lunch tray. Another worker was changing the blue pads under her bottom. I waited outside for a moment before deciding to get some lunch downstairs in the cafeteria.

A couple slices of warmed-up, soggy pepperoni pizza, and I was back in Cally's room. She had clean sheets, a clean room, and the baby had had a bath. Someone had taken the pink Baby Gap sleeper off and left it in a heap on the shelf under the bassinet.

"Who took off her sleeper?" I asked.

"I dunno," said Cally, and I knew she must have done it. "Well, they gave her a bath."

"Oh, shoot. I would have liked to see that."

"Yeah, it was pretty cute."

Later that afternoon, a nurse came in the room and announced, "Cally, I have a phone call for you at the nurses' desk. Did you want me to patch that through for you?"

"Oh," said Cally. "Sure, I guess."

"Okay," said the nurse. "Just answer when it rings, and that'll be him."

Him?

The nurse carried the landline phone over to Cally from the small side table near the empty bed.

"I guess I should get going," I said, noting it was close to five o'clock. "I have a few errands, and I'll try to come back tonight."

Cally's eyebrows fluttered up and down, but she may have had something in her eye. "Okay," she said, phone in her lap, waiting.

Then to the baby, I said in my involuntary baby voice, "Bye, little girl!" As I left the room, I heard the phone ring twice before Cally answered. I lingered a bit outside the room, to eavesdrop. Someone—a him—was calling her. I was curious who would be calling her in the hospital.

The nurses saw me standing there. One of them said, "Can we help you?"

"No thanks, I'm just leaving," I said, pulling my purse up to my shoulder.

"Do you need us to call you a taxi?" she asked.

"No, I have a car," I said, and suddenly, I couldn't wait to get out of there. In the parking ramp, I decided to take care of my last remaining errands. The first order of business was finishing the assembly of that car seat I'd left sitting loose in the backseat of my Jetta and buckling it in for good. After I tackled that monster, I hopped behind the wheel and raced to the grocery store to pick up a few days' worth of food, some ready-to-eat meals for the fridge and a few for the freezer. People had assured me that friends would bring us casseroles after the baby arrived, because everyone knows new parents don't have time to cook. But I wanted to stock up just in case. After I'd unpacked the groceries, I assembled the hanging mobile and searched the junk drawer for the hardware to install it.

Hal came home around seven-thirty, jolly and tired, and immediately ate one of the meals I had just purchased.

"Hal, come look what I've done," I called out proudly, waiting for him in the nursery.

I heard the squeak of Hal's recliner, and soon he was trudging over to join me.

"Look," I said pointing at the crib.

"It's wonderful, Poppy, but I don't see any difference."

"Look at the mobile." I gave it a spin.

Hal smiled.

"We're ready," I said, hugging Hal's midsection.

"As ready as we can be," he said.

"Should we go back over there tonight?" I looked up at his face, wondering if the baby's nose resembled his.

"The hospital? It's after eight."

"Is it too late?"

"Well, yeah, I think so. Don't you?"

"I guess."

"We'll be there first thing in the morning. Let's get some sleep. We're going to need it, Pop."

We walked arm in arm back to the living room, where I had a pile of to-do lists, people to call for the transfer ceremony, the minister, the social worker, and things to bring, the baby book for the foot-prints, the video camera, and the tiny gold cross from my mother's christening, which she'd given to me at mine.

"Did you remind the boys?"

"Yeah, but it's only Caleb, remember. Jake has his tournament."

"And Audrey's okay with swapping weekends?"

"No, but she's doing it." Hal smiled as he sat back in his chair and pulled up his crossword puzzle and pencil. The grandfather clock ticked, and soon giant snowflakes began to fall.

"Looks like a bit of snow is on the way," I said, pointing to the big window, the wintry scene outside.

Hal was busy filling in letters in squares. "They're forecasting three to six inches," he said without looking up.

"Geez," I said. "I guess we should take your SUV, then."

"Mm-hmm," he said, reading the next clue. "I'll move the car seat in the morning."

Twenty-Three

DIGGER

SATURDAY, DECEMBER 7, 2002

Evening

On the way back from Target, we were both hungry. We'd passed the Blue Anchor Grill on the way out of Superior. It looked pretty good, so we went there. Inside, Cally handed me the baby and went straight to the bathroom in back.

I found a booth and put the kid on the table so I could take off my coat. I sat down but kept my hand on the baby so she wouldn't fall. My dad liked to tell the story of this one time he was watching my brother Davey. While changing a dirty diaper, my dad looked away for a second, and Davey fell off the dresser. Dad said little Davey just bounced like a football when he hit the carpet. Deena always joked that's why Davey's the dumbest of us four kids. The oldest and the dumbest.

"You better stay put," I said to the kid.

"Hi, oh, what a cutie," said a waitress, setting down a couple of napkins and menus. "Can I get you something to drink?"

Cally showed up and slid into the other side of the booth. "Just water for now," she said, opening the menu.

"I'll be right back," said the waitress, leaving before I could order a beer.

"I could eat everything on here," said Cally.

"Me, too," I said, looking at photos of burgers and steak sandwiches and wings.

"I had the weirdest cravings when I was pregnant," she said. "Glad those are gone."

"Uh-huh."

Cally told me how she'd had strict rules for food. The nurse had given her a nutrition chart or some shit. She was supposed to eat healthy and count vitamins. Sounded like a lot of hassle. But now that the baby was here, Cally wanted a bacon cheeseburger and fries. And a Diet Coke.

"Don't you want a beer?" I said.

"No, but you go ahead." Cally took the baby off the table and handed the menus to the waitress.

I ordered two Leinies, and the waitress asked for my ID. She held it to the light and stared at it with a dumb look on her face.

"It's not fake," I said. "I'm twenty-three."

"No, I know." She laughed. "I was looking at your name. Dennis Wilkins."

"Yeah."

"This is weird, but are you related to Deena Wilkins?"

"That's my sister, why?" I looked at Cally.

"I just got a puppy from her last summer," said the waitress, big smile. "A Siberian husky!"

"I didn't know Deena was breeding dogs," said Cally.

"Neither did I."

"Oh, it's not a purebred," said the waitress. "She's a mix, but still so cute. Hi, I'm Bailey, by the way."

"That's cool, but can I get those beers?"

"Oh, sure, sorry," said Bailey, and off she went.

I knew Cally was gonna ask me a bunch of questions. About sled dogs, because she worked with all breeds and thought she knew so much. Or questions about Deena, whether she knew we'd broken up. Yes. Did she know about the surrogacy? No.

The waitress returned with two beers. "Here ya go," she said. "Be right back with your food."

"Two beers?" said Cally.

"Yeah," I said, sliding one over to her. "We're celebrating."

"What are we celebrating?" she said, using that voice again. "Are you gonna propose?"

"Ha-ha. You know that's never gonna happen." I took a drink.

"Believe me, I know. So then what is it?"

"I dunno. I thought you were happy about being with the kid for a couple of days. Being up here. Getting the stupid car seat and all that."

"Yeah, of course," she said, and she lifted the mug and smelled the beer.

"Cheers," I said, lifting mine and drinking.

"Cheers," she said. But she faked.

When the food came, we didn't talk much. Just ate and Cally paid and we left. She fed the baby on the way.

When we got back to the cabin, it was dark, and we unloaded the truck in the moonlight. If we dropped something in the snow, it was gone.

Cally spread out all the stuff and started to unwrap things, pull tags off, and tear off cardboard. We kept a pile of trash in the corner. To get the car seat out of the box, I had to turn it upside down. It slid out with a whoosh sound that Cally said reminded her of the birth.

"Gross. Don't tell me that," I said. The thing was navy blue and wrapped in plastic. There were a few parts that had to be snapped together, and lots of warnings and steps to follow, strap the kid in, rear-facing or front-facing. I put the instructions in the trash with the plastic wrap.

"Let's try it out," said Cally, picking up the baby and putting her in the car seat.

"She's not a doll for you to play with."

"I know," she said, pissy.

"There's a handle on top."

"Yeah, we can carry her in it."

The kid squirmed and fussed. "Looks like she doesn't like it much," I said.

Cally brought the baby to the rocking chair and rocked her. And fed her. Again. I finished unpacking the Target bags. The cabin felt smaller with all the new shit.

I got my toothbrush and walked outside. I wanted to brush my teeth in private, and Cally had been watching me. I didn't like it.

When I came back inside, Cally got up carefully from the rocker. The baby had fallen asleep, and I planned to do the same. Cally put her into the crate, and I blew out the candle and the oil lamp. Cally took off her pants but left on her T-shirt. In the glow of the wood-stove, her bare legs looked good. Her tits looked good under that T-shirt. Her stomach was slightly fat, but not bad, and anyway, I liked her curves.

I got down to my boxers. Cally watched me scratch my chest. She always told me she liked that I didn't have hair. And she didn't mind my scar. She used to follow it with her finger. From the top of my chest down to my waist. A line that divided my left from my right. A reminder I was a strong son of a bitch.

We crawled into bed, and I couldn't help but think about the last time we'd fucked. I couldn't help but wonder if we'd do it again. Was Cally thinking that? "Careful," I said as she swung her legs in and they rubbed up against mine. Her skin was soft. Her body was warm.

"You're cold," she said, unfolding the extra blankets from the end of the bed and covering us both. "This is a small bed, what is this, a double or a queen?"

"It ain't a queen," I said, rolling over and pulling the covers my way.

We lay there in the darkness, trying to sleep. The place got quiet. A log in the stove fell into smaller pieces, flaming.

"Digger," she said.

"Whuh?"

"Thank you."

Twenty-Four

HAL

SATURDAY, DECEMBER 7, 2002

Early Morning

Ruth was on a rampage. Pacing around the hospital conference room, she couldn't sit down. She'd been lecturing the director of patient relations, throwing her arms up. Ruth's voice was brusque. "I can't believe your hospital doesn't have procedures in place for this kind of—"

"Of course we have procedures," said the director of patient relations. "I can assure you—"

"A security system or something—" said Ruth.

"Yes, we have security. We have procedures in place," answered the director.

"Not very good ones," Ruth muttered.

"Ruth, come on. That's not helpful," I said. I didn't want to step in unless I had something to add.

The director remained composed. She explained, "We have patient wristbands, verbal confirmations, locked doors, cameras. We have state-of-the-art technology, including a matching DNA protocol for mothers and babies, and as I have already explained, for newborns, the ID bracelets are embedded with a security chip—"

"—that is tied to an alarm system, I know, I know—" said Ruth, exasperated.

"So if they leave before they are discharged, the alarm is triggered," said the director.

"But it only works when they go out the door," said Ruth. "Doesn't work for windows."

"Correct."

"Well, what is our remedy here?" I asked, trying to move us forward. "Cally broke your policy, so is there anything you can do about that?"

Ruth added, "I mean, she took the baby. She hadn't been discharged, right?"

The director of patient relations took a deep breath, smiled. Saying each word deliberately and gently, she explained, "Our patients are free to leave the building before they are discharged. It's not our preference, but it happens. More than you would think."

"Really?" I said, genuinely surprised if not skeptical. But also, I'd used this curiosity technique in my real estate negotiations. By asking questions, I'd keep the opposing party talking, and soon enough, they'd reveal a fact or weakness I could use.

"I know what you're doing, Hal," said Ruth. "And I hate it."

I put my hand on Ruth's shoulder, trying to get her on my side. She shook me off and gave me a glare.

"Yes, from time to time, patients leave without being discharged," said the director, as if about to share some outlandish hospital anecdotes.

Ruth couldn't take it anymore. "Oh, so people jump out windows all the time—"

"Well, no, not that extreme, but as I was explaining to your husband . . ." The director was calm and measured, which only seemed to make Ruth more distrustful.

"With a baby?" Ruth asked, as if wagering that ours was the most extreme public relations event this poor director had yet to deal with in her entire sad career.

"Ruth," I said, not knowing what else to say.

"What is it, Hal? Did you want to say something to me?" Ruth glowered, and I nodded, letting her know she couldn't scare me away. Letting her know I was on her side and strong enough to take these arrows. She slung another one. "Or did you want to speak *for* me, Hal?"

This was a reference to our first date, when I'd stupidly tried to order for her, an act I will forever regret. "Ruth," I said. "Come on, please."

The director looked away from us and sat back in her chair. After a few quiet moments, she set down her pen on her notepad. "Look, we're all on the same team here," she said. "And I can say with, you know . . . these types of situations—"

"These types of situations?" Ruth had gathered herself and sat up at attention. I wished the director had chosen her words more carefully. She didn't know she was speaking to a woman whose profession was words and meaning and truth. "What do you mean, exactly?" Ruth continued to press. "You mean surrogacy, don't you?"

This had been a sore spot for Ruth. She believed that, as the intended mother, she'd experienced second-class treatment and an undercurrent of disapproval at many of the stages of the process. She'd complained to me at night about the way the nurses stared at her, like she was, in her words, the freak at the circus. She'd caught them whispering. She felt they didn't view her as the baby's mom. And no matter how much I tried to convince her not to worry about others' opinions, she said she felt like she had a flashing neon sign over her head that said, "Infertile—Used a Surrogate."

"Yes, certainly," said the director, "with surrogacy situations, there is a greater degree of risk. A risk of this type of thing happening."

I sat with my head down, thinking. I was trying to find a solution. I was considering what our legal options might be and playing them out in my head. And I was listening.

"I mean the risk of having the birth mom change her mind," the director said with some delicacy. "We have teenage pregnancies, and it's not uncommon that we see a change of heart in adoption situations. It's very charged. It can be traumatic."

Oh, it had been plenty traumatic earlier this morning. When the phone had rung in the still-dark bedroom, and Ruth had switched on the lamp while I pressed the speakerphone button so we both could hear. The hospital had called to inform us, "We have difficult news," and "It appears she has taken the baby" and "We have alerted the hospital security team." "Do you have a way to reach Ms. Scott, because that may be the most effective way to resolve this," they'd asked. We'd given them her phone number, but there was no answer. We'd been listed as her emergency contacts, which seemed ridiculous in hindsight.

And now we were seated in a generic conference room in the office of the director of patient relations, Ms. Betsy Whittier. She had offered us weak coffee and room-temperature water to make us more comfortable. Ruth looked like a sleepwalker, with her messy hair and glasses, no time for makeup or contact lenses. I was in my sleep shirt and a pair of running pants I'd grabbed from the dirty-clothes bin. It was five o'clock in the morning, and it was still dark outside.

The director asked, "Do you think she might have mental or emotional challenges? Any instability?"

"No, nothing like that," I said. I wanted to nip that in the bud.

"Not that we're aware of," Ruth said, leaving open a crack of doubt.

"Well," said the director, "with hormones radically changed due to the birthing process, post-pregnancy, we have seen unpredictable moods, irrational behavior, that sort of thing."

"So you're saying this could be postpartum depression?" I said. I didn't want to jump to conclusions or use these terms casually. I knew all too well, with Audrey, that PPD was a serious matter.

"What about the parents, meaning us?" said Ruth, claiming her role. Completely composed, she held one of her used tissues in her hand, and pointed at me. "This man right here is the father of that baby. Today. Right now that is his child. Or are you going to argue with us about that, too?"

I sighed and shook my head. I appreciated Ruth's passion, but I didn't think there was much gain to be had by going down this particular road.

"I don't wish to argue with you, Mrs. Olson." The director rose and stood behind a chair. "I'm going to give you guys some privacy," she said. "I'll go to my office to see if there are any updates, and I will let you know, okay? I'll be back." The director left the conference room and closed the door behind her.

"We need to call the police," said Ruth. She scanned the conference room for a phone, but there wasn't one. Just a waste can, a box of tissues, and a lamp. The rose-colored walls were bare except for one framed poster of an eagle soaring over a waterfall.

"And tell them what?" I asked.

"That our child was kidnapped." She sighed, annoyed at my apparent stupidity.

I took a deep breath, cleared my throat, and drummed my fingers on the table. "Cally is still legally the mother of the baby. So technically, it's not kidnapping."

"I don't need your legalese, Hal." Ruth turned away. "I don't care what they call it. She's missing. We can give the police a description of her car. Put out an all-points bulletin."

"We don't know what car she's in," I reminded her. "We don't even know if she had a car. You're the one who drove her here."

"How do you think she got away? On foot?"

"Come on." I tried to take Ruth in my arms, to hold her. But she elbowed me as if I were a dummy in her self-defense class. I held open my arms for her.

"Stop it," she said through clenched teeth. "We'll file a missing person report."

"They can't really do much until seventy-two hours have passed." I moved closer to her, a peaceful approach.

"We can't wait that long, Hal," she said plaintively. "We have to find her."

"We will," I said, and she let me embrace her. "It's only been, what, seven hours?"

"I knew this would happen," she said, letting down her guard. "I knew it."

I frowned because I didn't enjoy what-ifs and why nots. There was usually nothing to do about them.

Still, she continued, and I knew she needed to get this out. "I told you weeks ago," she said. "At our anniversary dinner."

It was true. She'd said she was worried. The month before, we'd gone to the Winston steak house, where we'd had our first date five years earlier. We were celebrating three years of marriage, but nothing on the menu interested Ruth.

"I have a stomachache," she'd said. "Something's not right with Cally."

"What do you mean?" I was busy buttering my bread. They have the softest, freshest bread, impossible to resist.

"I think she is having doubts. I think she's attached," said Ruth.

"Well, that's natural, isn't it?" I said, looking up and making eye contact but also taking a bite of bread.

"Don't tell me what's natural. I understand what's natural," said Ruth, taking umbrage. She was sensitive to issues of maternal instinct and biology. "I think she might not go through with it."

My mouth was full, so I waited until I could swallow. "What makes you say that?" I asked.

"I've noticed things," she said. "At our Lamaze classes, for example. Cally's been getting close to this other pregnant gal, Sarah. They're always talking together, without me. Like they don't want me to hear what they're saying."

"So what?" I reached for more bread.

"What if Sarah's been trying to get her to change her mind, and giving her ideas—"

"Come on, Ruth," I said, taking a drink of wine. We were supposed to be celebrating.

"And Cally's been talking to her tummy a lot more lately, as if the baby can hear her."

"Babies can hear voices while in utero. That's a known fact," I said, and the waiter arrived for our orders.

"I'll just have a cup of wild rice soup," said Ruth.

"You sure?" I said, because I ordered a rib-eye steak and I wanted to enjoy it. The waiter took our menus and I tried to focus.

"And just last week, Cally asked me what I thought about the name Nell." Ruth made a quizzical face. "Why would she do that? She knows we having naming rights." Ruth bit into a piece of plain bread, not interested in butter.

"Yeah." I cleared my throat. These signs were not good.

"She knows we're leaning toward Elizabeth." Ruth took a long drink of water.

"What's your point?"

"My point is, we need to lock it down." Ruth looked around the restaurant as if there were a chorus of strangers who understood more about this than I did. The place was not busy on a Monday night, so there was no ready audience. "Make sure we get our child," she said, her eyes sad.

"We can't force her, you realize that." I sipped my wine.

"But she agreed. We have the contract," said Ruth, fidgeting with her silverware, and in this moment I was glad she only had a soup spoon and not a steak knife. "I'm just saying maybe we should speed up the transfer date."

"We can't do that," I said, wiping the crumbs off the thick white tablecloth.

"Yes, we can." She looked in the breadbasket, but it was empty.

"All right," I said, clarifying, "we shouldn't do that."

"We shouldn't? Why not?"

"For enforceability," I said in a tone of finality. I'd tried to explain enforceability to Ruth time and time again. She said she understood it, but she didn't agree.

"I guess I'll have to take your word for it," she said, motioning for the waiter to bring us more bread.

And now, as we sat in the conference room waiting for the director of patient relations to return, Ruth was on the same sorrowful wavelength. I tried to comfort her. "This isn't anyone's fault," I said, but I knew that if this deal went sour, I would certainly be the first one she'd blame.

The director knocked on the conference room door and walked in.

"Any news?" I asked, hopeful for a diversion.

The director clasped her hands. "I don't have anything specific just yet. But I have confirmed that we had security cameras on the areas that may have been involved."

"Good," said Ruth, standing up. "I want to see the footage."

"And I anticipated that request," said the director. "Our team is reviewing the footage in order to prepare it for viewing. It's protocol."

"How long will that take?" I asked.

"Not long," said the director. "I should have an answer for you by late afternoon or this evening. It's a Saturday, so we're reaching out to our various department heads and stakeholders."

"We understand," I said, hoping I could speak for us both.

"I want to see the room she was in. Now," said Ruth, gathering her things. "Take us to the room."

Twenty-Five

CALLY

Early Morning

In the middle of the night, early Sunday morning, I woke to Nell crying. My brain was doing that thing where it made me think the noises I heard were just a part of my dream. I was dreaming of wolves howling. At first they were far away, but they got closer and closer, like they had surrounded the cabin and were screeching at us through the gaps in the logs. The crying got so loud, Digger and I both woke up, and I realized the howling wasn't in my dream; it was inside the cabin. With us.

Before I knew who I was talking to, I sat up straight in bed and called out, "Okay, okay, you're all right."

"Make it stop!" Digger covered his ears with pillows.

I pulled off my covers and stepped out of bed to check the crate. Even in the dark, I could see Nell's mouth was wide open. I reached down to pick her up, and her back was arched. She'd come out of her blankets. Her fists and legs were stretching and shaking, like she was desperate and outraged and scared. I held her up to my shoulder, my neck, and I felt her tears on my skin.

"There, there," I said, bouncing. I was thinking that if Hal and

Ruth had taken Nell home with them, they'd be the ones waking up in the middle of the night, not me and Digger.

"Feed her or something, goddammit," said Digger.

I went to the rocking chair and crouched down on the old dusty cushion. I was wearing just my T-shirt and underpants. I held the wailing baby in one arm and raised up my T-shirt with the other. Her mouth was still open from screaming, so I just stuck it mid-scream onto my nipple. The crying stopped immediately.

"Thank God," said Digger.

"Yeah," I said, looking down at the baby. My bunched-up T-shirt blocked my view of her face, but I held her in place, her head and bottom in my two hands, my elbows on the armrests. I was afraid to move because she was quiet and I didn't want to jinx it. So I sat still, and the tingling happened again in my chest, almost like a sexual rush. That warm surge from my shoulders to my nipples, and my breasts were full. Luckily, Nell really started suckling. She gobbled and slurped while she ate, making noises like a French bulldog, not taking time to breathe.

"What time is it?" I asked.

"Aaaargggh mmmmphhh," said Digger. "I was just starting to sleep again."

"Well?"

"I can't see my watch," he said. Digger wore a watch and never took it off. Not to shower, not to sleep. Not when he lifted weights. Never. His watch was as much a part of him as the mole on his left thigh or his oddly shaped ears that I thought looked like a greyhound's. "It's too dark. Why do you care?"

"Come on, you can see it." I knew the hands glowed in the dark.

"For fuck's sake," he said, rolling over in bed and sitting up on one elbow. "It's two-forty-five, okay?"

"Thank you. That's about what I thought."

"Can I go back to sleep now?"

"Yes," I said. The baby leaned back, coughing and then smacking her lips. I pulled her wiggly body up to my shoulder and stood, pressing her against me enough with one arm so I could lean down and wipe off the rocker cushion. I'd felt something there, like a screw or a nail or a hardened piece of food. I thought about the story of the princess and the pea, which my dad used to read to me. The story he especially liked, because I was his Little Pea. And he told it whenever I was picky about whatever it happened to be, like not wanting my cheeseburger to touch my fries, or not wanting the seat belt pulled too tight, or not wanting calamine lotion on my mosquito bites. I grew up thinking it was better not to complain about my pet peeves, because I didn't want to be like the princess and the pea. Once I asked him if that was why my mother left us. He'd said, No, Caroline, my real name, the name he used when he was serious. I'd wanted to believe him, but I wondered if he was only trying to protect me.

I sat back down on the rocker, and the cushion felt nice and soft. No pebbles or peas. I leaned back and rocked with Nell at my shoulder, and I closed my eyes. She was gurgling and smushing her face on my neck, like she was trying to rub an itch. And then she burped, which surprised me and made me smile. It was the smallest little poof of a belch I'd ever heard. I opened my eyes and felt my other breast filling up and aching, the left one. She'd already sucked on the right breast, and the hospital nurse had told me to keep it equal, to even them out. But my own breast was telling me now, so I leaned forward and lowered the baby back down under my T-shirt. I stuck her face up against my left breast; she smacked her lips a few times like she wasn't ready, but then took hold of the nipple. Relief!

When I crawled back into bed, Digger was asleep, but he had rolled over to face my side of the bed. His arms were folded like he was praying, but I knew he wasn't. His left arm was on top, his watch facing up. My eyes had adjusted to the darkness and I could see like a cat. Almost too well. Would I be able to fall asleep? The watch read three-thirty.

He flinched and rolled back over, away from me. I pulled the covers up over my shoulders, positioning myself away from Digger and facing the crate on the floor. Nell breathed softly. I listened to each inhale.

I closed my eyes. The lumpy mattress poked at various parts of my body, and I shifted to try to fit in with the hills and valleys. The scratchy sheet tickled the back of my calves, my thighs, my arms. I wondered if the sheets were clean or if tiny bugs were biting me.

Suddenly thirsty, I pulled back the covers again and stood. Where was the water? I shuffled over to the kitchen area and sifted through the pantry. I opened a plastic jug of water and guzzled. I couldn't swallow quickly enough. I took breaks between chugs and drank until I'd quenched my mega-thirst. I looked out the window. I needed to pee but didn't want to walk all the way to the outhouse. I thought about the wolves in my dream. Were they really out there? They'd seemed so real.

I looked around for a bucket. Was there anything I could pee in? I banged around in the pots and pans but couldn't find a pail. I stood still and waited to hear if I'd woken Nell or Digger. No, they'd slept through, so I thought about my choices. I knew I had to go outside to pee. I stepped into my boots but didn't have time for pants.

I opened the door a crack and cold rushed in. I slipped outside as quickly as I could and closed the door behind me. I moved a few feet to the side, away from the entrance, spread my legs, and squatted. I pulled my undies to the side and peed. Yes! It felt so good; I didn't mind the frozen air on my bare legs and arms.

After I was done, I washed off with a handful of snow and wiped my hands on my T-shirt.

When I grabbed the doorknob, it wouldn't turn.

Twenty-Six

RUTH

SATURDAY, DECEMBER 7, 2002

Morning

Hal and I followed Betsy Whittier as she guided us from the patient relations conference room to Cally's recovery room. The three of us turned each corner with the precision of a pack of race cars, and as we cruised the long hallway, we passed the drinking fountain and the nurses' station. The night nurses were handing off to the seven a.m. shift. They ceased chatting to watch with serious faces.

"Good morning," I said without smiling.

Clip, clop, clip, clop. We strode past the faded construction-paper display board with all the same facts about all the same nurses. Everything was the same, and nothing was the same.

"I spent practically the whole day here yesterday," I said.

"I know," said Hal.

As we neared Cally's room, a part of me hoped that there had been a mistake, that she'd still be sitting there in bed, struggling to nurse the baby, and the baby would cry and we'd pick her up and she'd stop crying and we'd take her home and never come back, and all of this middle-of-the-night drama had simply been some kind of bad dream.

But that wasn't the case.

We slowed down as we approached her room and stopped in the doorway. I looked at the open bathroom door. Maybe she was in there and no one had remembered to check it. We walked all the way in and saw that the place was empty.

"That was fast," said Hal.

"For crying out loud. Will you look at that," I said, gaping. The room was unrecognizable: it had already been cleaned. The bed was made, there were no clothes, no personal effects, and no bassinet. The whiteboard was blank, and the window was intact. There was no sign of her ever having been there. I walked outside to check the room number again. Yep, this was it. "Where's her stuff?" I asked, looking in the small closets near the door.

"I'm sure if there were any items left behind," said the director, "they would have been placed in the hospital lost and found."

"How could you do this?" I said, looking in the bathroom.

"Do what, Mrs. Olson? Clean the room?" The director looked at her watch. "It's already seven o'clock on a Saturday morning. The rooms are cleaned first thing, standard procedure. I'm sure we'll have another patient very soon, that's how it goes, especially on maternity. I'm sure you understand."

"No, I don't understand." I sat on the bed.

"And we'll need to clean it again since we are in here," said the director. "It's no longer sterile."

"No longer *sterile*?"

"Ruth." Hal sat next to me and put his arm around me.

"I expected there to be, like, yellow tape cordoning off the area, to preserve the evidence."

"It's not a crime scene," said the director.

"Maybe not to you it isn't," I said.

"Mrs. Olson, a patient of this hospital gave birth to a child, which, according to the hospital's point of view, makes her the mother of the child, and she is free to do as she pleases with her own child," said the director. "And I believe that is correct according to the legalities of the state." The director looked at Hal, and Hal looked at the floor.

"We had an agreement with her," I said with as much self-control as I could muster.

"And that is between you and her," said the director. "As far as this hospital is concerned, this young woman—your surrogate—had every right to go wherever she wished to go."

"You shouldn't have let her." I got up and walked to the window.

"Forgive me, but that is not our job," she said. "You are implying that we had an obligation to keep her here. We did not."

"You knew she was a surrogate, that's all we're saying," said Hal, finally chiming in.

"Mr. Olson, I have seen many things in my line of work, and there is one thing I know for sure about human beings: they are unpredictable."

"We need to see the evidence." I paced each corner of the room, as if there might be clues in every nook and cranny.

Hal moved out of my way.

"What did it look like?" I said. "How did they know she was gone? What did they see?"

"It's possible there was foul play," said Hal without much conviction in his voice.

"As I said, we have notified our security team," said the director.

"I want to talk to them," I said.

"I'm sorry, talk to whom?" The director looked annoyed.

"Everyone," I said. "I want to talk to your security team, the janitors, the nurses. Who discovered she was gone? Who first saw the room? Who took the stuff out of here? I want their names."

Hal crossed his arms and leaned against the window ledge. He exhaled and looked at the floor.

"I'm afraid that's not part of our procedure, Mrs. Olson," said the director. "At least not at this stage."

"Okay, and what stage are we in here, exactly?"

There was a knock at the door and a friendly woman's voice trilling, "Helloooo," the same way a visitor would have sounded if I had been the new mom in the bed, holding her child.

"Hi, can we come in?" said a male voice. It was Jim, our social worker, and Carol, our minister. They had arrived early for the transfer ceremony.

"Oh, for cripe's sake! Carol, Jim," I said, rushing toward them. "I'm so sorry."

"What is it? Is everything all right?" said Carol, taking my hands in hers.

"You don't know?" I said.

"No, we . . ." Jim looked at Carol, and Carol finished his sentence: "Don't . . . know anything."

"Let's step out into the hall," said Hal, launching himself toward the door.

The director of patient relations excused herself, telling me she would contact us when she had more information, and meanwhile, she'd send in the cleaning crew. We could hear her high heels clicking as fast as her short legs could go, away from us and down the hallway.

"What's going on?" said Carol.

"Why don't we find a place to sit and talk?" said Hal.

"Let's go to the cafeteria," said Jim.

"Perfect," said Hal. "I could use a cup of coffee." He turned to me with his hand outstretched.

"You go ahead," I said. "I have some calls to make."

"Oh," said Hal. "Would you mind calling Caleb and telling him not to come?"

"Okay," I said, and Hal squeezed my shoulder before heading out the door to join Carol and Jim. As soon as he left, I went back to the window. Snowbanks below, a small parking lot, a few cars completely covered in snow. It wasn't as far down as I had feared. That gave me some comfort.

I went to the bed and sat, then swung my purse into my lap, digging for my address book and a pen. Since I'd already contaminated the room, I might as well take advantage. I picked up the bedside phone, the one that Cally had used to take the call yesterday afternoon as I was leaving. I dialed *69 and listened, pen in hand. An automated voice said, "The last number dialed from this extension was . . ." and "Stay on the line to hear this message again . . ." I hung up and looked at the number I'd scribbled on the front page of my address book. A St. Paul area code? Did I know that number? I flipped through the rest of my address book, thinking it might jump out at me. It didn't.

Meanwhile, I had several calls of my own to make. I used the phone freely and no one disturbed me. When I was done with my last call, I hung up, and the phone rang, startling me. Could this be the same person who'd called yesterday looking for Cally? I let it ring a second time, unsure what to do. On the third ring, I answered. "Hello?" I said quietly and checked the doorway to see if anyone was watching me.

"Yes, hello," said the man on the other end of the line. "This is Food Service calling. We are ready for your breakfast order, please?"

"No, there's no breakfast, thank you." I hung up.

A woman pushed a cart into the room, with a large bin for dirty laundry, clear plastic garbage pail liners, and a pile of clean sheets wrapped in cellophane. When she saw me, she stopped. "Oh, excuse me," she said. "I'll come back."

"No, it's fine," I said. "Can I ask you—did you, by any chance, did you clean this room earlier?" I stood up and smoothed the bedding where I'd been sitting.

"Yes, ma'am," she said.

"Hi, I'm Ruth." I reached out my hand and stepped a bit closer.

"Hello." She reached out and took just the ends of my fingertips and only briefly.

"Can I call you Marti?" I pointed to her name badge.

She touched the front of her smock and looked toward the open door to the hallway.

"It's okay," I said, "I am a family member of the woman who was in here." I walked to the window. "I'm trying to find out why she left."

"Oh, I'm sorry, ma'am." Marti lowered her head and moved closer to the bed I'd been sitting on, the one I'd made not sterile.

"What did the room look like when you found it?" I asked, setting my purse down on the window ledge, balancing it so it wouldn't fall. "It's very clean now, but what was it like this morning?" I folded my arms and leaned against the ledge. "It was very early in the morning, right?"

"Yes." The cleaning woman lifted the top layer from the bed and pulled it back. "I came on at five a.m."

"What did you see?"

"That window was open." She pointed at me.

"This window here?" I stepped away and pointed to the left side. The window was a slider, so there were technically two panes in the opening.

"Yes, that side, the left side." She pointed to the side nearest the bathroom door, in the corner. She turned back to the bed and continued pulling up sheets.

"Okay, what else?" I examined the window ledge outside. Brick. About eighteen inches deep, crusted with small drifts of snow.

Marti stopped to think. She pointed to the floor. "There was water there. Snow had blown in and melted. I cleaned it up."

"Uh-huh." I reached into my purse for something better to write on. I wished I had my recorder, but I found my journal instead. "And was the baby in the room? Or anyone else here?"

"No baby," she said, dumping an armful of sheets into the round bin attached to her cart. "No woman, nobody."

"The bassinet?"

"I don't remember." She bent down to the lower level of her cart and collected a tightly wrapped package of fresh linens.

"What else? What about the bed?" I gestured around the room, like a flight attendant demonstrating how lights will illuminate the aisle in the event of an emergency.

"Pillows and blankets on the bed, all in a pile, big pile on the bed. The sheets had blood and dirty pee pads. I threw those away and put the sheets and blankets in my bin. I put on clean ones." She held the packet in one arm and used her free arm to demonstrate what she remembered.

"Was that curtain open or closed?" I pointed to the aqua-colored privacy curtain that separated the two twin beds.

"I don't know." Marti tore open the cellophane packet and tossed the wrapping in a clear plastic garbage bag hooked onto her cart.

"Was there any food on this table or cups? Any notebooks or phone book?" I pointed to the table between the beds where the phone was.

"No." She shook out the sheets and let them billow down onto the bed. "Maybe there was trash I threw away."

I glanced at the trash container on Marti's cart.

"It's not there. I emptied that already." She preempted my next question.

"Anything in the bathroom or the closet?" I opened the bathroom door and switched on the light.

"I don't think so." She straightened as if to think more clearly. "No, because if I saw something in there, they'd put it in the lost and found."

"Uh-huh, and where is that?" I said.

"Excuse me." A nurse walked in. "What's going on here?"

Marti said nothing. I said nothing.

"Can you give us a minute?" the nurse said to Marti as she opened the door wide, and noise from the hallway spilled in.

"I'm sorry." Marti lowered her head and pushed her cart to the door.

"It's fine. Just come back in a few minutes, please." The nurse stood leaning on the rail of the bed closest to the door, with the other hand on her hip.

Marti nodded and left the room.

"Thank you, Marti," I called to her.

"I'm going to have to ask you to leave," said the nurse when we were alone.

"My name is Ruth Olson, and I am a reporter for the *Minneapolis*

Star." I reached out to shake her hand and noticed her name badge. "Actually, Rebecca, can I ask you some questions?"

"You'd have to call our media department." Rebecca walked to the bathroom and switched off the light. "I'm not authorized."

"How many nurses work on the night shift?"

"Well, that varies," said Rebecca, crossing her arms.

"How many were working last night?" I turned to a blank page and wrote Rebecca's name at the top.

"I'm not sure, and even if I knew, I wouldn't feel comfortable disclosing that kind of information."

"Let me ask you this: do you screen the visitors, or do you just let anyone in?"

"That's not our job as nurses, Miss . . ."

"Olson, and it's Mrs."

"Mrs. Olson," said Rebecca, sighing and shifting her weight to one side.

I wondered what she'd heard about me, about our situation. "Because I know you make us wear pink stickers that say the word 'visitor,' and obviously, we can write whatever name we want on there, but really, does anyone know who is here and who they really are?"

"Mrs. Olson, you're upset." Rebecca looked me in the eye.

"Do you have security on this floor? Or stationed outside the building? Where are they? Because I don't see any."

"You'd have to ask our security department, but I do know that we have security and safety procedures for all staff." Rebecca walked toward the door, as if doing so would lead me to follow her.

"Uh-huh, and how do you know when an intruder is in a patient's room?" I looked out the window.

"An intruder?" Rebecca turned to face me again.

"Do you realize over the last two days I walked into this room several times without anyone asking me who I was, and I sat here in this room holding a newborn baby for hours before anyone came into the room and saw me? I could have been anyone. Anyone could have waltzed in here and taken that baby out of that bassinet." I pointed to the empty place on the floor beside the bed where the bassinet had been.

"No one is accusing you of taking anyone's baby." Rebecca walked closer to me with one arm outstretched.

"How often are you supposed to check on the patients?" I stepped back.

"I don't think this is a productive conversation." She waved toward me as if gathering a group of tourists to come along with her.

"How many times have you had a patient kidnapped?"

"Come on, now." She nodded, still waving me toward her.

"How many times has a patient left without your knowledge?"

"Let's go now, so they can finish cleaning the room." She moved closer, trying to shepherd me from the window side of the room to the door and out into the hallway.

"Why won't you answer my questions?" I held up my notepad, showing that I was ready for her answer.

She shuffled behind me and placed one hand on my back.

"Don't touch me!" I jerked away, and Rebecca lifted both hands up as if to surrender. We stood frozen like that for one or two long seconds until we sensed another person enter.

"Mrs. Olson, I'm going to have to ask you to leave this room now."

I recognized the director's voice. Someone must have called her. "Hello, Betsy," I said. "I was just on my way out."

Twenty-Seven

CALLY

Early Morning

I pulled my T-shirt down around my undies and marched in place. It was freezing cold outside and the fucking door was locked. I'd jiggled the doorknob, but it was stiff, not budging. I tiptoed to the side of the cabin, half afraid there'd be a wolf standing there, or a bear. Every shadow looked like a monster, and I had to get inside. I peeked in the frosty window on the side by our bed. The woodburning stove had gone out, and there were only a few glowing embers. I knocked on the window, but not hard. I didn't want to wake Nell, because that would piss off Digger. Maybe I could find an extra key.

Lights flashed in the distance, by the road. I tucked myself behind the side of the cabin and peeked out. Car headlights were making the bend, and then they were gone.

I walked quickly back to the front door. "Digger," I called, and knocked on the door, harder. "Digger!"

Finally, the door opened. "What the hell," said Digger, rubbing his eyes.

I ran inside and he closed the door. "I had to pee." I snuggled myself into Digger's chest.

Instinctively, he put his arms around me. "You must have locked it on your way out."

"My legs are freezing. Can you get me some sweatpants or something?" I crawled into bed, shivering.

"What am I, your maid?" Digger hunted around in the piles and tossed me my sweatpants, and I put them on.

"Can you get me another blanket?"

"Jesus Christ," he said, and threw me a wool blanket from the sofa.

"Thanks, and try to be quieter," I said. Luckily, he hadn't woken the baby. Digger started getting dressed, and I worried he might be leaving us. "Where are you going?"

"To take a motherfucking piss, is that all right with you?" He stormed out the door. When it slammed, the cabin shook, and this time Nell woke. I picked her up and brought her into bed with me.

When Digger came back a few minutes later, the door was still locked. He knocked and called, "Cally!"

I rose as quickly as I could and shuffled to the door to unlock it. He stomped in with firewood in his arms and went to work at the woodburning stove.

"Oh, good," I said, and I put Nell up to my shoulder. She was fussing, so I changed her diaper. I'd been putting the dirty ones in the empty car seat box, our temporary trash can. I took the baby to the rocker and sat down gently. My underpants felt wet between my legs. I reached down and touched the wetness. I'd been noticing occasional bleeding that didn't seem to have any pattern or cause. The nurses had given me some paperwork with information about it, so I knew it was something to pay attention to.

Digger lit the fire, then sat on the bed, watching the flames catch.

"What time is it?" I said.

"Like five," he said. "I'm going back to bed."

We crawled in and stayed still in the darkness. The fire crackled, and the place warmed up. "Hey, do you think there are wolves out there?" I asked.

Digger grunted. "Why?"

"I just wondered. Thought I heard howling."

"There's animals around here, I guess. This whole area is, like, prime hunting grounds." He shifted around to get comfortable.

"They can't hunt wolves, though, can they?"

"I dunno. Maybe not. I thought they were endangered or some shit," said Digger.

"Well, I hope they don't come near us." I smiled, thinking that Digger would protect us. I wondered if he had a girlfriend down in Missouri or maybe one back home. He hadn't said anything and I hadn't asked.

"Nah. They're afraid of us more than we're afraid of them."

"Okay, that's good." I checked on Nell. She was quiet in the crate. I leaned over Digger to get a peek at his watch. He opened his eyes and startled me. "I was just checking the time," I said. The fire made a golden glow in the cabin, but it was still hard to see.

"Yeah, I didn't think you were about to jump my bones," he said.

"You wish," I said, waiting for a reaction, but there was none. "No, I'm way too sore," I said, pulling the covers up. "Besides, don't you have a girlfriend?"

"No comment," he said. "You dumped me, remember."

I thought about arguing that point but decided to let it go.

He said, "Why'd you have to bring that up?"

"What?"

"Having sex," he said. "Now I'm thinking about it."

"You're always thinking about it."

"True," he said, peeking to see me smile. "Just let me try to sleep."

"So what time is it?"

"It's five-fifteen, and why do you keep asking? We're in the fucking woods. Are you on a tight schedule or something?"

"I'm trying to keep track of when she's eating and peeing and things like that."

"You're not keeping this baby, why waste your time?"

"You don't know that," I said.

"Whoa whoa whoa," he said, sitting up. "You told me you would give me five grand after they paid you."

He was right. We'd made a deal during the drive north from the hospital. After Digger had seen the baby, he'd wanted to turn around and bring us back. He said he didn't want to get involved in whatever kind of trouble this was. He never wanted to be involved in the surrogacy at all. And now he was just getting his life in place, a good job working for his uncle, even though he never knew when or where the next project would be, but it was good money. He wanted to save enough to buy a house, a fixer-upper he could remodel, maybe rent it out, and eventually flip it. Maybe start a business flipping houses.

I'd needed help getting away from town, hiding out for a few days with the baby before I turned her over. I hadn't known I'd want to spend extra days with her. I wished I'd put that in the contract. So I offered him a piece of the money to help me. It was worth it. I didn't have anyone else to call. Maybe Sarah from birth class, but I didn't know her that well. And besides, I wanted Digger to see Nell. How cute she was. I wanted him to see that this had been a good idea, that I'd been a success.

Before we broke up, he'd wanted me to come down to Missouri with him while he worked. But what would I have done in Missouri? I wanted to go back to Inver Grove Community College. I had credits there. I'd picked out my courses. I'd picked a career. All I needed was the money.

"You're right," I said. "I agreed to pay you. And I will."

"With what?" he said. "If you don't turn over the kid, they're not gonna give you that money. And you'll have to pay them back what they already gave you, right?"

"No, I don't think so. Besides, I can't afford that."

"Damn straight," he said. "And don't even think about asking me for it."

This made me think Digger had made good money down there

working construction. He must have built up his savings. Good for him.

"The contract says I can change my mind," I said.

"Oh, no no no no no no," said Digger, sitting up again. "We talked about this."

"Relax. I could turn her over next week and they'll still want her. I have time."

"Twenty thousand dollars, Cally."

"I know," I said.

"Fifty, actually," he said. "In total, right?"

"Almost fifty-five," I said, thinking about that. "So . . . you don't think I should keep her?"

"Hell, no," he said. "Take the money. For college and shit." We sat there on the bed in the quiet cabin, thinking about fifty-five thousand dollars. "You could probably get more at this point," said Digger.

"No, that's the amount," I said. "I'm not gonna try to get more."

"I know, but you could. I'm just saying . . ."

"Can we talk about this later? I want to try and sleep while she's sleeping."

"Well, good luck with that, but now I can't sleep," he said, getting up off the bed and looking for his coat. "So I might as well take the trash over to the dump."

"The dump?" I said. "What time does it open on Sundays?"

"I know a way to get in."

"All right, but come right back."

"What? Are you afraid the wolves are gonna get you?"

"Ha-ha. Maybe I am," I said. "Can you believe I just like having you here?"

Digger scoffed and looked at me, tried to read my face. "All right. Well, I'm going to take the trash, and I'll be back." Digger picked up the big car seat box, hauled it outside, and threw it in the back of the truck. He hopped up into the driver's seat and lit up. The cigarette glowed as he took a couple drags. Maybe he was thinking about what

I'd said, about how I liked having him around. A few seconds later, he came back.

I opened the door, and he was just standing there with one hand on his waist and the other one propping him up against the doorframe. The cigarette was dangling from his mouth.

"What?" I asked.

He took the cigarette out and flicked off the ashes.

"Truck won't start," he said.

Twenty-Eight

HAL

Morning

Carol, Jim, and I had just finished a nice cup of hospital coffee when Ruth stormed into the cafeteria, determination in her face. Before we could greet her, she shrugged impatiently and barked, "What are you guys doing?"

"Ruth, sit down," I said. "We're discussing our options."

"We have no options," she said, not sitting. "We need to go to Cally's apartment. Now."

I apologized to Jim and Carol, who stood up and put on their coats, ready to leave. Clearly, they'd noticed our marital tension and took it as their cue. As they left, I thanked them for all their support and wise counsel.

On the way to Cally's apartment, the mood in the car was tense, as Ruth and I were both lost in our thoughts. Finally, Ruth spoke.

"We need advice," she said. "We should hire a lawyer."

"I am a lawyer, Ruth."

"But you do real estate. I'm talking about a surrogacy lawyer. You're always telling me that lawyers specialize and can't be experts in all areas."

These were fighting words and Ruth knew it. However, because I

was driving, I maintained my composure until I could put the vehicle
in park. As I approached Cally's street, I was lucky to find a parking
spot among the irregular piles of snow and the inadequate plowing.
"Here's a spot," I said, pulling over to the curb a few buildings short
of Cally's. I shifted into park and switched off the ignition. The fan
blower went silent. "I know the contract," I said firmly. "I wrote it."

We sat with that statement for a few moments. Then Ruth said
what she'd apparently been thinking this whole time. "We should've
had a real surrogacy lawyer write it."

I took a deep breath. A distinct unease filled the car. I opened the
door and cold rushed in, shaking us out of our battle positions. "Let's
go see what we can find," I said as I climbed out over a snowbank and
onto the sidewalk.

Ruth got out and followed in my footsteps. She motioned with her
mitten and we trudged along the frozen, snowy path, careful not to
slip or twist an ankle.

"Do you see her car anywhere?" I asked.

"Not yet," said Ruth, but I couldn't be certain how carefully she'd
been looking.

"It's red," I added, but Ruth knew that. "A four-door Chevy Cav-
alier." Maybe saying it would help us find it. We wandered up and
down the snowy street, searching for sedans, but most of them were
covered in snow, or the wrong color, or the wrong make.

"I'm going up," Ruth said as we gravitated back to the apartment
building entrance.

I pushed the button for 3F, and we waited, marching in place and
seeing our breath. I jiggled the front door just in case. Ruth pressed
her forehead up against the cold glass and peered in. There was a
wall of mailboxes, with envelopes sticking out of the box marked
3F, which would make sense, because Cally had been in the hospital
since Thursday.

"Her mail's still there," said Ruth.

"Didn't you say she gave you a key to her apartment," I asked, "in
case she needed something?"

"Yes, but it's at home, I think. Hang on." Ruth checked her purse, and it appeared we were back in sync. "It must be at home."

"Ruth." I sighed, frustrated that Ruth hadn't anticipated our need for the key. We could have stopped at our place first. We could have avoided this delay.

"Well, I'm sorry I wasn't thinking about breaking into her apartment this morning at five a.m. when I found out our baby was gone."

"Okay, okay, relax. Let's just go look in the back for her car," I said, trooping around the side of the apartment building. "It has to be here somewhere."

"Yeah," said Ruth, following me to the back parking lot. "I mean, where else could it be?" she added as we scanned the small row of cars by the alley. "I'm the one who drove her to the damn hospital."

Twenty-Nine

DIGGER

SUNDAY, DECEMBER 8, 2002

Morning

Cally was in my way, standing in the kitchen area, chugging water from the jug. She was blocking the shelves I needed to get to.

"Move," I said, bending down. "I gotta get in there." I reached around her into the shelves. Nothing but pans and plates and cans of Dinty Moore.

"What are you looking for?"

"Gas can," I said as I walked out the door.

Cally followed me and stood in the doorway. "You think it's out of gas?" she said.

"What the fuck else would I need a gas can for?"

"Could be the battery," she added, then closed the door.

"Won't know unless I try," I said, mimicking her voice, not caring whether or not she heard me.

I fished around in the shed and had to take out some shit: a shovel, some planks of plywood, a deflated, frozen inner tube, a cardboard box, and a coil of heavy-duty extension cord.

When I got back inside, the kettle was whistling.

"I'm making hot chocolate," said Cally.

"Uh-huh," I said, and I watched her pour hot water into a mug. "I found the gas can." I held it up to show her, but she wasn't impressed.

"I was thinking if you had a generator, you could charge the battery," she said.

"I know, but I'm getting gas first."

"Is there a leak? Because you put gas in Friday night."

"In fucking Rush City or wherever, a hundred miles or so away," I said. "And then we drove around a bunch yesterday."

"I'm just saying," said Cally.

"I need your credit card."

"What for?"

"What does it look like?" I picked up the gas can and threw it down. It made a hollow bouncing noise. The baby cried.

"Thanks a lot," said Cally. "Now the baby's up, and the place smells like gas."

"Just give me the card. Where is it?" I picked through her pile of clothes. Found her wallet and grabbed the Visa. "I'm going to the gas station."

"Lemme come with you," she said, pulling on her coat and grabbing the baby. "They might need my signature!"

I was out the door and halfway down the hill when I heard her yelling behind me. I turned around, and wouldn't you know, she was following me, her coat hanging open, wearing the boots I'd loaned her, and stepping in each of my footsteps. She had the baby in the car carrier, covered with a blanket.

I stopped to wait at the bottom of the hill. The main road hadn't been plowed. Finally, Cally caught up. Her face was red.

"You have ice on your face," she said.

"So do you," I said.

"Why'd you leave without us?"

"Because I didn't want you to come."

"Why not?" she said. We were standing next to the gate I'd opened two nights ago. Now it had drifted snow covering it.

"I wanted to make a phone call, okay?" I said. "Am I allowed to make a goddamn phone call?" I didn't wait for her to ask me who I wanted to call. I took off on the shoulder of the highway.

Cally followed, trying to keep up. "I don't care who you call, okay?" she said. "I thought since you had my credit card, they might want my signature!"

"You already said that." A car flashed their brights at us, so we stopped and moved farther back. The car drove past, slowly. I took the car carrier from Cally. It was only about a quarter mile to the Mobil.

Inside the gas station, it felt like a hundred degrees. I set down the car carrier. Cally took the blanket off the baby and unzipped the baby coat. The guy behind the counter looked bored out of his mind, but we were some entertainment.

"I'm gonna take a couple gallons of unleaded," I said, and he gave me a thumbs-up. I went out to the nearest pump and filled up the can. When I came back, Cally was looking for something in an aisle at the back. I waited by the front. There was a rack of Wisconsin maps, a small freezer with frozen candy bars, and a row of auto supplies. "Hey, if I need a jump, can you give me one?" I asked the guy behind the counter.

"Yeah, but I can't leave until two," he said. "When my replacement gets here."

I looked at my watch. "That's four hours from now."

"Sorry. I can't leave the shop unattended, ya know?"

The kid let out a screech like an animal and wiggled her arms and legs. Cally came over, picked up the carrier, and started swinging it.

"Fine," I said. "If that's the soonest you can come."

"And do you have a new battery we could buy in case ours won't take the charge?" asked Cally.

"Sure," said the clerk, looking at me. "I can throw one in the truck just in case."

Cally smiled because she always thought she knew more than me about cars. True, she could jump a battery practically with her eyes closed. And true, her dad had taught her about engines. So much that I'd given up on arguing about it with her. But I didn't have to like it.

"Give me your name and address?"

"Dennis Wilkins," I said, watching him write it on a scrap of paper. "Do you guys have a pay phone?"

"Yeah, it's outside," said the guy.

"What do I owe you for the gas?" I gave him the credit card.

"Wait," said Cally, "add in these." She placed a package of fucking maxi-pads on the counter.

"Sign here." The clerk pushed a slip forward.

I got out of the way so Cally could sign it. But while she was at the counter, I saw the back of her. I pulled her aside and whispered, "Your sweatpants are bloody."

"Fuck. Will you watch her?" Cally nodded at the baby carrier and then walked to the bathroom.

"Goddammit," I said. I didn't need this grief. When she was gone, I left the kid and went outside to the pay phone. I dialed my sister and she let it ring a bunch of times before she picked up.

"Why'd you wait so long to answer?"

"Digger?" she said.

"Yeah, and I'm standing outside in the goddamn freezing cold."

"Well, I didn't know that," said Deena. "Jesus. Are you okay?"

"Yeah," I said. "And uh . . . actually, I'm here. In Superior."

Deena wheezed. "Why didn't you tell me you were coming up?"

"I'm telling you now," I said. "It was a last-minute thing. I'm over at Charlie's cabin."

"Deer hunting?"

"No," I said. "I'm here with Cally." The fluorescent lights flickered above the gas pumps, and I could see my breath in the cold.

"Oh . . . so you two are back together?" said Deena, sounding skeptical, like my roommate. "I thought she dumped you."

"No, it's not like that. I mean, yeah, she dumped me. But we're not together." The pay phone meter clicked, reminding me to hurry up. "Look, I only have six minutes before I have to add money."

"Oh, believe me, you can piss me off in six minutes. Easy."

"Ha, funny." I leaned over as far as the metal cord would reach, to see into the store. The clerk was eating a bag of chips. No sign of Cally.

"Digger, do you have something to say, because this is like pulling teeth, and my show is on."

"I . . . um . . ." I couldn't think of what to say.

"Oh, God," said Deena, sounding concerned. "What did you do?" She'd helped me before when I'd done stupid shit. Nothing serious. Firecrackers, graffiti, a DUI.

"Nothing, nothing," I said, shivering.

"It doesn't sound like nothing."

"Look, are you home tonight?" I said. "Can I just come over there?"

"Sure, I'm home all night."

"Thanks."

"Mrs. Z's here, too," she said. Mrs. Z was Deena's ex-mother-in-law. "Hey, whatever it is, it can be dealt with, okay?"

I hung up and hustled back inside to get warm. The guy behind the counter was finishing a sandwich and a can of Coke. The baby was fussing. I picked up the carrier and gave it a swing, like Cally had done. It worked.

Cally came out of the bathroom. "I thought I heard the baby," she said.

"She's fine," I said, setting the car seat down.

Cally put on her coat and covered up the baby.

"See you around two," I said to the guy as we left. On the way back, I took the baby carrier and the gas can. Cally walked in front of me with her bag of maxi pads. "So, are you all right?" I said. "You got your period?"

"I don't think it's my period," she said. "I think it's just, you know, what happens after you have a baby."

"Okay, I don't wanna know," I said.

We walked in silence. At the base of the hill, she stopped and turned to me. "So, who did you call?"

A car slowed down and flashed its lights. It made crunch sounds in the snow, then stopped. An older woman on the passenger side rolled down her window. The driver was an older man. The woman asked, "Do you two need a lift?"

Thirty

RUTH

Afternoon

Eventually, Hal and I found Cally's car buried in snow in the parking lot behind her apartment building. With his wool-cloaked arm, Hal wiped off snow from the windshield and the driver's window, and we peered inside for clues. Nothing but used tissues, an empty Arby's cup and other trash, a Minnesota Gophers sweatshirt, a snow scraper, some papers that looked like junk mail. Nothing that indicated trouble or unusual circumstances.

"Look. There's a brochure from the community college on the passenger seat," I said.

"Okay, so we know she didn't drive herself away from the hospital," said Hal, like a lawyer.

"Couldn't she have come here somehow and then left the car?" I said, like a journalist.

"Well, from the accumulation up top, compared with the others, it looks like this car has been here for the six inches we got last night." Hal nodded at the perfectly formed meringue of snow on the Chevy's roof, then pointed around the lot.

"And there's no car seat," I added after checking the backseat again.

"Why would she have a car seat? We're the ones who need a car seat."

"I'm just noting it for the record, Counselor." I checked Hal's face to see if he appreciated my teasing. He didn't; he was too focused. I tried the door on the passenger side, and it opened. Snow fell into the car as I swung the door wide and leaned in, grabbing at the trash on the floor and in between the seats.

"What are you doing?" Hal stepped back from the car.

"Maybe she hid an extra key in here." I opened the glove compartment, combed through the papers, and closed it again. When I found incriminating evidence in the form of an empty Starbucks cup, I pulled it out and stood next to Hal.

"Anything?" he asked.

"Look at this," I said, holding the cup up to his face. "She was drinking coffee."

"So?"

"Aaarrgghhh!" I threw the cup back into the car. "I knew she couldn't stop with the caffeine."

"It's not a big deal, Ruth."

"The National Institutes of Health would disagree with you, Hal." We stood there thinking about Starbucks.

"How do you even know it's her coffee cup?" asked Hal.

"Who else's would it be?" I leaned into the car and pulled up the floor mat. No keys.

"Didn't she have a boyfriend?" asked Hal.

"How would you know that?" I stood up straight to see Hal's face.

"You told me. You said she broke up with her high school sweetheart." He shrugged.

"Okay, well, true. But they broke up a while ago, before she was even inseminated. Anyway, would her boyfriend wear lipstick?" I asked, turning the cup to show him that it had clearly been kissed with fuchsia lips.

"So what if she drank coffee? The baby's healthy."

"We put it in the contract, Hal. She blew it off." I leaned into the car again, tried the ashtray in the backseat, and bingo! Keys.

"It wasn't in the contract," said Hal somewhat meekly.

"Yes, it was. I specifically remember that one." I scooped up the keys and slid them into my pocket.

"It was, but then it wasn't."

I stood up slowly. "What?" I slammed the car door and turned to Hal. "You took it out?"

"She asked me to," he said, shrugging.

"When? Why didn't you tell me?" I spun around in place. I didn't know what to do with my frustration, my hurt.

"I didn't think it was a big deal," said Hal, palms up.

"Yes, it certainly is," I said. "And how, like, did she call you, or—?"

"Yeah, she called me. Or maybe it was an email. Anyway, I told her not to worry about it."

I stormed away from Hal and headed straight to the apartment building. I pulled out the key and opened the door. Hal followed and almost didn't make it into the building before the door slammed shut.

"Hey," he shouted.

I stomped up the first of three flights of stairs.

"Wait for me," he said, huffing behind me.

I unzipped my parka on the second floor. I wasn't in the best shape for stair climbing. Our footsteps hit beats that were not together, not synchronized, making noise, not music. "At least she didn't smoke," I said, reaching the third floor, "unless you took that out, too."

Hal stopped on the landing for a moment, taking that in before continuing up to join me. I knocked first, then unlocked the apartment and went in. The air smelled stale. We stood in the entryway and looked at the small living room. "What do you think?" Hal said, deferring to me.

"Doesn't look like anyone's been here in a while."

"No, it doesn't," Hal said in his calm voice, the voice that let me know he was done fighting. That let me know he was sorry. We both exhaled simultaneously. Hal opened his arms, and I collapsed into them. He kissed my head and rested his chin on the spot he had kissed.

From his embrace, I saw myself in the entryway mirror. "Look at that," I said.

"What?"

"That little sign over there." I pointed to an index card that was taped to the mirror, in the bottom corner. It said: "College Student Lives Here."

Hal raised his eyebrows. Was he puzzled or impressed?

"Look, there's another one." I moved into the living room. On the back of a closet door, a card said: "Move Forward So You Don't Go Back."

Hal followed me as we hunted for index cards, little signs all over her apartment, with affirmations and reminders. Some of them were relevant and useful, like the one on the refrigerator door, which said: "You are Cooking a Baby => Eat Better." I liked that one. Others were more vague or aspirational.

On the bathroom mirror: "You Are Good at Math."

In the bedroom: "Career Girls Are Sexy."

"What do you make of this? All these note cards?" I said, wondering what I thought of them myself.

"I take it to mean that Cally is an ambitious young woman," said Hal.

"I guess so," I said, continuing to survey the area. There were other clues scattered about. On the dining room table, I saw a pile of mail, some of it opened and some not. I saw a phone bill and a credit card statement and a gas bill with "past due" marked in red. I wanted to dig further in the pile of bills, but that would be too invasive. Best to keep to what was clearly visible. Next to the phone, two index cards were taped to the wall, as if they were everlasting phone messages. One read: "Call Sarah + Bob." They were friends I remembered from the birth classes. The other said: "Call Hal=> Internship."

"What's this about?" I asked.

"Oh, you know about that," said Hal, dismissing any concern. "We talked about that early on. I said I'd ask around."

"Look!" I said suddenly. "Her answering machine!" I pointed to the black device next to the phone. "The light is blinking. She has messages." I pushed the play button and the tape rewound.

Beep! "Hi, Cally, it's Ruth calling to see how you're doing today. Hope you're feeling well and getting lots of sleep and drinking lots of water. Give me a call when you get a chance, okay? Thanks." I cringed because my voice sounded so sugary and annoying.

The machine continued. Beep! "Hey, it's me . . ." said a low male voice. Hal and I looked at each other with wide eyes. I put my finger to my lips as we continued listening. "Um, so you said you needed a ride. Yeah, I guess I could do that, but just let me know when." The machine stopped.

"Her ex-boyfriend?" I said.

"I thought you said they were broken up?" said Hal.

"They were!" I said, furious. "Cally said they were done for good."

"Oh, man," said Hal.

"I'm gonna dial star-six-nine." I picked up Cally's phone and motioned for Hal to get me something to write with. I scrawled down the number. "I'm pretty sure this matches one of the numbers I got in her hospital room."

"Call it," said Hal, and it felt like we were a team again.

While I listened to the phone ringing, I asked, "What should I say if I get the machine?"

"Say you're looking for Cally," said Hal, as if that were obvious.

The phone rang and rang with no answer and no answering machine. "Nothing," I said, hanging up. "Should we go over there?"

"Over where? Do we know where he lives?" asked Hal.

"No, I guess not," I said, and it seemed we'd reached the end of this trail.

Hal shrugged and opened the door. I shuffled out into the landing, and we made our way slowly down the wet stairs, as the snow we'd tracked in was melting.

On the drive home, we brainstormed. What were our options? What were our next steps? In terms of calling the police, Hal wanted to wait until after we saw the security footage. We both knew the police would make us wait until Monday night before they'd do squat about anything. I insisted, respectfully, that we consult a surrogacy attorney, and I already had the name of a good one from Kristin's research. Hal vehemently disagreed with the idea, and I could sense the hurt behind his anger, but I wasn't backing down.

In addition, and I was on a roll, I informed Hal that I was going to call my brother, Raymond, and ask him for help. Hal had met my brother at our wedding. But I predicted that Hal might be threatened by Raymond's expertise: he was a detective (and Hal was not).

"Do you really need to drag Ray into this?" he said as we pulled into the tuck-under garage at our condo.

"Yes," I said without further elaboration.

Hal inhaled deeply. "All right, fine." He sighed his reluctant acceptance.

At home, there were no messages yet from the hospital, but it was midafternoon on a Saturday, so we weren't concerned. They'd probably had to call in additional staff who were off for the weekend.

Hal decided he'd make his goulash for me and Caleb, as we all could use some old-fashioned comfort food. And with a fire in the living room, we'd hunker down and wait. As Hal started the dinner, with the fire crackling, I slipped out and went upstairs to the guest room. There was a phone in there, and it was private.

"Hi, Raymond." I was sitting on the bed, swinging my dangling feet. "It's your little sis." I waited for a reaction. He laughed.

"What's so funny?" I smoothed out the wrinkles beside me on the bedspread.

"Nothing," he said. "You're the only one who calls me Raymond anymore."

"Ha!" I pulled my legs onto the bed and leaned back against the headboard. The overhead light was too bright, and the walls were bare. It felt oddly like a dorm room. "How's work?" I was stalling.

"Everybody good down at the station?" Even though Raymond was semi-retired, I knew he stayed close with the guys.

"They're good, but what's all this about?" he said. "I'm happy to hear from you, but it's not every day that—"

"I know. I'm sorry. I should call more often." I curled and uncurled the phone cord in my fingers. I looked out the window to the dark sky. We should put curtains up, I thought. "It's been a busy year, with the baby coming and everything," I said, and that was the truth.

"Eh." Raymond scoffed it off. "So what's up, Ru? I know there's something." He held the phone close to his mouth, and using his deep voice, he said, "I'm a detective, remember?"

"That's actually why I'm calling you, Raymond."

"Oh, boy," he said, and I could feel him smiling through the phone.

I was only able to give him the basics before Hal called, "Dinner's ready! Come and get it!"

Thirty-One

CALLY

OCTOBER 2002

Evening

It had been nice having a friend who was also pregnant. I met Sarah at the Lamaze classes Ruth made me attend on Tuesday nights. Since Ruth planned to be my birth coach, she wanted to learn the breathing and baby basics. Most of the other pregnant women were in their thirties, but Sarah looked closer to my age.

She walked up to me during a break one Tuesday night. "So are you guys, like, a couple?" She pointed to Ruth, who was getting a cookie from a platter by the bulletin board. Before the break, we'd been listening to a lecture about the cervix, and after the break, we'd be changing diapers on baby-sized dolls. "Your birth partner," said Sarah. "Is she, like, your significant other?"

"No, I'm not a lesbian," I said, smiling at the thought of me and Ruth.

"Oh, okay," she said, embarrassed. "My hubby is over there. See him in the yellow-striped shirt?" She pointed at a tall skinny man with bushy brown hair. He stood in the corner sipping from a Styrofoam cup. "That's Bob."

"Hi, Bob," I said, waving. He smiled and gave us the thumbs-up.

"So, is she your mom?" said Sarah. "Sorry. I shouldn't be asking all these personal questions."

"Ha, well, we're pretty much letting it all hang out anyway," I said, nodding to the posters on the wall showing women's body parts and nude shots of birth with blood and vaginas on display. "No, that's funny. She's not my mom. She's the intended mother of this baby I'm carrying."

Sarah scrunched up her face.

"I'm a surrogate."

"Ohhhhh," said Sarah, looking back and forth between me and Ruth. "Wow."

"Yeah, it's pretty cool," I said, rubbing my belly.

"Is that, like, what you do for a living?"

I didn't know how to answer. First of all, that was a rude question. I hadn't really known what to say about the money part of this. Before, people usually didn't ask me such nosy questions, but my being pregnant somehow gave them permission. Sarah was sweet and seemed more clueless than mean. "This is my first time," I said. "But I may do it again. We'll see how it goes."

"Must be tough on the body." She made a face.

"It's been pretty easy, actually."

"Just wait," she said, shaking her head. "After my first, I swore I wouldn't do it again. But here we are!"

"Wow. How old are you?"

"Twenty-four." Sarah laughed. "We had our first pretty young. And you?"

"Almost twenty-one."

"Oh, you'll get your body right back."

"I hope so," I said. We'd been sitting cross-legged on the floor mat, so it felt good to stand. I pushed my elbows back and rotated my shoulders, stretching. Some of the women bounced gently on exercise balls. Sarah wore a pink scoop-neck T-shirt, as wide as a poncho, and tight black pants. I was sure they were maternity pants. I was wearing them, too. No one ever would have guessed that under our flowing shirts, the tops of our pants were these ridiculous expandable, wide stretchy waistbands. They were hideous, and I loved them.

"I should look into that," said Sarah.

"Into what? Hiring a surrogate?"

"No, silly. Being one."

"Oh," I said, nodding. I didn't say more, because I wasn't sure if I would recommend the job. I thought about those women in the article I'd read in Dr. Salovich's office. If they interviewed me now, I'd say it's a big-time commitment with no privacy and plenty of physical risks but great pay. And it's really important that you like your intended parents, because if you like them, you'll feel much happier giving them the baby they always wanted.

"What will you do after the baby is born? Do you have another job?"

"I'm a trainer at a dog daycare in Minneapolis," I said.

"Oh, cool, I love dogs."

"I know," I said, "they're my babies."

"Until now." Sarah pointed at my belly.

"Ha, yeah," I said, looking down. This thing in my belly hadn't felt like a baby until about a month ago, when I was six months pregnant. I'd been at work, and it was around ten in the morning. My stomach suddenly growled, and I rubbed the area where I'd felt it. I assumed I was just craving food until it happened again and I saw it: a weirdly shaped roll flashed under my shirt, like those cartoons of a mole digging a trail under the dirt. And it felt like a tiny fist had punched me from the inside.

Sarah continued talking, but I wasn't paying attention. I thought about the many times the baby had kicked since that first time, and how I'd rubbed my belly and talked to it, trying to settle it down. Sometimes I imagined what the baby looked like, and the closer I got to my due date, the more excited I was to see her. Whenever I had thoughts like that, I tried not to get too attached. "It's a baby," I said, interrupting Sarah, "but not my baby."

"Oh, I'm sorry," said Sarah. "I didn't mean to hurt your feelings."

"No, that's okay," I said, reminding myself of the plan. "After it's born, I'm going to go back and finish college. To go into accounting."

"That's great," said Sarah. "Bob's an accountant."

"Awesome," I said, looking for Bob again. "Does he like it?"

"Yeah," said Sarah, also looking for Bob.

Ruth walked over and handed me a chocolate chip cookie and a cup of cold water.

"This is Sarah," I said.

"Nice to meet you," said Ruth, smiling at me like, Oh, what an accomplishment, for me to make a new friend.

The instructor called everyone to order. Ruth walked back to our spot on the floor, but I stayed to ask Sarah for her phone number. I was looking for a piece of paper and a pen when Ruth called my name and pointed at the diaper-changing area for the next lesson. I shook my head and told her to wait a second.

Sometimes I needed Ruth to give me more space.

Thirty-Two

HAL

Evening

Ruth was giving me a lot of grief about the credit card I'd set up for Cally. Ruth said we should find out where Cally had been using it, and this was a fair point. A good idea. So, after we ate my famous goulash, I called the credit card company.

Ruth sat across the kitchen table from me, clearly intending to participate in this venture; I put the phone on speaker so she could hear.

"Nice Muzak," I said when I was placed on hold. Ruth had no reaction.

"Okay, we've tracked your credit card to a couple of gas stations, a restaurant, and a Target," said the credit card representative when she finally clicked back on the line.

It was safe to assume that the Visa woman had no idea Ruth was listening in, but Ruth was waving her hands at me and mouthing things she wanted me to ask. It was terribly annoying.

"Ask where," Ruth whispered, poking my hand.

"Where, exactly?" I asked, slapping Ruth's hand away. I hated being poked.

"Well, it looks like Hinckley and Duluth in Minnesota, and then also in Superior, Wisconsin," said the Visa woman. "Does that make sense?"

"No," I said.

"Do you think the card was stolen?" asked Ruth, not whispering. I frowned and shushed her. She didn't like being shushed.

"Oh," said the credit card representative, clearly having heard Ruth's question. "I thought you said it had been stolen."

"Yes, we believe it was," I said, holding up my hand, signaling Ruth to stop. Clearly, she didn't think I could handle this call.

"Can you give us the addresses of these places where it was used?" asked Ruth in a voice that was louder than it needed to be.

There was a pause from the credit card representative. She must have determined that Ruth's voice was not mine. Perhaps she was checking her training manual for instructions on how to handle that. "Who is speaking, please?" the woman said finally.

"I'm Ruth Olson."

"Mr. Olson, since you are the named credit card holder, I am only authorized to release information to you. Do you authorize me to speak to Ruth Olson? Is that your wife?"

"Yes, yes, she is, and yes, I authorize it," I said.

"Thank you," said the voice.

"Thank you," said Ruth with as much fake sincerity as she could muster. She pulled out a pad and pen and found a clear space on the kitchen table next to the handheld receiver, which lay between us like a grenade.

"Can you repeat your question, Mrs. Olson?" said the woman after some clicking on a keyboard and a pause.

"The addresses of the places where the card was used," said Ruth.

"And the dates and times," I added.

The woman gave us the store names, store numbers, and street addresses. The dates and times were immediately after Cally's hospital stay. If someone had stolen the card from her hospital room, this would make sense.

"Would you like me to cancel the cards now?"

We looked at each other. I was inclined to say yes.

"Hang on." Ruth pressed the mute button.

"What are you doing?" I said, grabbing the phone from her.

"Let's leave the cards activated. That way, if it's Cally, we can track her and find the baby," said Ruth.

"Is that what Ray suggested?" I asked.

"Yes, but I also thought of it," Ruth said, unmuting the phone.

"Oh, Christ," I said.

"Let's leave the cards activated," Ruth said to the woman.

"So you are now saying the card has not been stolen?" The customer service woman must have been required to ask clarifying questions like that, in case her conversation had been recorded for training purposes. Or in case the cardholder's wife had an ulterior motive.

"We're not sure," said Ruth.

"Mr. Olson?" she asked. "Do you agree with that?"

I hung my head; I needed to think.

"Mr. Olson, are you there?" she asked. Perhaps she worried that Mrs. Olson had drugged me or taped my mouth shut or something.

"Yes," I said. "I'm here."

"May I suggest freezing the card until you can verify whether the purchases were authorized?" said the Visa woman.

"Would they be able to use the card?" I asked, lifting my head. This was an interesting option.

"No, they wouldn't," she said. "The account would be frozen, with the balance protected, and you could unfreeze it within the next thirty days."

"In that case, I think we should keep the card functioning, so we can track their purchases," I said, looking at Ruth for approval. She nodded vigorously.

"All right, but you will be responsible for those charges," said the representative.

"I understand," I said. Ruth smiled at me.

"I will add a note to your file reflecting this conversation. Is there anything else I can help you with?"

"No," we said in unison.

"Thank you," Ruth added.

After we hung up, we sat staring at each other across the table for a few seconds. The overhead light cast shadows that carved up our faces. Ruth stood up and gathered the stray newspapers that littered the table. Someone, possibly me, possibly the boys, had left a half-empty can of root beer on the table, and an old cereal bowl with a few swollen Cheerios floating in a few teaspoons of milk. This was one of Ruth's pet peeves. She'd been trying to get the boys to bring their bowls to the dishwasher. I'd say they remembered about thirty percent of the time.

"What if she is being held against her will? And she can't call us?" I asked, watching Ruth empty the cereal bowl into the sink.

"That is highly unlikely, and you know it." Ruth switched on the faucet, and the garbage disposal roared.

"Yeah," I said, and she was probably right.

Ruth walked over, wiping her hands on a kitchen towel, her favorite green one. "Hal, she took the baby."

I hated to think that. I hated to think Cally could have fooled us into believing she had good character, good motivations. It didn't make sense. "But she wants to finish college. She took the money."

"What does the contract say about this situation?"

"What situation?" I didn't know what Ruth was implying, but I didn't like the tone of her question. "You've read the contract."

"In the event that she changes her mind?" asked Ruth, softening. She must have sensed me bristle.

"Well, she'd forfeit the final payment," I explained. "And she'd have to pay us back. At least part of the money she's already received."

"Only part of the money?"

"Yes, Ruth, only part of the money. That's how the deal was structured," I snapped. She should have known that.

"Well, excuse me," Ruth said. "I didn't know."

"And we'd be lucky to get anything back, to be honest. She's probably spent it."

"Is that what you're worried about? The money?"

"No, of course not," I said, standing up and slamming my chair into the table. I didn't need to listen to more of this. The contract was valid. Thorough.

"Okay," said Ruth, as if trying to calm me down.

"We have rights under the contract," I said, leaning on the counter and facing away. "We can enforce our rights. I'll take her to court if I have to."

"Forget the contract, Hal." Ruth stood up. "That baby is yours."

"Not in the eyes of the law it isn't," I said, turning around to face her.

"You are the father in my eyes," she said, wrapping her arms around my waist and leaning her head on my chest.

"The court would have to recognize me as such and grant me parental rights." We stood rocking slightly, together.

"Okay, how do we get that?" she asked, looking up at me.

"A paternity test," we said in unison, as we sometimes did.

"That's ridiculous," Ruth added.

"That's the law," I said, fully accustomed to the dissonance between what's logical and what's statutory.

Suddenly, a drink seemed like a good idea. I opened the spice cabinet and reached to the highest shelf, the place where we kept the liquor. Jostling aside the bottles of olive oil and soy sauce, the disguise we used to hide our stash so the teenagers wouldn't get into the alcohol, I pulled down the green Jameson bottle and poured myself a double whiskey.

"What are you grumbling about?" Ruth asked.

"I really believed her." I took a drink and wiped my mouth with the back of my hand. "You want one?"

"Sure." She watched me pour her a whiskey.

"On the rocks?" I asked, but I knew, and I was already on my way to the freezer.

"Yes, please." She beat me to it, opened the freezer, grabbed a few ice cubes, and dropped them into the crystal highball glass. We clinked our glasses together and drank.

"I really didn't think Cally wanted children when she was so young," I said, and I was truly puzzling over this. "She wanted to start a career."

"That's what she told us," said Ruth.

"I gave her a list of accounting firms."

"I know."

"She even had that goal card about it," I added. "Remember? Posted on her bathroom mirror."

"I know, I know," said Ruth, and we drank in solidarity. Ruth grimaced with each burning sip.

"And she passed the psychologist's assessments," I said as we drank again and swallowed.

"Yeah." Ruth stroked the back of my shoulder. We'd taken precautions: we'd had Cally evaluated after extensive psychological interviews and written tests. "And Cally specifically told you she didn't think of the baby as hers during the pregnancy, right?" Ruth took a sip, then swirled the glass, watching the ice melt.

"Early on, yes," I said, remembering. "She pointed to her belly and said to me, 'Here's your baby.'" I lifted my glass and shook my head, incredulous.

"Yeah." Ruth pointed to her drink, so I topped us both off.

"There were times I wondered, though," I said, and maybe the alcohol had loosened a memory. "She said she was gonna miss us when this was over, or something like that. Do you remember?"

"Sort of," said Ruth unconvincingly. "I mean, we've spent a lot of time together, so it makes sense."

"And she said something about visiting the baby. Like she'd be there when the baby started talking or walking. I don't remember the context."

"Hmm," said Ruth, frowning. "I don't think you told me about this."

"Weren't you there?"

"I don't think so," said Ruth. "Was this when you gave her the list of accounting firms?"

"Maybe," I said. I didn't exactly know which conversation had oc-curred where and when. Was Ruth trying to take my deposition here or what?

"I wish you would have told me about that whole thing," she said.

"I must not have thought much about it at the time," I said. I knew that Ruth wasn't thrilled with the extra attention I'd given Cally re-garding her interest in accounting. I understood that.

Ruth wiped some crumbs off the counter. "We shouldn't have cho-sen her, Hal. We should have known."

"Maybe so," I said, although that was an outrageous assertion. I held my glass midair, as if anything were possible at this point. "Want another?"

Just then the phone rang; the receiver bounced slightly on the kitchen table. Was this grenade about to go off?

Thirty-Three

CALLY

Afternoon

The older couple in the car had pulled over and put on their hazard lights while they waited for us to answer. Their passenger window was open.

"No, we're fine," said Digger, charging ahead along the shoulder of the highway.

"Are you sure?" said the woman, noticing that Digger's hands were full, car seat in one, gas can in the other.

"Digger?" I said, trying to change his mind. "It would be a lot easier."

"We only gotta go up this hill," he said, nodding forward.

"Okay, then," said the older man behind the wheel. "Vera, they said no."

"It's so cold for the child," said Vera.

"She's bundled up good," I said.

"Is she?" said Vera, squinting at the car carrier.

"Roll up your window, Vera," said the older man.

"Okay, Stan, hold your horses," said Vera, rolling up her window and waving at us. That was the same phrase my dad used whenever I got impatient.

They drove away slowly as we walked in the opposite direction. "That was nice of them," I said to Digger's back. He marched with a rhythm, determined. Stubborn. It was cold enough that I could see his breath in the air around his head every three or four steps. A warm ride would have been nice.

"That old Buick wouldn't have made it up the hill anyway," said Digger.

I turned back to look at the Buick. A mauve-colored sedan, full-sized. It was turning into the Mobil station where we'd just been. The hazard lights were still on.

We plowed along in silence up the hill. "Hang on," I said, needing a rest. Digger kept marching. "Digger," I said louder, "wait!"

Digger sighed and turned around to see me. "Come on," he said, and kept going.

I continued behind him, slowly, so the cramping wouldn't get too bad. Finally, when we got inside, Digger set the carrier down next to the bed. I uncovered the baby's face, and she was asleep. "Look at her cheeks, they're so red," I said. "I hope she's okay."

"She's fine," said Digger, and we both stood looking at her, deciding he was right.

"I don't feel good," I said. "I'm gonna take a nap." I started taking off my wet clothes and looking for dry ones.

"The guy is gonna be here in like an hour," said Digger.

"What guy?" I said as I dressed.

"The guy from the fucking gas station that we just talked to. The guy who's gonna jump the truck."

"Oh yeah, I remember." I crawled into bed.

"I'm gonna put the gas in," said Digger.

"Okay, wake me up when he gets here," I said, and Digger walked out the door. I pulled the musty quilt up over my shoulders and melted into the mattress, closed my eyes, and ignored the creaky springs beneath me. My heavy head sank into the pillow, my mouth fell open, and I caught myself snore. I rolled over and fell into a deep and blissful sleep. I was gone.

When I woke up, I didn't recognize the wall or the quilt or the dirty window with cracked glass and spiderwebs in the corners. The glow of the oil lamp made angled shadows on the log walls. I must have overslept; where was I? I must have been out for a while but had no idea how long. I sat up and looked around, remembering, oh, yes, I was in the cabin. There was the rocking chair, my clothes on the floor, and what about Digger? Digger must have gone for a smoke but forgotten to wake me. Did the guy come to jump the truck? He must have been here and gone. If only I could see what time it was. I squinted at the dirty window. Dark outside, but in winter it could still be early evening. I guessed it was about five or six o'clock. So if the baby was asleep, then it had been a long nap and was time for a feeding. I looked for the baby carrier. We'd left it beside the bed, but where was it? Where was it? Not there. And the baby! Where was she?

I jumped out of bed, and my legs buckled. Dizzy, I grasped the bed frame to get my head straight. I looked in the crate. No! I stumbled to the front door, blinking. The truck was gone. No sign of Digger. The car seat was nowhere in sight.

The baby was gone.

I opened the front door. A gas can in the snowbank beside the spot where the truck had been. I pulled on my boots and ran outside to the outhouse and the shed. I ran a few steps down the hill, but everything was dark and empty. Bluish white surrounded by black evergreen trees. Shadows of tire tracks led back to the highway, but no sign of the truck or Digger or the tow truck or anyone.

"Digger!" I called down the driveway and into the woods.

I stumbled back up, weak against the doorjamb, and held my chest. I fell into the cabin and shut the front door. I lit a candle and scanned the remaining clothes and supplies on the floor, touching and separating them as if the baby might appear from between two pairs of pants or rise up out of the duffel bag. Where was she? Where did he take her? My heart was pounding hard and my breasts were solid as rocks. The woodburning stove had gone out, and the room was cold. I combed through the items. He'd taken all the important stuff: the diapers, the bottles, and the formula. My breasts hurt.

I put my hand on my aching chest and fell to the floor. Where was Nell? Was she hungry? Was she okay? I pulled my hand away and looked down. The wetness had leaked from my tingling breasts, and the front of my T-shirt was cold and damp.

"Digger!" I cried.

PART TWO

Thirty-Four

RUTH

Evening

Hal put down his drink and answered the grenade. "Hello?"

"Who is it?" I whispered, bouncing up and down. I was feeling a buzz.

"Shh," said Hal, frowning. Then, to the caller, he said, "Yes."

"Who would be calling on a Saturday night?" I whispered again, undeterred. I was guessing it was the credit card company calling back with more information.

"No." He waved me off, turned around, and put his finger in his other ear to help him hear better.

I leaned closer and could hear the "wamph-wah" sound of the voice on the other end of the line. A female voice. Businesslike.

"We will, thank you." Hal hung up the phone. "That was the director," he said. "She has seen the security footage."

I gasped. "And?"

"She wants us to meet her there to view it together."

"Is the baby okay?"

"I don't know." He walked to the front hall closet and pulled on his coat. "I don't know if either of them is okay."

I followed Hal out to the garage, and it occurred to me we'd both been drinking. "I should drive," I said.

"No, I'm fine."

"I think I'm better."

"You always think you're better." Hal unlocked the SUV and got into the driver's seat.

At the hospital, Ms. Whittier was waiting for us at the front desk. "Follow me," she said. We wound through the halls to a wing of the hospital we'd never been to before: the security office, where two men and one woman sat waiting in a conference room with a large video screen. They stood when we entered. Ms. Whittier introduced us to her team, including the director of security, a facilities manager, and a legal representative. Each of them handed us a business card, and we shook hands all around.

I asked, "Why is there a legal person here?"

Hal held up his hand to quiet me. Or perhaps to comfort me. "What do you have for us?" he asked the group, keeping his eye on the legal representative.

The security director said, "We'd like you to fill us in on any information you may have that can lend meaning to these images."

"Sure," said Hal, and we both sat down.

Ms. Whittier dimmed the lights; the facilities manager pressed play, and we all watched the dark and grainy video footage. The outside of the building. Light post. Lamplight over snow. Snowflakes falling. The camera switched to the parking lot.

"As you can see, our system catches various angles for us to put together," said the director of security. "So we have full coverage."

The view switched back to the outside of the building. Most of the windows were dark, but a few glowed with dim lights. In one room, a figure approached the window and slid it open. The figure disappeared, and the camera switched to the parking lot view. Most of the vehicles were covered in snow. Two were clean, and we could see exhaust coming from one of the clean ones, a truck with its engine running.

"Pause it here," said Ms. Whittier. "The south wall of Building C. That open window is the room where the patient, who was your surrogate, was assigned."

"Her name is Cally," said Hal.

Ms. Whittier slid a box of tissues toward me, and I ignored them.

"Let's keep watching," said the director of security, resuming the video. The figure returned to the window, leaned out, and placed a bundle on the ledge.

"What is that?" I said, stunned.

"Shh, let's watch," said Hal. The video switched to the parking lot. A tall figure emerged from the truck and walked toward the building. Snow fell heavily through the downcast light of the lamp. Back at the south wall, the figure climbed out the window, sat on the ledge, dropped the bundle a short distance into the arms of the other figure, and then jumped, tumbling onto a snowbank.

I let out a yelp and Hal reached over to hold me. "Come on," he said. "Keep watching." The camera switched to the parking lot as the two figures walked to the truck, loaded the bundle, and got in. The video switched back to the south wall and showed nothing further of interest. The next time we saw the parking lot, the truck was gone.

"Whose truck was that?" I asked.

"Did you get the license plate?" Hal asked. No one answered.

The facilities manager hit the stop button, then rewind. We listened to the VCR rev itself up to begin the rewind process. Ms. Whittier turned up the lights to bright.

The director of security stood in front of the screen as if to remind us of what we had just seen. "Ever see that truck before?" he said. "Any idea who the driver was? Any boyfriends or brothers, anything like that you're aware of?"

"No idea," I said, looking at Hal.

"I don't know, either," said Hal. "But what about the license plate?"

"We are reviewing other angles of the parking lot. We may be able to enlarge the image, possibly see the plates, but no guarantees on that."

This was sickening.

"The good news is that it appears the two people in the video are alive and well enough to walk and get into the vehicle."

"And the baby?" I said.

"We believe the baby might have been . . . in the bag that was dropped," said the director of security.

"And we surmise the child most likely survived the drop. Unharmed," said the legal representative.

"Because the distance of the drop was only about two feet," said the facilities manager.

"Are you serious?" I couldn't believe these people were saying these words.

"Oh, yes. In fact, we've been made aware of cases where very young children survived falls from even higher distances," said the legal representative. "Such as in houses that are on fire."

"Yes, they are very resilient," said Ms. Whittier.

"Are you kidding me?" I stood up. "Did I really just hear you say that?"

"Ruth," said Hal, pushing out his chair and standing up.

"None of you are concerned?"

"Of course we're concerned."

"It doesn't sound like it to me."

"Mrs. Olson," said the director of patient relations, looking around the room as if hoping someone else would speak. "It might be of some comfort to know that this dilemma with birth mothers—"

"Dilemma? What dilemma?" I said.

"With birth mothers, I'm only saying that it's not uncommon, in these types of situations, to have second thoughts, for example, in teen pregnancy and . . . surrogacy . . . situations."

"Teen pregnancy? This isn't anything like teen pregnancy."

"I didn't say that."

"Yes, you did. You said it before, and you just said it again." I felt the heat in my face. "I know you don't approve of us. For some reason, you have a problem with using a surrogate, Ms. Whittier—"

"I have never said anything one way or the other about surrogacy," said Ms. Whittier. "That would not be appropriate. That is not my place."

"You don't have to say it. I can feel it." I pointed to my chest so hard I might have drawn blood with my own fingernail. "And if anything, anything at all, happens to our child, if she's harmed in any way," I said, pivoting and pointing at the legal representative, "if she is hurt at ALL, you can expect a lawsuit from us."

"Ruth."

"Don't you dare shush me, Hal."

Hal sat down. There was a pause in the room, a cease-fire when we all took a moment to get our wits about us. I paced back and forth on my side of the table. "I'm sorry," I said. "I'm just a little upset."

"Of course you are," said Ms. Whittier.

"Maybe we can switch gears for a moment," said the director of security. "Do you have any idea on the identity of the driver of that truck?"

Hal and I shook our heads.

"That's fine. I just thought I'd ask."

"We wanted to share what we had and provide you with as much transparency as we could," said the legal representative.

"Is there any footage from inside the room?" I asked.

"Unfortunately not," said the director of security.

"We can't put cameras in the rooms," said the facilities manager.

"Patient privacy," said the legal representative.

We sat stupefied as the VCR stopped rewinding, ejected the tape, and switched off. The noise of the machine was a reminder of our being humans, imperfect and powerless. The experts in the room were saying words, nodding in somber agreement. In our experience. Events of this nature. Protocol. Next steps. Our best information. Hal kept his head down and his hands folded as if in prayer. I had one thing on my mind: I had to get this video, and the credit card information, to Raymond. Now.

Thirty-Five

DIGGER

Evening

When I took the kid, she was sound asleep in her car seat, and Cally was sawing logs on the bed. I loaded the supplies into the truck, but trying to get that damn carrier into the fucking base was a shit show. While I was dicking around with the latch, the baby woke up and started wailing. I said screw it. I put the thing on the base unlatched, with a seat belt across to hold it. Good enough. How the hell people do that multiple times a day, I will never know.

I hauled ass down the hill and onto the main road. The little freak was screaming, and I tried everything. I slowed down for her. I sped up. I reached back and jiggled her. She kept bawling.

"Shut up!" I said. "Shut up!"

How did other people put up with howling babies? Women didn't seem to mind it. Were they saints or deaf? I cranked up the radio to drown out the noise. This was going to be a painful half hour to Deena's house.

My sister's farm was just east of Superior, and I got up there about once a year. Usually during hunting season. Tonight the roads were okay, but I put it in four-wheel drive just in case. George Strait came on, and I tapped on the wheel as I kept an eye out for cops. On a

Sunday evening, I thought I'd be fine, but Wisconsin police were pricks.

With the nonstop crying in the backseat, I was afraid my head was gonna burst. I tried to ignore it. Then halfway there, whattya know? I looked in the rearview mirror. The lunatic was asleep. Must have been the country music.

"Thank God," I said, squinting at the upcoming intersection. Most of the roads were unmarked. Was this the left turn or was it the next one? In the dark, it was hard to tell.

Finally, I saw the old billboard for Midwest Bank. That was the landmark I used to signal my turn. Another left at the T-stop, then take the second right. As my headlights moved over the long drive-way, I saw Deena's big white farmhouse ahead. I slowed down to try and fool her sled dogs. But the motion-sensor floodlights flashed on. All four huskies ran out from their winter kennels. They jumped up at the chain-link fence. They whined and barked. Soon a full-on howl got going. Sure enough, the porch light went on. I put the truck in park and saw Deena peeking out the curtains on the little window of her big front door.

"Stay asleep," I said to the blanket-covered lump in the backseat. As soon as I put the truck in park, the baby woke up and started fussing. "Oh, for fuck's sake," I said, and I fished around in the stupid bag for a pacifier. Found one and stuck it in the kid's mouth.

Deena trudged out the door in her oversize parka and her dead husband's duck boots. Her mother-in-law, Mrs. Z, stood in the open doorway, clutching her blue robe at the neck.

"Quiet, Trapper! Quiet, Baz!" said Deena. The dogs bounded to-ward her as she got near the fence. She was bossy but calm. She said each name. "Quiet, Nathan, quiet, Pops." They settled down, and she tossed them each a treat.

"Hey." I nodded as I got out of the truck and shut the door. I waved at Mrs. Z, and she waved back, then moved away from the window.

"Hey ya, pipsqueak." Deena walked to me and gave me a slap on the shoulder. She always called me that because she's five years older. But it's been a long time since I was smaller than her.

"The dogs seem good," I said, shifting my weight.

"My boys," Deena said, beaming at her dogs, watching them play. "You gonna come in?" She started up the front steps. Her voice was raspy. She coughed.

"Yeah." I looked back at the truck. The kid would be fine for a few minutes.

"What is it?" Deena noticed me looking at the truck. "You got a dead body in there?"

"No," I said, but I must not have sounded too confident.

"The hell?" Deena sounded suspicious. She came back down the steps and started toward the truck. "You're not moving in, are ya?" She winked. She'd taken me in one summer when I had to get away from Mom and Dad. I'd stolen a hundred bucks from the cookie jar where our mother hid her stash. Deena'd given me a room and fed me, while I helped out with the chickens and dogs. Did repairs and shit.

"I was gonna tell you about that," I said, looking at the ground.

"Holy SHIT," she said as she pressed her forehead against the tinted backseat window to see what I had. "So this is what you called me about?"

"Yeah."

"Jesus, Digger." She opened the door and unbuckled the seat belt. "You were gonna leave him out here? Is it a him or a her?"

"Her. And I was gonna come and get her. I wanted to tell you first."

"Tell me what?" Deena said as she lifted the car carrier out of the truck. "Never mind. I don't wanna know. Let's just get her inside."

I picked up the bag of supplies, closed the truck door, and followed up the steps. "You got anything to eat?"

Deena stopped outside the front door and sighed. "Yeah," she said. "Just get inside, and don't say nothing stupid to Mrs. Z."

We trudged inside and stomped off our boots. Deena swooped the baby carrier straight into the kitchen, so Mrs. Z might not notice.

"Hello, Dennis." Mrs. Z had been waiting in the living room. She reached her arm out and wiggled her hand in a spastic wave, as if she could reach me from her comfy chair, twenty feet away.

"How are you, Mrs. Z?" I smiled and bent my head down.

"I'm alive, Dennis." She closed her eyes for dramatic effect.

"Aww, Mrs. Z," I said, keeping a side-eye on Deena down the hall. She'd set the baby carrier on the kitchen table.

"My arthritis is acting up," said Mrs. Z. "But I'm still going."

"Like the Energizer Bunny, right?" Deena walked into the living room and stood behind Mrs. Z, patting her shoulders.

The baby fussed, then cranked up into a full cry.

"Oh my!" Mrs. Z clapped her hands. "A baby! Yours, Digger?"

"Surprise," said Deena, going to the kitchen and taking the baby out of the carrier, while Mrs. Z chirped like a crazy bird.

Eunice Zimmerman was her real name, Deena's mother-in-law. She liked to tell the story over and over. How she was the youngest of six children, survived the Depression, grew up during World War II. Deena married Mrs. Z's only son, who'd bought this old farmhouse thinking they could raise chickens and breed dogs and maybe have a kid or two of their own. They built a coop and bred a few huskies. But their only child died at eight months. Heart problem. Then Frank OD'd, and everyone agreed it was accidental. After that, Mrs. Z moved in, and they've lived together for the last couple years. Neither of them were city people, and they kept each other company.

I was raiding the fridge.

Mrs. Z, a large lady, waddled into the kitchen to see the baby. Taking her away from Deena, she wedged her spotted hands underneath the thing's head and butt and lifted her up onto her fleshy shoulder. "Do you have a bottle, Dennis?" she said.

"In that blue bag." I nodded toward the bag on the floor.

"Get your lazy ass over there and pick it up," said Deena.

"I'm hungry," I said as I picked up the bag and tossed it to Deena.

"Thanks a lot, asshole," she scoffed as she dug in the bag for a bottle and formula.

"Welcome." I pulled out some bread and salami from the fridge and made myself a couple sandwiches.

Mrs. Z had taken the baby back to her comfy chair in the living room. She sat there waiting for Deena to heat up the bottle and bring it to her. Talking to the baby, having an imaginary conversation, she said, "You do? . . . Oh, I see . . . What else? . . . Uh-huh . . ."

As soon as the bottle got into the kid's mouth, the noise stopped, thank God. Deena put on her jacket and motioned for me to follow her outside for a smoke.

"We'll be out on the porch, Z," said Deena, closing the back door behind us.

We lit up and exhaled into the backyard. Acres of dark fields, the outline of the chicken coops, occasional barks from the dogs.

"I heard you sold some puppies," I said.

"Just the runt."

"Well, the waitress at the Blue Anchor is pretty happy about it."

"Oh yeah? So you're going around town talking about me? You in the market for a sled dog or what?" said Deena.

"No, she carded me and saw my name."

"I changed mine back to Wilkins."

"Makes sense," I said. We smoked and let it sit.

"So what's with the baby? Is that my early Christmas present, because it ain't what I asked for," she said with her hand on her hip.

"First of all, it's not mine," I said.

"Well, that's good, because Ma would skin you alive if she knew you knocked up some girl," said Deena.

Our mother had lectured me and my brothers to put money in the bank, and above all, don't get anyone pregnant. In high school, whenever I had a girl in my bedroom, Mother would march up the stairs and yell, "Use a rubber!" It was annoying as hell.

Mother believed girls were out to get me. Wanted to trap me with a baby. Mother said it'd ruin my life. Like it ruined hers, I guess. After Deena's little boy died, I realized it also had to do with that genetic heart sickness. The same reason I'd had surgery as a baby. And the scar to remind me. I guess I was the lucky one.

I'd always used a condom. But Cally hated when Mother bothered us, yelling at the door. That's why Cally didn't like having sex at my house. Or if we did, she'd want to avoid seeing Mother afterward, so she'd escape out my window where the roof connected to our garage. She got pretty good at taking out the screen and sneaking out the window.

"So it's Cally's?" said Deena.

"Yeah."

"And what the fuck are you doing with it?"

The back door opened and Mrs. Z was holding the baby. "Help me, please," she said, waddling around in the kitchen, searching aimlessly. "I need a diaper!"

"Coming, Eunice." Deena threw me a look, and we went back inside.

Thirty-Six

CALLY

Evening

I opened my duffel bag and emptied my backpack onto the floor so I could see the stuff I had to work with. Wool was better than cotton. Layers. Water bottle, wallet. I loaded up my backpack. Pads, underwear. Where were the papers from the hospital? Socks. I checked under the bed. I pulled out Digger's flannel shirt: it would be my face mask.

Putting on my hat and boots, I hoisted up my backpack and took one last look around the cabin. Was there anything else? I grabbed a pacifier from the table and stashed it in my pocket.

I was out the front door and down the hill in one motion. In the dark of winter, the snow reflected the moonlight, and my eyes adjusted as I walked. At the bottom of the hill, I turned onto the main road and trudged toward the same gas station where Digger and I had been earlier in the day. Our old footsteps were there, but the snow was crunchier, more frozen. I squinted in the cold air and pulled up the flannel shirt, which I'd tied around my neck, to cover my nose and mouth. I checked for cars. I was trying to think straight.

At the gas station, bells rang when I entered. I hadn't remembered that from earlier. I stomped my boots and shook off the wet; pulled off my hat and swept back my sweaty hair.

"Hey there," said the clerk. This was a female voice. She was young; she looked about my age and like she had a lot more energy than this job required.

"Hi," I said, out of breath. "Did you see a guy in here with a baby in a car seat?" I untied the flannel shirt and set down my backpack.

"Uh, no, but I came on at two. What time was he here?" she asked.

"I don't know if he was," I said. "That's why I'm asking."

"I can call Tim. He worked the shift before me."

"Okay, maybe," I said, moving to the back. "I'm just gonna use your bathroom."

"Oh, sure," the clerk said, pointing.

Inside the bathroom, I caught my breath and exhaled. I hung my backpack on a hook and shook out my hair. I looked in the mirror. No makeup. Bags under my eyes. I hadn't had a chance to clean myself or any place to do it, and I looked scary. I splashed my face with cold water and dried it with a paper towel, more to help me think than anything else.

Where would Digger go? He didn't know Hal and Ruth's last name or address or anything about them except that Hal was a lawyer and Ruth worked for the paper. He didn't know where the fertility clinic was or anything like that. He only knew which hospital I'd given birth in. Would he take her there?

The door opened, and the clerk walked into the bathroom.

"Sorry," she said. "I have to pee." She headed to the handicapped toilet stall. My backpack was still hanging on the hook in there, but she didn't seem to care. I listened to her rustle her pants down and then the trickle sound. Suddenly, I had to go, too, and I took the second stall.

"So," said the clerk from her stall, "where're you from?"

"Minneapolis." I didn't plan to say much, because I hate talking to people in bathroom stalls. Also the Olsons were probably out looking for me and the baby, or maybe they'd called the police on me. But

I didn't know what my options were at this point. Maybe I needed to call the cops on Digger. But what would I say?

"Yeah. When we get people in here from out of town, they're usually from the Cities." The clerk flushed and flung open her stall door, then scuffed along to the sink. "I'm Amanda, by the way."

"Okay." I didn't want to give her my name. I waited while she washed her hands and pulled down a paper towel.

"So, no gas for you?" she asked.

I flushed and came out of the stall. "No," I said, washing my hands.

"I know," she said, chucking her used towel in the trash. "I saw you walking."

"Actually, I need to call a taxi," I said.

"Thought so," she said, flinging open the door. "I'll see you out there."

As soon as she left, I took out a maxi-pad and made a quick change. The bleeding came randomly but could have been triggered by my trek. My boobs were still hurting, so I locked the bathroom door. I needed to get the milk out, but I didn't want Amanda barging in on me.

At the sink, I lifted my shirt and pulled up my bra, exposing the first breast. I grabbed it with both hands, like a double cheeseburger, squeezed, and pointed it down to the drain, until finally, the thin white line of milk streamed out from one of the ducts in the nipple. Sometimes a few ducts would shoot out at once and spray like a sprinkler or squirt me in the face. I wasn't good at this yet. I took out the second breast and got to work.

When I'd put myself back together, I walked out and saw Amanda sitting at the little desk behind the counter.

"Everything all right?" she asked.

"Yeah, I'm fine," I said. Suddenly thirsty again, I pulled a bottle of water out of the small refrigerated selection. "I'm taking this."

"Okay."

I noticed a prepackaged turkey sandwich. "This, too," I said, opening the package and taking a bite.

"Fine."

"So can I use your phone?" I pointed to the desk behind the counter.

"Sure." Amanda got up from the chair and gestured for me to sit.

I dialed Digger's apartment. His roommate answered and seemed surprised to hear from me. Digger wasn't there. "I thought he was with you," the roommate said, and I hung up.

"Do you have any phone books?" I asked Amanda.

She opened a drawer and pulled out both a White Pages and a Yellow Pages. I looked up Taxi. I looked up Blue Anchor Grill. I looked up Police. Who to call first? I dialed the police.

Amanda leaned in and clearly tried to eavesdrop, but I turned away so she'd get the hint that I wanted privacy. I cupped my hand over the receiver.

"Superior Police," a woman answered.

"Hi, um," I said, trying to keep my voice down. "I'm calling because . . ."

"Can you speak up, please?"

"My ex-boyfriend took my baby," I said a bit louder.

"All right. Can I have your name and address, please?"

"Cally Scott, but I don't live up here. I was just . . . staying up here with . . . my daughter." I heard myself say those words, and I had to stop for a second.

"Yes?" she said.

I continued, "So, anyway, I was taking a nap, and when I woke up, my ex-boyfriend and the baby were gone." I could hear the lady typing.

"Okay, when did this happen?" she asked.

"This afternoon. I'd say three o'clock? Maybe four."

She asked for Digger's name and where I thought they might be. I said I didn't know, that was why I was calling. She said that without an address, all they could do was put her in their missing child database. She asked for a physical description and the birth certificate. I said I didn't have it because she was only three days old.

"Okay, the officers will need proof that she is your child and that you are the authorized custodial parent. Usually, there is a court order or at least a birth certificate."

"Well, I don't know what to tell you," I said, annoyed.

"You might want to apply for the birth certificate and expedite it. Do you have an attorney?"

"No, I mean . . . no," I said. Hal was the only attorney I knew.

"I'll give you the number for Legal Aid, and they can get you a volunteer lawyer, okay?"

"Okay."

"You'll need a court order from Douglas County Court, okay? Because once we locate your daughter, we'll need documentation before the child can be released from temporary placement or foster care."

"Foster care? Are you serious?"

"Yes, miss. That's why it's usually more successful, if a parent can convince their partner, boyfriend, whomever is involved in the domestic dispute, to voluntarily hand over the child. That way, you can gain immediate custody."

"Yeah," I said. Obviously.

"So I have made a record of this report, and I have placed your information into our database," said the woman. "We'll contact you if we have anything, and please call back if you have more details, okay?"

After I hung up, I turned around and saw that Amanda must have heard every word I said. She looked at me with raised eyebrows, a combination of pity and fascination.

"So do you need a ride?" she asked.

"I need to get to the Blue Anchor Grill," I said. "Can you take me?"

"No, I'm working, but my grandma can. She has a local ride service." Amanda swooped over to the desk, picked up the phone I'd been using, and started dialing.

"Your grandma? How old is she?" I needed a young person, someone who could drive fast. In the snow.

"She's like sixty, why?" said Amanda. "Hi, Gram." She smiled at me and carried on her phone conversation. Then to me she said, "We only live about a mile and a half away."

"Okay," I said. I grabbed the White Pages and looked up Wilkins. No listings.

"She's on her way," said Amanda, hanging up and grinning.

"Have you heard of the Wilkins Farm? Or Deena Wilkins?" I said.

"No, why?"

"I think my boyfriend is there, and I need to find him."

"Where is it? Near here?" asked Amanda.

"I don't know. That's why I have to go to the Blue Anchor Grill," I said. "I think somebody who works there might know."

Thirty-Seven

RUTH

Afternoon

Cally had been missing for thirty-six hours, and our daughter was three days old when my brother, Raymond, arrived in Minneapolis from San Francisco. He wouldn't let me pick him up at the airport; he rented a car, and I was ready to go. I'd packed my overnight bag and gathered the credit card information. I cued up our copy of the hospital video, made coffee, and waited.

I sat in my favorite blue chair, a wingback, the one that has a view to the front walk. Squirrels hopped over snow and disappeared up into the trees. Cars whizzed by, too fast through narrow neighborhood roads. The man across the street shoveled his driveway and sprinkled salt over the whole thing. He didn't miss an inch. In the light wind, a pink balloon bobbed weakly as if discouraged. It had been tied to a skinny tree in our modest front yard, next to a small sign that said, "It's a Girl." I wondered if our neighbors had been watching me, like I sometimes watched them, and whether they wondered where our baby was. Or why I didn't look pregnant. An icicle fell from the gutter and vanished in the snow below. And finally, a silver Honda Accord appeared, slowing down as it approached our address, then pulled over to park at the curb. Raymond.

I stood up, close to the window. Raymond had never been to our new place. He saw me and waved. I pressed my hand to the glass and mouthed, "Hi." And as he trudged along the sidewalk, hunching forward against the cold, a rush of heat flushed my neck. Big brother who loves me. The expert come to help.

"Raymond!" I scurried to the front door and opened it before he had a chance to ring the bell. He smiled and stepped inside, carefully wiping his feet on the mat and allowing me to hug him. I took his coat and he bent over to remove the rubbers from his shoes. "Thank you for coming."

"Anything for my baby sister." Raymond was seven years older, and Mother had always said that when I was little, Raymond treated me like a doll. "How are you, Ru?"

"So happy to see you." I squeezed his arms and examined his lined face. "How was the flight?"

"What goes up must come down," he said, shrugging. Raymond was never one for small talk.

"Come in, I have banana bread," I said. "People keep bringing us food."

"Don't fight it," he said, surveying the place. "Nice joint you got here. Living room's big."

"Yeah, Hal calls it a double-wide because it's two condos remodeled into one." I peeled the cellophane off the banana bread and reached for a knife.

"Is he here?"

"No, he had to meet a client at the office." I sliced the banana bread.

"On a Sunday?"

"That's how it goes." I put the slice of bread on a napkin. "He's sorry he couldn't be here, but he'll see you when we get back."

Raymond nodded and half smiled, taking in the information. "Can I see the video?" He took a bite.

"Yes, it's all cued up." I dashed to the VCR in the living room, and he followed at his own pace. As we watched, I sat on the floor next to the screen, pointing and explaining what I knew, what we'd been told, and what my hunches were.

Raymond watched carefully but didn't say anything. He just nodded and asked to watch it one more time, and we did. At the end, he said, "All right. Ready to go?" and he popped in one last bite of banana bread.

"Absolutely."

"I'll throw this away." He collected our dirty napkins and looked for a bin.

"It's here." I pulled open the trash drawer for him. His hair looked healthy and thick, almost all silver now, and his hairline had receded slightly since the last time I saw him.

"Oh, hang on, lemme use the biffy," he said, zooming toward the front hall. "Grab what you need for a couple of nights," he called out.

I wasn't sure how many nights we'd be gone. The plan was for Hal to stay home in case news came that Cally was in town or the hospital needed us or any other leads developed down here. I'd already packed two shirts, two sweaters, two pairs of pants, vitamins, necessities, my Day-Timer, and my journal. "Should I look for my map of Minnesota?" I yelled back.

"No," he said calmly as he emerged from the bathroom. "I've already got that taken care of."

I switched off the lights and glanced out the window. The sky had cleared; the roads should be good by now.

In Raymond's rental car, he had set up his own galaxy. A car phone, a GPS system, a portable laptop computer, a full-size spiral-bound AAA TripTik, organized in sections, highlighted, and circled in color-coded symbols.

"Whoa," I said, surveying the landscape.

"You'll navigate, okay?" He smiled and put the car in gear.

We headed north on I-35, the familiar artery traveled so often by city dwellers escaping north on weekends. Hal and I had been this way many times for romantic getaways at Lutsen or Naniboujou

Lodge. I'd gone up north to follow stories and interview sources. Our news group had done team building in Duluth, and a good friend had been married in Grand Marais. Everyone in Minnesota knew about the tradition of stopping for cinnamon rolls at Tobie's restaurant, located halfway between Minneapolis and Duluth.

But this time, with Raymond, the road looked new and foreign. The car was a fortress, and we were warriors in a strange land. Information was our weapon, our nourishment, our fuel.

"What's this mean?" I pointed to a light blue triangle on the map.

Raymond had made an investigative guide, a trail of locations of interest and notes of names or purchases he said he'd like to check out. He glanced over and looked at the map.

"That's a bread crumb," he said, and returned his focus to the road. "I thought we'd take them in order. Follow the crumbs."

According to the chart of bread crumbs, the most recent credit card purchase was at a restaurant in Superior, Wisconsin. Superior was twenty minutes past Duluth, and Duluth was three hours north. I wanted to go straight to the restaurant, but Raymond wanted to stop at the places in the same order that the credit card had been used: first a mini-mart, then a Target, and finally, the restaurant, with each clue leading to the next.

After an hour or so, the traffic thinned out and the billboards began to change, became more specific, more revealing. Advertising for deer stands and filtered water systems. The casino and local politicians. Facts about a fetus's beating heart, with a photo of an adorable baby.

"Pro-life up here, eh?" Raymond said, not really a question.

"Pretty much," I said. Tension rose in the car as the billboards with pro-life statistics cast a spotlight on the secret between us. Raymond was the only person in the world who knew. He was the one I'd called, and he was the one who'd helped me. At seventeen. I'd been on the pill, but it gave me migraines and made my breasts hurt. So I stopped the pill and instead insisted on condoms. But still I got pregnant. I couldn't believe it, and I couldn't tell anyone. Raymond drove me to the clinic, waited, then drove me home. We never spoke about it after that. I wouldn't dare bring it up now.

I wondered what his stance was on surrogacy. I'd told him the entire story, everything I knew about Cally, the insemination, the pregnancy and birth, and the first couple of days in the hospital. He didn't react one way or the other. He had a perfect poker face, a true professional. And he wasn't judgmental. He had a calmness that made you feel like confessing. A good quality in a detective.

"I hope you don't own a gun," he joked, breaking the silence in the car and nodding toward another hunting-related billboard.

"Ha-ha, no," I said, but it occurred to me that Raymond might be carrying a handgun. I glanced at his waistline but couldn't see.

"Probably for the best." He smiled.

I smiled in agreement and looked down at my hands in my lap. I folded them one way, then the other. We'd talked about everything that we could talk about. We had our game plan. I closed my eyes and let my torso rock with the bumps in the road. I felt myself falling asleep, so I reminded Raymond of our exit number and let myself nap. I'd been feeling extra-tired all week, and I was sure the stress was wearing me down. I rested until I felt the car slow down and heard the ticking turn signal.

"Okay, here's our first stop," said Raymond, pulling off the highway. "Bread crumb number one: the mini-mart." He switched off the ignition. "Cally spent seventy-eight dollars here, and we're gonna talk to that cashier."

Thirty-Eight

CALLY

Evening

While we waited for Amanda's grandmother to get there, I ate another sandwich and put a water bottle in my backpack. Amanda seemed relieved when I pulled out my credit card. Like I was gonna steal all that stuff.

"What time is it?" I asked, looking around for a clock.

"Like six-fifteen."

"Has anyone used the pay phone since your shift started?"

"I don't remember seeing anyone, no."

"Hang on," I said, leaving my stuff by the counter and running out to the pay phone. It was dark outside, and I could see Amanda in the light of the store, watching me. I dialed *69 and wrote down the number, then returned to the warmth of the little store.

"There's my gram," said Amanda, pointing out the window at the car that had pulled in.

I saw only headlights and snow against a purple-blue background. The overhead lights shining down on the gas pumps made us like a bright oasis in a winter desert. When the car stopped in front of the gas station building, I got a better look at it. "Oh," I said, realizing this was the same sedan that had pulled over to help me and Digger earlier today.

The driver got out and slapped her woolly gloves together, then waved. I stood squinting, waiting for some sign that this was the right step. Would this eager old lady be of any use to me? "I'm Vera." She stuck out her hand and walked around the car toward me.

"Cally." I shook her hand.

"You look familiar." Vera opened the door for me. "Have I given you a ride before?"

"No."

"Well, it'll come to me, I never forget a face." She marched to her side of the car and got in. The car smelled like pine air freshener.

"Breath mint?" She offered me a piece of candy, red and white, wrapped in cellophane.

"No, thanks." I didn't care if my breath was bad.

"Where are we headed today?" She turned on the ignition and the wipers came alive, along with the heat, which was cranked too high for her to hear me. I waited for her to turn it down before I answered.

"Blue Anch—"

"Blue Anchor Grill it is," Vera said. She pulled the gearshift into drive and took her foot off the brake. She inched toward the driveway, and the car gently rocked over the lumpy snow. "My granddaughter told me," she said.

"Great." I looked back at the gas station, and Amanda was waving goodbye.

"What's at the Blue Anchor Grill? Because there are a few other local dives serving better food, unless you had a hankering for a greasy hamburger."

"My boyfriend and our baby went out a while ago and haven't come back, and I'm worried about them."

"That's it!" She slapped the dashboard, remembering. "You're the couple walking on the shoulder with the baby. Earlier today?"

"Yeah," I said.

"I knew you looked familiar," she said. "Stan and I pulled over to ask if you needed any help. Remember?"

"Yeah, of course," I said, flashing a smile. "Thank you."

We got on the two-lane highway and Vera turned up the heat fan. "Is this good? Are you warm enough?"

"Actually, could we turn left here?" I pointed to the road that led to our cabin. "I want to see if they might have come back."

"Sure thing." The car fishtailed and the rear wheels couldn't grab. "Oh dear. Hang on," she said. She maneuvered the car in reverse, put her arm on the seat rest behind my head, and looked out the back window. I'd seen my father do this so many times, and it always made me feel like he was holding me and not just the back of my seat. While Vera focused past me and out the rear window, I studied her face. Wrinkles, droopy lids, small and tired-looking eyes. "Just lemme get a good run-up to it."

"Does this have front-wheel drive?" I asked, looking at the automatic gearshift. Her choices were D, 1, and 2. I remembered Digger saying this car wouldn't make it up the hill.

"Yes, it does, don't you worry." Vera smiled and shifted into 2, her lowest gear. She drove confidently, like she had experience in snow. We bolted up the hill, skidding and slipping, but stopped at the top, next to the cabin. Her car sat in the spot where Digger's truck had been. A couple of deer perked up, spooked, and ran away into the woods, their white tails flashing a warning. "How long have your baby and your beau been gone?" asked Vera.

"Like three or four hours, I think," I said. It was obvious they weren't in the cabin.

"Oh, I'm sure they're fine," said Vera. "We women don't give men enough credit with babies. I know daddies can be clumsy, but they can handle it. Sometimes we just have to get out of their way. Give 'em a chance."

"We can go now," I said, feeling stupid for thinking they might be in that freezing cabin. And I felt stupid when we got to the Blue

Anchor Grill, because there was no sign of anyone or anything helpful. The blond waitress wasn't working that night, but the bartender
said she'd be in the next day.

Vera said she'd be happy to drive me there again in the morning,
and she offered to let me stay at her place overnight. I said okay.
I didn't know what else to do. My stomach hurt. My head hurt. It
would be nice to take a hot shower. On the ride back to Vera's, I
leaned back and stared out my window, counting the passing telephone poles and green mile markers like I had done as a kid when
I'd ride with my dad on long highways that seemed to go nowhere.
I'd gaze up at the never-ending black night and ask him how much
longer, how much longer, and he'd make up games for me. I hoped
Vera was right: I hoped Digger could handle this.

When we pulled up to Vera's, she helped me through their front
door and into their warm home. Her husband got up from his chair.
"Who do we have here?" he said, as if Vera often brought home stray
strangers.

"This is Cally," said Vera. "A friend of Amanda's. She's going to
stay the night."

We walked through the kitchen and upstairs to the guest room.
She switched on an antique lamp. The walls were covered in yellow
pineapples and the bedspread in pastel pink. A NordicTrack sat in the
corner next to some boxes and piles of books.

"Never mind the junk," she said.

I sat on the bed and immediately lay down. The pillowcase smelled
like laundry soap, and lacy trim scratched my face.

"I'll get you some towels and point you in the direction of the
shower," she said, reading my mind.

"Thank you," I mumbled, and I hoped she heard me. She was already out in the hallway.

The shower was heaven. I hadn't been clean in days. The warm
water on my head, the feel of clean hair, the smell of shampoo, it was
like a new start. Afterward, I crawled into bed with wet hair and let
myself drift off. I dreamed of sleeping. I dreamed of holding Nell,

finding her there beside me, in a wide white bed. I touched her face, and she smiled her first smile. I put my finger under her matchstick fingers and thumb, and she squeezed. I watched her rosy lips open wide in a miniature yawn. I inhaled her flowery, soapy scent. But when I rolled over, she was gone, and I was alone in the bed, which had grown to fill the room. I tried to get up but couldn't walk on the mushy surface. I kept falling down, and with each step I took, my foot sank deeper and deeper until I disappeared into the mattress.

The next morning, I woke up to voices and laughter. It was light outside, so I must have slept more than twelve hours. Amanda was bellowing in the kitchen; I could hear her all the way upstairs. I stood up slowly, just in case. My clothes were in a pile on the dresser. Had Vera washed and neatly folded them? How embarrassing! It felt amazing to slip my legs into clean pants, clean socks. I quickly dressed and tiptoed down to see what was going on.

I didn't want to stay. I needed to get to the Blue Anchor, but I also didn't want to seem ungrateful. From the bottom of the stairs, I saw the living room in the light of day. A grandfather clock, a cabinet of china figurines and fancy glasses. A painting of a loon. A crocheted blanket draped over the armchair. Stacks of newspapers and a basket of yarn.

Amanda peeked around the corner and saw me. "You're alive," she said, smiling.

"Yeah, I was really tired," I said.

"Your hair looks good," said Amanda. "I wish mine was thick and wavy like that."

"I always wanted it straight, like yours," I said, smoothing my hair.

"I washed your things," said Vera as she came around the corner with a dish towel. "I hope that's all right."

"You didn't have to, but thank you," I said. Vera smiled.

"I'm going to work," said Amanda. "I hope you find your people."

"Bye, dear," said Vera from the kitchen.

"I should get going, too," I said.

"Not so fast," said Vera. "The Blue Anchor doesn't open until eleven, so you've got time."

"Oh," I said, looking down. She could have told me that last night.

"And just how did you think you were gonna get there? I'm your driver today," she said, looking at her tiny gold wristwatch. "How about some oatmeal, or would you prefer scrambled eggs?"

"You don't have to cook for me."

"It's throwing eggs in a pan." She'd already opened the fridge and the egg carton. "Just sit, stay where you are. Do you want some tea?"

It was frustrating to be stuck like this. "Can I call my voicemail?" I said, and she pointed to the cordless phone hanging on the wall. I'd been checking, but there was nothing new.

As Vera set down a plate of eggs in front of me, I dialed the number for Legal Aid. "I need a lawyer," I said to the person who answered.

Thirty-Nine

DIGGER

Night

Deena dug around in the blue bag to find a clean diaper while Mrs. Z placed the baby on some kitchen towels she'd spread out on the table. The kid wiggled and Mrs. Z held her still. She called, "Come watch this, Dennis."

Deena laughed at me. I took off my coat and rubbed my eyes. This was the last thing I wanted to do.

Mrs. Z unsnapped the baby clothes. "Cute little jammies," she said, pointing to the moons-and-cows pattern.

"Yeah, real cute," I said, leaning on a kitchen chair.

Mrs. Z gave me a lecture: first you do this, then you do that. She opened the dirty diaper.

"Holy hell." I turned away. "Jesus, Eunice!"

Mrs. Z handed the dirty one to Deena. She balled it up and tossed it in the trash. They stuck a fresh one under the kid. "Got any wipes?" said Mrs. Z.

Deena handed her what she'd found in the bag. They cleaned her up, put the new thing on. Got her all back together and snapped her up. Wrapped her in the blanket.

"Glad that's over." I grabbed a beer from the fridge and looked for a bottle opener.

"Dennis," said Mrs. Z, and I got the feeling I was in trouble. "I want to show you something."

"But isn't it your bedtime, Mrs. Z?" I looked at my watch. "Almost nine."

"I'll be quick."

"Okay," I said, taking a swig.

"Come here," said Mrs. Z, nodding. The baby was still on the kitchen table, wrapped up like a burrito. Mrs. Z took away my beer and set it down.

"Hey!" I said.

Mrs. Z yanked at my arms like I was a damn mannequin. "Like this," she said, positioning my arms and hands. "Now," she said, "I'm going to show you how to hold a newborn."

"Oh, God," I said, rolling my eyes. But I had a weakness for Mrs. Z. There was something about her that made me obey, made me just go along with whatever stupid-ass thing she wanted to do, or wanted to say, or whatever. So there I stood with my arms out, like an idiot. And Deena was loving it.

Mrs. Z stood close to me. Put the thing in my stiff arms as slowly as she could. Talked about how to support the head and neck. Adjusted my fingers. "There," she said, like she'd just finished frosting a cake. Proud of her work.

"Okay," I said, with the Slinky in my arms.

"Now. Just give her a little bounce, bend your knees a bit," said Mrs. Z.

I bounced. Deena was really enjoying this. I was afraid she was gonna take a picture and torture me with it for the rest of my life.

"All right," said Mrs. Z. "I'm off to bed."

"Hey!" I said, feeling duped. She left me there with the baby like a cheap magician's trick.

When we heard Mrs. Z make it to the top of the stairs, Deena turned to me and said, "Go sit in the living room. I'm gonna make up a little bed for her. And I'll get another bottle ready."

"Fine," I moaned. Still holding the bundle, I walked into the living room and sat in the chair Mrs. Z had been sitting in.

"We'll see if we can get her to sleep," said Deena, putting a pan of water on the stove. "And then you'll tell me what the hell is going on."

Deena disappeared to the basement, then came back up with an empty dresser drawer. She put it on the floor and wiped it out. Then she dashed upstairs. She came back with a bath towel and a blanket and sat on the floor, folding the blanket this way and that. Then she positioned them in the drawer, but she wasn't happy. She took them out and put them in another way. She stood up and ran to the kitchen. Was she singing? She came back to the living room with a bottle, shook a drop onto her wrist, and handed it to me.

"Nuh-uh. You do it," I said.

"All right," she said, taking the baby, and we switched places. "But only so you can do the talking."

"Okay," I said as I paced the living room, back and forth.

"Just start at the beginning," she said. I told Deena the whole story, all the stuff Cally had told me about college, the sperm donor, everything. "Fifty grand?" she said when I told her about the rich-ass lawyer and the contract, the credit card. Deena put the baby on her shoulder to make her burp. I could see the wheels turning in Deena's head.

"So we broke up, and I went down to Missouri with Uncle Joey—"

"Yeah."

"—because he had all that construction work. And I made like thirty-five grand, just between March and October."

"Uh-huh." Deena stood up and bounced with the baby.

"When I got back to town, I moved in with Danno over in St. Paul. You remember Danno?"

"The line cook or the one with the tattoo of the pope?" She looked at me, eyebrows up, bouncing.

"Tattoo of the pope."

"Okay." Deena took the kid over to the empty dresser drawer she'd just finished fixing up. She lowered the sleeping thing, the size of a football, and set it in the drawer so carefully you'd think it was a bundle of dynamite.

"And out of the blue, Cally called," I said. "Long story short, she had the baby, but she wanted more time. Asked me to help."

"So you brought her up here," Deena said, standing up and wiping her shirt.

"To the hunting cabin, yeah."

"And what's in it for you?" Deena crossed her arms.

"Five grand," I said.

Deena made a face like she was impressed. "So what's the plan?" she said, moving to the kitchen.

"What do you mean?" I said, following her.

"For getting your money? When do you get your five grand?" She handed me my beer and opened the fridge to get one for herself.

"Oh, um . . ." I took a swig.

"And why isn't Cally with you?"

"Um . . ." I swallowed and cleared my throat, trying to think of what to say.

"I don't like the sound of that." Deena opened her beer, keeping her eyes on me the whole time.

"She's back at the cabin," I said.

Deena swallowed. "Why?" she said.

"Because I left her there."

"What the hell, Digger?" Deena rolled her eyes. "Does she know you're here?"

I shook my head.

Deena put her beer down. "Then why are you here?"

"I panicked," I said, shrugging.

"Oh, Jesus." Deena turned away. We'd been leaning against the counters, but Deena picked up her beer and walked over to the kitchen table and sat down. She pulled out a cigarette and lit up.

I followed her and sat across the table. "Cally's been acting like she wasn't gonna go through with it," I said. "And saying things."

"Like what?" Deena took a drag.

"Like she wants to keep the baby."

Deena exhaled. "Shoulda got the money in advance."

"No shit," I said.

Deena just shrugged and took another swig of beer. "So you thought it'd be a good idea if you kidnapped the baby instead?"

"What the hell? I didn't kidnap shit."

"Yeah, you did." Deena pointed her cigarette in the direction of the living room.

"No," I said. I felt my teeth clench. "I'm *returning* the fucking thing."

"And who do you think is gonna pay you?" said Deena, but she didn't wait for me to answer. "Because it sure isn't gonna be Cally now that you've taken the kid. Without telling her."

"Maybe we just went for a drive?" I said. My beer was warm.

Deena shook her head and looked down. She'd pulled her feet up onto the chair and was hugging her knees, cigarette in one hand. The smoke rose up and mixed with the light from the fixture that hung over the kitchen table, just like when we were kids and our mother sat and chain-smoked all day. "Don't be stupid," she said.

In one motion, I stood up and shook the table. I hated when Deena—or anyone—called me stupid.

Deena didn't flinch. Just grabbed our beers so they wouldn't tip over. The baby fussed. "Now you woke her up," said Deena, taking a sip.

I paced around the kitchen, trying to calm down. "There's proba-bly a reward or some shit. More than five grand."

"Is there or isn't there? Or are you just guessing?"

"I don't know," I said. "But I bet that lawyer and his wife would pay dearly. They were gonna pay Cally, so why not?"

"Okay, so take it to them." Deena put out her cigarette as she stood up. The baby was crying. Deena put a pan of water on. Started another bottle. "You can't leave her here with me, that's for damn sure."

"I know," I said. "My plan is to bring the kid to them."

"Then go do it. What are you waiting for?" She finished her beer. The baby's cries were getting louder.

"What are you waiting for?" I mocked her voice. So annoying. "I'll tell you what I'm waiting for: I don't know who they are or where they live."

"Oh my Lord," said Deena, walking out of the kitchen and into the living room, toward the baby. "You're stupider than I thought."

"God DAMN it, Deena." I slammed my palm on the table.

The baby stopped crying for a second. Everything was still.

Deena came back. She stood in the doorway, holding the baby. Finally, she said, "So you want me to help you?"

I took a deep breath and exhaled.

"That's why you're here, isn't it?"

"Yes," I said finally. "Yes, goddammit."

The baby wailed. Like she'd forgotten and then remembered what she was mad about. Then cried harder, to make up for it.

"If I do this," said Deena, pointing at me, "I get half the money."

Forty

CALLY

Afternoon

On the drive to the Blue Anchor Grill, I wanted to believe I was wrong. Maybe Digger would come back to the cabin. Maybe he'd gone for a very good reason. Maybe he wanted to let me sleep or just went to get some beer. But I knew he wasn't coming back. He'd taken too much with him.

The police weren't very helpful. Since I didn't have the birth certificate. Or a court order. At least I was being matched with a lawyer from Legal Aid, but that would take a day or two, they said. So I had to find her on my own. I had to stop Digger if he was going to do something stupid. Like bring the baby to Hal and Ruth? But he wouldn't know how to find them. Would he take the baby somewhere else and do what? Leave her on the firehouse steps? He wouldn't get his money that way.

I should have known better. He'd been so strongly against this. I wished I hadn't called him. I wished I hadn't fallen asleep. And I shouldn't have helped him diagnose his dead battery. I didn't say any of this to Vera, of course. I just kept it in my head. But she'd been listening to my call with Legal Aid. And I was sure Amanda had told her about my call to the police last night. I was shifting in my seat and not in the mood to talk as we made our way to the Blue Anchor.

"Where do you live in Minneapolis?" Vera asked as she drove, occasionally glancing at me.

"Cedar Park."

"That's nice. My niece lives near the art museum."

No answer. I had a lot to think about.

"Are you a student down there," said Vera, "because Amanda was undecided about college, and I told her you're never too old to get an education."

"Yeah." I couldn't focus on conversation. I stared at the shoulder and the passing woods, wondering what might be out there, hiding.

Once, when I was out driving with my dad, his truck hit a deer that jumped out from nowhere, and I fell to the floor. Hit my head on the glove compartment. My dad yelled, and I thought it was my fault. I stayed in the hospital for a week with a concussion. He visited me every day and brought me dolls and chocolate. There was a Santa Claus in the lobby, and kids in wheelchairs with bald heads. I was the only kid without a mother. I thought everyone was looking at me. I wanted to go home. After that, I was always skittish, like something could jump out at any moment.

So I watched the sides of the highway for any signs of deer. I didn't tell Vera what I was looking for. She was happy to take what she could get. When we got to the Blue Anchor, the place was getting busy for the lunch rush. Several cars and trucks in the parking lot. I didn't see Digger's, but I was hoping Bailey was working.

"Will you wait for me here?" I asked Vera.

"No, ma'am, I will not," she said. "I am coming in there with you." Vera put the car in park and pulled the keys out of the ignition. I tumbled out of the car, and she followed me.

Inside was warm and dim. It took a few seconds for my eyes to adjust, and the noise gave me a headache. Loud conversation. Overhead music. I scanned the guys sitting at the bar. A good-looking bartender was drying glasses and stacking them. He smiled at me when we made eye contact.

Then the booths. Tall wooden booths lined the edges of the place, and I grabbed hold of each one to brace myself as I walked down the aisle.

"I'll be right with you," said a waitress, squeezing past me and carrying a tray of beers. It wasn't Bailey.

Neon lights and televisions flashed red and blue. The dark-paneled walls were covered in framed newspaper clippings and black-and-white photos. The floor was sticky. The women's bathroom was occupied. I went into the men's and locked it. The outside sounds were immediately muffled, and I leaned against the porcelain sink.

Someone knocked and jiggled the doorknob.

"Busy," I yelled.

"Cally?" said the voice. It was Vera. "Are you all right? Let me in."

"No."

"There's a baby out here." She jiggled the doorknob again. "There's a baby!" she yelled.

My thighs tightened. My tummy seized, and I leaned over. I wobbled to the door and unlocked it. "I'm cramping," I said.

Vera came in and closed the door behind her. She held on to one side of me to keep me from falling. "Okay, move over here, sit down." She walked me to the toilet. She was so strong for a grandma. The toilet lid was up, and the bowl was covered in urine. Vera lowered the lid and wiped it off. "There, it's okay."

I sat and leaned over in pain.

"Take a deep breath." She leaned down and tried to see my eyes. "Do you feel faint?" She put her hand on my forehead. "You're sweaty."

"No, I'll be okay," I said. "I just need to . . . change my pad."

"All right." She glanced at my backpack, dropped on the floor. "I'll wait outside the door."

I'd been changing my pads every hour, but this time I changed it, and it immediately filled up again. I put on another clean one and stuffed my pants with paper towels as extra backup.

"Okay," I said loudly, and Vera came in. She put her arm around me and guided me back out into the bar. When we shuffled to the front, I saw the baby Vera had found, sitting in a high chair. This baby was much older; she looked like a giant compared to Nell. "That's not her," I told Vera. "She's way too big." I had no idea how babies looked at various ages. This one looked like she was three times the size of Nell. "That baby is practically a kid."

"Well, I'm sorry about that," said Vera.

We both stood there staring at the young family. The mother at the table finally caught our eyes and raised her eyebrows as if to shoo us away. Vera pulled me toward the door. I turned back to look for Bailey. I saw a burly busboy, that same handsome bartender, and then there she was, coming out of the kitchen. Tall and blond, she carried three burger platters, one balanced in the crook of her elbow, as she strode confidently to one of the booths.

"That's her," I said.

"Who?" asked Vera.

"The waitress. Ow!" Pangs throbbed in my groin, and I felt a gush; my pad was soaked already, and something was running down my legs. My pants were definitely wet, and my thighs were sticking together.

"We need to get you to the doctor."

"No, I need to talk to her." I yanked myself away and moved toward the waitress. She had stopped at the wait station while the good-looking bartender sprayed soda into the glasses on her tray.

"Hey," I said, getting her attention as I moved closer and finally grabbed the edge of the bar. "Excuse me, miss."

"Can I help you?" she said, focused on the drinks.

"I was here yesterday," I said.

"Okay . . ." She sounded unsure.

"With a baby. And Digger—er, Dennis Wilkins. You're Bailey, right? You waited on us."

"Oh, yeah, okay, I remember," she said with a worried look. Maybe she noticed my wet pants, or maybe she wondered why I was leaning over. "Sorry, what can I, um?" she said, looking at Vera, who had joined us at the wait station.

The bartender had stopped pouring drinks and was watching us. "Is everything okay?" he said. He had a nice voice.

"You said you know Deena Wilkins?" I said. I was having trouble getting enough air to make my voice say the words. "For the huskies."

"Sam, you'd better come out here," the waitress said to the bartender, and he did.

"Can you give me Deena's address?" I said, louder than I meant to. Another warm rush ran down my legs and I held on to my midsection.

"Um, I guess," Bailey said, looking at Vera. "Is she okay?"

I sensed bodies around us, people crowding me. "I need the address," I said, dizzying. My legs gave way, and I buckled toward the floor. I felt someone catch me and help me stand up.

A male voice said, "Whoa, there, are you okay?"

My eyes flashed black.

Forty-One

RUTH

Evening

Raymond and I had already pieced together several clues. The cashier remembered a disheveled young woman with a newborn coming into the mini-mart and a man with her in a pickup truck. The cashier and her two women friends, who were keeping her company that night, remembered the evening well and could describe the truck and the baby. It stood out in their minds because it seemed to them that the young couple was in trouble. The women still had a red mitten they believed belonged to the couple, and best of all: these women had written down the license number of the man's truck.

I immediately memorized the Minnesota plate: NVB381A. I planned to scour the city and the license plate of every truck until I found my baby. But when we got to Duluth, and the Target where Cally had made purchases, we didn't find the truck or any other useful information. It was late when we checked in to our motel, so we went straight to our rooms.

Early Monday morning, I got a call from Kristin. She'd arranged for me and Hal to meet a surrogacy lawyer that afternoon, which meant I'd have to fly back to Minneapolis as soon as possible.

"Well, that was quick." Raymond spread syrup on the crusty waffle he'd made in the breakfast nook at the North Family Inn just outside of Duluth.

"Yeah, I hate leaving right now, we're so close!" I said. "But we need this lawyer, and I don't trust Hal to accept the guy's advice. I want to hear it directly from the horse's mouth."

"So to speak." Raymond winked.

I smiled as I took a bite of toast and a sip of dishwater-flavored coffee from a Styrofoam cup. "I'll fly right back late tonight or first thing Tuesday morning."

"It's fine, Ru," Raymond said as he broke his plastic knife trying to cut the waffle.

"You'll probably do better up here without me getting in your way," I said, handing him my knife.

"Maybe," he said, smiling and cutting the waffle.

"Well, you could have at least pretended you needed me here," I said.

Raymond's fork snapped, and he gave up. He grabbed the waffle with his hands and took a bite. "Of course I do!" He winked.

We finished our terrible breakfasts, and Raymond drove me to the airport to catch my flight. The plan was he would continue following his leads without me, starting with the Blue Anchor Grill, and I would return as soon as I could.

At the delightfully small Duluth airport, I used a public phone and my calling card to touch base with Hal. He answered on the first ring.

"I have good news," I said.

"So do I."

"What is it?"

"You go first," he said.

"We have the truck's license plate number. What's yours?"

"Not as good as that, but the credit card company reported another location. Purchases at a Mobil gas station in Superior, Wisconsin."

"Oh, that's amazing. Can you fax it to Raymond at the motel? It's the North Family Inn."

"Already did."

"Great." I watched as travelers dragged their roller bags to the waiting area at gate three. My phone carrel was across the aisle from my departure gate, so I could keep an eye on the boarding. A young mother pushed a stroller with one hand and gripped a rambunctious toddler with the other. "I'm flying home. I'm at the airport."

"Yes, I got that message. Apparently, we're meeting with someone named Sol Bakerfield this afternoon?" Hal enunciated each syllable of Sol's name.

"Yeah," I said. "He's a family lawyer." The mother struggled to get the baby out of the stroller and ran after the toddler, with her purse and the baby's legs dangling from her arm as she ran.

"Why do you need a family lawyer? Are you divorcing me?"

"Don't be ridiculous." I cupped my hand over the phone. "He handles surrogacy . . . situations."

Hal sighed, sounding exasperated. The breath was magnified in my ear. "I told you, that's not necessary," he said. His voice sounded smaller, and I wondered if he'd prefer talking about divorce. At least he'd had experience with that.

"He's going to help us get the baby." I lowered my voice. "You do real estate."

"I know the bloomin' area of law I practice."

There was an announcement from the speakers in the ceiling, and the crowd of travelers tightened around the gate. The young mother was out of my view. The empty stroller was a mess and looked like it had been used as a shopping cart. Blanket askew, coat draped over, bags stashed underneath, and toys dangling.

"Let's just hear his advice," I said. The woman, baby, and toddler emerged intact and returned to the stroller, which no one had touched.

There was a pause on the other end of the line. Another announcement from above.

"I gotta go. My plane's boarding." As I hung up, I heard Hal saying something, but I'd cut him off. If I'd hurt his feelings, I could apologize in person in about an hour.

As soon as the airplane took off, it was only a matter of minutes before we began the descent. Hal picked me up, and we proceeded directly to the meeting with Sol Bakerfield. His law office was in the stretch of town between Minneapolis and St. Paul, in a quaint historic mansion that had been converted for commercial use, including a coffee shop and a small restaurant that served traditional English tea with scones and cucumber sandwiches.

"This is too cutesy for me." Hal gestured to the rose garden decor, dried floral arrangements, and patterned wallpaper.

"Give him a chance," I said. But he was right: the decor was abysmal. We waited in the lobby next to a small military cannon surrounded by framed war medals and flags. Clearly, Mr. Bakerfield was a fan of the Civil War.

Finally, he emerged and introduced himself. He was closer to my height than Hal's, about five-nine, and solidly built. He wore brown pants and a brown corduroy vest over a mattress-striped cotton shirt with his sleeves rolled up as high as they could go. With his shaggy hair and sandy brown mustache, he resembled a sheepdog with glasses. He brought us into his office, which was adorned with even more Civil War memorabilia.

Hal looked for a place to hang his overcoat but, seeing none, draped it over the back of a chair. I did the same with my jacket. There was a chill between me and Hal, as we had repeated the same arguments on the car ride from the airport, until there was nothing more to say and we rode the rest of the way without speaking.

"Please sit," said Mr. Bakerfield, gesturing.

We took the two visitor chairs opposite the oversize desk, which was covered in piles of folders.

"I've looked over the papers you sent me," said Mr. Bakerfield. He shuffled through a stack and pulled out a tattered Redrope folder.

"What'd you send him?" Hal asked me, sounding defensive, as if he were being graded. I wondered if he knew of any weaknesses in the contract.

I leaned toward Hal and said, "Pat sent him a copy of the whole agreement, and what else? Kristin faxed over my notes from interviewing the hospital, stuff about the security tape, the credit card report."

"I didn't actually need all of that, but it's good to err on the side of providing it," said Mr. Bakerfield.

"Okay," said Hal, as if the quantity of information were keeping us afloat rather than the quality.

"And it was helpful background." Mr. Bakerfield placed in front of us a piece of paper. "This is a time line I've put together. I'd like you to review its accuracy and fill in the missing points of data. I understand you are an attorney, Mr. Olson, so you'll be familiar with much of this."

"But not *family* law," I said.

"Yes, well, in any case, I need to compare the parties' actions against what was contractually agreed upon."

"Isn't the contract enforceable on its face?" said Hal.

"Hold that thought." Mr. Bakerfield held up his index finger. "We'll get to that, but we'll also identify any evidence of abuse or neglect, poor judgment, or mishandling we can use in the event that we need to argue best interests of the child."

"Best interests of the child?" I murmured, wondering what it meant in this context. Such a vague and subjective concept. How could anyone really know what was best for our child? Or anyone else's?

"Isn't that a custody standard?" said Hal.

"Yes. Very good," said Mr. Bakerfield.

"He's divorced, so we're familiar," I said.

"Mm-hmm." Mr. Bakerfield looked over his glasses at us, then continued, "In the event some aspects of the surrogacy agreement are not enforceable or are deemed to be void, for example."

"That would be outrageous, no reasonable court would deny me the . . . the benefit of our bargain," said Hal.

"We'll see, we'll see, but for the sake of argument, if a court did, then we would shift our focus to prove paternity and then move for custody or, at the very minimum, visitation rights."

"What?" I was stunned.

"All of that would also include, potentially, child support, but not in the traditional sense, because"—he chuckled—"we didn't get here the traditional way, did we?"

"No," I said. Hal and I were not laughing at the joke.

"All the same, the child is entitled to the benefit of support, regardless of method of conception."

"Child support?" said Hal. "That doesn't seem right. If we don't get the baby, we shouldn't have to support it." We sat silent for a few seconds, taking in the coldness of the comment. It occurred to me, even as a non-lawyer, that this baby was just as much a child of Hal's as were his two sons, and I was stunned by the inequality in his thinking: he would never abandon his sons like this, financially.

"Oh, I think you'll get the baby," said Mr. Bakerfield.

"Why do you say it like that? You sound certain," I said.

"My initial reaction is that the act of exiting the hospital with the baby, via the window, does show, at a minimum, poor judgment and could also be construed as reckless endangerment of a child, and I would certainly argue that it was," said Mr. Bakerfield.

"I would agree with that," said Hal without hesitation.

"Do we know where the birth mother took the baby?" asked Mr. Bakerfield.

"Yes," I said. "She's in the Duluth/Superior area."

"Do we have an address?" said Mr. Bakerfield, pen in hand.

"Not yet, but my brother, who is a detective, is very close to finding it. And we have a license plate number," I said. "What will you do with an address?"

"On your behalf, I'd file a request for injunctive relief, a court order, and get the local protective services folks to pick up your daughter."

"What will happen to her then?"

"She'll be taken care of, either at an on-site facility or, if needed, in a short-term foster placement until we can sort it all out."

"Holy crap," I said. The image of our baby girl in a foster home was gruesome and completely unexpected.

"Fine. So we can get the papers ready and serve them on her as soon as we get a location. Did you hire a private investigator?"

"No, Ruth's brother," said Hal.

"Oh, that's right. You told me that."

Hal sighed, annoyed that Mr. Bakerfield had already forgotten a simple piece of information. "What about the contract?" He leaned forward in his chair. "Shouldn't we start an action to enforce it?"

"I think we should, yes." Mr. Bakerfield leaned forward, mirroring Hal, and said, "I'll draft a complaint for your review."

"Good." Hal slapped the table and scooted to the front of his chair, readying himself to stand.

Now that Sol hadn't directly criticized the terms of our agreement with Cally, Hal seemed strangely proud that his precious contract could be the centerpiece of a lawsuit to enforce our rights, even though it meant our new baby might end up in foster care. I wanted to slap my hand on the table and shout, No, not good! Raymond and I have nearly found the baby with no lawsuit, and no one needs to go to foster care if we do it our way.

Mr. Bakerfield stood, indicating our meeting was concluded. "I need you to get in as soon as you can for a blood test, Mr. Olson. You can have the clinic send your blood report to my office." He handed us his business card.

"Call me Hal." He stood up and reached out his hand.

"Call me Sol." The two men shook hands.

"Thank you." Hal lifted his coat and swung his arms into it. "We'll get you that address as soon as we can, so she can be served with papers."

I said nothing as we walked out the colonial-style doors and into the parking lot. Hal tried to put his arm around me, but I was walking too quickly, and he didn't keep up with me.

"I need to get back to Duluth," I said once we found our car and got in. "Can you drive me to the airport?"

Forty-Two

CALLY

Afternoon

A handsome face hovered above me. I saw his lips moving. I wanted to talk, but my throat didn't work. I felt weak and just needed to sleep. I closed my eyes. Over the next hour, I was aware of voices and sirens, footsteps, the cold air outside, men's hands on me, a flashlight in my face, Vera's voice, pain in my groin, wetness in my pants. At the hospital, they wheeled me down the hall.

"One, two, three," said the ambulance men as they transferred me from a cart onto the bed. There were IVs and tubes and tests. They interviewed me over and over. What day is it? Monday. Who is the president? George Bush.

Nurses helped me take off my clothes and get into a gown. They hooked me up and drew blood; they poked my tummy and checked my eyes and ears and mouth. They looked up my nose and checked my temperature. Someone asked for my regular doctor's name. I said Dr. Salovich, but he was the fertility doctor. I struggled to think of another doctor I'd seen. They said not to worry, they'd find out.

The doctors and nurses all looked alike. Each nurse had a different job, which they announced when they entered the room and rubbed sanitizing foam on their hands.

"Can I have a drink of water?" I asked one of them.

"Not yet," she said. "We're gonna check you out first. In case you need surgery."

"Surgery," I mumbled, hoping somebody would explain.

"I'll get you some ice chips," the nurse said.

A different woman walked in and sat on a stool next to my bed. She wore a white coat with her name embroidered on it. "I'm Dr. Sheldon," she said. "You can call me Alice if you like."

I stared at the blue pens in the pocket of her coat and the stethoscope around her neck.

"This is Mark." She nodded at the young man beside her. He had a laptop on a wheeled cart, and he stood behind it, typing. "He's gonna be taking notes, okay? Can you tell me where you are right now?"

"The hospital," I said with a sigh. How long was this gonna take?

"That's right. You're at St. Mary's hospital in Duluth," she said. "How long ago did you give birth?"

"I don't know. Thursday," I said. It felt like a month ago. I needed to find Nell.

"Were there any complications?" She placed her hand on my forearm, gently.

"Well . . . I was a surrogate, so . . ." I wondered if I was in trouble.

She nodded, taking that in. "We'll get to that. But I meant, were there any problems in the birth?" She used a sweet voice, low and calm, as if this were just a get-to-know-you session. "Everything go all right with the placenta, as far as you know?"

"I think so, yeah."

"Good." She looked at Mark as if to make sure he was still taking notes. She put in her earpieces and placed the stethoscope on my chest. "Was there excessive amniotic fluid? Lean forward, please." She moved the stethoscope to my back and I felt its cold weight.

I hugged my chest and my breasts were full. "Oh, God, I think I'm leaking." I looked down at my robe.

"Oh, are you breastfeeding?"

"I—I . . ." I stammered, trying to think where to start. I explained what had happened as well as I could. She nodded compassionately, and Mark typed my words. Or his words. Who knows what version of events he typed. Dr. Sheldon kept eye contact with me as she listened. Good bedside manner. When I finished, she spoke slowly. "I'm sorry you've been through so much, Cally." She waited to let that sink in.

"Thanks," I said.

"There are a number of birth-related complications I'd like to rule out. But I won't know until I take a look. So I'd like to keep you overnight and run some tests."

"What? No, I can't stay here that long."

"Well, I recommend against your leaving in the condition you're in. With your bleeding and fainting, it wouldn't be safe."

"I need to make a phone call," I said, trying to get up.

"Not quite yet," said Dr. Sheldon as she guided me back into bed. She placed her hands on my belly and pressed hard.

"Ow," I said.

"Your uterus is still rather large."

I wasn't worried about my uterus, but this doctor was. She asked me to rate my pain and point to where it hurt. She lifted my hospital gown and peeked in like it was a tent. "Just checking for rashes." She put my gown back in place and asked if I had any trouble urinating.

"No," I said. "I really need to make a call."

"Okay, one of the nurses can help you with that." She was done with her exam. "They're going to move you to a regular room so you can sleep. I'll check on you in the morning."

"Can you get me another blanket?"

"I'll send someone in to take care of that," she said, and Mark closed the curtain behind them.

Alone again in the room, I looked at the labels on the cabinet doors, the receptacle for used needles, the canisters of tongue depressors, and a small sink for washing hands or pouring water into tiny paper cups. I imagined sticking an index card on the mirror. If I had a marker, I would write, "Come Back, Nell."

The nurse came in and covered me with a clean sheet and two heavy blankets, warmed and toasty, like they'd just come out of the dryer. She pulled them up to my neck. Heaven. I closed my eyes and, despite the fluorescent lights, felt the earth pulling me down. I felt I could sleep here for a long time.

Once I fell asleep in the back of Digger's pickup. During the summer after I'd graduated from high school (and Digger had almost finished), we went for a drive. He had a different truck back then, his first of several. He'd fix each one up and sell it for a better one, like what he wanted to do with flipping houses. That first truck was a Ford in turquoise blue. It had rust on the wheel wells and a mismatched dirty white tailgate. He worked on it every chance he got, every day after school. He replaced parts by scouring the junkyard for what he needed, a rearview mirror, a latch for the glove box, a heat fan mechanism, even a new seat cushion. He took the thing apart and put it back together. It was his.

And one warm day, he took me on a drive to a wide-open field. We didn't have a plan, just followed roads he hadn't been on before, turning here and there, following dandelions. Finally, he drove off the pavement onto a gravel road and then into the field, where he parked amid the wilderness. When he switched off the ignition, he turned to me and smiled. We took our lunches to the flatbed, where he had a mattress and a few boxes on their way to somewhere. We leaned against the boxes and stretched out our legs while we ate our sandwiches. I remember the sound of our paper bags crunching, birdcalls we tried to identify, and green flies buzzing by, but no people. Just us, under the hot sun.

And after we were full and roasted, we made love in the sweltering heat, then we slid down onto the warm mattress and slept, as if the sun and the sex had hypnotized us. It was delicious. When we eventually woke, our bodies were stiff, and I forgot where I was. The flatbed looked foreign to me, like I'd been kidnapped or drugged. We laughed when we remembered we were safe. My skin was dry and tight, probably burned, but I loved it. We kissed and kissed and finally woke ourselves up, woke up enough to go home.

That was the same kind of heavy pull I felt in the hospital bed, that feeling of not knowing where I was, exactly, but that I could, without doing anything at all, go somewhere deep and far away.

Forty-Three

RUTH

MONDAY, DECEMBER 9, 2002

Night

When I arrived back at our Duluth motel late Monday night, I hoped I'd have a voicemail from Raymond. I could hardly get into my room fast enough to get to the phone and press play. And what an update! Raymond had been to the Mobil gas station where Cally had made several charges. He'd interviewed two employees, and based on what they'd told him, Raymond had scoped out two possible locations where Cally might be hiding. One was a cabin, but it was vacant. The other was a suburban home not far from the Mobil station. I called Raymond's car phone.

"I'm back, and I got your message," I said, barely able to hold my excitement.

"Good," said Raymond.

"Where are you now?"

"I'm outside the home," he said.

"Oh my God, what have you seen so far?" My heart was pounding with hope, and I wanted to go straight over there. But even if I'd jumped in a taxi right that instant and found Cally there in the flesh, I wasn't sure how I'd feel when I saw her. Was she the same person I'd thought I'd known, the one who held the key to our dreams coming true? "Is she there?" I asked, breathless.

"Yes, Ruth, she's here. I saw her come out of this address, and I saw her go back in. She is staying with these people."

"Is she all right? I mean, can you tell if she and the baby are okay?"

"She hasn't brought the baby outside, but Cally herself looks fine."

I wasn't sure how I felt about this information. Part of me wanted Cally to be sick and crazed with some ailment that had invaded her senses and caused her to take our baby. "Is she with anyone? Is the truck there?" I asked. Perhaps she was under the influence of a cult master or an abusive boyfriend.

"It looks like she's with a young woman, early twenties, and an older woman and man, sixties or early seventies. No sign of the truck. Does she have family up here, Ru?"

"I don't know!" I was angry that I didn't know more about her. Hal and I had believed we'd done sufficient research on her medical and psychological profile, but we hadn't been able to uncover much about her family history. If these people were her relatives, we knew nothing about them. Who knew what else she might have been covering up?

"Don't worry about it," said Raymond. "I've already phoned Hal with this address. He's passing it on to your lawyer."

"Gosh, that was fast," I said.

"How did the meeting go? Must have been productive, from the way Hal talked about it."

"Yes, we liked him," I said. "And he knows his stuff . . . it's just that the baby will probably have to go to temporary foster—[beep]—"

"What?" said Raymond.

"Hang on. I'm getting another call," I said when the beeps continued.

"Go ahead and take it," said Raymond.

"I'll call you back." I pressed the button to answer the other line. It was Hal. He was agitated, flustered. He may have been crying. I heard a woman's voice in the background, shrieking. "Is that Audrey?"

"Yes," Hal sobbed, but it also sounded like an order.

"What's going on? Are you okay?" I sat down, bracing myself.

"Jake's been in a . . . car accident." Hal's voice was low and gravelly. Then, before sobbing, he barely choked out the words, "He's in a coma."

"Oh, no," I said. "Jesus. Hal, I'm so sorry."

Hal sniffled and made noises that weren't words. Sitting on the edge of my motel bed, I pressed the receiver as hard as I could to my ear, as if this would help me understand why this had happened.

"Honey, it's gonna be okay, okay?" I said, not knowing anything about anything. "What happened? Can you tell me?"

Hal explained that Jake had been at the snowboarding event in Lutsen, which was almost two hours north of Duluth. I knew, because this was the competition that was going to keep him from attending the transfer ceremony. "Yes, I remember, but I thought it ended on Sunday?"

"It did." Hal could barely get the words out. He choked and whimpered, and when he composed himself again, he added, painfully, "But he asked . . . if he could stay up there . . . with friends . . . for another night."

"Oh, honey, yeah, I remember that now."

"And they were driving back . . . tonight . . . and his friend Tommy was driving, you know Tommy?"

"No, but that's okay," I said.

"I thought you'd met him," said Hal, sniffling and blowing his nose. "They hit a patch of . . . ice and slid sideways, the officers said, and . . . they got hit by a . . . semi . . ." Hal gasped, and I thought he might hyperventilate.

"And he's in a coma? Do they think he'll come out of it . . . soon?"

"They don't know . . . I don't know anything more," said Hal, and I could hear Audrey in the back, tugging at him. "We're coming up there."

"Good," I said. "Can you drive?"

"Yes, I'll be fine," said Hal. "We're bringing Caleb."

"How is he?"

"He's hanging in there. It's tough," said Hal. "Ruth, can you meet us at the hospital?"

"Yes, of course, I'll go over there right away. Which one is it?"

"St. Mary's. We won't be there for . . . a few hours," Hal said, losing his strength momentarily. "But if you could go . . . and see him . . . speak to him . . ." He stopped at that idea, then continued as soon as he was able. "If you could, that would mean a lot . . . to me."

"I will, I will," I promised, and we said goodbye. Before I dialed a taxi, I called Raymond to let him know.

This was my new priority, and I was on my way.

Forty-Four

DIGGER

MONDAY, DECEMBER 9, 2002

Morning

It'd been too late to leave for the Cities and return the kid on Sunday night, so Deena set me up in her guest room. I slept like a rock. Deena and Mrs. Z must have taken care of the baby. Or maybe she didn't cry. Either way, I didn't hear a thing all night. In the morning, I remembered all the shit I was in. I went downstairs. Deena was sitting at the kitchen table, reading the paper.

"Look who's awake," said Deena, eyes peeled on the horoscopes.

"Is there coffee?" I said.

"In the maker," she said, pointing. "You might wanna warm it up."

"Where is she?" I pulled down a mug and poured the cold coffee in.

"The baby? Mrs. Z has her."

"Okay." I stuck my coffee in the microwave and punched the buttons.

"That kid sure sleeps a lot," said Deena.

"Thank God," I said. I peeked into the living room. Mrs. Z had the thing asleep on her lap. Like it was a cat. She spied me and waved. Why did she always have to wave at me? Did that mean I was supposed to wave back? I waved back.

The microwave beeped, and I brought my coffee to the kitchen table. I sat across from Deena. When we both still lived at home, mornings at the kitchen table were the times we'd see each other most. And our mother. She loved to read the whole paper. And smoke her half a pack. And drink her Folgers coffee with almond-flavored creamer. And I think she liked seeing us before school, even though she never said anything like that.

"I'm about to head out to work," said Deena.

"But I thought we were gonna go down to . . . ya know." I nodded toward the living room. "Take her to Minneapolis."

"I'll be back at four," she said. "We can go then."

"Okay, I guess." I didn't have much choice.

"There's eggs and cheese in the fridge. Or we got Cheerios. I know you like that." Deena brought her dishes to the sink. "Plenty of chores to keep you busy while I'm gone." She began loading the dishwasher. "Rake the roof, for one. I haven't had a chance after that snow. The roof rake is in the shed. And you can take the dogs for a walk, if you like. But leave Baz. She has to go separately. And give 'em fresh water. You'll see the buckets. And if you still need something to do, you can fix the drip in the bathroom sink upstairs."

"Jesus," I said. "Anything else?"

"I think that's enough." Deena winked at me, got her coat on, and went out the back door. Like she didn't have a care in the world. Like she was enjoying this. She sat in her car for a couple minutes, warming it up, then drove away.

I was stuck here with the kid and Mrs. Z. And a shitload of work. I thought about taking the baby and heading down to the Cities by myself. Just take my chances. But I didn't want to be alone with the kid in the truck for three hours. It would be easier with Deena. And I had no fucking clue where or how to do this. So I'd have to wait till Deena got back. She had the upper hand. And she knew it.

When she got home, I was napping on the living room sofa. I'd done everything except the bathroom drip. I heard her come in and rustle with grocery bags. Chopping sounds. Hissing. Then something smelled good. She walked into the living room and laughed at me. I opened my eyes, and she threw a kitchen towel at my head.

"Hey," I said.

"You did good out there," she said. "I took a peek before I came in."

"Checking up on me?" I sat up and rubbed my face.

"You never know." She shrugged and went back into the kitchen. "Is Z at cribbage?"

"Yeah," I said, yawning. While I was outside working, Mrs. Z had been watching the baby. When I came back in, the kid was asleep in the dresser drawer, and Mrs. Z said she was going to the senior center. Said she'd be back for supper.

"You wanna help me with this?" Deena said.

"No." I walked into the kitchen. "But I'll eat one of these." I opened a package and grabbed a biscuit.

"Hey, that's for the chicken à la king," she said, chopping mushrooms.

"We should get going," I said, eating another one. "It's already four-thirty."

"After dinner," said Deena. "Let's eat, and then I'll get ready to go."

I sighed. Deena was always better at making plans. But I hated feeling this helpless.

The front door opened and Mrs. Z walked in. "Hello," she called out. "I've got cookies from the senior center."

The baby cried and Deena motioned for me to go get her. "Jesus," I said, but I went.

"Someone's hungry," said Mrs. Z, taking off her coat and watching me struggle with the baby.

"How was cribbage?" asked Deena. I brought the baby into the kitchen and Mrs. Z followed. Deena was taking the bottle out of the pan. The screams were loud.

"Here." I handed the kid to Mrs. Z, and she sat on a kitchen chair, waiting for Deena and the bottle. I couldn't take the noise. I busted out the back door. Nice cold air. I needed a smoke. I lit up and inhaled. Needed my brain to kick in. My nerves to calm. I watched the cloud of exhale in the dark. I used to make smoke rings for Cally, and she'd thought that was cool. Deena's dogs came over to check me out. I walked down the steps, closer to their fence. They started whimpering. Maybe they thought I'd harness them up and take them out for a sled.

"Hey, Baz, Trapper," I said. "Good boy, Pops. Hey, Nathan. Check it out." I made a few smoke rings for the dogs. They howled, so I made a few more.

I tried to think of everything I knew about that couple. His name was Hal. I remembered that because my buddy Eric's dad's name was Hal, and he was a dick. We used to call him "Hal the Pal, Douche Canal." But what was his last name? Johnson? Smith? It was something boring. He was a lawyer, but I didn't know anything more than that. And the wife? She worked for the newspaper downtown. Cally really liked that about her. Ruth something. Did she have the same last name as the lawyer? I wasn't sure. I couldn't think of it, anyway.

I walked back up the steps to the porch. Nice view over the back acres. Dark sky. I liked the sky at night. You could see more without all that sun. I remembered Cally had some papers in all her shit from the hospital. Was the guy's name and address on that? I didn't look at it that close. I stubbed out my cigarette and went back into the house. No one was in the kitchen. Dinner was set out buffet-style and half eaten. Dirty plates in the sink. They'd gone ahead without me. I loaded a clean plate and ate quickly. I was loading a second helping when it started.

"DEENA!" called Mrs. Z. "DENNIS!"

I went to the living room. Mrs. Z was sitting in the chair with the baby. The bottle was on the floor. "Find Deena!" she said.

"DEENA!" I called to the ceiling. "Is she in the shower?"

"I'm not sure."

I yelled up the stairs, "DEENA, MRS. Z NEEDS YOU."

"Dennis, look." Mrs. Z held the baby out for me to see.

"Why is she all stiff like that?" I said.

Mrs. Z shook her head. "Take her," she said.

"I don't wanna take her," I said. She looked greenish and had spit up all over herself.

"What's all the yelling?" Deena finally came down.

Mrs. Z waddled to the stairs. "Look, look," she said as she held the baby out for Deena to see.

"Something's wrong. She's green," I said.

"More like yellow," said Deena. "What did you do to her?"

"Nothing!" Mrs. Z fretted. "I was burping her, and she spit up, and when I was wiping her up, she arched her back and went stiff."

"Shit." Deena ran her hand through her hair.

Mrs. Z cried, "I don't think she's breathing, Deen."

"I'm calling 911," I said.

"No," Deena said. "We have to go now." She marched to the hallway, pulled on her coat, and grabbed her purse.

"To the hospital?" I said.

Mrs. Z took the blanket out of the dresser-drawer bed and wrapped it around the baby.

"Now, now, go." Deena waved me into the hallway. She put the baby in the car carrier as we hustled out the door and into the truck.

"Where am I going?" I pulled out the driveway, past the howling dogs.

"St. Mary's. I'll tell you the way," said Deena.

Forty-Five

CALLY

Evening

I woke up in a different room. It was dark outside. For a moment, I thought the bassinet would be nearby, and I sat up and scanned the room in a panic, as if I were still in Minneapolis and hadn't gone out the window yet. But I was alone, and I remembered about Vera and the ambulance. Where was Nell? Was she hungry? Was she okay? I sank back into the bed and tried to think.

Monitors beeped around me, and there was a bag of liquid on a pole, dripping something into my veins. I grabbed the call box and pressed the big red button. Rip. The curtain opened and a red-haired nurse walked in, rubbing her hands in sanitizer foam.

"I need to use the bathroom," I said. There wasn't one in my room.

"I can certainly help you with that," she said, fussing with the IV pole and organizing the tubes. She guided me out of bed and held on to my arm. "Just push this pole along with you, and we'll walk."

When we got to the hallway, the lights were bright. The building was shaped like a U, with lots of glass. I was drawn to the hall across from me, where I saw a slumpy gray figure shuffling along in a ratty hat. Digger? My heart jumped and I froze in place.

"Is that . . ." I pulled the pole with me as I strode toward the other hallway.

"No, no, no," said the nurse, chasing me. "This way." Another nurse blocked me and I had to stop.

"What's over there?" I said, peering, but I couldn't see him any-more. Maybe he'd gone into a room. Maybe it wasn't him.

"Come on," said the red-haired nurse, directing me along by my shoulders. "It's fine."

My legs were weak, and I felt one of my socks coming off. I stopped and looked down. "What are these socks?" I pulled the fuzzy lime-green thing back on.

"You like those?" she said. "Hospital-issue." She kept one hand on my back and focused on the bathroom door as we resumed walk-ing. "Here we are."

She waited and I went in. When I came out, I wanted to look for the slumpy person. Was it Digger? The nurse asked if I'd had more bleeding and I told her no. She seemed happy about that and we re-traced our steps, but there was no sign of the slumpy person. Inside my dark room, a woman was sitting in my guest chair. I gasped, because for a split second, I thought . . .

"Ruth?" I said, and the person stood up. Shorter than Ruth.

The nurse switched on the light.

"Sorry to scare you dear," said Vera.

"Oh my God." I sighed, and the nurse helped me into bed again.

"And Sam's here, too," said Vera. "I hope that's okay."

"Who?" I said.

"From the Blue Anchor. The kind soul who caught you."

"He's here?" I pulled up my covers and the nurse adjusted my tubes.

"He wanted to make sure you were okay. Very sweet," said Vera.

As if on cue, a tall, handsome guy walked into the room, and I instantly recognized him. "You're the bartender," I said.

"Guilty." He raised one hand and bowed his head briefly. "I'm

Sam." He had warm brown eyes and dimples. A nice build, definitely strong. Maybe a few years older than me.

"This young man knew to bring you here," said Vera.

"St. Mary's has the bigger ER," he said. "And I think it's better."

"Thank you so much," I said, suddenly self-conscious. My lips were dry, and I licked them.

"I was glad I could help," said Sam.

"But you didn't need to come." I looked around for a pitcher of water.

"How are you feeling?" Sam asked, helping me look, then pouring me a cup.

I took a sip. "I feel . . . good," I said, surprised at my own words.

"They probably gave you something to help with that," he said, smiling at me. His laugh was gentle, and there was a twinkle in his eye. I smiled back, wondering where that twinkle came from, or maybe I was imagining it.

"I'm just tired, that's all," I said, wondering what I looked like. I wished I could have fixed myself up a bit.

"I'm going to find the ladies' room. I'll be back," said Vera, moving toward the door. "Sam rode in the ambulance with you," she added before leaving.

"You did?" I asked. Wow, this guy was going above and beyond.

He nodded. "I'm training to be an EMT, so those guys know me."

"Oh," I said. Maybe that explained why he was so comfortable. "You'll be good at it."

"Thanks," he said, looking down. His hair was a rich brown, loose and wavy.

"Bartending probably helps, too. In dealing with all sorts of people," I said. "And situations."

"Yes, it does," he said, smiling and nodding. This guy smiled a lot. I liked it.

"I have something for you," he said while Vera was out of the room. "I thought you'd want this." He held a piece of torn paper with handwriting, numbers, an address. "The address you asked Bailey for," said Sam. "Remember? Before you fainted."

I looked at the numbers. "Deena Wilkins's house," I said, holding the paper to my chest. There was that smile again. I held the paper, thinking what to do next. This guy had helped me, and he seemed to like me, so maybe he could help me even more. "Hey," I said. "Can you take me there?" I tried to sit up and figure out the tubes that were plugged into my hand.

"Now? Tonight?" said Sam.

"Yeah, did Vera tell you about my ex taking my baby?"

"I don't think you can leave," said Sam, looking around.

Vera returned to the room. "Leave and go where?" she said.

"I need a ride to Deena Wilkins's house," I said.

Sam and Vera looked at each other as if they didn't understand the language I was speaking. As if they were trying to figure out which one of them would give me the bad news. Sam stood up and put on his coat.

"I'm afraid you can't leave, dear," said Vera, taking her time. "You're having surgery in the morning."

And yes, I remembered. Dr. Sheldon was concerned about the bleeding, maybe a clot. They were concerned about damage. She'd asked about the syringe insemination. She'd asked if they had done a pregnancy test first, and I'd said yes. Dr. Sheldon said they'd have to go in and see what they found. They wanted me to be prepared for the worst and hope for the best. They said they needed to act quickly.

"It'll be very early in the morning." Vera moved close to my bed and stroked my shoulder. "Is there someone we should call for you? A family member?"

"My parents are both gone," I said. In the background, Sam lowered his head, as if out of respect for the dead. I wanted to tell him, No, it's fine, my mom's not dead, she took off. And last I heard, she was a travel agent somewhere in California. And before that, she was a hotel manager in a small town in Montana. And before that, she worked the rental counter at a ski resort. Probably wore a cowboy hat, or maybe that was a photo I saw of her.

"I'm sorry to hear that," said Vera. "Are there any siblings?"

"Oh, I've probably got a few half siblings by now," I said. "But I don't know their names."

Sam shifted his weight and turned around to read a poster about giving the Heimlich maneuver.

"All right." Vera paused and tightened her mouth to think. She was not going to let me off the hook. "How about a roommate or a friend?"

I thought about Sarah from birth class. I had her number on an index card at my apartment. But what could she do? She had two kids and a life.

"No," I said. "I already signed a form giving the doctor permission to talk with you, if you don't mind."

"Oh," said Vera, eyebrows raised, then smiling. "I don't mind at all."

"Okay," I said, relieved.

Sam cleared his throat and moved to the door. "I should get going," he said. "I'll see you tomorrow."

"You will?"

"Yeah," he said, like that was a given. His EMT training, or maybe he wanted to see me.

Vera kept hold of the metal bar on the side of my bed. "Get some rest," she said, pulling the blankets up and tucking me in. "I'll be back in the morning after your procedure, when you're waking up." She patted my shoulder.

"Vera," I said quietly. Sam must have noticed we were having a private conversation, because he walked out the door and into the hallway.

Vera leaned in closer to hear me. "What is it?" she said.

"I think I saw Digger," I said. "Across the way on the other side of the hospital."

"Really?" Vera covered her mouth with one hand, and her eyes flashed to the side. The skin on her hand was wrinkled and spotty. "I don't think so, dear. You've had some pain medication."

"Will you look for him out there?"

"I'll do my best," she said. "Now try not to worry."

Then she did the most outrageous thing: she leaned down and kissed my forehead. Her lips were thin and wispy soft. I couldn't move because my hand was attached to tubes and needles and all of me was tucked underneath the blankets. She smelled like roses and cinnamon, but too much of it. The scent was so sweet, it stung.

Forty-Six

DIGGER

Night

Deena gave me directions to St. Mary's hospital. This was the one she'd taken her little boy to when he was sick. She told me to drive faster. I told her to watch for cops. She was in the backseat with the baby. The overhead light was on so she could see the kid's face. She was giving me updates, which I hadn't asked for.

"Still clenched up, same color," she said.

"Just watch for cops," I said, looking in the rearview. I was relieved Deena was helping me turn over the baby and get a reward. Hopefully five grand, or more if we could. Right now I just needed the thing to stay alive. "Is she breathing?" I asked.

"She must be, just barely."

I made a left and swerved wide. Deena grabbed the overhead strap and leaned over on the seat.

"Jesus, you could be an ambulance driver," she said.

"No, thanks," I said. "But it would be nice to have the road cleared out."

"We're almost there," she said, like a fucking kid on a car trip.

The only car trips our parents took us on were across the state border to buy fireworks every July. We used to beg them to take us to Wisconsin Dells. They said it was too far. So the summer after I got my license, I took a road trip out there with a couple of guys. The drive was only three hours. My parents were lazy.

I pulled up to the emergency room. Deena hopped out with the kid. I parked in the small lot on the side. The place was quiet. One guy holding an ice pack on his arm. Two other people holding a sleeping little kid.

"Can I help you?" The triage nurse stood up. When she saw the baby, she called to another person. That person had a stethoscope around her neck. Serious look on her face.

"How long has she been like this?" she asked.

"Fifteen or twenty minutes?" said Deena.

"Come with me." The nurse led us through the security door and into the examination rooms. She put us in a room with sliding-glass doors. The first nurse came in and handed me a clipboard with a form on it. Pen on a chain.

"The hell?" I took the clipboard.

"Just fill out as much as you can," she said, scrunching up her face. Like we were cheating.

"Thanks." I stared at the paper and fumbled with the chain. Papers and questions reminded me of everything I hated about school. Which was almost everything. From as far back as I could remember. Teachers telling me I had poor penmanship, calling it "chicken scratch" and "hieroglyphics." They urged me to practice at home. Like that was going to happen. They said bullshit like good penmanship was a key to success in life. Only once did I believe a teacher was worthy of me trying to write neatly: mechanical drawing. That was the one class I liked. That was the one teacher who knew how to teach. Making pencil drawings of buildings and machines, using rulers and straightedges. Measuring perfect angles. I got my highest grade in that class: a B-minus. The only problem was the need to print block letters. All caps, all the same size. Evenly spaced. But if I took it slow, I could do it. I loved the finished product, but it was hard.

"I don't know what to say here." I nudged Deena.

"For what?"

"Everything, address, when did symptoms start, pain level." I read the questions out loud. This whole thing was chapping my ass. "Medical history? I don't know her medical history." I tossed the clipboard.

"She doesn't have one yet, calm yourself." Deena handed the baby to me. She picked up the clipboard and filled out what she could. "There," she said. "It's as good as it's gonna get."

I gave Deena the baby and took the clipboard back out to the nurse at the front desk in the waiting area. The television on the wall was muted. I sat down and watched it with no sound, just closed-captioning. Commercials about car insurance, dog chow, and medications with horrible side effects. I wished I could snap my fingers and be back in my old life, watching television in my crappy apartment, with a beer in my hand and no responsibilities. I never should have taken that baby. I wasn't gonna get away with it. Every bone in my body suddenly wanted to run out the door, drive away, and never look back.

"Digger?" said a woman's voice.

"Huh?"

"Is there a Digger?" the voice called again. A nurse was standing at the security door.

"Yeah," I said.

"Can you come with me?" she said. "Your sister was asking for you."

"Okay."

Another family had entered the waiting room, and they had a wailing little kid and a mopey-looking older kid. More proof that being a dad would be a pain in the ass.

The nurse led me back to the room. The baby looked much better. She wasn't rigid anymore.

"Still yellow, but that's jaundice, and it'll go away," said Deena.

"What about the stiff back?" I said.

"It could have been an upset tummy. Maybe an allergy to formula," said the nurse. "I've given your sister another brand to try. But we'd like to take some blood tests in case there was a seizure or something else."

"Like what?"

"I'll let the doctor go over all of that with you," said the nurse. "But we recommend more frequent burping and holding the infant upright for longer periods of time, especially while feeding. I've shown your sister here how to do it." The nurse nodded toward Deena.

"Okay," I said.

"I'll leave you alone," said the nurse as she was going, then added, "The doctor will be in as soon as he can."

Deena sat on the bed, which filled practically the whole space. I sat on the stool. Where the nurse had been.

"Have you seen her ears?" Deena asked.

"Yeah I guess."

"Look." She peeled up the pink hat. "They're like yours. Little triangle ears."

I smirked and shook my head. "Ears are ears," I said, looking at the baby's. I could see what she meant. But I hated when Deena teased me about mine.

"Hi, everyone," said a man who walked in. He clicked a pen in his left hand and stuck out his right. "I'm Dr. Jefferson, how are we tonight?"

I looked at the floor as the doctor explained what he knew. The baby was dehydrated.

"And the yellow color is indicative of jaundice. Fairly common at this age," the doctor said. "What is she, about a week or a few days old?"

"Yeah," I said. I looked at my hands. The finger with no nail. I turned my hands up and down, the palm, the back. The scars and calluses. My stubby fingernails. It would be good to get back to work. But I had two months until the job in Florida.

The doctor was going on about crap. Using medical lingo. They were concerned about her getting enough to eat. They wanted to observe her, maybe give her fluids. He said they would run some tests. Get a sense of what was going on. Could be allergies. Could be more serious. He talked like a game-show host or some shit. Casual. Upbeat.

"How much longer will this take?" I asked.

"That's hard to say. Several hours, at least," said the doctor, taking off his glasses.

"But it's almost midnight."

The doctor explained our options. He could admit the baby for observation. In that scenario, we'd sleep in a hospital room. Or we could wait in the ER for the tests, which might take several hours.

"Is there a place to sleep in the ER?" asked Deena.

"No, unfortunately. And in the emergency room, we can't guarantee that you'll be our top priority," he said. "That will depend on who else happens to walk in those doors at any given moment."

"We understand," said Deena. She hated people explaining things she already knew.

"I'll leave you to it," said the doctor, and he was gone.

"What do you want to do?" asked Deena.

"If I'm gonna stay, I need a place to sleep," I said.

"So the room with the foldout bed."

I shrugged, like, Isn't it obvious?

"CODE BLUE, CODE BLUE, response team to Level One," said a loud voice. Over the speakers.

"Clear the way!" someone yelled.

A cluster of medics, nurses, and doctors wheeled a patient down the hallway. I watched him pass. Looked like a teenager. Looked unconscious. Serious shit. They were hustling and giving each other orders. Like something on TV.

Forty-Seven

RUTH

TUESDAY, DECEMBER 10, 2002

Very Early Morning

When I reached St. Mary's, having rushed over in a taxi, it occurred to me how many times I'd been in hospitals in the last five days. I'd become an expert. And now I was confident I could conquer this place, too. Here, in Duluth, in the wee hours of the morning. But since it was after midnight, the security desk was unstaffed and the front doors were locked. A sign instructed visitors to check in at the emergency room.

At the triage desk, I asked the room number for Jake Olson and explained that he was in a coma, so he might be in ICU. The triage clerk typed Jake's name into the computer and nodded, then asked, "Yes, and you are his mother?"

"Um, well," I stammered, "I'm his stepmother."

"Stepmother?"

"Yes, his father is my husband, who is on his way up here from Minneapolis, along with Jake's brother and his mom, and they asked me to come over and sit with him until they get here, which could be three hours or maybe two and a half. Can you tell me where to find him?"

"Uh." The clerk looked confused. "Sorry, are you a legal guardian?"

"No." I was taken aback.

"Gary?" he asked the next cubicle. Then to me, he said, "One moment, please."

I stood waiting while the clerk held whispered negotiations with Gary, whoever that was. This wasn't a new experience for me. When I'd taken the boys to their doctor or dentist appointments, or called to excuse them for being absent from school, I was always asked this question: Who do you think you are?

Soon Gary approached. "I'm sorry, ma'am, but because it's after visiting hours, we can't allow anyone into ICU who's not immediate family."

I glanced around to see how many people were witnessing this humiliation. Only three souls in the waiting area. "Even though the immediate family asked me to be here until they arrive?"

"Yes, I'm sorry, ma'am." Gary and the triage clerk stood next to each other, firm in their policy but both making sad faces to show how compassionate they were.

I turned around and left, waiting outside in the cold until the next available taxi driver noticed me and pulled up to the curb. In the cab, I was fighting the rising well in my chest, the familiar burn of exclusion, of not being enough, all of it taking over until I couldn't stop from crying, at first a whimper, then letting it fall out in sobs. The driver asked if I was okay, and I choked out an unconvincing "yes." He handed me a handkerchief, an old-fashioned gesture that I appreciated, and somehow his kindness made me weep a little bit more.

I returned to my dark motel room, dropped my purse and keys, and crawled into bed, in my clothes, with unbrushed teeth. I pulled up the covers and let the crying fade into my pillow, to sleep.

The telephone startled me awake. In my dark room, the loud ring was overkill, like a fire alarm, and it was Hal. They were at the hospital, and he sounded disappointed in me. I explained what had happened and Hal was apologetic, although it wasn't his fault. He said there wasn't any change in Jake's condition, but they were glad to be near him. I was glad, too, but I told Hal I'd like to get some sleep. The red glowing time was 3:44 a.m. The weight of fatigue was like flood-sized sandbags on my chest, arms and forehead, keeping me horizontal. I felt as helpless as Gulliver and gave in to it. All of a sudden I couldn't remember when I'd really slept or for how long. Before hanging up, I mumbled to Hal there was a key to my room waiting for him at the front desk.

When I awoke again, it was almost nine in the morning, and I was alone in my room. Hal must have spent the night at the hospital. I needed to get over there, too. Out of the shower, I noticed the message light: news from Raymond.

He had called to report that a legal messenger, a "process server," had arrived at the suburban home where Cally was staying. The messenger had delivered the legal papers for Cally by leaving them with the older woman who'd answered the door. So, the lawsuit had begun. This could lead to us getting a custody decree. This was big news and I was thrilled. Raymond said he would call if he had anything more and asked me to please do the same.

I stopped at the breakfast nook to see if anything caught my eye. The too-sweet smell of waffles cooking overpowered me, and I felt briefly nauseated, but it passed. The coffee was too terrible to drink, but I was still a bit groggy, so I took a half cup. Maybe a Styrofoam bowl of Froot Loops or Raisin Bran with two percent milk? I saw my cab pull up outside, so I grabbed a bagel, took a bite, and tucked the rest in my purse.

The taxi took me to St. Mary's, where I'd been last night, where Hal and Audrey sat with Jake, but now I was seeing the place in the light of day. Four stories tall, surrounded by parking lots, with an emergency room around back. I prayed there was a decent coffee shop inside.

"You can drop me at the main entrance," I said, wanting to avoid the triage desk or any of the staff from the ER. But the taxi driver had missed the turn for the main entrance and apologized profusely.

He explained he would turn around in the next parking lot, which happened to be for the ER. "Fine," I said, distracted by digging in my purse for my lipstick and finding the bagel.

When I looked up, I couldn't believe what I saw parked in the lot: a truck, the same make and model as the one in the video. "Can you pull over there, to the right?" I said.

"But we are going to the main entrance or no?"

"No, to the right, go toward that pickup truck there, see the reddish one?"

The driver crept closer, not sure what I was asking him to do.

But I saw the plate. The license number. This was it: Cally's getaway truck! The baby was here; they had to be inside. I jumped out of the taxi before he had a chance to stop. The driver yelled out his window, "Hey, you gotta pay me!"

I ran back frantically and leaned against the taxi, purse perched on the edge of his open window. Digging for my wallet. "Here, here you go." I stuffed a wad of cash into his face and turned back to the hospital.

Where was I? Which entrance was this? Oh, nuts, it was the ER. I burst into the waiting room and looked around for Cally and the baby. Not there. I ran back outside and down the sidewalk to the main entrance. Where are they, where are they? Why are they here? Why is my baby here? Where is my baby?

As I hurried along the miserable, snowy sidewalk, tears streaming down my face, I imagined getting inside and running past all the rooms, finding Jake in a coma with Hal and Audrey standing next to him, or locked in an embrace, telling me I wasn't wanted and that they were getting back together, then finding the baby but seeing that she was having open-heart surgery, or finding Cally and her friend Sarah nursing their babies together and laughing at me.

But I had to get my head back to reality. Focus.

Several nurses leaned out from their desks as they saw me roaming the halls. They got up and intercepted me. "Ma'am, can we help you, ma'am?"

I took a moment to gather my breath. "I'm looking for Hal Olson, he's my husband."

"Have you checked in?"

I shook my head, still trying to look into rooms.

"This way, ma'am." They pointed me down the hall and to the right, to the visitor check-in. "You can inquire about your patient there, okay, ma'am?"

"Thank you," I said, wondering, as I walked to the visitor desk and got in line, whether I wanted to see Hal first or go straight to Cally.

"Cally Scott?" said a woman's voice.

The woman ahead of me in line had asked for Cally. The clerk at the visitor desk said, "Just a moment." She typed into her computer while the woman ahead of me filled out a pink visitor badge.

"Cally Scott. Room 310," said the clerk, and the woman walked toward the elevator. The clerk turned to me. "Can I help you?"

"Um, actually," I said. "I'm gonna get some coffee first. I'll be right back." I walked away, trying to act calm. When I was out of sight of the clerk, I swerved back around to the elevator bank just in time to hop in with the woman who'd been asking for Cally. She pressed the button for the third floor.

She got off and I followed her. 322, 320, then 302, 304: this was like looking for hotel rooms. The numbers made no sense. Finally, we got to 310. I swooped past the other lady and charged into Room 310 with full adrenaline pumping. There she was: Cally. In the hospital bed.

She glanced up, and I saw her recognize me.

"Oh my God, Ruth," said Cally, looking pale. She seemed to be in shock.

"Where is she?" I demanded, walking closer to her bed.

"Whoa." A handsome young man stood up. I hadn't noticed him sitting there. He hustled around the bed and came to my side of the room. He put himself between me and Cally.

"Where's the baby, Cally? And what in the hell is going on here? Do you have any idea what you've done?"

"Hey, hey," said the man, holding his hands up like stop signs.

"Get away from me," I said.

He exited the room in a hurry.

"Cally, do you know this woman?" asked the older woman I'd followed on the elevator.

"Yes, Vera," said Cally.

"Oh, she knows me," I said to Vera. "She knows me all too well."

"Please lower your voice," said Vera.

"Where the fuck is my daughter, huh?" I said to Cally. "Answer me!"

"You're upsetting her," said Vera. "Please calm down."

"Tell me, Cally."

She didn't answer. Her mouth was open. She looked like she was choking. "I don't know," she stammered. "I . . . don't have her, Ruth, I'm sorry . . ." She cried, "I don't know where she is . . . I don't. . . ." She trailed off and leaned back. She looked like she might faint.

I stepped back from her bed. She looked so weak. There was a yellow stain on her face and a cup with a straw next to her pillow. Monitors and IVs. Her hair was slicked back. I wondered who those two people were. What had happened here?

"Are you all right?" I asked. Vera was at Cally's side, stroking her arm. The young man returned and joined Vera.

"CODE GRAY, CODE GRAY, Level Three," said a voice from the ceiling. Next thing I knew, a handful of men and women entered the room and escorted me out.

I cooperated. No one needed to get hurt. Nothing to get upset about. "What happened to her?" I asked the security people as they guided me down the hall.

"Here we go, ma'am." They shoveled me into the elevator.

As the doors closed, I saw an unknown woman walking by with a baby. Was that my baby? Was I crazy?

"This way, ma'am," my escorts said as the doors opened. They brought me down to the visitor desk on the first floor. We stopped while they had a chat with the clerk. She looked at me. Then other people looked at me. Like I was a criminal.

"I need to see my husband and our family, please."

"Ma'am, I'm going to ask you to have a seat over here." They pointed to the seating area just inside the sliding entry doors. Two henchmen accompanied me: one was tall and the other was short and burly. We sat down, and as outrageously as they were behaving, I sensed that it was in my best interests to play the game. I stayed as calm and polite as an usher in church.

Eventually, I said, "I'm fine now. And I want to apologize for my behavior back there. I was worked up, but I'm much better."

"That's good," said the short security guard. "But we're going to need you to stay away from the third floor for the rest of the day."

"I will. I will," I said, not necessarily meaning it. "But would it be possible—I mean, my son is in the ICU with my husband."

"Hang on. Stay right here."

The tall guard stayed to watch me while the smaller one went to the visitor desk and had another chat with the clerk.

When he returned he said, "Ma'am, we will escort you to the ICU for your visit. That's on the second floor. Come along."

As we walked past the visitor desk, everyone was watching us again, like we were the most interesting thing they'd ever seen. "I don't need a chaperone," I said.

They said nothing. In the elevator, the tall guard pressed 2.

"I was only upset about my friend, the sick woman on the third floor, Cally Scott. That's why they called you to take me away. I was simply worried about her." I paused to see if they were convinced. No reaction. "Do you know what happened to her?" I asked, but how would they know. They wouldn't tell me if they did.

"Here we go, ma'am." They accompanied me into the ICU, flashing badges to open doors and nodding at nurses like we were some kind of celebrity entourage. "We'll be waiting outside the door. Fifteen minutes. Any disturbance, and we will remove you from the premises," the short guard said. These were their terms.

I smiled politely and nodded. This was some grade-A baloney, but I wasn't letting on. "Hal," I said, so relieved to see him when I got in Jake's room. Hal practically ran to hold me, then leaned on me so heavily, I thought I'd crumple. What was this? He started to cry. "Oh, Hal, it's okay," I said, trying to hug him but also making sure he could balance on his own.

Audrey sat in the chair, and Caleb was on the floor in a swirl of jackets, hats, and backpack. Game Boy Advance in hand. Eyes on Game Boy Advance.

"Hi, guys," I said, with Hal still slumped on me. I kissed him and said, "I'm so sorry, honey."

Audrey flashed a smile, then a worried look.

"Any news?" I asked the group.

Finally, Hal stood up straight, wiped his face, and shook his head to reset himself. In this moment, I was grateful my security detail was out of sight.

"Nothing new," said Audrey.

"He's been stable," said Hal, blinking and inhaling deeply. "And we've been talking to him. Telling him we love him." Hal sounded like he was getting weepy again, and I patted his chest, trying my best to comfort him.

"I'm sure he hears you; he knows you're there," I said, and I believed it.

"Yeah." Hal seemed to believe it, too.

"Hal," I whispered, pulling his head down to hear me. "I need to tell you something."

"What?" he said in his normal voice, not whispering. He could see the urgency in my face, but I held back because it felt wrong to be too excited.

"Cally is here." I looked in his eyes, hoping he'd be happy, even in the midst of this room of sorrow.

"What?" he said too loudly.

Audrey looked at us, as if this were a germane matter that needed her attention. I realized I wouldn't be able to keep it a secret.

"Cally is here," I said to everyone. "In this hospital. I just saw her."

"Oh, wow," said Audrey with only the slightest interest.

"Why? What's . . . Is the baby okay?" asked Hal.

"The baby wasn't with her, and I couldn't get any answers." I thought about my escorts and wondered if they were eavesdropping. "So I need you to go and ask her."

Hal tilted his head and pulled it back as if both confused and suspicious.

"She's in Room 310," I said, nodding to the door.

Forty-Eight

CALLY

Morning

Waking up after surgery was like being underwater, how slow every-thing was, and how out of reach. A heaviness on my chest. I was asking my arms to move, but they wouldn't. Asking my lips to open.

Sam was there. Beside me. And light behind him. The window was a frame around him. A portrait. I may have been saying non-sense words. "It's okay," he said. "Just stay asleep."

I wanted to tell him so many things. I wanted to ask why he liked me. All I'd been to him so far was a girl in trouble, a mess. Noth-ing made sense. The other side of the room was dark, with a spot of light, then shadows. Beeps and dripping. My head was sand. Pulling thoughts from sand. I needed to wake up.

A woman walked in. Spoke loudly. Checked the bags of liquid hanging beside me. Took my finger in a pinching machine. Words and numbers. Cheerful questions. When she left, her shoes made loud scuffle sounds. Like sandpaper. I must have giggled.

"What's so funny, Cally?" asked Sam.

"Is that you?" I said. "You're nice."

"Thanks. I try."

"And easy on the eyes," I said. I felt drunk. Was I drunk?

"Very nice of you to say," he said. "You're not so bad yourself."

That made me smile. "Can we go home now?" I said.

"I don't think they'll let you. Gotta wake up a bit more."

"Come on, let's go." I tried to twist myself to get up.

Sam reached out to hold me down, rubbing my arms. His hands were warm. And strong.

"Okay," I mumbled, leaning back. The lights were dim in my room, and soon I fell asleep again and dreamed about me and Sam. We were holding hands and running through a busy intersection, trying to get to a concert, and we were late, and all the lights were red, and our legs were stuck to the concrete, like it was wet and hardening with us in it, and we had to get out of there, pulling and pulling.

When I woke up next, it was with a big inhale. A relief. My head was clearer, and my stomach hurt. I opened my eyes and Sam was there, asleep in the guest chair. I pressed the nurse button, but no one came for a long time. When a nurse did come, she was with the doctor.

Sam woke up when he heard the voices and footsteps. "I'll give you some privacy," he said, winking as he walked out the door.

"How's the pain?" asked Dr. Sheldon, poking my belly and sides.

"Worse when you poke me," I said.

Dr. Sheldon smiled patiently, then sat down to explain what was going on. She'd performed a procedure to seal the blood vessels and stop the bleeding. In a calm yet serious voice, she slowed down to explain this next part: a second placenta had been "present in the uterus" and had "failed to completely detach." This was the cause of the bleeding.

"A second placenta?" I wasn't sure I'd heard her correctly.

The doctor nodded, explaining the rare condition, called "superfetation." Apparently, I'd already been pregnant for about two weeks when my body released another egg. The pregnancy test must have been a false negative, she said, almost like she was apologizing. So when they inseminated me with Hal's sperm, two babies started to grow, each with its own placenta. "Very early into the pregnancies,

one of the fetuses died," she said gently, "and was expelled with minor bleeding, unnoticeable." But remnants of the placenta stayed attached, which caused the hemorrhaging.

I must have looked confused. The doctor paused to let it all sink
in. "We are trying to avoid a hysterectomy," she added.

"So . . . can I go home?"

"Afraid not," said Dr. Sheldon, standing up. "You're stuck with us
for another day, at least. You can go for a walk down the hall. Walking will help you recover faster."

I thought about walking all the way out the front door.

The nurse helped me pee and got me back into bed before Sam
returned, which was good timing. He offered to take me for a walk
later, when I was up to it.

Sam had been sitting by my side when Ruth barged in and yelled
at me. How'd she know I was here? I rubbed my stomach; something
about seeing her made my incision hurt. I was in shock, and I might
have passed out for a bit. Had she followed me?

I explained everything to Sam. And Vera. Vera had come in during
the chaos of Ruth. "That was her," I said, when things were calm.
"She's the intended mother. The one who hired me. To be her surrogate."

"Yes, dear, that was the sense we were getting." Vera seemed worried.

"I don't know how she found me," I said, squinting at the doorway. "Where'd she go?"

"The security people took her," said Vera. "She was making quite
a scene."

"And I hope those guards keep her away," said Sam. "You don't
need that kind of stress."

"But where'd they go?" I wanted to find her. I needed to tell her
about Digger and the cabin and Deena's address. Maybe she could
find Nell.

"I believe I heard her say ICU," said Sam.

"Where is that?" I said, sitting up and reaching for the IV pole on wheels. My head was light, but I felt a rush of adrenaline and purpose in my chest.

"Second floor, why?" said Sam, watching me prepare to get out of bed. Concerned.

"Where's that paper you gave me with the address?" I looked around my bed and found it under an extra pillow. I pulled the clip off my finger and unbuckled the monitor from my waist. I felt a flash of shyness as I stood in front of Sam. Under my hospital gown, I was naked, but I'd put on a second one, so I was covered. "I'll be back," I said.

"What? No," said Vera. She sat forward in her chair with a manila envelope in her lap and a concerned look on her face. "Sam, do something," she said, as if Sam could have stopped me, even if he'd wanted to.

Sam merely shrugged and stood up. He escorted me to the door. "Do you want me to come with you?" he said.

"No," I said, "stay here and tell them I went to the bathroom or something."

Sam nodded, and I took off alone, scuffling and wheeling my IV pole as quickly as I could. When I came to the nurses' station, I slowed down and tried to act like an innocent sick patient. As I turned the corner, I picked up the pace. My legs and stomach were weak, but I needed to find Ruth.

Finally, I reached the elevator, got in, and pressed 2.

Forty-Nine

RUTH

Morning

Hal was clearly torn. He wanted to stay with Jake. And Audrey. But I needed him to go see Cally. Now. And get answers. He didn't understand why I couldn't go do it myself. His brain was so full of Jake's situation that he didn't have enough space to comprehend that I'd been banned from the third floor.

"Something's wrong with Cally," I said. "She's had some kind of operation."

"Something's wrong with Jake, too," said Audrey.

"I wasn't talking to you, Audrey," I said.

"Ruth, come on, now," said Hal, moving closer to Audrey as if I might attack her. "I need to stay with Jake."

"Fine," I said. "I'll ask Raymond to do it."

"Cally's not gonna talk to him," said Hal. "Why can't you do it?"

"I told you. I'm not allowed on the third floor."

"Holy cow, Ruth," said Hal, as if all I did was make trouble.

"Excuse me, but I've been a bit stressed out," I said.

Nodding toward the hallway, Hal ushered me out of the room. "Let's go somewhere private," he said. We walked past the hoodlums outside Jake's room. They must have thought I'd be okay as long as

Hal was watching me, because they headed for the elevators without a word.

"In here." I pushed open the door to the stairwell. We scurried in and let the door close behind us. Hal turned to me and opened his arms; I moved inside the space he made, leaning my dried-teary face against his weary-solid chest, and he closed his long arms around me. This was our ritual for connection and comfort. This was how we reminded ourselves that we were on the same team. That we needed each other. For thirty seconds, we embraced, wordless on the cement landing in the hollow gray-and-white stairwell.

Hal pulled away. "Okay, what's going on?"

"Cally's here! Do you understand how crazy that is?"

"Yes, but what am I supposed to do about that?" Hal's voice echoed in the empty stairwell.

"Go talk to her. Find out where our baby is."

Hal made a face like he was thinking about it.

"Why not? What do *you* think we should do?" I said.

"Nothing right now," said Hal.

I exhaled, exasperated. "I don't understand you. I feel like I've been doing everything I can to get our daughter back. Unlike you."

"What's that supposed to mean?" Hal rubbed his forehead as if he'd come down with a sudden headache.

"You know what it means. You haven't been half as concerned as I have through this whole thing."

"I wrote the agreement, didn't I?"

"Oh, here we go again with the blasted contract."

"And I paid the money?"

"We paid the money together. Why aren't you more upset? It's like you don't want to find her."

"Of course I want to find her," said Hal.

"You don't act like it."

"How do you want me to act?"

"Like you care!" I said. "Please go talk to Cally."

"Look. I didn't ask for this. This was your deal."

"My deal?" I said, and my heart was breaking. "This is our child. Our daughter to raise together, Hal. Remember? You said I would be a spectacular mom, and you wanted to make a family with me." I was crying.

"I did say that. And I do." Hal tried to take my hands in his. I pushed them away. "But things have changed dramatically," he said. "Look around you."

"Jake? I know," I said. "But he's stable. He's being looked after."

"Ruth, he's my SON!" said Hal, his voice booming in the stairwell.

"And Elizabeth is your daughter," I said, not backing down.

Hal spun around, frustrated. He had a pained expression. "Not yet, she isn't," he said.

"Yes, she is," I said, certain as the sky is blue.

"No," he said. "We don't know that."

"We don't?" I said. "Well, then, what else do you call it when your sperm is used to fertilize an egg that grows into a real-live baby?"

"We don't know it was my sperm, okay?" said Hal, sounding defeated. Perhaps he was relieved to get this off his chest.

"Wait a minute, WHAT?" I said, and it felt like the world had stopped still. "What are you talking about? What in the hell are you talking about, Hal?"

Hal looked down. "I took out the provision where she couldn't have sex."

For a moment, the stairwell was so quiet, I felt I had superhuman hearing. The click of Hal's heel on the concrete floor, the swoosh of his hand as he swept back his coat, and the squeak of his fingers landing on his leather belt. He stood facing me with his hand on his waist, readying himself for what came next. His necktie seemed to rise to his chin as he inhaled, deep and long, but suddenly, I felt I had no oxygen in me.

"Why would you do that?" I said. "And when?"

"When she asked about the coffee clause, okay?" Hal spoke, and it was like we'd been stuck in slow motion, but now our regular timing had returned. "The main reason she called me was about the sex clause. She wanted that removed." His tone sounded like he thought it was reasonable and he'd had no choice.

"Oh my God," I said, looking away. My throat was tight and I felt a throbbing in my neck. I turned around and squinted as if that would help me understand. I pointed at Hal and asked, in as controlled a voice as I could, "What in the world . . . would make you think . . . that that was even a little bit . . . okay?"

Hal held up his hands as if in surrender. Then he used his most rational voice. "She promised she'd use birth control."

I snapped at him, "Why didn't you tell me?"

"I honestly don't know." Hal put his hand on his chin and covered his mouth. Maybe he was trying to keep something inside. "Obviously, I should have."

"I can't believe this." I paced around the stairwell, suddenly feeling nauseated.

"Yeah . . ." Hal rubbed the shadowy whiskers on his cheek as if he wished he could change the past.

"Sex?" I said. "But she didn't have a boyfriend."

"Well . . ." said Hal sheepishly.

"She did?"

"They were on and off, as I understood it," said Hal, sighing and crossing his arms.

"How in the world do you know that?"

"She told me," he said. "But I didn't want to worry you."

"Worry me?" It was as if the words didn't have meaning. "So this baby might not be yours? Might be some random guy's?"

"Might be," said Hal. "But it's probably mine."

"I cannot believe this." I was furious. What were the odds that Cally had used birth control? What were the odds that the birth control had failed? I thought about how I had required my lovers to use condoms. I'd been certain that I could control it, that I'd decide when to get pregnant, but it didn't work out that way.

"I'm sorry," said Hal. "But you understand: if she won't sign over parental rights, the baby's hers, whoever the father is. And we'll have very few options."

"We don't have to take it if it's not your child, do we? Because I sure as crap don't want some other guy's baby," I said.

"I realize."

"But if it is yours, Hal . . ." I said, but I couldn't go on.

"I can assert paternity, and I'm already scheduled for the blood test. We'll find out for sure whether it's mine."

"Yeah, but how long will that take?" Everything about this process had been out of our control, subject to the whims and rules of others, the system.

"Couple of weeks to get the court to order testing on the baby. Once we know it's mine, we can try for full custody, but that's unlikely. At best, we'd have joint custody or some visitation rights, and that is by no means guaranteed."

"So you've talked with Sol about this," I said. Another secret conversation.

"A bit."

"Did you tell him about the sex clause?"

Hal nodded.

"So I'm the last to know." We stood in silence, the tension amplified by the emptiness of the stairwell. Suddenly, I needed to get away from Hal. I yanked open the stairwell door and marched into the hallway. Hal followed me. I stopped when I saw my brother leaning against the wall. "Raymond!" I said, so happy at the sight of his face.

"What are you doing here?" Hal was taken aback when he saw Raymond.

"Looks like it's the place to be," said my brother.

"Did you hear what we were saying in there?" asked Hal.

"Pretty hard not to," said Raymond.

"You'll excuse me." Hal walked away, waving his hand in dismissal, like he needed to be alone. I remembered again the night we first met, when Hal had waved his wineglass up in the air as he left, as if toasting me, and how different this felt.

"Your lawsuit was served on Cally," said Raymond. "For breach of contract. Sol confirmed it."

"Holy crap, that was fast," I said.

"What's with him?" Raymond nodded toward Hal's shrinking outline.

"Oh, he can't deal with this. He needs to be with Jake."

"How's Jake doing?"

"The same."

"Well, Sol says you should have your emergency court order within the hour."

"That's amazing." I grabbed Raymond and pulled him with me. "We have to go down to the parking lot."

"Okay," said Raymond as we hustled to the elevator. "What now, boss?"

"We have to find this truck," I said, pushing the button. "And follow it."

The elevator doors opened, and at first I thought it was a ghost: Cally, out of breath, holding an IV pole and leaning against the open doors, wearing a pale mint hospital gown and socks.

"Ruth!" she said. "I was . . . looking for you. . . . Please, I need you . . ."

"Cally, my God! Are you all right? What's going on?" I asked.

Cally's face was flushed and sweaty. Her lips were dry and her dark hair hung in her face, wild. She looked desperate, like a crazy person in a B-movie: the feverish patient roaming the halls, a menace.

"Here," she said, handing me a piece of paper, head down, weak and wheezing. "I don't know where she is . . . but she might be at this address . . . Hurry."

I stood there, mouth gaping, holding the scrap of paper. As the doors started to close, Raymond and I pushed them open, got in the elevator with Cally, and pressed 1. On the ride down, Cally leaned against the wall to rest. She looked smaller and soft, not so crazy anymore. I wondered what she'd been through and what the heck was going on with her body. The three of us rode quietly, not knowing where to start. I examined the scrap of paper. "Whose house is this?" I asked.

"Digger's . . . sister, Deena," she said.

"Digger, your ex-boyfriend?" I said, wondering if he was the one Cally had wanted to have sex with, and the elevator doors opened.

"Yeah." She nodded and breathed heavily as she exited with us, forcing herself to take a few steps forward, like a runner after a marathon. We three stood outside the elevator on the first floor. We were all in a kind of haze. Cally said, "He took the baby, Ruth . . . and I've been . . . trying to find them . . . I thought I saw him here." She pointed to the ceiling and gestured to the general surroundings.

"Here? Yes, he is!" I said. "I saw his truck. In the parking lot."

Raymond and I took hold of Cally and helped her waddle into the lobby. "Let's get you to a chair," said Raymond.

"No," she said. "Where'd you see . . . the truck? Is it still here?"

"Out there." I pointed at the tall glass-pane windows toward the parking lot, where the truck had been. I scanned for it. "Second row . . ." I looked, but the spot was empty. "It's gone!" I said.

"Hurry," said Cally, feebly pushing me and the piece of paper toward the door. "Go to Deena's . . . Please!"

"Miss? Miss?" A nurse approached to retrieve Cally, who was clearly out of place and struggling, and I waved goodbye and headed to the parking lot with Raymond.

Fifty

DIGGER

Late Morning

Finally, the doctor said we could leave. Nothing wrong with the baby. I'd slept on the foldout chairbed. Horrible. Not comfortable at all. Deena had a sofa in the lounge. In the morning, she made some calls. Deena had a friend who worked at the courthouse in Duluth. She would see what she could find in their computer system. Trying to find out how to get ahold of the sperm lawyer and the Ruth woman. Get their last names and numbers.

Deena said she'd come with me to the Cities. Help me with the kid on the drive down. Then we'd bring her to the parents, if we could. Or, if we had to, we'd go to the media. Get some attention. But first we needed to swing by Deena's place and get some clothes and shit, pick up some lunch, the baby supplies, and other crap. We'd left the house so fast the night before, we hadn't grabbed anything.

We took the kid out to the parking lot. The temperature had dipped below zero, and I had some trouble starting the truck. I blasted the heat. Just cold air, but I left it on. And I fiddled with the radio while Deena loaded the baby in the backseat. Finally, she plopped down in the front next to me. "Okay." She tugged on her seat belt.

I yanked the gear into drive and sped the hell out of there. Someone honked, and I slammed on the brakes. A voice yelled, "Idiot! Learn to drive!" I swore at the asshole and laid on the horn.

"Stop it." Deena turned around to see if the baby was okay. I looked in the rearview mirror. On cue, the baby started to fuss, then broke into a full cry.

"Goddammit!" I said. I was thinking Cally would have been able to make the kid be quiet.

But Deena sat staring straight ahead. The wailing continued, and Deena leaned her head back and closed her eyes, clearly willing herself to be calm. Or disappear. At a stoplight, I turned around. The baby's mouth was open and red. No teeth, just gums. The thing was choking and screaming. It was driving me nuts.

"Do something," I said.

"Do you have a pacifier back there?" said Deena, fishing around. "Pull over."

"What, no," I said, annoyed, but the crying was too much. I pulled over and lit up a cigarette.

Deena hopped into the back and got the kid to quiet down. "Okay, you can go."

The rest of the drive was fine. When I turned down Deena's driveway, the dogs ran to the fence. Like they always did. We decided we could leave the kid in there for a couple minutes while we went inside. I had to take a piss, and Deena only needed to grab a couple things. Wouldn't take more than five.

As we walked past the dogs, we heard a car, so we stopped and turned around. "Who's that?" she said.

A silver sedan made its way down the driveway.

"Hell if I know," I said.

The car stopped in front of us. A white-haired man got out and then a dark-haired woman. "Is that your truck there?" asked the white-haired man.

"Yeah, so what?"

"So you're Digger," said the woman.

"Who wants to know?"

"Where's the baby, huh?" she said, walking past me and over to the truck.

I pushed the lock button on my key fob. Click! When she tried to pull open the door, it was locked. "Don't touch my truck, please."

The woman pressed her forehead against the tinted window and cried, "Raymond, she's there!"

"Can I help you with something?" said Deena, walking closer. "Or do I need to call the cops?"

"By all means, please. Call the police," said the woman. "My name is Ruth Olson, and that baby in your truck is my daughter."

"Oh, Olson," I said to myself. Hal Olson, that was the sperm's name.

"Yes, so I would appreciate it if you would unlock that door," said Ruth.

"As I understand it," said Deena, "you are not the mother of that child. Yet."

Ruth exhaled, and we saw the cloud of her breath in the cold air. Like a mean-ass dragon. They stared at each other. For a second, I hoped she and Deena might start swinging.

"What do you mean by that?" said Ruth.

"I believe you owe some money to your surrogate, isn't that right, Digger? Or do I have that wrong?" said Deena.

"Yeah, that's right," I said. "Cally needs the rest of that money."

"And you are hoping to collect Cally's money for her, is that what you're saying?" said Ruth.

"I'm sure we can work something out," I said, like a smooth operator.

"Are you threatening me?" said Ruth, like she couldn't believe she had to deal with us. Like we were chumps. She looked at the white-haired man as if he'd be interested in this.

"No, we're trying to help you," said Deena. "Without the cops or anybody else getting in the way."

"Very civilized," I added, showing her I wasn't a total idiot. Couldn't she see this was a better deal?

Mrs. Z was peering at us from inside the house. Nosy, as usual. Then we all turned to look at the driveway when we heard the noise. The crack of car tires on cold snow.

"Who the fuck is that?" I said.

"That would be the police," said the white-haired guy. "With your court order, Ruth."

We stood there as a black van pulled up, followed by a dark blue car. We watched them slow down, park, and get out. "Dennis Wilkins?" said one of them, walking toward me and holding up his ID.

All I could think about was how much I hated cops. "What can I help you with, sir?" I said.

"This your vehicle?" said the cop. "Mind if we take a look inside?"

"Matter of fact, I do," I said. I stared at the white-haired guy. He must have had something to do with this.

"All right," said the main cop. "Wendy, can you bring me the order?"

I heard buzzing and squawks, voices jabbering from the police radio. One of the cops had left the door open. The dogs barked and howled. "Shut up!" I yelled.

There were four officers: one female and three male. In the frigid driveway, all of them showed us their IDs. All of them acted like this was a big federal case. Two cops and two caseworkers from the Department of Social Services. They had a court order and a search warrant. They gave me a copy of the papers, which I stuffed in my pocket. They took my driver's license and ran a check on it. They asked for Deena's ID, and she said yes, this was her property, and they said they were here to take custody of the "infant child" who was "believed to be in this vehicle and/or residing at this location."

The cops ordered me to unlock the truck, then opened the door and unbuckled the kid. They lifted her out of the car seat, and she woke up, wailing and squirming. Ruth followed every step they took, standing a foot behind them. Asking, "Can I hold her, is she okay, where are you taking her?"

The female caseworker carried the kid to the van. Loaded her in and closed the door. She got in with the baby and closed the door, and we couldn't see anything. All that tinted glass.

The male caseworker asked where we'd been, what'd been done to the child, and whether we'd given her any medications. Deena gave them the papers from the hospital. Then I went in the house and grabbed all the kid's supplies. Brought those out and handed them over.

The cops told us what was going on. Ruth was upset and leaning on the white-haired man. He was watching and listening to the officers.

"The infant will be placed into protective care, most likely with a foster family, for a forty-eight-hour hold, and after that, all interested parties will have the opportunity to appear in court and make claims or assert any rights they have or provide any further information to the court." The officer handed me and Ruth each a business card with a phone number circled on it. "Any questions, call that number," he said.

The officers got in their vehicles and went down the driveway. The dogs barked. The rest of us stood there like statues. Watching until the cars turned onto the main road and were gone.

Fifty-One

CALLY

TUESDAY, DECEMBER 10, 2002

Afternoon

After I found Ruth and sent her to Deena's, a nurse guided me from the lobby back onto the elevator and up to my room. After she left, I felt an enormous wave of relief and hope. Vera helped me into bed, and Sam attached the pulse clip to my finger. I liked the feel of his hand touching mine. While I was gone, he said, he'd made small talk with the nurse, letting her believe I was down the hall on a walk. I was sure his charm hadn't hurt, either.

Sam gave me a few sips of water. "Shouldn't take risks like that," he said.

"I had to," I said, smiling because I'd passed on Deena's address to Ruth, like it was a relay baton. Hopefully, Ruth would carry the next leg. If she could find Digger, she'd find the baby. I thought she might be able to stop him from doing whatever he was gonna do. Maybe convince him to give her the baby. He wouldn't have listened to me. I prayed Nell was okay. She had to be okay.

"Well, I'm sorry to be the bearer of bad news, dear," said Vera, explaining that while she'd been home, a man, whom she'd described as an "unpleasant goon," had rung her doorbell. And when she opened the door, apparently, he'd shoved a thick manila envelope into her hands. It was addressed to me. "He snarled at me," said Vera, imitating his deep voice, "'Tell Caroline Ruby Scott she's been served,' and he walked away."

I opened the envelope and it was legal papers. I'd seen things like that on TV; I was being sued by Hal and Ruth. The top of the first page said:

SUMMONS AND COMPLAINT

State of Minnesota
In Re: Baby Girl Olson

Harold Olson and Ruth Olson v. Caroline Ruby Scott

I skimmed the first few pages. Breach of contract. Child endangerment. They wanted their money back. "What am I gonna do?" I said.

"Call your lawyer," said Sam.

Vera took the lawsuit papers away. "All in due time," she said. "Don't fret about it, just focus on resting." She stashed the papers in her purse, but they were hard to forget about.

Sam suggested I try eating some of the food on the tray that the lunch guy had delivered. I took a few bites of cottage cheese and green Jell-O. Drank a few sips of milk. Vera asked Sam to tell us some stories, trying to change the subject and lighten the mood. "What should I tell you?" he said.

"Tell us about being a bartender," said Vera. "You must see a lot of different things."

Sam smiled slyly and nodded. He must have had tons to choose from. He started with funny things said by customers, pickup lines. The code language for drink orders. Pranks on the manager. Soon I was feeling stronger and clearheaded. Sam took me and my IV pole for a walk down the hallway. He told me not to leave the hospital before they discharged me. He had medical knowledge. And he seemed to care.

Back in my room, I called my voicemail. Legal Aid had found a lawyer for me who would work for free. Nothing from the police department. I called the volunteer lawyer back. I told him everything. I gave him Deena's address. I told him about the double pregnancy. And the chance that the baby was Digger's. About the need for a court order and a birth certificate. About the surrogacy agreement and what I had done. And I told him about the lawsuit.

He said he would try to get the court order, but it might take a day. He would try a local lawyer here in Duluth who could get it faster. He said we'd need to do DNA testing to prove I was the mother, and the test would also show who was or wasn't the father. I wasn't sure I wanted to know that, but of course it had to happen. But first the police and Social Services would have to find the baby and take custody of her. And I was pretty sure they were at Deena's.

While I was on the phone, Sam got up and said he had to go to work. "Hang on," I said. "Can you go to Deena's and see what's happening?"

Sam nodded as he swung his coat on. "I was already planning on it."

I got a warm feeling inside.

"I'll go check it out," he said. "And I'll see you later."

I looked at Vera, and she was beaming, as if she and Sam had silently passed some batons of their own. I finished my call with the lawyer, leaned back, and exhaled. This was my team, and Nell was my child. I knew it, and they knew it. I'd follow my lawyer's advice and my doctor's orders, and I'd get my body as healthy as it could be, so I'd have the best chance possible to be Nell's mom.

PART THREE

Fifty-Two

RUTH

/

FEBRUARY 2003

The next time I saw our daughter, she was not as I remembered. She was different and so was I. Worlds had passed between us, or maybe I saw her through different eyes. She was two months older and so much bigger. She seemed to have traveled to a place I'd never know and she'd never tell me about. Maybe I saw her through Hal's eyes, with all that he'd been through, but she was further away even than that. Maybe I saw her through Cally's eyes, the eyes of a parent, after watching Hal flounder in his helplessness. Jake had come out of the coma, but he'd lost the use of his legs. It was devastating. It would take years for him and us to adjust to the new reality. And maybe I'd suffered my own form of paralysis. Maybe my spirit was simply too weak to hold Elizabeth now, too weak to lift her up and take her away from there.

Hal and I were at the social services office. In Duluth. The lawyers had us meet there as a neutral place. Little Elizabeth was in a crib, wrapped up tight and alone. Neither of us was bold enough to touch her in front of the caseworkers. We were being observed. I feared I'd make her cry. I wanted so badly to pick her up and hold her close. This was what I'd been waiting for, but I stood stiff, in shock.

Like rushing to an old boyfriend, then stopping short, seeing him married to someone else.

I remembered our baby being smaller, redder, more wrinkled. The last time I'd seen her, she'd been brand-new. She'd been a creature wholly dependent on us, wholly vulnerable. Her alien eyes had been closed, straining to open. Nothing was to scale. The head and big tummy but miniature bottom, slight shoulders. Petite limbs tucked in, creased skin. That first day, I'd stretched out her bent arms like little bat wings. I'd unfolded her accordion legs, and when I'd let go, they'd folded back into her body, mechanically, as if some part of her knew she might return to the womb.

Who was she, then, when she was mine? It seemed absurd that so much could have changed. That this particular coldness had descended. Perhaps I'd missed some window. I'd had my chance to be her mother, and who was I now? All I had to do was pick her up. Was that it? Was that how it would be?

I looked at Hal, but he wasn't there. He'd taken a detour. He was in his own mind, his list of what-ifs, and he was dwelling on versions of failure. He was dark and gray. Nothing took front seat to the tragedy with Jake's legs. Not this baby, not me, not anyone. Maybe he didn't want her anymore. Maybe he never had. Had he done it all for me? Or did he have a sense, even then, that she wasn't really ours, was never meant to be our child? Maybe he'd come back and claim her someday in the future, and we'd become who we planned to be. But for now, and for weeks, he had been elsewhere, and I was alone. With her.

Raymond had gone back to California to be with Mom, and I'd already booked my flight to visit them. Before he left Minnesota, I'd thanked Raymond so many times and so profusely that he couldn't stand it anymore. He finally asked me to stop thanking him and instead come visit. He was right. I planned to see them both on a regular basis. I couldn't have asked for a better brother, and I promised I'd be there for him in the way he'd been here for me.

Hal and I had been awarded temporary custody of Elizabeth, as the paternity test had shown that Hal was the biological father. But the arrangement was only tentative, pending the court's determination of the "best interests of the child." This irritated Hal, when he spent the emotional energy to pay attention to it. He was irked not only because we had a clear contract that should have ended the inquiry, in his opinion, but also because, in his view, the best interests of the child were clearly served by her living with us. Where, he said, she'd have a stable home, two parents, and abundant resources.

The court was also considering our breach-of-contract lawsuit. Legally, we couldn't force Cally to sign over parental rights, but if the judge found in our favor, we could require her to pay back the money she'd received (other than medical expenses), plus pay for our legal costs. Motions had been filed on both sides. Cally had a lawyer from Legal Aid, the organization responsible for my meeting Hal in the first place. I'm sure the irony wasn't lost on Hal. Certainly it wasn't on me.

I'd hoped that when Hal saw the baby, she would heal him, even if only in small places. That he'd melt with new love and forget his grief for a moment. But he didn't want to look at her, and why? Because he was afraid she'd grow up and lose the use of her legs, too? Because she reminded him of Jake when he was still full of potential? Or perhaps Hal knew, on some level, he wasn't able to be a father to her. He wasn't talking. I was only guessing at what was going on inside. Even when we brought her home, Hal was distracted, absentminded. I was afraid he might drop her inadvertently, or scare her with one of his rants about God and the meaninglessness of life. Some days his eyes went wide and he'd say she looked just like Jake, but other days he railed because he couldn't see the resemblance.

Meanwhile, when I held our daughter, she cried. It seemed nothing I did could console her. No matter how much I tried, it felt like I was getting it wrong. It was disheartening, to say the least. The crying wore me down in every way. And I was tired all the time, which didn't help, and then I'd get suddenly sad or irritated when I looked at her. I'd fall asleep in the living room with her on my chest, even if she was crying. I'd be too lethargic to move.

When she woke up five or six times a night, I'd try to wake Hal and ask him to help, but often he didn't want to. Especially on days when he had something big at work. And when he did get up, he'd hold her like a zombie, half asleep while bouncing, and I was afraid she'd roll out of his arms and he wouldn't even notice. He didn't like when I adjusted his arms or asked him to keep an eye on her. He reminded me he'd done it all before and knew the drill. These things hurt my feelings, and he got gruffer and more bristly with me until I finally decided I'd rather handle it myself. I'd change her. I'd do the feedings.

During diaper changes, she'd go stiff, stick her arms out, and turn red. Then she'd scream in pain. The doctors said it was a normal reflex, a primitive instinct like a reaction to falling or losing balance. It was triggered by being startled or sudden stimulation, they said. They showed me techniques to calm her and said it would go away in time.

After her bottle, she'd spit up, multiple times a day. I had her tested for reflux, but the doctors explained that reflux was normal for healthy babies as long as there were no gastroesophageal concerns that needed treatment. They didn't find any. Although she wasn't gaining as much weight as we might have liked, she was gaining enough that the doctors weren't alarmed. They told me I shouldn't be, either.

I'd walk around the condo with her, and bounce and sing to her, but she'd arch her back, hold her breath, and turn blue. Afterward, she'd cry as if in pain. I became terrified to touch her, convinced she was holding her breath on purpose. To punish me? I read books for advice but was afraid or ashamed to ask my friends. I'd never heard of anything like this before. The doctor said it was normal for babies to stop breathing, something called "periodic breathing," and that most babies achieve regular breathing after the age of four or five months. What about turning blue? As long as it was only for a minute or so, it was normal for her age, they said. The medical community called it "apparent life-threatening event," or ALTE, which was not a diagnosis but a catchall label for a series of symptoms. And the label was not at all comforting.

But after bringing her in again and again, with the tests never finding any problems, I became discouraged, depressed. It seemed I was in a constant state of being sick. Was she making me sick? At the doctors' suggestion, we tried every kind of formula and even started her on some solids. Nothing helped. We tried holding her differently and for different periods of time. We changed the sheets and blankets and clothes to different fabrics. We had our home desensitized. Gave her different baths, exposed her to sounds. Increased humidity, smaller spaces. Nothing helped. I was afraid one day she'd die. I feared I was going to kill my child, kill her by not being the right kind of mother. I didn't know what to do.

And I thought about Cally. What were her days like? Her nights across town? Did she get up with me in the wee hours, woken by the cries of a ghost baby miles away; did she roam the halls too? Somehow I believed she knew what was happening in the darkness of our home, and our narrow hallways and creaky floors where I paced with the stiff infant, listening for our baby's breath, praying for her to sleep. In the black moonlit nights, as I turned each corner, I half expected to find Cally standing in the next room, her arms extended, ready to take back her baby. Ready to be her mother.

But night after night, she wasn't there. Just me and the moonlight, the crying and the going stiff, with Hal sleeping soundly. And me, needing to.

Fifty-Three

CALLY

I thought about Nell every day. Three months without her had been like hell. Sam had driven me back to Minneapolis, and I was alone in my apartment. I'd been ordered to take it easy and not risk my recovery. I was fully healed from the surgery and the postpartum hemorrhaging, but I went in for checkups with my new gynecologist, a woman I really liked. She wanted me to pump and express milk so my uterus would continue to contract and heal. She told me she was cautiously optimistic that someday I would be able to carry another child to term.

But even if I could have another child someday, it wouldn't be Nell. Longing for her, missing her, the hurt was excruciating. My lawyer was working every angle to get the custody hearing moved up. He said I wouldn't get my final payment, and I might have to pay some back. I couldn't think about that. I'd registered for a full load of classes in the fall and a couple courses over the summer. Focusing on college was the only way I could keep from going crazy.

But I thought about Nell all the time. And what I'd done wrong. The judge said I'd put the baby in danger, and he gave temporary custody to Hal and Ruth. And somehow it was my fault that Digger had taken her from the cabin. My lawyer argued my side of the story but lost. Our only hope was in the final custody hearing.

My plan was to show the judge how stable I'd become. Returning to school. Getting a part-time job as a secretary for a CPA. Doing research on my future accounting career. And a social worker came to check out my apartment and ask me parenting questions. Hopefully, the judge would see that I'd be a loving and good mom, able to care for a baby by myself.

My lawyer wanted me to bring a counter-lawsuit against Hal and Ruth because of the physical damage to my body. And the emotional pain. He was using it as a negotiation strategy. He said I should protect my rights and expand my options. My counter-lawsuit would give me bargaining power, he said. I wasn't used to having any kind of power, and I was starting to like it.

Digger was out of my life for good. I was pissed at him, but I was sure he was happy in Florida. He and Deena both signed a paper saying they promised to leave me alone and not come after me for money. And I agreed not to press charges. But I realized I couldn't hold a grudge against Digger; we'd been friends for so long. And I'd been the one who asked him to get into this whole thing in the first place. I was surprised by my sadness when I found out that one of the fetuses, the one who died, was actually Digger's. We'd never get married and have a kid together. And that was a loss, in some strange, unrealistic way, the way my younger self would have thought about it. I felt like I had aged ten years in three months.

Sarah and I spent a lot of time together, and she was a good friend to me. She'd had a baby boy and named him Lucas. They came to see me every Tuesday, just like our birth class, but in the mornings. Sarah put her baby boy in my lap and let me hold him, but he was so different from Nell. He smelled different. He had no hair. He didn't make eye contact with me like Nell did, not that deep stare. I didn't even think he could see me. I always believed that Nell could recognize me when I held her. We'd gaze into each other's eyes, and I felt

I knew her in a way I'd never known anyone else. But not this baby. He wasn't mine.

Sarah seemed happy but exhausted. She complained about everything: It's so hard, so much work. She whined about all the feedings, the bathing, the diapers. She talked about every baby noise, every rash. Was he getting enough to eat? She showed me how she clipped his paper-thin fingernails and explained the belly-button thing. She was careful about keeping everything clean. And was the stool the right color? I wondered how I would have coped with all that stress. I hoped Ruth didn't worry too much. I didn't think all that worrying was good for Lucas or Nell or any baby, but what did I know.

Sam and I talked almost every night. I was trying to convince him to move to Minneapolis, but he thought I should move to Superior. I said I didn't think there were enough job opportunities up there for me. And it had bad memories. I thought he'd really like Minneapolis. He could be a bartender down here, and also an EMT. He said he was thinking about it. Meanwhile, we'd see each other in person at least once a month. I kept in touch with Vera, too. She and Stan visited me when they visited their other relatives in the city.

One day, the doorbell rang and I thought it might be Vera, coming to surprise me. And I was surprised, but it wasn't Vera.

It was Ruth.

She was holding Nell.

Fifty-Four

RUTH

On that day, I packed up the essentials in a large tote bag: diapers and wipes, formula, bottles, several changes of clothes, a few books and toys, a teething ring for later, and the medical kit. My heart was pounding as I loaded all her stuff into the car, and I shook as I carried her out the door. Hal had gone to work, and Elizabeth had just woken from her morning nap. I buckled her into the car seat and glanced around the neighborhood. Someone should be watching this. My neighbors across the street who shoveled their driveway meticulously. They must have seen the pink sign and pink balloon in our yard announcing our daughter's arrival, and surely they'd noticed that it took us two months to actually bring her home. Maybe they'd guessed it was surrogacy or adoption, and maybe they judged me for it. Had they seen us, our lamps on, in the middle of the night and in the early morning, pacing and bouncing and failing to soothe her? And could they have known how hard this was? In that moment, I didn't care what they thought. I was doing what my instincts told me. For Elizabeth.

I got in the driver's seat and buckled up. As I started the car, I paused. In the rearview mirror, Elizabeth stared into space in utter innocence, unaware of what I was feeling or where we were going.

Suddenly, she spit up on the cotton blanket I'd draped over her chest. I put the car in gear, tears streaming down my face. "Here we go." I looked at her in the mirror. She scrunched her nose and shook her head, unhappy and unpleasant. She didn't look well. "We didn't ask you, did we?" I said. "We didn't ask what you wanted."

I'd started a story. In my head. A story about surrogates. And the babies they carry. About the ways in which it is different from adoption. And I'd made lists of places to start my research, interviews I'd want to take with the women and doctors, ethicists, psychologists. Maybe Professor Judith could help me with the economic inequities angle. When I got back to work.

And I wondered about the medical risks to surrogates. Cally had suffered postpartum hemorrhaging and had to undergo surgery, but I hadn't thought about that as a possible risk before we signed the contract. Had she? And I hadn't thought about the intended parents' liability for harm to their surrogates. I planned to research the medical risk issues for my article. And I was curious to see how Hal's contract addressed it. I looked for a clause that said either we were or weren't legally responsible for medical risks or any damage to her health. I didn't find any, but I wanted to be sure. On a cold day the prior week, I dialed Hal's office and Pat answered.

"I'm sorry, but Hal's in a mediation. Can I help you with something?"

"As a matter of fact, yes," I said, thinking this was a perfect opportunity to get an objective answer. "You have the most recent version of our surrogacy contract, right?"

"Of course," she said, and I could hear her typing.

I asked Pat to look for any provision in the agreement that absolved us from liability. She put me on hold, and the music was an instrumental version of Barry Manilow. Ready to take a chance again. Finally, Pat came back. "Ruth?" she said.

"Yes."

"I don't see anything in here that absolves or relieves the intended parents from liability for physical harm or medical damage to the surrogate. Nothing like that. But I also don't see anything that says you *are* responsible. It's silent. It just doesn't address it either way."

"And how do you think the court would interpret that?" I asked.

"Oh, they'll hold it against whoever wrote the contract," said Pat, pausing to let that sink in, and we both knew who wrote the contract. "They'll say that since Hal wrote it, if he wanted to escape liability, he should have put the language in the contract. And since he didn't, he can't now claim it."

"Making him, and us, legally responsible?" I asked.

"Correct," said Pat. "Does that help? But I'm not a lawyer. I can't give legal advice."

"I know, I know," I said. As I hung up, I smiled because I'd gotten exactly what I'd wanted, and it wasn't legal advice: it was a solution.

Fifty-Five

RUTH AND CALLY

MARCH 2003

By the time Ruth pulled up outside Cally's building, the baby was asleep, and Ruth wondered how she could prove her troubles now. Had she made it all up? All the misery. The colic. In Ruth's vision of this moment, the way she had rehearsed it in her head, she would present the crying baby, holding her out, as if showing Cally the evidence. Then Cally would take the child and the pain would be relieved. But with the baby sound asleep, Ruth simply unbuckled the car carrier and lugged it to the front door. She rang the buzzer.

"Hello?" said a voice tentatively.

"Um, it's me. Ruth." There was a pause on the other end of the static. Squinting against the sun, Ruth wondered if there was a security camera capturing her on Cally's steps. Ruth wiped her face and took a deep breath. The air was wetter and milder, with a sweetness in its slow promise of spring.

"I'll be right down," said Cally finally. When she opened the building's front door, her mouth dropped. She covered her face, clearly not expecting that Ruth would have brought the baby with her. "What are you doing here?" They hadn't seen each other since the temporary custody hearing, and the baby hadn't been in the courtroom.

"Can we come in?" said Ruth, barging through the doorway.

Cally stepped backward into the entryway to make room for Ruth and the car seat. The baby was bigger than she'd been in Cally's memories. She looked so much older, like someone had put a first-grader into a shrinking machine. Her little head had grown from an orange to a musk melon. Her legs were chunky. She looked like she could step out of that car carrier, march down the stairs, and run away. Cally's mother was a runner; maybe Nell would be, too.

"Thanks," said Ruth, letting the heavy door close behind her. The entryway became darker without the bright sun. Ruth took off her hat and ran a hand through her hair.

"Do you wanna come up?" Cally studied Ruth. Her worried forehead and tense chin. She'd gained weight. Her arms and attitude were strong as she carried the car seat. And there was the sleeping baby, but Cally wondered what else had changed: was this the Ruth she'd known and the child she'd carried? Ruth nodded, and Cally began the climb, in a numb state of disbelief.

Leading the way, Cally tromped up the stairs as loud as she liked, as if the stomping motion were helping her think, steeling her for whatever misfortune this visit might bring. Behind her, Ruth walked softly up the stairs, matching her right and left feet to Cally's as a soldier would. Ruth touched her back and Cally stopped. She turned around.

"What?" said Cally.

"Please walk quietly. I don't want to wake her up," said Ruth.

"Oh. Sorry," said Cally, standing mid-stair, her hand firmly on the railing as if she might lose her balance. "Why are you here?"

"Keep going," said Ruth, gesturing for Cally to move it, continue up two more floors. "I'll tell you."

Cally turned back to climb the remaining steps more quietly, just another example of Ruth instructing her on what to do. This would not be like the Tuesday-morning visits from her friend Sarah and baby Lucas. This would not be like a visit from Stan and Vera, who'd come twice already, each time bringing a pan of brownies with chocolate chips. This would be serious. This would be painful.

On the third floor, the women filed into Cally's apartment, and Ruth set down the baby carrier. The place was mostly the same. Maybe the sofa had been relocated. Maybe there was a new armchair. Textbooks covered the dinette table. A pizza box on the floor.

A man with a coffee mug emerged from the kitchen, then stopped short. "Oh," he said.

"Ruth, you remember Sam," said Cally. "From . . . the hospital."

"I don't think we were formally introduced." Ruth reached out her hand and Sam shook it. She said, "I'm sorry and very embarrassed about my behavior at the hospital. Truly."

"Don't worry about it," said Sam. He turned to Cally and said, "Hey, I was just about to go on a run." Sam must have noticed the tension in the room and clearly was looking for a way to get out of it.

As he moved past her, Ruth caught a glimpse of the kitchen cabinets and what looked like a note card taped to one of them. Was it a leftover from three months ago, or was there a new one? Perhaps it was about the baby. "Nice to see you, Sam," said Ruth, but there was nothing nice about this.

"Look at her." Cally was fixated on the baby. "She's so much bigger. And so sweet."

"Hi, little lady," said Sam to the child before nodding goodbye to the adults and heading out the door.

"She looks so different," said Cally.

"Does she?" asked Ruth.

"Yeah, can't you see it? Her hair, her lips. Look how much chubbier her fingers are."

The baby's hands were resting on her chest and draped over the car seat's shoulder straps as if she had been struggling to break free but then got tired and fell asleep.

"Now I wish she were awake," said Ruth. Normally, she was wishing for the opposite, wishing this child would sleep. It occurred to Ruth that she was upside down in this moment, a negative image of the real photograph.

"You're not supposed to be here," said Cally.

"I know."

"Is everything all right? You don't look so good."

"Everything is fine. And not fine," said Ruth, not ready to say what she'd come to say. "Sam seems nice."

"Yeah, he's great," said Cally, staring at the baby asleep in the carrier on the floor in front of her. "That's the one thing about this—I mean, I'm really glad I met him."

"I'm sorry to show up like this," Ruth said with a choke in her voice. "I'm sorry about everything."

"Um . . . it's okay, I guess," said Cally, not sure at all. "Does Hal know you're here?"

"Oh," said Ruth, and there was the familiar burn. "Yes, he knows." The truth was Hal didn't know she was there. Hal didn't know much about what Ruth was up to or how she'd come to feel about raising this child more or less alone.

"Okay," said Cally.

"How are you? Have you recovered?" asked Ruth.

"Mostly," said Cally, wary of this interview. Her lawyer had warned her not to talk to the Olsons without him present. She should neither admit nor deny anything.

"This is so hard," said Ruth, "but um . . . I'm really having . . . a lot of trouble." Her voice cracked and she took a moment to gather herself. "A lot of trouble with her . . . It's been . . . really hard . . ."

Cally made a face, both confused and concerned.

"And I know that sounds stupid, because obviously, this whole thing must be hard for you, too," Ruth said, and the pitch of her voice rose higher as she fought to get the words out.

"Very hard," said Cally in a quiet voice. "Horrible."

"And I'm so sorry about that," Ruth cried.

"I mean, it's . . . okay," Cally said, even though it wasn't. "And how is Jake, and Hal and everything with that?"

Ruth shook her head, unable to speak. "It's not good," she said. "Hal's devastated . . . Jake is in . . . physical therapy, but it's . . . not . . ."

"Oh, I'm sorry," said Cally, looking around for a tissue. "Here." She slid a box to Ruth. They'd been sitting in the living room, and Cally had been staring at the baby nonstop since they'd arrived. "Can I . . . Would it be all right if I held her?"

Ruth nodded, still a bit weepy, and helped to unbuckle the child.

Cally slid her hands underneath and lifted the sleeping baby up out of the seat, amazed at her long legs. "She's heavier," she said.

"Not as heavy as she should be," Ruth sobbed. "She's not . . . eating as much and . . . not growing like . . . she should . . ."

"Really?" Cally found that hard to believe. In her arms, this child was bigger than she remembered, in the way that everything changes when you've been away from it.

Ruth placed a burp cloth on Cally's shoulder so she could hold the baby up there and be protected just in case. "She's been spitting up . . . so much," said Ruth.

"Oh yeah?" said Cally to the baby, cooing sweetly. "What's going on, my Little Pea?" Cally brought the baby down to her lap and the baby's eyes opened. Cally smiled at her and touched her cheek.

"Oh dear, I'm not feeling so well." Ruth got suddenly dizzy and nauseated. "Do you mind if I use the toilet?"

"Yeah, sure, it's in there." Cally pointed. "It's a mess."

Ruth stood and rubbed her stomach as she walked to the tiny bathroom. She glanced into Cally's bedroom and was tempted to go in and look for index cards. But her stomach lurched, and she hurried to close the bathroom door before she vomited into the toilet. Any second now, the baby would start wailing, she thought.

Ruth washed her face, rinsed out her mouth, and dabbed at the puffy bags under her red eyes. "Get it together," she said to her reflection.

Cally called out to Ruth, asking if she was okay. Ruth made a quip about perimenopause, then asked for a drink of water or tea and maybe a cracker, but said she could get it herself. She didn't want to disturb the baby. And maybe she'd find some new index cards in the kitchen.

When Ruth returned to the living room, she froze at the sight: Cally was holding the baby and rocking side to side and singing something quietly. Tears rolled down Cally's face. Ruth slipped into the side chair without a word.

The women exchanged glances.

Finally, Cally spoke. "She smells so good," she said.

Ruth nodded, even though she hadn't noticed the baby's smell, and she yearned to understand what that meant. To her, this infant smelled of whatever Ruth had put on her, talcum powder, fresh cotton jammies, or Desitin. Or worse, of the baby's own spit-up or urine.

"Cally," said Ruth, gathering her courage. "What would you think about . . . having full custody of her? Of Nell."

Cally's face lit up. "What?" She inhaled. She looked confused, grateful, incredulous. "I would love it. Are you serious?"

Ruth nodded.

"But what about—"

"Hal, I know," said Ruth, cutting her off before she had to hear that question one more time. "Here's my idea . . ."

Ruth explained Hal's distance and distraction. Her theory that this lawsuit was keeping him in a state of perpetual grief, like the coma had kept Jake in an unconscious state. That Ruth thought Hal was only doing it for her. And how Hal needed to be freed from this fight, for himself and for the sake of their marriage. She told Cally about her own trouble with the baby and asked if Cally had any interest in restarting nursing, if possible. Yes, she did.

Ruth went further and mentioned her idea about the article. Asked if Cally would agree to be interviewed. And about Ruth's strategy for settling all of this legal business with a mutual agreement. She told her what Pat had said about the surrogacy contract and liability for harm done to Cally's health. Cally said her lawyer was already exploring that, and Ruth said good. Do that.

And while Ruth talked about her exciting ideas, Cally was holding the baby, swaying and cuddling her, and Cally felt a rising lightness inside, a clarity and confidence. It was as if they were all in their right places in this moment. Buoyed by Ruth's passion and earnestness, Cally gathered her own courage to visualize her life anew, a future as she might design it: with college, career, Sam, and Nell.

And now, with Nell in her arms, her baby's soft skin as familiar to Cally as her own, she knew, in that deep place of knowing, the very place where Nell had lived inside her, that she would never let her go. And she could see that Ruth knew it, too.

Fifty-Six

RUTH

OCTOBER 2003

For all those months when Cally was pregnant with Nell, I'd been asking her to explain what it felt like. She couldn't. Especially the birth. She couldn't find words.

And now I understood why. Because you can't really explain what it feels like to give birth. Oh, sure, everyone says it hurts. Everyone says it's the best day of their life. But no one can explain how it feels inside. How the cramps and contractions get worse and worse, building up, maybe for hours, but you lose track of time as you toss and turn on scratchy sheets and nurses try to position you, and they say, "Are you comfortable?" and "Is this better?" and you're just groaning because nothing feels better, and they feed you ice chips, check your blood pressure, the beeping fetal heartbeat, they stroke your forehead, and they constantly check you down below, then snap off the rubber gloves without really telling you anything that you understand. Centimeters?

And no one can explain that moment. When the beast rises up from the center of the earth and bursts through all the layers of the ground and up into your body. This terrifying thing like a giant fist grabs hold of you from inside and yanks at the womb like it wants to take you back down to the center of the earth, it yanks at the baby to get going, pushes and pulls at the two of you until it happens. And you have lost all control. There is nothing you can do about it. Nothing in the world. You are gone. And all the tubes and beeps and needles and wipes and ice chips and nurses and blue paper sheets, none of that matters. It all goes away, and there is only you and the beast, and you'd better let it go. Let go and help it, ride on it, let it be.

And then the heat arrives. As if a solar flare has landed between your legs, radiating in the very birth canal, to direct your attention (and your pushing) directly into that sun. And you'd better just join with it—don't fight—just push and push into the hot center. The nurses will say, "Another one now," and "One more," and "A big one now," and—! Out slides the slippery blob, the rubbery miniature human, wet and pasty blue, arms and legs folded, hair slick, squinty eyes, wrinkly cheeks, and the busy people will cut the thick and twisty purple cord and swoop the new thing away.

And all you want to do is stare at it, figure out what happened, what this is, this silky new life, this chalky blue angel with black eyes and red mouth, you want to stare at it, be near it, touch it, but you can't because the people take it and urgently fuss with it, weighing, sponging, wiping, measuring, and suctioning it. And you can do nothing but watch them work. And wait.

They don't talk to you, they just talk to each other. And you just lie there, still connected to the new person but also apart, helpless in this sacred moment, peeking around the equipment to catch a glimpse of your newborn darling, needing it near you.

For the rest of your life.

My baby was born on September 13, 2003. I'd had a high-risk pregnancy, but I hadn't been worried. I felt this was meant to be. And I'd been having dreams where the baby would tell me to be confident, because the baby was strong and would come out fully gestated and ready to breathe. So the baby and I had made a pact, and we had made it happen.

Meanwhile, Hal and I made our own pact. When I told Hal I wanted to withdraw our lawsuit for custody and settle with Cally, including settling her medical claims against us, he said he was relieved. Letting go of this fight allowed him to devote himself entirely to his boys. He lightened in a way I hadn't seen since before Elizabeth was born. Our settlement allowed Cally to go back to school and raise her daughter with modest support payments from Hal and friendly informal visitation for us.

Jake had been getting used to his wheelchair, and the doctors were always on to a new study, a new hope for regeneration and animation of his legs. He was looking for a college with a para sports program and eventually planned to compete in para snowboarding. When all was said and done, Hal was simply grateful that Jake was alive. The accident had thrust us all into a slow-motion shock, a gradual acceptance, and also a new clarity. We felt the need to cling to every bit of life and connection we had. We felt the need to appreciate our bodies.

And then I discovered I was four months pregnant. I'd noticed the symptoms but thought it was perimenopause or hyper-stress or both. Hal was thrilled. It was as if this was what he'd wanted all along but hadn't known it. Or hadn't felt able to say so. The idea of making a baby together, in my own womb, with my old egg, was a new—and unexpected—joy for us both.

When I was seven months pregnant, I received another surprise. I'd been nominated by the Society for Professional Journalism for their Excellence in Health Reporting Award for my surrogacy story, published in the *Minneapolis Star.* A great honor, for which I would embark on a quest to find a sufficiently festive maternity gown to wear at the awards dinner and gala. And on the night of the big event, in an amusing role reversal, Hal insisted on bringing my old camera bag so he could play the part of "sexy photographer," as he put it. I couldn't help smiling as I walked onstage to accept the prize, my belly like a basketball, and there he was in the front row, clicking shot after blurry shot of me, his award-winning, very pregnant wife. And as on the night we first met, the sparks were flying.

We were a team again. He'd acquiesced to my handling of the Cally matter. He'd said everything he needed to say; he'd been trying to make me happy. But we both saw how much happier the baby was in Cally's arms. We would remain in the background, help her when needed, and it felt right to work together, not fight. And since Cally had full legal and physical custody, she had the prerogative to name the baby. I was deeply touched when Cally chose Nell Elizabeth.

Hal and I named our little boy Raymond August Olson, and he is as sweet as pie. I could have kept most of the nursery decor in place, because who doesn't love an underwater ocean motif? But we decided to give baby Ray his own theme.

And start over.

ACKNOWLEDGMENTS

This book started on the first day of the first writing class I ever took, and was inspired by a "postcard prompt" from our teacher, Laurel Ostrow. The postcard featured a snowy cabin in the woods, with the words "Welcome to Wisconsin" plastered across the image. Laurel gave us three minutes to write, and that's when this story began to flow.

In that class, I met my first writing group, who have been my dear friends ever since. Bridgit Colleran Albrecht, Judie Mattison, and Romelle Adkins, thank you for your enduring support through many early chapters.

To Brier Miller, who encouraged me to write in the first place: thank you for your generous care.

To my fellow mentees in the 2013 Loft Mentor Series: I am fortunate to have met you and I treasure our connection. Thanks also to the mentors for bringing us together, teaching us about the craft, and showing us how to be a community.

To the Loft Literary Center, its staff, teachers, and students: thank you for the vibrant literary universe you continue to foster. I am lucky to live in a city with such a haven for writers and readers.

Speaking of which, I am forever grateful to my agent, Marly Rusoff, who started the Loft many years ago. Thank you for believing in me and in this book. In our early emails and phone calls, I felt an instant connection with you, which has only deepened. Your vision and tenacity are a wonder. I can't believe how lucky I am to work with you. And to the uber-talented Julie Mosow: this work would not be what it is without your developmental engagement with these characters and their story.

To my wonderful editor, Sara Nelson at HarperCollins: thank you for taking a chance on me. Your deep knowledge and keen insights have been invaluable. From our first conversation, I knew I was in great hands. I am profoundly grateful for the way you understood these characters and expertly shepherded this book into the world. And thank you to Mary Gaule and the amazing members of the Harper team, for all the million things you do behind the scenes.

This novel would not have happened if not for my coconspirators in the Friday Morning Writing Group. Chapter by chapter, you lovingly critiqued it. Thank you for your outstanding feedback and limitless encouragement, Roxanne Sadovsky, Tom Schierholz, Heidi Schneider, Rachel Jensen, Margaret Peterson, Gretchen Van Hauer, Heather Awad, Dawn Hill, Gillian Brecker, Paula Shames, and Melanie Brening. I can't wait to see those "Team Digger" T-shirts.

To Rosalie O'Brien, Mary Finley, Makenzie Krause, and Corissa Pennow: thank you for taking the time to carefully read and comment on an early version of the manuscript. Let me put it this way: you were right, and I am in your debt.

Other brave early readers include Rachel Awes, Sam Awes, and my dearly loved and recently departed uncle Mel and aunt Sue, who wrote me the most supportive email I have ever received. To my entire family, book club sisters, and sweet friends far and wide: thank you for your inspiration and love.

To my dad, Michael Halleen: you are the writer who taught me to appreciate words and story and grammar, and, most of all, to trust myself. I hear your wise and tender voice encouraging me when I have doubts.

Thank you, Milo Bunting, for reading my short stories when you were just a kid. I can't wait to read your books someday.

Pearce Bunting: Remember the time we all took turns reading the manuscript while on vacation in Florida? I'll never forget that morning when you finished it and showed up at my door, moved with emotion. Thank you for your fierce love and bounteous reading. Your energy could fuel a small nation.

Stephanie Halleen, my sister and longest friend: thank you for always being there, always helping, and always reading. I trust your eye and judgment, as does everyone else who has ever worked with you. What a gift to be able to collaborate with you.

Thank you, Barb Halleen, for your smart and tireless help with this book, including your excellent editing. Mom, I love how you write and think, and I cherish the memories of us reading every word aloud, again and again, making it real.

Larry Schaefer, you are the best reader and best everything in the world. I can't do any of this without you and I don't want to. Thank you for being my husband.

ABOUT THE AUTHOR

Toni Halleen worked for many years as an employment law attorney. She was born and raised in the Midwest and earned a BA in women's studies from Mount Holyoke College, and a JD from the University of Minnesota. Toni won a Mentor Prize in fiction from the Loft Literary Center, and her writing has appeared in *Wigleaf*, *Structo*, *Gravel*, and elsewhere. She lives in Minneapolis with her family.